STARS OVER EDEN FALLS

A CLEAN, FRIENDS TO LOVE ROMANCE

TINA NEWCOMB

I dedicate this book to the lovely ladies in my critique group.

We brainstorm, we laugh, we cry, we share, we encourage, we cheer.

Best of all, we're friends.

To Becky, Dawn, Kay, Lori, and Mary

Hugs!

CHAPTER 1

Stella Adams pulled back the silky curtain of the dressing room, feeling like a princess thanks to the bride-to-be—who happened to be one of her best friends—and the fifteen pounds she lost due to starvation.

She threw her arms around Carolyn West, soon to be Mrs. JT Garrett. "Thank you, thank you, *thank you* for picking bridesmaid dresses that don't make me look like I've strapped two beach balls to my butt. I love you."

Carolyn hugged her tight. "You have a body I've envied since we were kids."

She held Carolyn at arm's length. "Are you nuts? You have the body of a—"

"Boy."

Stella snorted—a bad habit she really should try to overcome, but a snort made a certain point no other sound could make. "I was going to say superstar fashion model."

Carolyn laughed. "Now you're the one who's nuts." She turned Stella toward the huge floor to ceiling mirror. "I love that color on you."

"I love it too." Stella turned from side to side. The

burgundy lace over nude looked pretty perfect with her skin color and dark hair. Stella ran her hands over her stomach. "I don't know about you ladies, but I look gorgeous," she said loud enough for the four friends still in their dressing rooms to hear.

Jillian Saunders held the curtain to her dressing room aside. Of course, the dress looked fabulous on her model-thin, personal-trainer-toned body. She tugged at the hem. "I thought the dress was supposed to hit at the knee."

"Holy moly, your legs go on forever." Stella lifted the hem of Jillian's dress even higher. "Can you share about two inches with me?"

Jillian shimmied the dress back into place. "I wish I could."

"It does hit at your knee," Carolyn said. "You're just used to wearing yoga pants that cover your whole leg." She turned Jillian toward the mirror so she could see the full effect. "Your shapely calf muscles will be the envy of every woman at the wedding."

Jillian pivoted to see her profile. "I do love this dress. It hides all my flaws."

"What flaws?" Stella retorted.

Jillian pointed at her flat stomach and Stella rolled her eyes.

Carolyn twisted Stella's long hair into a knot. "You should wear your hair up for the wedding. You have a pretty neck."

Stella glanced at her reflection. *Len never tells me I have a pretty neck or anything else for that matter.* One more item for the ever-growing Con column of her Len Pros and Cons list.

Tiny Alex McCreed slid her dressing room curtain open. "You two look absolutely perfect." She turned to the huge wall mirror. "Me, on the other hand…"

Alex's five-foot-nothing made Stella appreciate her additional three inches. Still, Alex looked like a miniature beauty queen with her sunlight smile, mossy green eyes, and messy blond top-knot. "You're darling as ever."

Alex slipped on the four-inch heels she'd brought along. "That's a little better. At least I don't look like the little sister playing dress-up."

Jolie Klein and Misty Garrett emerged at the same time. Jolie adjusted her ample breasts while Misty spun around, her mass of midnight black hair in a fist. "Zip me, Stella."

"What's the magic word?" Stella asked, treating Misty like one of her second graders.

"*Please*," Misty whined.

Exactly like a second grader.

Carolyn lined them up in front of the mirror. "You all look gorgeous."

Stella tugged Carolyn into their lineup. "Forever friends," she said. Which was true. They had all been friends since kindergarten, except for latecomer Carolyn, who joined the group when she moved to Eden Falls during third grade.

"Forever friends," they repeated.

Misty pulled away and clapped her hands. "Okay, enough of the mushy stuff. If we're done, let's change and get to the restaurant. I'm starving."

The six of them hadn't been to Seattle together in years. They decided, after their dress fittings, they'd indulge in a special girls' night out. One last hurrah before Carolyn's big day.

After changing, they climbed into the SUV Alex's *New York Times* best-selling author husband just bought for her and headed to the waterfront for a seafood dinner.

From the very back seat—sometimes having shorter legs wasn't a blessing—Stella looked over her friends. If Len didn't show at this wedding, she would be the *only* one there without a plus-one. In that moment she decided if he cancelled, as he so often did, next Saturday would be the last time he stood her up.

That thought left her with mixed feelings.

The last time he visited her apartment, a small box—perfect engagement-ring size—fell to the floor when she moved his jacket from the back of the sofa to the coat rack. She scooped the box off the floor, tempted to take a peek inside. Instead, she tucked it away in its hiding spot.

She'd waited for Len to propose for over a year. Now that the time was here, she wasn't sure marrying him was the right decision. He'd disappointed her so many times over the course of their relationship.

She hadn't mentioned the ring to her friends. They were more skeptical of Len than she was. Without voicing their opinions aloud, she knew they thought Len would hurt her, believed his excuses for missing events were unbelievable. At times, she thought the same. Then he'd come over and chase all her fears away with tender kisses and promises to do better.

She'd spent more time than she should dreaming about the how and when of Len's proposal. He wasn't terribly inventive, so she didn't expect anything spectacular. Maybe he'd pop the question after the wedding next weekend. Or as soon as tomorrow, when he came over for a home-cooked dinner. Seeing him two times in one week was unusual, but he'd made a promise and she was holding him to it.

You're waffling back and forth about this guy, whispered a white-clad angel as she fluffed her tutu.

Len doesn't make loving him easy. In fact, he turns something that should come naturally into a chore like cleaning toilets or scrubbing the kitchen floor.

When was the last time you did either of those things?

I clean. Sometimes.

A romantic fantasy unfolded in living color. The first

week of June would be a beautiful time to get engaged. Four months to plan a colorful autumn wedding, or six months for an enchanting Christmas wedding.

You're waffling again.

A ring would prove my friends are wrong about Len. Maybe it would ease her apprehensions, too. A ring would mean he was serious.

Len seemed to be holding back a piece of himself, and she was curious about that piece. Was he ashamed of where he lived or how he was raised? Did he like to stay in rather than go out because he wrestled with a mountain of debt? Maybe he supported a sick mother she didn't know about or a sibling in financial trouble.

Deeply in debt didn't fit the scenario though. He dressed well and drove a newer model car, so he wasn't broke. When they did go out, he always took her to nice places and paid with cash. Stella didn't consider herself a complex or high-maintenance person. Happily self-sufficient, she made a decent living and paid her bills on time. A roof over her head, a car that ran, an occasional vacation, money in savings, and she was perfectly content.

He'll change. Once he proposes, he'll be more open and giving of his time. We'll discuss the part he keeps hidden, and my feelings of unease will dissolve.

But what if your unease doesn't go away, and what if he doesn't open up? The chirpy voice chimed in. *You've been dating for two years and you've never met his family, or any of his friends.*

Stella flicked the pest off her shoulder. *Aren't you supposed to be positive? Maybe he's embarrassed by his family. Who isn't at one time or another?* She thought of her four sisters and how many times they'd embarrassed her over the years.

The angel dusted off her halo and climbed back into place. *If that's the case, why doesn't he talk to you about it? Especially if he's ready to propose? You can't start a marriage with secrets. After two years, don't you deserve more? Your friends don't trust him.*

Another moment of doubt bubbled in her stomach. *Only because they don't know him.*

Whose fault is that? How many times have you invited him to meet your friends, and he's only shown up for a handful of those occasions?

Her little irritant was right. Len had plenty of opportunities, and he cancelled on most of them. Stella wiggled her shoulder, trying to unseat her passenger. *My friends will support me.*

Alex pulled into the restaurant parking lot and they piled out of the SUV. Inside, pictures of lighthouses lined the walls and large lanterns hung from the ceiling, providing a cozy ambiance. The yummy smells coming from the kitchen teased Stella's grumbling stomach. She'd have to be very careful about what she ate. Those fifteen pounds hadn't just fallen off of their own accord.

Carolyn stopped at the reservation desk and gave her name.

The hostess flashed a bright smile. "Welcome. Your table is almost ready."

As they waited, a ruckus drew Stella's attention to the dining room. She leaned to the right and spotted two boys in a family of five fighting over a plastic superhero. She started to lean back when a familiar voice reprimanding the boys hit her like a quick punch to the gut.

Len.

Her chest tightened enough that she couldn't take a full breath. A loud buzzing silenced all the background noise, everything but Len's harsh tone.

The man who had a ring box in his coat pocket, the same one who was supposed to be playing basketball with buddies tonight, was sitting in this restaurant, trying to break up an argument between two little boys who looked suspiciously like him. A woman sat across the table cradling an adorable little girl with ringlets in her hair.

Misty pointed past her. "Hey, isn't that what's-his-name?"

Stella felt more than she heard the commotion around them, a tug on her arm, a hand on her shoulder, another at her waist. She sidestepped them all, her feet taking her toward the family despite her quaking knees.

Her mind screamed *NO!* yet her eyes weren't deceiving her. Same hair, same nose, same mole on his right cheek. She stopped next to the table, so close she could reach out and touch him. He glanced up and his expression shifted from frustration to alarm.

"I-I think we've met…at a teachers' conference." Stella was surprised the voice was hers, surprised she was able to speak at all.

"Uh…"—a quick glance at the woman across from him—"Yes, maybe. You look familiar."

You look familiar. The skin on her cheeks prickled with heat and the buzzing grew louder. "Len, right?"

His alarm turned to dread as his gaze darted from the woman to her, then to somewhere over her shoulder where she assumed her friends stood. "Uh, no."

"No?" Stella jerked her arm from a clasping hand. "I could have sworn you said your name was Len Barlow."

"You must have my husband mixed up with someone else," said the woman.

Out of curiosity, Stella offered her a glance. "I usually don't forget a face."

"His name is Jerry Winters." The woman smiled. Sweet. Unsuspecting. Her hair was wavy brown, her cheeks flushed with a rosy glow of family bliss. She had insanely long eyelashes and lips the color of pink rose petals. And a cute dimple. She probably had naturally skinny hips, too.

"Jerry. Winters." Stella pronounced first and last name slowly, distinctly. Her gaze moved back to Len. "And this is your wife?"

"I'm Anna Winters." The woman ran a hand over her daughter's brown curls. "This is Zoe, and the two heathens disrupting everyone's dinner are Benjamin and Michael."

Lovely family. Stella tried to smile, but her mouth wouldn't cooperate. Len seemed just as paralyzed.

"Where did you meet Jerry?"

The blood was rushing through her body so fast she had a hard time hearing over the roar in her ears. "In Tacoma two years ago. Right, *Jerry?*"

He looked down at his plate as a muscle in his jaw bunched. "Yes, I believe that's right."

"Jerry teaches in Greenwood, but we live in Seattle." Anna ran a hand over Zoe's hair again, and her diamond wedding ring sparkled under the dopey lantern light.

I thought you liked the ambiance.

Shut up. Stella flicked her shoulder to dethrone her irritant.

"Do you teach in Seattle?" Anna Winters asked.

"No, Eden Falls."

"Oh, I love Eden Falls." Anna leaned forward and confiscated the action figure from one of the boys. "We've driven through a couple of times, but Jerry never wants to stop."

Because you might run into me.

"I obviously have my details wrong." Stella squeezed her eyes shut as the lies began to build along with a pain at the base of her skull. "I could have sworn you taught in Harrisville."

Jerry shook his head still looking at his plate.

"Jerry's always taught in Greenwood." Anna smiled at her husband. "Maybe you have a doppelgänger, honey."

Jerry cleared his throat. "Maybe."

"Stella, we should probably go so this *family* can finish their dinner." Alex's tone hinted she was worried Stella would say something to hurt Len's—*Jerry's*—wife and kids.

Anna glanced behind Stella. "Looks like you're celebrating something."

"A friend's upcoming wedding," Stella said.

"Who's the bride?"

Someone must have indicated Carolyn, because Anna smiled. "Best wishes for a happy marriage."

"Thank you," Carolyn said quietly.

Her friends had her back. From almost the first time they met Len—*Jerry. Will I ever get used to that name?*—they kept telling her something wasn't right about him. She'd refused to listen. She'd given him the benefit of the doubt. Believed him. Believed *in* him. Her jaw felt numb. So did her fingertips. And the top of her head.

"Come on, Stella," Jolie coaxed.

Her friends were afraid she'd cause a scene. And she might if her head started to spin on her shoulders. "Sorry to interrupt your dinner."

"Yep." Jerry occupied himself with one of the boys. "Nice to see you again."

Stella stood her ground for a long moment, staring at the cheating husband and the unsuspecting wife. Jerry glanced back at her, and she could see the fear in his eyes. Instead of providing satisfaction, his palpable fear made her stomach twist in an I'm-going-to-throw-up kind of knot.

Stella pushed through her friends and headed for the door as the noise of the restaurant resumed. She wasn't sure if anyone had followed until she reached Alex's car. Jillian opened the back door and hurried her inside. "Let's grab something to eat on our way home."

Misty slid in next to her. "I told you there was something off about that guy."

"Misty," Alex warned, climbing behind the wheel.

"I don't see why we're leaving," Misty argued. "We should sit at the vacant table next to *Len* and make the rest of his night miserable."

He looked miserable enough," Carolyn said.

"Let it go, Misty." Alex glared in the rearview mirror.

Stella shut out her friends. Their angry comments about *Jerry*, and their attempts to comfort grated on her nerves. The two-and-a-half-hour drive home was a blur as she tried to focus on breathing. Inhale. Exhale. She stared at the distorted scenery while she fought threatening tears. She would not cry in front of them.

Breathe in. Breathe out.

Anna Winters' innocent smile branded Stella with a bitter memory, one she wouldn't forget any time soon. Not Len Barlow. Jerry Winters. There was no Len. Only Jerry, who had a wife and three kids. Two sons, one with his eyes, and a daughter who inherited his smile.

Inhale. Exhale. Inhale. Exhale.

She was aware when Alex pulled into a fast food restaurant and ordered burgers and fries. Stella didn't dare eat for fear she'd throw up in Alex's shiny new SUV. She held a hand over her nose and mouth to keep from smelling the food and tried to empty her mind.

When Alex finally pulled to a stop in front of Stella's apartment, her sister was waiting at the curb. One of her friends must have sent a text full of information, because Phoebe watched her with pity, much like the expressions her friends wore.

Jillian and Carolyn helped her out of the car as if she was an invalid. Shrugging their hands away, she knew once she was inside, they would talk about her, discuss how they'd been right all along.

They were right all along.

Stella glared at her white-clad, winged nuisance. *Go away.* She wanted to go inside, shut the door on the world, and pretend the past two years had never happened.

~

*R*owdy Garrett entered his bar and grill by the back door, stopping long enough to drop a book in his office. He hummed to the country music coming from the speaker behind his desk. As always, a sense of satisfaction settled over him. The first week of summer, and his place was hopping with tourists and locals alike. His employees wouldn't have another slow night until mid-November.

He sat on the inheritance his grandparents left for four years before buying and gutting the boarded-up building not too far from Town Square. His parents weren't happy with his decision. His mom worried the name would bring in the wrong crowd, and sometimes it did. She said she would forever regret bestowing the nickname Rowdy on him when he was three, but Jefferson's Bar and Grill just didn't have the same ring.

He stopped in the kitchen and greeted the cook and dishwasher before taking his place behind the bar. He filled drink orders for customers on the floor while Mike Stettler worked the bar. Loading a tray for Rachel, he glanced up just as his cousin Alex entered, followed by her friends. JT told him earlier that his soon to be bride and her friends went to Seattle for dress fittings and dinner before the upcoming wedding. They must have had a change of plans, because they were back early.

He counted heads as they filed past. Alex, Misty, Carolyn, Jillian, and Jolie. Stella was missing.

Alex waved after taking a seat at a table in the back. He

nodded. One of his wait staff would have to fill their drinks and usual order of extra-hot nachos tonight.

Mike Stettler moved down the bar efficiently, and Kyle was due in to help in another ten minutes. Rowdy wasn't sure what he would do without Mike. He worked for the forest service during the week, but gave up his weekends for the bar and grill. Kyle was a big help, but replacing Mike was going to be impossible. He was the best bartender Rowdy had ever employed.

While he filled a tray with drinks for Alex's table, the raised voices of an imminent brawl competed with the usual roar and music. Rowdy spotted two men on the far side of the room who were exchanging insults nearly nose-to-nose.

"Rachel," he called. When she looked his way, he held up eight fingers to identify the table and made a slashing motion across his throat. "Cut them off."

She nodded.

"You're slammed tonight."

"Hey, Low-Rider," he said to his pint-sized cousin. "JT was whining and moaning earlier that you whisked Carolyn away for a girls' night out in Seattle, yet here you are."

Alex leaned forearms on the bar. "Yeah, well, our plans changed when Stella confronted her boyfriend, Len Barlow —whose real name is Jerry Winters—with his wife and three kids at the restaurant."

Rowdy closed his gaping jaw, but not before his cousin's face lit up like a Christmas tree.

"I knew it. You've had a thing for Stella the whole time she's been chasing after that jerk."

He shook his head as he filled a glass with ice. "You don't know what you're talking about."

"Oh, but I do." She flashed another I-knew-it smirk.

Alex had caught him staring at Stella too many times to

let him continue to deny his attraction. "How is she?" he asked.

"About how you'd expect. Jillian texted ahead, so Phoebe was waiting when we dropped her off at her apartment. I suspect after a short period of mourning, she'll be right as rain and ready to date a tall, handsome bar and grill owner. Do you happen to know anyone who fits that description?"

"I'm kinda busy here, Alex."

Raised voices caught his attention again. Rowdy grabbed the baseball bat off the shelf behind the bar—the one he never used but kept handy for intimidation purposes—and hopped over the bar just as the fight broke out.

Alex would have to get her teasing jollies somewhere else tonight.

CHAPTER 2

*R*owdy rolled over and blinked his eyes open when a big weight nudged his back. He pushed aside the giant paw that hit his chest. "Morning, Moose."

"*Woof.*"

"Does that mean breakfast or outside?"

"*Rororoo woof.*"

"Outside it is." Rowdy swung his legs over the side of his bed and gave Moose a good rubdown. "You like that, boy? Huh? Okay, let's go."

As soon as Rowdy stood, his Saint Bernard jumped around like a puppy instead of the hundred-and-seventy-pound grown dog he was.

After he let Moose out, he went into the laundry room to fill the dog bowls with food and water, then headed into the kitchen for coffee. The next hour was spent at the table on paperwork he'd hoped to finish last night, but never got the chance.

His cell phone rang, and he jumped up to get it from the charger on the counter. "Hey, bro," he said, when Beam's face appeared on his screen.

"Hey yourself. I'm taking Sophia to Noelle's Café for lunch. Want to meet us?"

"I don't want to horn in on your date."

Beam laughed. "She likes you better than me."

"Of course she does. I don't make her take baths, eat mashed-up peas, or go to bed before dark. What time?"

"Around one-ish."

"See you then." Rowdy disconnected the call and opened the back door to let Moose in. The Saint Bernard nearly knocked him flat charging for his breakfast.

Rowdy filled a bowl with sugary cereal and added milk. He stood at the laundry room door while they both wolfed down their breakfast. After eating, they took a walk up the mountain trail behind the house. At a fork in the path—right took them around a ridge, left led them past a cave—Moose picked left. For some reason he loved sniffing around the small cavity in the rock.

Rowdy, Beam, and JT discovered the cave way back in their running-the-hills-as-carefree-kids days. The indentation went back about a hundred feet, and the ceiling rose nine feet up, except for a tube near the entrance that showered sunlight down during certain times of the day. As kids, they'd built their fires at the entrance to allow the smoke to escape. He looked over the valley below while Moose nosed nearby. His parents taught him and Beam to appreciate nature, and he visited his favorite trails and vistas every chance he got.

Once they got home, Rowdy washed a load of laundry, showered, made the bed, and played ball with Moose before driving down the mountain road into his hometown. Eden Falls, Washington, was small and quaint, a place where everybody knew everybody else's business, but he couldn't imagine living anywhere else.

He parked behind the bar and grill so he could drop off

the new knife he'd ordered for Juan before heading to Noelle's.

Town Square was busy. People buzzed in and out of shops and wandered through the park, which covered two blocks in the center of town. Maude Stapleton had a crowd in front of Pages Bookstore. A sign over the door read Post Memorial Day Sale in big red letters. He stopped at a table, scanned the marked-down books, and picked one out. The back blurb hinted at war and ruination.

"That's a good book."

Rowdy smiled at the feisty redheaded owner of Pages. "Yeah?"

"It's book one of a series."

"How many books are in the series?"

"Three."

"Are they on sale, too?"

Maude lifted her drawn-on eyebrows. "I'm here to make money, Rowdy. You buy book one on sale, get hooked, and come back for the other two at full price."

"Got any of Colton McCreed's books on sale?"

She looked up at him as if he'd lost his mind. "Since Colton McCreed moved here and married your cousin, I sell more of his books than any other author. Do you think I'd put the books that feed me on sale?"

"Stupid me." He set the book on the table. "I'll come back after lunch."

"You meeting your girlfriend? Oh wait." Maude barked out a laugh. "You don't have one."

"Stop. You're making me laugh so hard I'm getting a stitch in my side," he said keeping a straight face.

Rowdy crossed the street before he spotted his cousin, in full police chief uniform, standing on the steps of Town Hall, which also served as the police station.

"Hey, JT. How's it going?"

JT nodded toward the park. A group of Goth-dressed kids lounged in the shade of a pine tree. "They're taunting me."

The tree was a replacement for the original Eden Falls' Christmas pine that arsonists set fire to a year earlier. A cell phone belonging to one of the kids was found under the tree, but the police couldn't prove he lost it the night of the fire.

An orange-haired kid who went by the name of Blaze stared at them. JT believed one or more of the kids had also burned down the hardware store and lumberyard, and started two other fires around town. Heavy snow put out the one set in a dumpster behind Noelle's Café, and a firefighter discovered the other one behind Patsy's Pastries and called for help before the blaze did much damage.

Rowdy, along with many other shop owners, had installed security cameras in an attempt to catch the arsonists and protect their property.

Rowdy stared back at Blaze. "Defiant little bugger, isn't he?"

"Yep. Rance called to say they just left The Fly Shop. He's pretty certain that little one put something in his pocket while one of the girls distracted him, but Rance didn't see it happen."

The leader of the Goth gang, a guy named Thorn, sat apart from the rest, looking like a vampire with his white skin and black makeup.

"Need me to stay with you?"

JT glanced at him for the first time. "No. Mac's across the square and Layne is circling back around in a patrol car."

"I don't imagine you want to join me and Beam for lunch."

As if on cue, JT's stomach grumbled. He chuckled. "If you're still there when these kids move on, I'll join you."

Rowdy looked back at the kids. They didn't look like they

were leaving anytime soon. "Want me to put in an order to go?"

"Nah, I'll eat when I'm sure they're gone. Thanks though."

"If you decide you need help, just text. I'll be in Noelle's."

~

The sound of drape rings scraping along the curtain rod grated against Stella's nerve endings. Without opening her eyes, she gritted her teeth and rolled away from the bright light filling her room.

"Time to get up. I've let you wallow in bed for three days. You promised to help Alex with the flowers for Carolyn's wedding."

Stella yanked the covers over her head.

A cold hand grabbed her foot.

She jerked out of her sister's grasp. "Go away, Phoebe."

"Not gonna happen. Alex needs your help. If I knew how to arrange flowers, I'd go for you, but I don't, which means you have to get up."

"What time is it?"

"Eleven. Come on, Stella. You can't stay in bed forever."

On the pain scale from one to ten, this was her ten. Her chest felt hollowed out. How did someone recover from such deceit and heartache?

Stella felt the bed dip, a strong indication that Phoebe wasn't going anywhere. She lowered the covers and squinted, one-eyed, against the bright light.

Phoebe lifted a brow. "You look like crap."

Stella rolled her eyes. "Thanks so much. I appreciate your tender concern."

Phoebe's expression softened. "I say that in the most loving way." She patted Stella's leg. "I know you're hurting, but Len—"

"Jerry. The jerk's name is *Jer-ry*." Stella said the name slowly like she was pronouncing a hard word for one of her students.

"*Jer-ry* isn't worth any more of your tears."

Stella's lip trembled, and she bit down hard. She would not cry in front of her strong police officer sister. "Did you tell Mom and Dad?"

"They were concerned when you weren't in church Sunday." Phoebe reached under the covers and rubbed her leg. "I told them what happened. Mom wanted to come over, but I talked her into giving you a couple of days. She stopped by this morning with a batch of your favorite cookies."

"Peanut butter?" Stella asked, hopeful. But that hope turned dark an instant later. "Just what my wide hips need."

"To help out, I ate one. Okay, two." Phoebe blew out a breath. "And a half. Leo had the other half."

"If you don't want any, I'll take them," said a familiar male voice.

Stella glanced at the door. Leo Sawyer grinned. She turned a glare on her sister. "You told Leo?"

He pushed away from the doorjamb with a shoulder while shoving a bite of *her* peanut butter goodness into his mouth. "Of course she told me. I'm her best friend—her smart friend. You look terrible. When was the last time you brushed your teeth?" He glanced around. "Or cleaned your room?"

Stella grabbed a pillow and launched it at the ridiculously handsome man. He caught it with a laugh and launched it back, hitting Stella in the head. "You need a shower and I need another cookie."

"Leave me at least five or six!" she yelled at Leo's retreating back. She glanced at Phoebe. "Thanks for that."

Phoebe lifted a shoulder. "Eden Falls is a small town. He would have heard eventually."

"I don't get you two. You have the weirdest relationship ever. What woman has a guy for a best friend? An annoying guy," she added.

Phoebe wrinkled her nose like a little bunny, an endearing habit she'd carried over from childhood. "He can be annoying, but he's a great cook, and he always fixes my computer. In fact, he can fix anything. And he smells good."

"He does smell good." Stella smiled. "You know everyone in town thinks you're secretly sleeping together."

"Then they won't be shocked when they find out we are."

"What?" Stella sat up so fast her head spun.

Your equilibrium is off. The angel climbed out from under the sheet after taking a tumble. *That's what happens when you lie around in bed for three days.*

"For the quadrillionth time, we're just friends." Phoebe stood. "Now get up. Alex needs your help. The flowers for Carolyn and JT's wedding are going to take the rest of the week."

Stella fell back into the pillows. *Oh joy. Just how I want to spend my week, working on someone else's wedding flowers.*

Stop being so dramatic. You weren't even sure you wanted to continue dating the guy.

Stella dropped a pillow on the haloed cutie.

Two hours, approximately eight hundred calories in cookies, and a shower later, Stella walked into Pretty Posies. The bell over the door tinkled merrily, making her want to smack the happiness out of it. Normally, she loved this place.

Today…not so much.

Tatum Ellis's smile faltered when she spotted Stella. "Hey!" she said too brightly. "How are you?"

"Fabulous."

Goth girl Tatum wore a black veil over her black and purple-striped hair. Since she was working behind the counter, Stella couldn't see what she wore with the black lace top that was more holes than fabric. "I'm sorry about what happened," Tatum said, her enthusiasm fading.

Stella waved her hand as she glanced around the shop Alex had inherited from her grandmother. The fragrances of roses, lilies, and earthy moss enveloped her like a comforting blanket. Every nook and cranny of the place was bursting with wonderful things to see and touch and smell. Along with flowers, Alex sold unique knickknacks and crafts from local artists.

"It might not help"—Tatum lifted her shoulders in an apologetic shrug—"but I always thought you were too pretty and fun to be with Len."

"His real name is *Jerry*," she said with attitude, and then felt terrible. "Sorry, Tatum. It does help a little. Turns out Jerry had a good reason for being such a stick-in-the-mud. I'm sure it's kind of hard to get out with a wife and three kids at home."

Tatum laughed, then slapped a hand over her mouth. "Sorry. That's not funny."

Stella was done discussing her bad choice in men. "Is Alex in the back?"

Tatum bit down on the pencil she'd been using. "She didn't think you'd be in today, so she ran to the wholesale flower market in Seattle for a few things."

"Phoebe," Stella growled. Her sister had lied to get her out of bed.

"She said she'd be ready to start tomorrow."

When Stella yanked the door open, the bell jingled. She jumped to slap it down, but she was about three—or six— inches too short. *Stupid bell.*

With nowhere she had to be, she crossed the street to Town Square and sat on an empty bench. For three days she had sulked in bed with images of Jerry's happy family running through her mind.

The endless broken dates made sense now. He had a perfectly reasonable I-have-a-wife-and-kids excuse for never inviting her to his house or introducing her to his family and friends. He'd been attending soccer games and school plays and performing honey-dos.

He lied to her for two years, and not once had she suspected. All the telltale signs blazed bright, right in front of her nose, and she'd ignored every one. Now that she knew the truth, everything became so blinking-neon-sign clear.

She had realized one important thing while lying in bed. She wasn't as heartbroken as she should be over losing the man she'd expected to propose. That part of this ordeal was a surprising relief. If he *had* asked her to marry him, would she have accepted or would she have gone with her heart and said no?

On top of all the lies and deceit, the part that really bothered her was that Jerry had turned her into the Other Woman. He'd cheated her out of the choice she would have made had she known the truth. Shame and guilt made her stomach churn like a washing machine.

She should have listened to her friends and family. Her mom and dad hadn't warmed up to Jerry. They were polite, but never treated him in the easy way they'd treated other boyfriends.

Alex never trusted Jerry. Carolyn thought he might be abusive like her own ex-husband. Misty had taunted her when Len came up with an excuse to miss Alex and Colton's wedding. *"On Valentine's Day, Len couldn't make it? Doesn't that seem a bit odd to you?"* She'd suggested a background check. *"He's probably a drug dealer with major mafia connections."*

Well, Misty had been wrong about him being a drug dealer, but she was right about the bit odd part. Stella should have done her own checking when Misty suggested it, but she'd been too stubborn, too trusting, too certain she'd one day prove them all wrong.

"Hey, Stella!"

Stella closed her eyes at Leo's imitation of Marlon Brando. He'd greeted her that way since she was little. Long before she knew about *A Streetcar Named Desire.*

"Not going to answer me?"

"Did Phoebe send you here to keep an eye on me?"

He plopped down on the bench and wrapped an arm around her shoulder. "Do I need to keep an eye on you?"

"Did you know she was lying when she said Alex was expecting me?"

"Do you think we discuss you all the time?"

"Why are you answering my questions with questions?"

"We're three for three. Want to keep going?"

"Do you?"

He held up his hand in surrender. "You win this round, but only because you're all sad and gloomy."

She almost argued but decided not to bother. She was sad and gloomy and completely disgusted with herself, and she wanted to be alone. "So now you've checked on me, you can go away. And tell Phoebe I don't appreciate being lied to by her any more than I appreciated it from Jerry."

"Technically she didn't lie, she just didn't tell you Alex said you could start tomorrow."

"Same as."

"She simply stretched the truth a little for your own good. You needed a shower."

"Go away."

He stretched his long legs out, making it clear that he wasn't going anywhere. "But I have a fun afternoon planned for us. We'll have such a great time, you'll forget all about Len in your joy and happiness overload. *Len,*" he scoffed. "Where in the world did he come up with that name?"

She settled back against Leo's arm. Despite her snarky comments, she didn't mind him hanging around. He was like the brother she never had. He and Phoebe had been best friends since grade school. Growing up, he'd been a fixture at their house—kind of like a comfy chair or a mattress molded to your body—preferring the Adams' home to the communal atmosphere where he was raised by hippie parents.

"Ha! Your name isn't much different."

"No, but I was given the name Leonard by my tie-dyed, bead-wearing parents who named me after a rock band. The hospital made the mistake with the spelling of Lynyrd. Jerry, on the other hand, came up with Len all by himself without any… medicinal help."

Stella lifted a shoulder. "Maybe he thought Len sounded smart."

"Yeah, he's real smart," Leo said with disgust.

Smart enough to fool me.

"Stop defending the jackass."

"I'm not."

"Yes, you are. I see the tickertape running across your forehead."

Stella rubbed her forehead as if she could wipe away visible thoughts. *Time to change the subject.* She looked into Leo's kind, amazingly blue eyes and grabbed the first thing that came to mind. "Why don't you and my gorgeous sister get married? You'd make beautiful babies."

Leo flashed his devastating grin, the one that made women all over the state of Washington swoon. "Your gorgeous sister and I would make beautiful babies, but we're just friends, as we've both told you many, many, *many* times. In fact, I believe your gorgeous sister told you that very thing"—he glanced at his watch—"two point five hours ago."

"No one believes you're just friends, you know. The whole town thinks you guys are sleeping together."

"We are."

Stella slapped her thigh and pantomimed laughter. "You're as hilarious as Phoebe."

"Do you think having a repeat conversation will make it true?"

"Were you standing in the hall listening?"

He thumped her softly on the top of the head. "Stella. You live in an apartment with paper-thin walls. I could be next door and hear what you and Phoebe are saying."

Stella blew out a breath. "I just don't get how you can be together all the time and not be attracted to each other."

"She's very attracted to me. She tells me how handsome I am all the time." Leo laughed. "Your eye-roll says you don't believe me, but it's true. She thinks I'm unbelievably handsome."

"And conceited."

"I'm only conceited if I believe her."

"Do you?"

Leo swept a hand down in front of himself as if that was all the answer she needed.

She snorted.

"I've always thought that snort was one of your most attractive features."

"A snort isn't a feature. It's a habit."

An extremely bad habit according to your mother.

Stella wiggled her shoulder to unseat her tiny annoyance.

"Let's get pancakes."

Stella turned Leo's wrist so she could read his watch. "It's two o'clock in the afternoon."

Leo stood, grabbed her hands, and pulled her to her feet in one swift motion. "It's two-twenty-four, which is the perfect time for pancakes." With her hand in his, he led her through the park. At the corner, they crossed the street and entered Noelle's Café.

Noelle met them with a sad smile, which told Stella the news had been thoroughly discussed in the café like everywhere else in town. "Table for two?"

"Yes, please." Leo waited until Stella slid onto a booth bench like he was afraid she might bolt. Again, she had nowhere else to be. She hadn't eaten much in the last three days, and the smells coming from the kitchen made her stomach growl. She imagined a juicy burger and a huge plate of fries…

"What can I get you?" Noelle asked tugging an order pad out of her apron pocket and a pencil from behind her ear.

…or a club sandwich and some of Albert's potato salad or maybe…

Leo slid into the opposite side of the booth. "Stella will have buttermilk pancakes with blueberry compote and maple syrup. I'll have chocolate strawberry pancakes. We'll need two glasses of milk and one side of bacon."

"We don't serve breakfast past eleven," Noelle said.

"I hate pancakes," Stella said at the same time.

"Noelle"—he indicated Stella—"look at that sad face and tell me Albert wouldn't make an exception." He shook his head at Stella. "And nobody hates pancakes."

"I do," Stella said.

Noelle sighed. "Leo, you would make life for me and Albert so much easier if you'd order what's listed on the menu."

"You and Albert would make my life easier if you expanded your menu to include chocolate strawberry pancakes."

Noelle tucked her pencil behind her ear. "I'll see if my cook is *willing* to make that exception."

"Being rich has made you high-maintenance," Stella said after Noelle disappeared through the swinging kitchen door.

Leo had dropped out of college, developed a dot-com

company, and moved to Silicon Valley. A few years later he sold the company for millions, moved back to Eden Falls, and lived a quiet yet anything-but-lonely life. He always had a string of women chasing him.

"I'm not high-maintenance. I just want what I want."

"High-maintenance." She propped her elbow on the table and leaned her cheek on her hand. "I hope you're hungry, because I really do hate pancakes."

"How is that even possible?"

Stella shrugged. "They're squishy when they're dry and mushy after they've sat in syrup."

"We'll put syrup on one bite at a time. If you don't like them, you can eat the bacon."

Just what the old hips need, her tiny nuisance muttered.

Hey, I didn't order the pancakes or the bacon.

Leo cell phone chimed with an incoming text. He read the message then typed a reply.

Probably Phoebe checking up on me. Stella turned to the window and the beautiful day. Her mood called for dark clouds and thunder echoing off the surrounding mountains. A few lightning strikes would top things off. *Yay, me. I have all summer to wallow in my own Jerry-induced misery.*

Was he worried she'd rat him out to his wife? But how could she without revealing the part she played?

"Quit. It."

She jumped at Leo's brisk command. "Quit what?"

"Thinking about that loser. Quit with the what-ifs and the I-should-haves. It's over. You made a mistake." He narrowed his eyes. "Hopefully you learned from that mistake. Always ask a man if he's married before you accept his tongue."

"Gross."

Leo drummed the table with his palms. "Let it go, Stella."

"Easier said than done. I dated the married man for two years." *How do I come back from that?*

"Any guy who cheats on his wife isn't a man."

"The point is—"

"The point is he's trash."

"Yeah, but his wife—"

"Want to know something about me that only Phoebe knows?"

Stella held up a hand. "No."

Leo leaned back on the red vinyl bench. She could tell he was going to reveal his secret anyway. He was raised on a farm where his parents grew and sold organic vegetables—among other things they'd been arrested for. Leo was a total geek in school. For years, his only friend had been Phoebe.

"When I lived in California, I met someone special. The one. Or at least I thought she was. Later, almost too late, I found out she was only after my money. We were engaged when I found out." His phone chimed. He glanced at the screen, then set it facedown on the table.

"You were actually engaged, with a ring and everything?"

"Yep."

"Was it pretty?"

"What?"

Stella leaned forward. "The ring. Was it pretty?"

Leo lifted a shoulder. "It was big and shiny and cost me a lot of money."

When he didn't offer any more information, she rolled her hand. "So…how'd you find out she was only after your money?"

"Charging roughly two to three thousand dollars on a credit card and expecting me to pay the bill was a huge giveaway."

"Two to three thousand dollars is like…what? A sofa?"

"A day."

Stella's mouth dropped open. "She was charging two to three thousand dollars a day? For what?"

"Clothes, shoes, makeup, hair. Whatever she could buy while I was at work."

Stella fell back against the booth seat. "Did you pay it?"

"I paid off what she bought while we were together."

"Then you broke off the engagement?"

"Yep."

"Did she keep the ring?"

"Would you?"

Stella rolled her eyes. "It wasn't the same with me and Jerry. He wasn't after my money, because I have none."

"My point is anyone can be duped." He leaned forward, crossing his arms on the table. "We all want to believe the best of a person, but everyone lives by a different moral compass. Life is a learning process. Hopefully, we learn from our mistakes and move on."

"Thanks for the lecture, Dad." Stella stared at him for a moment. "Was that even a true story?"

The corner of his mouth twitched. "Mostly."

"What part wasn't?"

"The part where I was engaged and the part where she was spending two to three thousand dollars a day."

Stella snorted. "Which part was true?"

He lifted a shoulder. "She did like to spend money and she wore a lot of makeup."

She shook her head. Still, he deserved an A for effort.

Noelle appeared with a tray. She set a side of bacon, two glasses of milk, and two huge plates of pancakes on the table. "Albert did his best. *Bon appétit.*"

Suddenly Stella was ravenous. Despite her abhorrence of pancakes, she dug in like she hadn't eaten in weeks. Halfway through hers, she reached across the table and helped herself to a forkful of Leo's choice. "Yum..."

"For someone who doesn't like pancakes, you've put a

pretty big dent in that plateful." After two more bites, he raised a brow. "Stella, you're going to be sick."

"I want to make sure you get your money's worth," she mumbled around a mouthful. "You owe Albert a gigantic tip for indulging in quirks."

He lifted a comical eyebrow. "I don't have quirks."

After too short a time, she sat back and rubbed her stomach. "Ohmygosh, I can't eat another bite."

"Are you sure you don't want to lick that little bit of blueberry compote off the plate?"

"Shut up. You're the one who ordered for me." She put a hand to her mouth to stifle a burp.

He leaned away. "You're not going to throw up, are you?"

"Nope." She slid out of the booth. "Thanks for the pancakes, the stimulating conversation, and for sharing your sad love story that was a gigantic lie. For a millionaire, you're not as stuffy as everyone says."

He frowned. "I think there were several masked insults in there somewhere."

"Stimulating, sharing, and not stuffy. All compliments. See ya around, Leo."

"I think I'm supposed to be babysitting all afternoon," she heard him shout as the door closed behind her.

Not happenin'. She turned toward home.

CHAPTER 3

Stella wandered around her and Phoebe's apartment feeling lost. She should have accepted Leo's babysitting offer. She might have finagled a free movie and some popcorn out of the afternoon. Not that she could eat another bite.

The pancakes had settled like a lump in her stomach.

Her cell phone rang and Jillian's cute face popped up on her screen. She didn't feel like talking, but she also didn't want to sit alone in the quiet. She connected the call. "Hi, Jillian."

"Hey girlfriend. How are you doing?"

Yes. How are you doing?

She frowned at the nuisance next to her ear. *You are very annoying.*

"Stella?"

"I'm here. I'm fine. Well, pretty fine."

"I just got off work. Want to meet at Noelle's for a piece of pie?"

Stella swallowed, the pancakes threatening a reappearance at the mention of food. "Thanks, but I just ate."

"Are you just saying that?"

Stella paced her small living room. "No. I was just at Noelle's with Leo eating pancakes."

"Wait," Jillian said, her voice full of suspicion. "You hate pancakes."

Stella swallowed, once more forcing the pancakes down. "Leo ordered and I was hungry." *I won't make that mistake again.*

"Do you want to do something else? We could go for a ride or see a movie."

She stopped at the bathroom door and looked over the mess she'd left this morning. "Thanks, but I think I'll surprise Phoebe and clean up around the apartment."

"Want some help? I'm great at cleaning."

"As much as I'd love the help, Phoebe will razz me forever if I don't do this myself."

"Okay." Jillian blew out a breath. "Will you promise to call me if you change your mind? I'll be at home. I'm worried about you, Stella."

"I truly am fine. I love you for checking on me."

"I love you back. Call if you need anything."

After disconnecting from Jillian, she picked her still-damp towel off the bathroom floor, wishing one of her other sisters was around. Georgiana lived a perfect married life in Chicago with her surgeon husband. Isadora was in northern California working at an art gallery. Baby sister Adelaide, affectionately called Oops because she was eight years younger than Stella, and a surprise to them all, was apprenticing for a top publishing company in New York between her junior and senior years at Western Connecticut State University.

Stella went to the kitchen for glass cleaner and paper towels. As she misted the bathroom mirror, she thought about how different this summer would be from the one she'd planned.

She loved the school year and teaching her little second graders, but she also loved her summers off and helping Alex at the only flower shop in town. They arranged bouquets for weddings, birthdays, and anniversaries. As much as she loved the momentous occasions, her favorite arrangements were for the tables at the senior center's luncheons once a week. Those ladies sure loved their flowers.

She'd always been able to occupy her summer days. When Alex didn't need her, she took Alex's son swimming at the public pool or spent time with her mom. She'd go to the gym for a workout or plan a day tubing down the river. There was always something to do around Eden Falls, but this summer would be different. When not working, all her friends would be with someone else.

Maybe she should get another part-time job so she wouldn't have time to think. Keeping busy would stop her from dwelling on Jerry, on his wife Anna, on the two years she'd wasted. Yep, Jerry's summer would be a lot different than he'd planned, too.

She could help out at summer recreation, a program run by high school seniors for college credits. Surely they could use a supervisor or someone to come up with craft ideas. Alex's mom might teach her to knit or crochet, something she'd always wanted to learn. She could make booties for newborns at Harrisville Regional Hospital or doggy coats for the animal shelter. She could serve ice cream at One Scoop or Two or donuts at Patsy's Pastries.

Why the sudden urge to be needed?

Stella stared at her reflection in the now-clean mirror. *It's not need. It's reparation.*

She yanked open her designated vanity drawer and threw

her brush, dental floss, and a tube of mascara inside. She gathered all the towels and dumped them in the washer. Fresh towels would shoot Phoebe over the moon with happiness.

The doorbell rang and she groaned. Leo was here to bug her. Then again, Leo's company was better than finishing the bathroom or sitting alone feeling sorry for herself. She ran through the living room and flung open the door, then just as quickly tried to slam it shut. Jerry's foot was faster.

"Let me in, Stella. We need to talk."

"No, we don't." She put all her weight into shoving on the door. Sure she'd lost fifteen pounds, but with all the pancake carbs she just consumed, she had to have gained several back.

"Let me explain."

"I don't want to hear anything you have to say."

"Stella, you love me."

She tried to laugh but the sound stuck in her throat, throbbing with the pain of betrayal. "*Loved.* Past tense. I hate you now."

"Love doesn't disappear that quickly, sweetheart. It's still there, just under the surface. I see it in your eyes."

"What you see is disgust and loathing. Disgust that you not only deceived me, but you're deceiving your wife. Loathing that I allowed it to happen. Any other feelings I had for you are dead." She put her shoulder against the door and pushed. "Get away from my apartment."

"When we met, Anna and I were having problems in our marriage. We still are."

"You are the only problem Anna is having. How could you do that to her? To your children?" *To me?*

Putting yourself into that equation is selfish.

Shut up! Stella pushed harder.

"Will you let me in so we can talk?"

"No. We are never talking again. Now get your foot out of my door." With two kids the age of his, he was older than he'd led her to believe. Another lie. The lies were stacking up, too deep to wade through. She'd been so gullible, so…

Pathetic?

I don't need any help from you.

"Stella," he said, his voice softening. "Can this stay between us for now? I don't want to hurt my wife needlessly. My marriage is over. It has been for a long time, but until—"

"You are the most despicable human being on the face of the earth. Even now you're spouting lies. Your marriage isn't close to over. It wouldn't matter to me if it was. I never want to see you again. You are a snake, No, you're lower than a snake. You're a vile, despicable, cheating pig. Nope. Still not bad enough to describe you. You're—"

"Stella—"

She opened the door quickly and he fell on all fours. She glared down into his eyes. The eyes she thought she'd be gazing into forever.

He scrambled to his feet, but before he could catch his balance, she hit him in the chest with both hands, knocking him back outside. Still he was able to stick his foot over the threshold again.

"You turned me into the other woman. The home-wrecker. Have you even considered your wife's feelings? And what about your children? Have you considered—no you haven't, because you're a selfish, self-centered, lying pig."

She stomped on his instep as hard as possible. He yelped and lifted his foot back. She slammed and locked the door. "Get away from my apartment or I'll call the police. My sister is on duty. She'd love to throw you in jail. Or shoot you."

She slid to the floor, her whole body shaking. What she told him was true. She was totally disgusted by him and disgusted that she ever loved him. What had she seen in him? His eyes were too close together, his eyebrows too perfect, and his nose too small and narrow for his face. His earlobes were too long, and he had a high forehead. And bad breath. "You have bad breath," she yelled in case he was still outside the door.

She glanced at her perky little pest. *Too over the top?*

Her angel tipped her hand back and forth a couple of times.

In reality, outrage should be reserved for Anna, but Jerry had cheated his wife out of that emotion by sneaking behind her back. He'd cheated his family out of so much. All the times he was in Eden Falls when he should have been home with his wife and kids. The poor woman lived in dark, blissful ignorance, believing her husband was faithful.

A stab of memory punctured her thoughts. She jumped up and opened the door.

Shoot, he's gone.

You wanted to see him again?

Just long enough to ask what was in the jewelry box. I hope it was something beautiful for his wife.

Aww...

Stella slammed the door and trudged down the hall to the bathroom, picking up the paper towels she dropped in her rush to answer the door. Instead of resuming, she decided to get out of the apartment. The walls were crushing her into oblivion.

But where to go? She wasn't ready to face her parents or their sympathetic looks and the myriad of questions that would follow her arrival. She'd received calls and texts from each one of her friends, but she wasn't ready to deal with them, either. Misty's I-told-you-so would have to wait.

She slipped into sneakers, grabbed a sweater, and left. With the sun on her face, she listened to birds twittering in surrounding trees as she headed into town. A breeze teased her with the smell of freshly mown grass, a summer favorite, and something flowery.

She could shop for a new outfit at The Clothes Barn—spending money always helped heal a wounded soul—or she could stop at Patsy's Pastries and add a dozen donuts to the pancakes she gorged on earlier. She had no one to impress anymore. Two more inches around her waist and hips, and she could justify buying a whole new wardrobe.

You have a bridesmaid dress you have to fit into, her companion sing-songed.

Right. The donuts would have to wait until after the wedding.

The sidewalks were crowded with people popping in and out of shops. She stopped in front of Pages and glanced over the titles for sale.

Maude came out and put an arm around her waist. "You okay?"

The shop owner and her husband had lived next door to Stella's parents since before she was born. The couple didn't have children and often invited one or more of the five Adams girls over for dinner and a movie. "I will be. Got any books about cheating spouses getting what's coming to them while the "other woman" helps the wife achieve justice?"

"I got a better idea." Maude lifted an eyebrow. "I know a hit man."

Stella's laugh faded when Maude didn't join in. "Seriously? No, Maude. He has a family."

Maude shrugged slender shoulders. "Just sayin'."

Slightly disturbed by the elderly lady's suggestion, Stella waved and moved on.

Instead of going inside when she reached The Clothes Barn, she continued down the street. At Rowdy's Bar and Grill she paused, listening to the country crooning coming from within. The Zac Brown Band calmed her inner turmoil.

An order of onion rings would taste good.

Her angel smiled. *No need to skip them anymore since there won't be any kissing.*

Stella nodded. *I've missed onion rings.*

Inside, she bellied up to the bar.

Mike Stettler stopped in front of her and glanced at his watch. "It's a little early to be meeting the girls."

"I'm on my own tonight. I'll have a Diet Coke with a twist of lime." Her stomach was still too full of pancakes for the onion rings, but in an hour... She watched Mike, busy behind the bar. She heard through the gossip grapevine that he'd moved to town after his fiancée ran off with his best friend. She wondered if it would be appropriate to ask how long it had taken him to get over that kind of hurt. Though, if he was still hurting, her questions might only dredge up fresh pain.

"You okay?" Mike set her drink in front of her. "You look like you've lost your last friend."

"Not my last." She lifted her glass. "You haven't heard?"

He planted palms on the bar. "Heard what?"

So word hadn't reached everyone in town yet.

"Want to talk about it?" he asked when she didn't answer. "Rowdy made me take a class in listening before he hired me."

"Really?"

"No," he said with a chuckle. "Just a joke. Obviously not a very funny one."

She held out her hand. "Hi, I'm Gullible Adams. Nice to meet you."

"Sorry, Stella. We're all a little gullible sometimes. Anything I can do to help?"

She twisted her lips in thought as she tapped her fingers on the wooden bar. *Matter of fact, there is something he can do.*

No!

"Yes." Stella brushed away her conscience. "You can give me a shot of whiskey."

Mike's frown was instant. "You don't drink alcohol."

"I don't—haven't…yet. But there's always a first."

"There doesn't have to be."

She rubbed her temples with index fingers. "Can I just get a shot, please?"

"Alcohol isn't an answer to—"

"I didn't ask for a lecture. I asked for a shot."

With narrowed eyes, Mike set a tiny glass in front of her and added amber liquid.

Stella lifted the shot to her nose and sniffed. The biting scent was strong. "An acquired smell, like sulfur or skunk spray."

Mike shook his head.

She touched the tip of her tongue to the liquid.

Yuck. Stop now.

Go away.

She'd seen people just toss a shot back, so that's what she did. The liquor burned a hole through her tongue, her esophagus, then the lining of her stomach, sending her into a coughing fit. Tears filled her eyes and spilled down her cheeks. She put a hand to her throat as she sucked in a wheezing gasp of air.

Mike was next to her in a second, concern etched across his features. "You okay?"

"Fine," she rasped out while swiping away the tears. "I'll have another."

"Stella…"

She stopped him with a do-not-mess-with-me look. "Pour me another."

~

*A*fter storing the bank bag in the bar and grill's safe, Rowdy went into the kitchen and opened the walk-in freezer door. Good, the meat delivery came in this afternoon. Same story in the pantry. The shelves were well stocked.

He shifted a couple of boxes around. His cook would shift them back. They didn't agree on the layout of the pantry. Most of the time he let Juan have his way, but a shift every once in a while kept his fussy cook on his toes.

Back in the kitchen, he joked with a waitress, razzed the dishwasher, then helped himself to a spoonful of the potato salad Juan made to accompany the French dip sandwiches on special for dinner.

He thanked his lucky stars every day that he'd been able to see beyond the dilapidated building that used to be where his bar and grill now stood. He'd renovated with lots of wood—walls, bar, floor—giving it a welcoming sense of warmth that still spoke to him on a visceral level. He hoped others felt the same when they walked through the door.

Out front, Mike stood near the register with a worried expression. Rowdy followed his bartender's gaze to Stella, who glared from a seat at the end of the bar. Chin in palm, she picked up a shot glass with her other hand and slammed it down with a bang. "I-I wann...annnother shot...a whiskey."

Rowdy was shocked to hear Stella slurring like a drunk.

Mike shook his head. "I can't serve you another one, Stella. I'm sorry."

Rowdy rounded the bar and stopped next to Mike, his gaze on Stella. "How many has she had?"

"Too many. She's been here since about four thirty. I've tried to pace her." Mike shook his head. "I surprised she's still sitting upright."

"I know you're talking about me while I'm sitting *up right* here." Stella beat the glass on the bar with each carefully punctuated word. "I'm a paying customer, Rowdy Garrett. I want another shot."

Rowdy walked around the bar and caught Stella just as she slipped off the stool. He lifted her in his arms. "See if you can find Phoebe," he said to Mike.

"Phee-bee is wor-king." She giggled. "My liiipsss are nummmb."

"Try her at the station," Rowdy said.

Mike nodded and picked up the phone near the register.

Rowdy turned toward his office with Stella tucked close to his chest. She smelled like oranges, whiskey, and maple syrup, a strangely beguiling combination.

"Put me down. I'm too fat to carry."

"First of all, you're not fat. Second, you're too drunk to walk."

"Rowdy." She snorted. "Rrr-ow-dee. I never noticed how funny your name is. Why can't I have another drink, Rrr-ow-dee?"

"I have a hard and fast rule. If you can't stand, you can't have another drink."

"I can stand."

"You can barely talk. What makes you think you can stand?"

"I can talk." Her eyebrows bunched together in a cute frown. "And I can talk."

He chuckled. "You mean walk."

"Yeah, I can walk, too. Put me down and I'll show you. Hey, that rhy…" Her eyebrows puckered again. "Too and you sound the same."

"Yes, they do."

"Where are we going?"

"My office."

"Is that where you seduce women?"

He felt a frown pucker his own brows. "No, Stella. I don't take drunk women to my office and seduce them."

"Too bad." She tucked her cute little nose against his neck and sniffed. "Because you smell amazing. Masculine. Macho. Jerry never smelled this good. He wears stinky cologne," she stage-whispered.

"Stinky, huh?"

She nodded vigorously.

"You smell nice too. Like maple syrup."

"Did you hear my boyfriend is married?" she asked running a finger from his jaw to his Adam's apple.

"Yes. I'm sorry you got hurt."

She looked up at him with an adorable but goofy grin a moment before she turned green and spewed vomit all over both of them.

CHAPTER 4

Stella blinked her eyes open, then quickly squeezed them shut when a jackhammer pounded into her left temple. She tried to swallow, but the same someone who ground sand into her eyeballs had shoved a hairball down her throat.

She forced one eye open a slit. Butterscotch. Lifting a finger, she ran the tip over the color. Butter soft butterscotch. Scotch, the word turned her stomach a fuzzy green with squishy tentacles. She pressed the palm of her hand against the softness in front of her eye. Leather. She was looking at leather. Turning her head inch by inch, her gaze moved up the back of a sofa to…*stars?*

Where am I?

Floating through space.

That's not funny.

She winced when the jackhammer moved to her right temple. She slammed her eyes shut for several heartbeats and sucked in a ragged breath, hoping to calm her queasy stomach. Blinking slowly, hoping her eyes and head would adjust to the dim light without exploding, she stared at the solar system and beyond above her. *I'm floating through space on a butterscotch-colored leather sofa.*

She grabbed the sides of the cushions, terrified she might fall over the edge into nothingness. *I'm dreaming. This has to be a dream.*

Not a dream. Her pest pointed upward. *There's Saturn.*

A cold fear that she was floating through space splashed over her like a bucket of cold water, and she shivered.

A sound on her left startled her, then relief replaced fear. At least she wasn't alone. Turning her head a fraction at a time, she tried to keep the jackhammer at medium speed rather than full blast.

Oh, look. I'm in space with Rowdy.

He sat behind an old wooden desk. Shoulders bare, head down, he was scratching away with a pen. *I'm in space with a naked Rowdy.* Turning her head a bit farther…

Nope. He wore white socks and something on his legs—could be jeans. She squinted to see through the dim light.

Or an awful lot of hair. Which reminded her of the hairball in her throat.

"Do you have pants on?"

He looked up and their eyes met. A slow grin moved across his face. "I can take them off if you'd like."

Did I say that out loud?

Yep.

Rowdy set his pen aside. "Are you in the land of the living?"

Am I?

Her angel laughed way too loud. *I don't think so.*

Stella's last memory was demanding a drink from Mike and him refusing. She closed her eyes, hoping for relief from the drill that had taken the jackhammer's place in her forehead.

"How do you feel?"

"You don't have to yell."

His chuckle was softer than his voice had been. "I'm not yelling."

The universe still whirled above her when she opened her eyes, and she grabbed for the sofa cushions again. "Why are we in space?"

"We're not in space. You're in my office." He pushed back from his desk. His chair scratching against the wood floor sounded like a metal boat being dragged along concrete. He looked down at her with his familiar smirk. At least that part of this dream was right. "You look terrible."

She pressed palms to her pounding head. "Wow. Sweet pillow talk. You sure know how to sweep a girl off her feet."

He lifted a brow. "Would you rather I lie?"

"I'd rather you stop talking."

He sat beside her, scooting her against the back of the sofa with his hip.

Eyes closed, the room spun, but eyes open was too painful. She tried one open, one closed. "Do you work bare-chested often?" she asked with as much snark as she could muster.

He leaned back, pinning her legs. "Only when someone throws up on me."

A swift, terrible memory flooded her mind, and she groaned. "Oh…I did."

"Yep, you did. Vomited all over the front of both of us."

She lifted her head enough to see she wore a man's oxford button-down. Her legs were bare. Luckily, because of Rowdy's height and her lack thereof, the shirt hit low on her thighs.

"Don't worry. I didn't tarnish your reputation."

Too late. I'm a home-wrecker.

You didn't know he was married.

"Phoebe took a quick break from work. She cleaned you up and dressed you."

More bits and pieces came back. Phoebe pulling her T-shirt over her head, wiping her face with wet, scratchy paper towels, and washing her hair in the bar and grill's bathroom sink with hand soap. She owed her sister big for this one. "Why didn't she just take me home?"

"We didn't think you should be alone, and she didn't want to call your parents. She tried to get ahold of Leo, but he was out." Stella picked at the men's oxford with her fingertips. "You always keep a change of shirts handy?"

"I own a bar. You aren't the first woman to throw up on me."

She rolled her eyes and was immediately sorry when the jackhammer went back to work. "No, I don't imagine I am. Though I'm sure you probably keep extra clothes here for other reasons."

Rowdy half turned to her. "Was that an implied insult?"

"It wasn't meant to be implied."

"I'll have you know you're the only female to ever grace this sofa in a reclining position."

"Whatever," she mumbled, rubbing her temples. Everyone in town knew Rowdy's reputation as a player.

"Speaking of whatever. Whatever you ate before you came here was disgusting."

Late lunch with Leo. "Pancakes with blueberry something. I can't remember the fancy word Leo used when he ordered."

"Well, that fancy word is never coming out of *my* shirt."

She opened both eyes to stare at him. "Eww. You'd want to wear a shirt I threw up on?"

"I just bought that shirt. Thanks for christening it on its debut night. I looked great in that color," he mumbled.

She wasn't about to roll her eyes again. "I'll buy you a new one." Stella turned so she faced the back of the sofa and closed her eyes, hoping to relieve the sand scratching her corneas. "I'm sorry I threw up on you."

"That's what happens when you drink too much, too fast, on a stomach full of pancakes. Especially when you've never had alcohol before."

"Could you please stop mentioning food? This is all Leo's fault. I told him I *hate* pancakes."

Rowdy chuckled. "Why would you eat pancakes if you hate them?"

"He ordered for me and I was hungry." She ran a hand over the soft leather. "Nice sofa, by the way. It's comfortable."

"Thanks." She felt him shift. "So, what happened?"

Unable to look him in the face, especially when his tone turned from teasing to empathetic, she stared at the butter-scotch leather. "I'm sure you heard Len Barlow is really Jerry Winters, he's married, and has three kids."

"Everyone has."

Tears burned. Maybe a good, cleansing cry would wash away the sand scraping her eyeballs every time she blinked. "He had the nerve to show up at my door earlier today. He said his marriage was in trouble, but it didn't look that way to me on Friday night when he was sitting in a restaurant with his family."

"Did you let him in?"

His tone had changed, and she turned to look at him, but couldn't read his expression. "No."

"Good."

She pointed up. "Why do you have a poster of stars on the ceiling?"

Rowdy leaned his head back on the sofa, his gaze fixed on the ceiling. Stella studied his rugged profile. His square jaw matched his straight, well-defined nose. A strand of leather secured his long hair at the nape of his neck.

He glanced at her. His mossy green eyes, which were as

much a Garrett family trait as handsomeness, focused on her face. "When I get out of here at night, I'm usually too tired to spend much time stargazing, so I lie where you are and stare at my ceiling when I get a chance."

"Are you interested in the stars?"

"Space fascinates me. Always has." He sat forward, resting his forearms on his knees. "Do you want to try and sit up? I can get you a cup of tea and a slice of bread."

Her stomach flipped. She shook her head. "I can sit up, but I don't want anything to eat. I just want to go home." *Fall into bed and sleep for a week. Or a month. Or maybe all summer.*

Rowdy stood and held out his hand. "Come on. I'll give you a ride."

She started to protest, but remembered she'd walked here and she only wore a man's shirt.

He pulled her to her feet. "You okay?" he asked, holding her hands.

She looked down at her bare feet and wiggled her toes.

Wrapping an arm around her shoulders, he walked her to the back door. "Here are your shoes. They were the only item of clothing not covered in vomit."

Phoebe is going to kill me.

～

*R*owdy was having a hard time being the gentleman his mom taught him to be. Stella sat in the passenger seat of his truck looking all sleepy-eyed and sexy, with all kinds of cute thrown in. Cute wasn't a word he normally included in his vocabulary unless he was talking about his niece, but that's the only way he could describe Stella in his oversized shirt. A familiar desire rippled through him. He tightened his hold on the steering wheel.

She closed her eyes and rubbed a hand across her forehead. He could only imagine the headache she was suffering. As far as he knew, she'd never had a drop of alcohol before tonight.

He parked in front of her apartment. "Wait there." He got out and hurried around the back of his truck, but not before she opened her door.

"I can get out by my—"

He grabbed her and swung her into his arms before she hit the ground in a full face-plant. "I said to wait. You had a lot to drink, Stella."

"I can walk."

"Oh, but this is so much more fun."

She groaned and dropped her head back, exposing her graceful neck. "I bet I owe Mike an apology. I don't think I was very nice."

"He's used to belligerent customers."

"If you're trying to make me feel better, it's not working." She gave in, wrapped her arms around his neck, and tucked her nose close. The whisper of her breath tickled his skin, making mincemeat of his trying-to-be-a-gentleman intentions. "I like your cologne."

"You told me that earlier."

"I did?"

"Right before you threw up on me."

"Ahh, that's why it's mixed with vomit fragrance."

"Yeah, thanks for that. Where are your keys?"

"There's one under the flowerpot on the shelf next to the door."

"Hold on." She tightened her hold around his neck when he reached up to move the flowerpot. "This is a real safe place to keep a key."

"My sister's a cop."

"I don't care who your sister is, you two need to start

carrying keys with you instead of hiding them right next to the front door."

"Okay, Dad."

Rowdy frowned at her cute—there was no other word that fit—smirk before he unlocked the front door and pushed it open. He carried her down the short hall and set her on her feet at the bathroom door, holding her by the shoulders to make sure she was steady. "Take a shower."

"I just want to crawl into bed."

"You need a shower. The steam will help. Plus you still smell like vomit yourself."

She stepped into the room and smiled for the first time, the tiniest bit of sparkle lighting her eyes.

He raised a brow. "You need any help?"

The smile fell away and she shut the door in his face.

As soon as he heard the shower start, he went to the kitchen and filled two tall glasses and a juice glass with water. In the juice glass he dropped two tablets from his jeans pocket. Alka-Seltzer was the hangover remedy his father gave him when he came home drunk as a skunk as a teen. He lifted the fizzing water to his nose. Hopefully this would do the trick. He rummaged through her cupboards until he found a sleeve of saltines. He tucked the crackers between his forearm and body, picked up the three glasses, and carried them down the hall in search of Stella's bedroom.

The room on the left was neat and tidy, the bed carefully made. The one on the right looked like a cyclone had blown through. As often as he'd heard Phoebe complain about her messy sister, he could only assume the room on the right was Stella's.

After knocking several books to the floor in order to make room, he set the glasses and sleeve of crackers on the nightstand. Restacking the books, he glanced around. At least the chaos was colorful. The quilt on the unmade bed was red with big yellow flowers. A desk and shelves on the opposite wall were painted blue, a red rug sat under a yellow dresser. *Primary colors for an elementary teacher.* The floor was covered with clothes. Bras, also colorful, hung from the closet doorknobs, half-empty bottles of water, along with bracelets, necklaces, and earrings, littered the dresser. His fingers itched to create some order.

He closed the dusty blinds, flipped on the nightstand lamp, and turned off the overhead. Dim light would be easier on her head and eyes. He wandered to the shelves and picked up a book and then another. Self-help, weight loss, motivational, more weight loss—her selection of reading material surprised him. He'd expected bare-chested men on the covers of romance novels.

He straightened a few of the framed pictures on the walls, Stella posing with her friends or family in most. She and her four sisters modeling their Easter best. Her with her friends striking crazy poses at their high school graduation, another of her in cap and gown holding up her college diploma.

He ran a finger over her face, then laughed at himself. He hadn't looked at another woman in more than two years— ever since he started noticing Stella. Of course, she'd just met her idiot boyfriend. Ironic how things like that happened. Other than college years, they'd lived in the same town their whole lives, and he only became acutely aware of her just when she began dating someone else.

He heard the shower turn off. A few minutes later the bathroom door opened. Stella padded into her room wrapped in a bright pink robe. That he was still here, and in her bedroom, didn't seem to faze her. The scent of perfumed soap and shampoo swirled around him, triggering a pleasant, heady sensation.

He fought an overwhelming urge to pull her into his arms and kiss her silly, but now wasn't the time. He could tell the shower hadn't helped her headache much. And he wanted her fully aware of what was happening when he did kiss her. "Did you brush your teeth?"

"I'm not a three-year-old, Rowdy."

"You sure? When was the last time you made your bed?"

"None of your business." She picked a towel off the floor and ruffled it through her hair while eyeing his bare chest. "Thanks for the view tonight. This has been the best nightmare I've had in years."

To distract them both, he pulled open the sleeve of crackers. "Eat a couple of these and then drink this." He held out the glass with Alka-Seltzer, which was still fizzing.

She sniffed the contents and wrinkled her nose. "What is this?"

"Just drink it, straight down. I promise it will help your headache."

She shoved a cracker in her mouth, chewed and swallowed, then drank the fizzy water as he directed. She covered her mouth and coughed. "It tastes worse than the whiskey."

"You're a glutton for punishment tonight. Eating pancakes that you hate and drinking whiskey that tastes bad. Why did you do either?"

"I told you, I ate the pancakes because I was hungry." She sank to the edge of the bed. "I drank because...I don't know why. I just had the urge to do something I've never done before. Something different and defiant and maybe a little dangerous."

"Next time buy a book on the fundamentals of decision-making." He could see the raw hurt around her eyes and wanted to punch the guy who put it there. "Or call me. I'll take you to the river and put a fishing pole in your hands."

She snorted out an adorable laugh. "I've lived in Eden Falls my whole life. If Alex can't get me in the river, you can't."

"How do you know you won't like fishing if you've never tried?"

"You sound like a dad again."

She flashed an impish grin, and the urge to kiss her swept over him, stronger than before. He had to get out of here before he did something he'd regret.

He tore his gaze away from her mouth and handed her another cracker. "Eat this and drink at least one of those glasses of water before you go to sleep."

"Thanks, Rowdy. I can't think of a nicer guy to throw up on." She picked up one of the glasses. "I'll get your shirt washed and back to you in a day or two."

He stopped at her bedroom door. "If you don't want to try fishing, clean your room the next time you want to do something new."

"Will do, Dad."

On his way out, he picked up his shirt from the bathroom floor, where she dropped it before her shower.

CHAPTER 5

A pounding headache reminded Stella of her night as soon as she blinked her eyes open. Memories of her time with Len collided with visions of Jerry and his family. That she'd been dreaming about him nauseated her.

She rolled onto her back and covered her eyes with her forearm. Emotions warred with each other in her heart and in her head. So much time wasted, so much trust lost. Were there any good guys left in the world?

She'd suffered the same puppy love as her friends in high school, but Len was her first grown-up love. Her first this-could-be-forever relationship. And her first mature heartbreak.

She looked up the grieving process steps. Yes, someone actually came up with steps one through five—or seven, depending on which site you believed. She wasn't doing any of the steps right, or in order. Everything was backward. Anger. Depression. Loneliness. None of which were part of her makeup.

She didn't always look on the bright side of the penny, but she did like to take an optimistic approach to most things. So, how to turn this experience into a positive? Never date was the only answer that came to her, but she was much too practical to believe she'd never date again. She enjoyed kissing too much.

She rubbed her temples as memory snippets of drinks at Rowdy's replaced Jerry. She owed Mike a huge tip and an apology. Rowdy deserved a new shirt and an apology, and Phoebe would get a clean apartment and an apology. She had a busy day ahead of her.

The bang of a pan in the kitchen pulled her out of bed. With a hand to her head, she stumbled down the hall in her pink bathrobe, relieved her headache wasn't worse. She vaguely remembered Rowdy carrying her into the apartment, insisting she shower, then tucking her into bed after a couple of crackers and a terrible fizzing drink. The sun was blazing through a west window, which confused Stella.

Phoebe stood at the stove, stirring something that smelled interesting. Asian. "Hey."

"Hey yourself," her sister said without turning. "Am I making too much noise?"

"No. What time is it?"

Phoebe stepped back so the stove clock was visible.

"It's four o'clock in the afternoon? Why didn't you wake me? I was supposed to help Alex."

"I tried. You bit me."

"Phoebe—"

"Relax. News of your escapades traveled fast. Alex knew you'd be in no condition to help today."

Fudge brownie with frosting on top.

Phoebe glanced over her shoulder. Stella saw the disappointment mixed with concern in her sister's eyes. "How do you feel?"

"Dizzy. Headachy. Strangely ravenous."

Phoebe turned back to the stove. "With all the vomit

Rowdy and I cleaned up last night, I understand the ravenous part."

Stella flashed on the look on Rowdy's face when she lost her late lunch all over him. His astonished blink before wide-eyed horror. An uncontrollable snicker worked its way up her throat, sounding more horse than human. Why she laughed, she had no idea. Nothing about last night was funny.

Phoebe lifted the wok and turned off the red burner. "What did Leo feed you before you decided to be stupid?"

"Pancakes." Stella dropped into a chair at their small kitchen table. Just the mention turned her stomach. "Which I'll never eat again for as long as I live."

"Ahh, right. He told me." Her sister sprinkled something on top of her concoction. Stella suspected sesame seeds. Like their mother, Phoebe was a great cook. A talent Stella hadn't inherited. "How bad is your headache?"

"It hurts in a blurry, dust-bunny kind of way. Rowdy gave me something he said would help."

"He owns a bar, so he should know." Phoebe opened a cupboard and pulled out a couple of bowls. "Want some stir-fry?"

Stella nodded. "As long as it doesn't have tofu, blueberries, or maple syrup in it."

Using a big wooden spoon, Phoebe scooped a portion of her wok concoction into a bowl and set it in front of Stella.

"Why are you home? I thought you worked tonight."

"I traded shifts with Eli. I didn't want to leave you alone."

And the apologies just keep piling up.

I don't need any reminders from you. Stella wiggled her shoulder. *Where was my pesky little conscience last night?*

I needed a night off.

Stella stood. Her head spun and she dropped back into her chair.

"Stay put. I'll get everything," Phoebe said, shooting her another look of concern. She grabbed chopsticks and napkins and set everything on the table. "Want something to drink?"

"Just water."

While Phoebe filled two glasses with ice water, Stella leaned over and sniffed the stir-fry. The sweet, spicy scent rising from the bowl made her stomach growl, and flip like a grounded fish at the same time. She set her chopsticks aside and leaned back in her chair. "I don't think I can eat after all."

Phoebe set the water on the table and took a seat across from Stella. "I'm not surprised."

Stella looked away from her beautiful sister with her long blond hair and enormous brown eyes. No one who met Phoebe on the street would believe she was a cop. She was taller than Stella by three inches, and slender. The oldest of five sisters, she was the wise one. Stella had always looked to Phoebe for advice about school, parents, and guys. Until Jerry. Then she ignored Phoebe's warnings and suggestions to break up with someone who cancelled more dates than he kept. "Sorry about last night."

"I'm trying to understand, Stella." Phoebe popped a shrimp in her mouth.

Phoebe wasn't asking about what led Stella to drink, but why she would break the vow she and her sisters had made after their alcoholic Grandma Adams drove her car over a cliff, killing herself and their grandpa. After the funeral all five sisters, including five-year-old Adelaide, had sworn to never drink. As far as Stella knew, they'd all kept their word. Until last night. She was suffering from a lot of "untils" lately. "Can we keep my lapse of judgment between us?"

"You know word will get out."

"Yeah, but it doesn't have to get out to the sisters. At least not yet."

"What happened?"

"Jerry came over."

"Please tell me you didn't let that worm into our apartment," Phoebe said through gritted teeth.

Stella rolled her eyes. "I didn't, but after he left, I just couldn't stay here alone. I felt like I was smothering."

Phoebe fished through her bowl with her chopsticks. "Why didn't you go over to a friend's house? Why Rowdy's?"

She pushed her bowl away. *Because I'm embarrassed to face my friends. Because I feel like a loser. Because I wanted to forget.* "They're all engaged or married. They're busy taking care of kids, fighting morning sickness, or planning weddings."

Her little pest cupped a hand to her ear. *Is that self-pity I hear?*

If it is, so what? I'm not allowed to feel sorry for myself after what happened?

"You're sounding a little like your students. This isn't a great guy you lost. Be grateful you were in the right place at the right time. You discovered Jerry for the scumbag he is. If you'd broken up with a great guy, I'd say stumble around in a funk for a while, but Jerry isn't a great guy. He isn't even a good guy. Now why didn't you go see one of your friends rather than go to Rowdy's? Wouldn't you drop everything to help if one of them needed you?"

"Of course, but it's not the same."

"It's exactly the same. When Colton left town, you kept Alex company until the stupid lug decided he couldn't live without her. When Misty ran away from home, despite how you felt about her at the time, you sent her a birthday text. When Carolyn came back to town, you helped her move into her house, supported her through the ex-husband-stalker mess. You were there for Jillian and Jolie when they needed you. You've helped all your friends. Why would you think this isn't exactly the same kind of situation?"

Stella looked at the ceiling to escape Phoebe's intense scrutiny. "Like you, they all warned me. Almost from the start, they said something wasn't right with Jerry. I didn't listen." Her chin dropped. "I was so sure I could prove them wrong."

"Okay, little sister, time to stop beating yourself up. You made a mistake. We all do. Jerry what's-his-face isn't worth any more of your time, your tears, your guilt."

The front door opened. "Hellooo. Oh man, what smells so great?"

"We're in the kitchen and you're in luck. It doesn't look like Stella's going to eat her dinner."

Phoebe grabbed a clean set of chopsticks and a napkin before Leo walked into the room followed by a droopy one-eyed dog. She pointed with the chopsticks. "Uh…who is this?"

"A stray that followed me home from Mom and Dad's farm. We just left the vet, where he had a complete physical, shots, and a flea bath."

The dog walked over to Stella and rested its head on her thigh. "Aww." She stroked his yellow fur. "Hi, doggy. What's your name?"

"I haven't named him yet." Leo picked up Stella's bowl and accepted the chopsticks Phoebe held out. "Looks like he gravitates to the forlorn."

Stella lifted the dog's head from her lap. "What happened to his eye?"

"The vet suspects some kind of infection."

Stella tried to twist in her chair and look under the dog. "Him or her?"

"Him," Leo said around a mouthful. He stabbed at the bowl with his chopsticks. "This is great, Phoebs."

Stella ran both hands down the dog's sides. "I think you look like a Leo."

Leo made the sound of a buzzer on a game show. "That name's taken."

Stella fought a smile. "Okay, how about Willy?"

"Hey, like One-Eyed Willy from *The Goonies*," Phoebe said.

"Willy it is." Leo flashed Stella a smirk. "Heard you spent the night on Rowdy's sofa."

"You already heard?"

"The story was in the Eden Falls Chronicle this morning."

"What?" Stella cried.

Phoebe elbowed Leo in the stomach. "He's kidding, Stella. I told him."

"Do you think Mom and Dad know yet?"

Phoebe glanced at her watch. "It's four-thirty, so my guess is yes."

Leo chuckled. "Guess you shouldn't have ordered those pancakes for lunch, huh?"

"First, I didn't order the pancakes." Stella pressed her fingertips to her forehead. "And second, can you *never* use the word pancakes around me again? Like forever?"

∼

*R*owdy scrolled through the contacts in his cell phone twice before he realized he had the number of every business and person in Eden Falls except Stella.

After he dropped her home, he snuck in a shower and a nap before heading back to the bar for his afternoon shift. On his way, he considered stopping by her apartment to check on her, but decided against it. If she drank as much as Mike said, she would be recovering all day.

He scrolled through his contacts one more time and stopped on Phoebe's number. He'd just make a friendly call and ask how Stella was doing. He didn't want Phoebe to become suspicious of his interest. Though being a cop, Phoebe most likely had suspicious down to a science.

He should have attached a note to the sleeve of crackers asking Stella to call and let him know how she was feeling. Then again, based on the state of her room, those crackers were probably already buried under a pile of colorful underwear.

"You're a thousand miles away."

JT's voice brought Rowdy back to the present. "Hey." He slipped the phone into his jeans pocket and planted palms on the bar in front of his cousin. "Where's your lovely bride-to-be?"

JT slid onto a stool. "She had an appointment at Dahlia's Salon, so I thought I'd walk over to ask a favor."

"Sure."

"Father's Day."

JT had been holding an annual Father's Day barbecue for years. Except this year he and Carolyn would be cruising the Caribbean on their honeymoon. "I was wondering how you were going to work that out."

"I know it's a lot to ask…"

"I don't mind. How are we going to let people know it's at my place this year instead of yours?"

"I can announce it at the reception Saturday night. Almost everyone will be there. Hopefully word will spread to the people who aren't."

"Stop at the post office and tell Rita Reynolds. Everyone will know within twenty-four hours."

JT laughed, then grew serious. "You know, that's not a bad idea."

What started as a small Father's Day celebration in JT's backyard for just a handful of guests had grown astronomically. JT provided the burgers and hotdogs. Everyone else brought buns, side dishes, and desserts to share.

"I can bring over some hamburger and—"

Rowdy waved the offer away. "Consider it your wedding present, since I have no idea what to buy."

"Thanks, Rowdy. By the way, I heard Stella had a private party here last night."

Rowdy shook his head. Life in a small town. "What would we do without the Eden Falls human telegraph?"

"Keeps us in the know. How's Stella doing today?"

"I haven't heard." Rowdy rubbed a hand along his jaw. "I was about to call Phoebe to check."

"Maybe we should take a trip to Seattle and put a little fear into the ex-boyfriend."

Rowdy raised a brow. "This coming from the chief of police?"

JT leaned forward, resting forearms on the polished wood of the bar. "Stella's like a sister to me. I want to pound the guy for hurting her."

"Yeah." She wasn't like a sister to him, but Rowdy decided to keep his feelings to himself. Being a cop and all, his cousin was pretty quick on the uptake, and Rowdy didn't need people speculating about his feelings. Besides, it would take Stella a while to get over the hurt. "Maybe just a warning he shouldn't come around anymore."

"Is that why Stella was drinking? He showed up in Eden Falls?"

"Stella said he came by her apartment. He's probably nervous that Stella will tell his wife."

"Someone should."

Rowdy shrugged.

JT humphed out a breath like an old woman. "You think the wife shouldn't find out? Alex said they have three kids."

"I don't know the answer to that, JT." Rowdy studied his cousin a moment. "Would you want to know?"

"Yeah. I'd want to know. What about you?"

"Yes, I'd want to know, but that doesn't make knowing right for every situation. Do you tell the wife and possibly break up the family, or keep quiet and hope the guy never strays again?"

JT shook his head. "I don't think he's that type of guy."

Neither did Rowdy. "You want a drink? Something to eat? Juan has pulled pork sandwiches as the special tonight."

"No. I just stopped by to ask about the barbecue." He thumbed over his shoulder. "I think I'll take a walk around Town Square. Carolyn's only getting her hair cut, so she shouldn't be long."

His cousin headed out into the early evening. Rowdy knew JT would end up impatiently waiting for Carolyn in front of Dahlia's Salon. His cousin was as bad as a lovesick teenager.

Rowdy never thought the bug would bite him. He'd never been in love, never even wanted to be in love, but he was experiencing the sharp gnawing of unfamiliar feelings working their way under his skin. He'd been unable to get Stella off his mind for a long time now. Strangely, he didn't want to either.

"Hey, Kyle. I'll be in my office for a few. Holler if you need help."

"Will do," Kyle said with a wave.

Rowdy rounded the bar and headed down the short hall that still smelled like vomit. The cleaning crew was due tomorrow morning. He'd leave a detailed note to give the hall and women's bathroom an extra-good scrubbing.

In his office, he tugged his cell phone out and scrolled to Phoebe's number before he sat behind his desk. She answered on the second ring. "Hi, Rowdy. Do you still smell like puke?"

"No, but the hall does."

"Sorry," she said with a laugh.

He put his heels up on his desk. "How's your patient doing?"

"She's still green around the gills, not eating much, but she looks like she'll survive. Here, you can talk to her," Phoebe said, saving him from having to ask.

A chair scraped against the floor, and a man laughed. Sounded like Leo.

"Hi, Rowdy."

He imagined her as he'd last seen her, fresh-faced from the shower, wrapped in a pink robe. "Hey, Stella. How're you feeling?"

Stella exhaled into the phone. "I'm okay."

Her voice sounded hesitant, un-Stella-like. "Headache?"

"Yes, but I bet it would be worse without that fizzy stuff you made me drink."

"That fizzy stuff works wonders."

"I think I told you last night—though my memory is pretty fuzzy—I really am sorry I threw up on you." She either cleared her throat or giggled.

"I would say all part of the job, but I'd rather skip that part. I am glad you're feeling okay."

"Thanks."

She must have walked into another room because Phoebe's voice and Leo's laughter faded away in the background. This time he didn't mistake her muffled giggle.

"What's so funny?"

"Sorry. Nothing."

"Tell me."

Snicker. "There is absolutely nothing funny. I can't believe I'm laughing. Last night was *so* not funny."

"Something's funny, because you're giggling like Sophia when I tickle her neck. Tell me."

"I keep picturing the split-second look on your face when I threw up all over you. The horror..." Her giggles turned into full-blown laughter.

"Again, thanks for that."

"I-I'm sooo sorry. I..." She snorted. "Nothing—nothing is funny, but..." She was laughing so hard she couldn't finish her sentence.

He chuckled at her giddiness, glad she'd turned a bad situation humorous.

Just as quickly as her giggles turned to laughter, her laughter turned to sobs. "Thank you f-for bringing me h-home."

His chest constricted. *Aw, please don't cry, Stella.*

"Give me the phone, honey." Phoebe's voice said from a distance. "Sorry, Rowdy. We're having a mini breakdown. Gotta go."

The call disconnected.

Rowdy lowered his heels from his desk and sat forward. With the office lights low, he could only pick out a few constellations on his huge map of the stars on the ceiling. His first reaction was to rush over and hold Stella, try to heal her hurt or tease the sad out of her. But he knew she wasn't ready for that yet. She needed time to cry and mourn the worthless liar who'd shattered her world.

CHAPTER 6

*S*tella arrived at Pretty Posies early. She'd promised to help with the flowers for Carolyn's wedding, which was in two days, but spent yesterday in bed getting over the damage she inflicted the night before. Alex depended on her, and she'd dropped the ball.

The front door was already propped open with buckets of flowers when she climbed out of her car and glanced around. Eden Falls was just coming awake. Customers were going in and out of The Roasted Bean, Noelle's Café, and Patsy's Pastries. Police Chief JT Garrett, in uniform, stood on the steps of the police station surveying his domain. He held up a hand when he spotted her. An extrovert, she wasn't embarrassed often, but after what happened at Rowdy's...

Actually, the emotion dogging her wasn't embarrassment, but shame. She heaped shame on top of the guilt she already wore like an iron necklace. Guilt that she'd dated a married man for two years and didn't have a clue.

She glanced at the cloudless blue sky and wondered why the weather refused to match her gloomy mood. Phoebe said working on flowers for her friend's wedding would be a good way to take her mind off her own misery. Stella knew nothing could distract her enough to free her of the weight she wore.

Walking into the flower shop gave her a temporary sense of peace that she accepted gratefully. Though it would be short-lived, being in this place helped her feel calm and centered. She always felt at home here and in her classroom.

Tatum was busy with an early morning customer. She motioned Stella to the backroom. She followed the laughter around the counter. Alex and her mom, Alice, and Carolyn stood around Alex's worktable. By Carolyn's blush, she was the one being teased, probably about her soon-to-be husband. After Carolyn's Saturday wedding, the three of them would be sister or mother and daughter in-laws.

All tied together with a pretty Garrett bow.

Her angel fluffed her wings. *That's not nice.*

I know. I'm being selfish again.

Carolyn's only family was an estranged sister living in Tacoma who turned down the wedding invitation with, "I have a hair appointment that day." Carolyn would fit into the Garrett family nicely, because they wrapped welcoming arms around newcomers as if they'd always been members of their fold.

As soon as Carolyn spotted her, she tugged her into a hug. "I've been worried about you. You haven't returned any of my calls."

"I haven't returned anyone's calls, so don't feel left out." At Carolyn's hurt look, she added, "But I appreciate that you called."

Alex hugged her next. "We're here for you, sweet friend, but you have to answer your phone."

"I know. I'm sorry." *But wallowing is a solitary activity.*

Sweet Alice was third in line with a tight hug. She was like a second mother...or a third or fourth. Many years ago, her own mom had joined forces with Jillian's, Jolie's, and Alex's, mothering all the girls as if they were their own. Carolyn's mother died in an accident when she was eleven, and Misty's mother left Eden Falls when Misty was six.

"I'm so sorry about what happened, sweetheart."

Stella held on for a long moment. "Thanks, Alice. I'm okay. Promise."

Alice shook her slightly by the shoulders. "You're going to be better than okay. You're strong and beautiful, and that strength, added to your compassion, will get you through this."

Stella felt the sting of tears. "You have more faith in me than I do."

"Don't question yourself and what you know to be true. Or he wins."

That was something Stella wouldn't allow. Jerry didn't get to win.

After Carolyn left for her job at Patsy's Pastries, the four of them got busy assembling bouquets for the bride and her attendants. Stella had learned a lot about flowers from Alex over the years, but she still would never attempt an arrangement without her friend's advice and supervision. Alex created the most stunning bouquets in the state of Washington.

Carolyn's colors were blush, celery, chocolate, and orchid. Alex, who learned the Victorian language of flowers from her grandmother, used blossoms that spoke when assembling arrangements. She placed pale pink roses, which meant grace, green orchids for good health and longevity, and soft purple callas for refined beauty. They wrapped the green stems with chocolate-colored ribbon. The end result was soft, fresh, and very Carolyn.

When the bouquets were complete, they started on four

large arrangements for the church. Alex built one. Alice, Tatum, and Stella followed along flower by flower.

"We'll tackle the centerpieces for the reception tables tomorrow," Alex said late in the afternoon.

Phoebe was right as usual. Being so focused on work had distracted Stella enough that she forgot her problems. They hadn't gone away, but at least they faded into the background for a while. While she worked, she kept Alice's insights close. Stella was strong, but it wasn't her strength she was worried about. It was the hurt Jerry's wife would experience if she ever found out.

After she left the flower shop, she put on her big-girl panties and drove to her mom and dad's house. Talking to them would be awkward. Not that her parents expected more than their daughters doing their best. Still, she'd always worked hard to make them proud. With four other sisters, there was the usual good-natured—and sometimes not—competitive-ness and sibling rivalry, but the Adams girls tried to keep their brawls to a minimum. At least in front of their parents.

Thanks to Jerry, she'd toppled off every pedestal she ever crawled to the top of in order to beat out a sister.

She walked through the kitchen door and inhaled deeply. The scent of freshly baked cookies was a norm in the Adams family kitchen. Today sugar cookies cooled in their usual spot on the countertop.

Her mother rounded the corner from the family room, stopped when she spotted Stella, then opened her arms. Stella rushed into her mom's comforting embrace and let the tears flow.

"It's okay, baby." Her mother smoothed a hand over Stella's hair. "Breakups are painful but not as painful as staying in a relationship that makes you unhappy." She held Stella out by the shoulders exactly as Alice had. "And you weren't truly happy with Jerry. You probably won't believe this now, but you will come through this a better person."

Stella laughed on a choked sob. "Have you and Alice been talking?"

"Aww, I'm hurt Alice got to console you before I could."

"Don't be hurt. I didn't seek her out. She came to help with Carolyn's wedding flowers this morning."

"Well, I haven't talked to Alice, but I'm sure she told you the same thing because we both believe in you."

Stella swiped under her eyes. "I'm sorry I disappointed you and Dad."

Her mom tugged her in for another hug. "Oh, baby. You didn't disappoint me or your father. We all have storms that push us off course. The important part is steering back in the right direction. Hurt and disappointment are part of life. What happened is big." She took Stella's face between her palms. "I don't mean to make light of what you're going through, but you're so much stronger than you know."

Her dad entered the kitchen through the back door and immediately engulfed them both in his strong, loving arms. "I'm sorry, my sweet cupcake."

Her poor dad should be sainted after enduring the hormones of six females living in the same house with only two bathrooms. He was still enduring those hormones as he dabbed a tear off her cheek.

"Enough. You were made for better. One day you'll look back and be grateful things didn't work out. You might even be grateful you went through the experience."

"I don't think I will ever be grateful for dating Jerry."

"You'll be a stronger, more sympathetic woman because of it."

Would she? At this moment she couldn't imagine being grateful for anything associated with Jerry.

· · ·

The last stop on her list was Rowdy's Bar and Grill. She stepped inside and let her eyes adjust from the bright sunshine. It was too early for the dinner crowd, so very few tables were occupied and only one person sat at the bar.

She slid onto a stool at the far end and smiled at Kyle when he approached.

"Hey, Stella. How are you feeling?"

She palmed her forehead. "Is there anyone in town who doesn't know?"

He shook his head. "Probably not."

"Is Mike in the back?"

Kyle leaned a hip against the bar. "He only works Friday and Saturday nights."

She lifted her head. "Not true. He was here Tuesday night…or did I just imagine all those horrible shots I demanded from him?"

"He traded shifts with me that night."

Fudge brownie.

Her little annoyance giggled. *Means you have to wear big girl panties again tomorrow.*

Yep.

"Can I get you something to drink?"

Stella rolled her eyes as she slid off the stool. "I can't believe you just asked me that."

～

Other than church on Sundays, and only then because his mom insisted, Rowdy wasn't much into dressing up. He was way more comfortable in jeans and a T-shirt, but JT and Carolyn were pretty adamant that he wear a suit to their rehearsal dinner.

He parked in front of the church, climbed out of his truck, and took a minute to appreciate the perfect weather and his hometown. He could hear the river still rushing with spring runoff and the laughter of kids in some nearby back-yard. The scent of pines and Russian olive trees blended nicely, a reminder it was summer in Washington. Luckily, the hot temperatures hadn't hit yet. Low seventies was ideal. The snow-covered mountain peaks were a sharp contrast to the blue of the early evening sky. In his opinion, there was no prettier place on earth than Eden Falls.

He strolled into the church and about twenty people turned to stare.

"You're late."

He glanced at his watch with a frown. "You said five-thirty."

JT crossed his arms. "I said five."

"I could have sworn you said a thirty in there somewhere."

"Nope. No thirty anywhere in five o'clock."

"Well, I'm here now." He clapped his hands. "Let's get this show on the road."

Preacher Brenner made a shooing motion, guiding the group into the foyer. "Now that everyone is here, let's start from the beginning. Line up as you did before. Rowdy, you're here, next to Stella."

Suddenly being one of the groomsmen wasn't so bad. He knew Stella would be here, but not that he'd be paired with her.

Beam wrapped him in a headlock. "You never were any good at following instructions."

Rowdy lightly punched his older brother in the stomach. "Of course not. Look who I had as an example."

Stella took her place behind Alex and Colton.

"Where do I stand?"

She pointed at the floor. "Right here."

He indicated the same spot. "Right here?"

She rolled her eyes as only Stella could.

"Okay, everybody. When the music starts, you proceed down the aisle. Wait until the couple in front of you separates at the podium before you follow." Preacher Brenner looked at Rowdy. "Understand?"

"This isn't my first rodeo, Josh."

"Right. You've been down this aisle before."

Alex turned with a grin. "Maybe the next time you walk down the aisle it will be for your own wedding."

"I'll bet your body would fit in that old trunk Grandpa Garrett gave me. The one with the big, rusty padlock."

She turned back around, mumbling something about him being ornery.

He looked down at Stella when the music started. "You look better than the last time I saw you."

"I took a shower. Phoebe said I should try that rather than whiskey," she said, not quite meeting his gaze.

"Smart sister."

Pink touched her cheeks. "Sorry I burst into tears when you called the other night."

"No apology necessary."

"I appreciate all you did for me Tuesday night," she said, still not making eye contact. "I feel bad you had to stay with me. Shirtless. Thanks for that, too, by the way. Best part of the night."

He chuckled. In her easy way, Stella could always lighten the mood. "Glad I could help."

"I have a confession." They took a step forward. "I couldn't find the shirt you loaned me to wear home."

"Yeah, I found it on your bathroom floor and took it with me."

She finally glanced at him, a spark of life in her pretty eyes. "You didn't trust me to bring it back to you."

They took another step forward. "Based on the state of your room, I figured it would be months before you found it."

She crossed her arms and raised her chin like a petulant child. "My room is not that bad."

"Not that bad?" He laughed. "It looks like a tornado blew through there and upchucked your junk and your neighbors', too."

"Could you skip any references to throwing up, vomiting, or upchucking, please?"

"Sure."

They reached the threshold of the chapel and he held out his arm. When she slipped her hand through the crook of his elbow, he tucked it close to his side.

As they started down the aisle, he glanced at her in time to see the corners of her mouth wobble in a my-heart-is-breaking smile. Her step faltered, and he squeezed her hand. "Hang on, darlin'. This will all be over soon."

Her nod was almost imperceptible. She swallowed, swiped a finger under her eye, and pasted on a steady smile.

He squeezed her hand again.

*A*fter the rehearsal they all met in the back room at East Winds for Chinese. Rowdy was lucky enough to sit next to Stella—though it took a little elbowing to get there—and unlucky enough to have his cousin Alex across the table from him. Every time he glanced her way, she grinned. Now was her time to gloat. And gloat she did.

Stella was quiet through the rehearsal and talked even less during dinner. She wasn't gloomy and she did make comments, but she wasn't her usual bubbly, full-on snarky self. Rowdy did receive several eye rolls and a couple of dangerous scowls, which he laughed off, trying to lighten the mood. He hated seeing her so broken up over a guy who hadn't been worth her time.

Since he'd never been in love, Rowdy had no idea how long it took to get over someone after a breakup. Alex didn't date for five years after her husband's death. If he asked her how long he should wait to ask Stella out, she'd bug him incessantly. His cousin wasn't a meddler, but, being the mayor, she felt she had a right to know what was going on in her town, even if the situation wasn't Eden Falls-related or any of her business.

His attraction to Stella went against everything Rowdy had ever practiced. He, Beam, and JT were very careful never to date local girls. They lived in a small town, and people generally took sides after a breakup. Yet a year and a half ago, Beam married Misty, who was local, and JT was marrying Carolyn tomorrow. She'd been a local before moving to San Francisco for culinary school.

Here he sat, gazing down at a local who was no doubt thinking about the married man she used to date. He glanced across the table, and Alex smiled.

Yep. Life had a way of shoving your world into a topsy-turvy mess, scooping a dab more whipped cream on for giggles, then throwing the whole pile in your face.

~

On the sidewalk outside East Winds, Stella turned toward Riverside Park, not ready to go home to an empty apartment. Phoebe was out with a new guy, and her friends had someone else to be with. She and lonely Friday nights were about to become best friends.

This self-pity thing is getting ridiculous.

During the wallowing period, self-pity is allowed.

That is a completely made up rule.

Stella knocked her irksome guest off her shoulder.

Hey, you bent my halo!

She would also be going to Carolyn and JT's wedding alone. The thought depleted her energy. She wished she could just climb into bed and bury herself under the covers until all the engagement parties, weddings, and babies' births were over.

The park was busy with visitors, both young and not, sitting on the grass or on benches, strolling along the riverbank hand in hand. Stella had been here a few times with Jerry, but mostly they dated outside of Eden Falls, so at least she wouldn't be bombarded with endearing or enduring memories every time she walked down a street or entered a restaurant.

She sat on a boulder at the river's edge and slipped off her shoes. The water was icy, in a maybe-this-will-freeze-my-heart-beyond-feeling sort of way. She shivered.

"You knew it would be cold."

Stella whirled around with a hand to her chest. "Geez! You scared me, Rowdy. What are you doing here?"

"It's a public park."

He stood a few feet away with hands in the pockets of his dress pants, his hair pulled back in the usual ponytail. "You look out of place."

"Excuse me?"

Throwing Rowdy off balance was nearly impossible. She gloated a moment at the look on his face. "It's just that you're dressed up and not in church."

He glanced down at his clothes like he'd forgotten what he was wearing. "Dressing up for tonight was not my idea."

"So…" She rolled her hand. "…what are you doing here?"

"I saw you leave East Winds alone and decided to follow."

She slipped her shoes on. "I think that's called stalking."

Rowdy lifted a shoulder. "Okay, if you want to slap a label on it, I'm going to call it singles sticking together."

"You don't have some bombshell waiting for you at the bar?"

He snapped his fingers in a darn-it manner. "No bombshells tonight."

"You have the whole night off?" She took his offered hand and let him pull her to her feet.

"I have the whole weekend off for the wedding."

"Thanks." She let go and tugged on the hem of her dress. "I bet you don't get many days off when you own a business. I know Alex doesn't take much time off."

"I usually take a couple of weeks a year."

"Don't trust Mike to handle things for longer?"

"I trust Mike completely, but he works another job, so he can't always be there when I'm not." He held out his hand again as they started up the slight incline from the river.

Accepting his offered support, she noticed his callused palm, so unlike Jerry's, whose hands were baby smooth. She kind of liked the texture of working hands.

"It's hard for me to turn over the reins for very long."

She understood. It was hard for her to take a sick day during the school year, because she was sure no one could teach her class the way she did. "How did you get calluses?"

"What?" he asked, quirking a brow at her.

She liked that she'd thrown him off balance a second time. She turned his hand over and ran her fingertips along the ridges of his palm. "How did you get these?"

He lifted a shoulder. "Working. Fishing. I have no idea. Why?"

His hand was large, his fingers long and warm and… She placed her hand palm to palm against his.

"I like them."

"You're weird, Stella."

Rowdy laced their fingers together and led her to an empty bench. They sat close beside each other. She'd known Rowdy her whole life and felt as comfortable around him as she did with Leo or JT. For the first time in a week, she allowed herself to relax.

The moonlight lit a path across the river. Stella kicked her shoes off and swished the bottom of her feet back and forth over the soft grass. "Since moving into the apartment with Phoebe I haven't walked barefoot through the grass as much as I like."

"Why haven't you and Phoebe bought a house together?"

She leaned her head against the arm he'd stretched along the back of the bench. "We've talked about it, but that's as far as we get. Buying a house together is so…permanent. We'll be considered the weird old-maid sisters of Eden Falls. We'll have to collect cats, grow strange herbs in our garden, and scare little kids at Halloween. Teenagers will try to break in and take pictures of us in our underwear to sell on the internet. We'll have to shop after dark to avoid the awkward stares."

Rowdy started chuckling even before the mention of underwear. "Who thinks like this?"

"Old maids."

"Stella…" He sounded like a dad scolding a disobedient kid. "You're not an old maid. You're not even thirty."

"I will be. Soon. Before you know it, I'll be hoarding spoons."

He glanced at her, a puzzled expression on his handsome face. "Why spoons?"

She shrugged. "I have no idea. Just sounds like something an old maid would collect."

"You're nuts." He extended his long legs and looked up at the sky.

"What got you interested in the stars?"

"I took an astronomy class in college."

"Were you interested before that?"

He flexed and released his bicep hard enough to bounce her head. "Only enough to get a girl alone in the dark."

She liked his profile. And the way he smelled. And the color of his eyes, even though she couldn't make them out in the night light. She'd always found the Garretts' mossy green eyes intriguing. As a child, she'd wanted eyes the same color as Alex's. "Did it work?"

He looked at her, his white teeth flashing with his familiar grin. "Let's see… you, me, in the dark, under a blanket of stars…. You tell me if it's working."

She groaned, knowing he couldn't see her eye-roll. "Men."

~

Rowdy didn't want the conversation to digress so much that she'd start obsessing over the ex, so he wrapped his arm around her neck, enjoying the way her subtle perfume swirled around his head, drawing him in, making him want to nestle his nose against her neck. He drew in a deep breath and pointed to the sky. "See the bright star to the right of the moon?"

Stella nodded.

"That's Jupiter."

"Jupiter," she repeated, a little awe in her tone. "Isn't it amazing that we can see an actual planet?"

"Venus, Mercury, Saturn, and Mars are all bright enough to be seen with the naked eye."

"Where's Venus?"

With his arm still hooked around her neck, Rowdy pointed. "Venus, the Goddess of Love is right over there."

"What about Mercury?"

"Mercury is easier to spot right after sunset."

She turned to look at him. If he leaned forward eight inches their lips would meet. Instead he settled for being close enough to see the moonlight sparkle in her eyes.

"I'm amazed that you know so much about the planets."

"Why?"

"I just never figured you to be a star man. I should have you talk to my second graders next year."

"Anytime."

She intertwined their fingers like she might move closer. Instead, she lifted his arm over her head. "Thanks for the astronomy lesson. Maybe you can show me some more another night."

"If you play your cards right, I can teach you all kinds of things."

"I'll bet you can." She pushed up from the bench with a laugh. "See you tomorrow, Rowdy."

"'Night, Stella."

CHAPTER 7

Stella took her position at the back of the chapel, walked down the aisle, and cheerfully performed her duty as one of Carolyn's five bridesmaids. She smiled for pictures, nodded at the appropriate times, and donned a happy attitude for one of her best friends, even as her heart shrank like a cotton shirt in a hot dryer.

She was supposed to be blissful today, ecstatic, possibly wearing a ring of her own. Instead she was bitter, lonely, and the last single of their group. Jolie married Nate, Alex married Colton, Misty married Beam, Jillian was engaged to Brandt, and now Carolyn was married to JT. Then there was Stella. The outsider. The odd person. The eleventh spoke in the wheel, the girl who made things wobbly and uncomfortable. She'd be the one who stood out if they all went bowling or to a movie or played cards. Not that they ever did any of those things together, but they might. Someday.

Everyone would go overboard to include her and sit by her to make sure she felt like part of the group, like she belonged even if she was alone, which would only create a more uncomfortable situation.

Since they weren't dating anyone special at the moment, Phoebe and Leo came to the wedding together. Even single, Phoebe had someone who filled in, someone she could count on.

The reception was held in JT's mountain home backyard. White lights were strung around the perimeter of an open space with a small creek running through the middle. A dance floor had been constructed, and a band played from the wooden deck above the backyard. Under a white tent, the bride and groom greeted their guests, which consisted of most of the town.

Carolyn looked gorgeous in her white lace over tulle A-line gown. The scalloped neckline and lace hem looked so feminine with Carolyn's red hair and spatter of freckles. She and her dark-haired police chief husband, who couldn't keep his hands off his new wife, made a stunning couple. Their smiles were a testament to their deep love.

Carolyn deserved all kinds of happiness after what she'd been through with her abusive first husband, and JT would treat her like a queen.

After the receiving line broke up and the dancing started, Stella wandered to the edge of the yard to watch the sun disappear behind the mountain peaks. The sky held onto the last colors of day, the golden glow fading to cotton candy swirls of pink, soft yellow, and baby blue.

She turned to watch JT and Carolyn circle the dance floor in each other's arms, silly, beautiful, I-adore-you smiles on their faces.

The contemporary house in the woods that JT inherited from his Garrett grandparents would be Carolyn's new home. He'd carefully renovated the interior room by room until he reached the kitchen, which he left for Carolyn, his chef fiancée, to design. The house fit Carolyn. She'd already added a vegetable garden in the back and flower beds along the driveway. Stella knew her friend would be incredibly happy here in her hideaway mountain home.

A hurt crawled over Stella, so deep it ached from the inside out. How did she get here? How could she have been stupid enough to believe Jerry's lies? He'd displayed every warning sign and she ignored them all, hoping he'd redeem his follies with a wedding ring and complete commitment.

Yet some little twinge in the back of her mind told her that she wouldn't have accepted his proposal. The doubt was real, very tangible.

She walked to a small bench on the outskirts of JT's yard, wondering why it was so far from the house. Once she sat, she knew the answer. The waterfall was visible between two trees, and beyond that the whole of Eden Falls lay in the distance, the lights of town just blinking on.

Stella imagined JT's grandparents situating the bench in this exact spot many years ago, so they could watch while the population of their small place in the world grew from five hundred to fifteen hundred to three thousand.

Summer was here. Hot days. Long, lonely nights. She had two and a half more months, approximately seventy-five days, to immerse in self-pity and guilt before school resumed and she could lose herself among her students.

Her cell phone buzzed in her hand. She glanced at the screen and set the phone facedown on her lap. Jerry still called a couple of times every day, intent on making her misery a bit more agonizing. She'd thought if she didn't answer he'd give up. No such luck.

Footsteps approached, and she knew it was Phoebe before she rounded the bench.

"What are you doing out here?"

Trying to enjoy the quiet.

Be nice.

"Enjoying the night," she said aloud.

"One of your best friends just got married."

Stella exhaled loudly, tired of feeling judged by her perfect sister, who never stumbled after a relationship breakup. "I covered my responsibility today, Phoebe. I walked down the aisle, I smiled, I congratulated, I smiled some more, all from the bottom of my heart, so get off my back."

Phoebe tucked a lock of Stella's hair behind her ear. "Sorry, I'm just worried about you, Stella-bella. Being sad is so not you. You've never taken a breakup this hard. And Jerry is not worth the time you're investing in him. He's a dirtbag. Any guy who dates someone while he's married is like the fuzzy green mold that grows on old cheese. No. He's the foam hanging from the corner of cows' mouths. No, wait—give me a minute and I'll come up with something truly disgusting." Phoebe laughed. "I can hear you rolling your eyes."

Stella was not in the mood for company or her older sister trying to cheer her up by thinking of disgusting ways to describe Jerry. Especially because she hadn't been able to come up with anything disgusting enough herself. "I know he's not worth it, Phoebe, but I dated the guy for two years. How was he able to cover up the fact that he was married so completely that I didn't have a clue?" She hung her head and stared at the phone in her lap. "I dated another woman's husband. That makes *me* the disgusting one."

"But you didn't know."

"That doesn't make me feel better. I should have known. I don't know how, but I somehow should have known."

Phoebe wrapped her arm around Stella's shoulder and tucked her close. "I'm sorry you're hurting. If he lived in Eden Falls, I'd arrest him. And believe me, his jail time wouldn't be pleasant." She lifted Stella's chin with an index finger. "Leo will beat him up for you."

Stella snorted a laugh—sort of. At least it started as a laugh that turned into tears. Phoebe lowered her cheek to Stella's hair. "Please don't cry. You'll make me cry, things will start to run, and then everything will get ugly. He is not worth another thought, another tear."

"How do I forgive myself for dating someone else's husband? How do I stop worrying about his wife and their three children? Does my ignorance make my sin forgivable? How do I move past what I did?"

"Maybe you should talk to Preacher Brenner. He could probably help with the forgiving stuff."

"Hey, Stella!" Leo came around the front of the bench, picked up the phone in her lap, and tossed it to Phoebe, before pulling her to her feet. "I need a dance partner."

"Go dance with the bride."

He laughed, a contagious sound of merriment. "You're kidding, right? JT won't let another male within twenty feet of Carolyn. And he carries a gun."

Stella tugged, trying to free her hands. "There are plenty of other women to dance with."

Leo's incredible grin flashed with mischief. "Oh, but none as attractive as you with your puffy red eyes and"—he pointed—"that liquid trickling from your nose. Every man here will be so jealous. But hey, I'm the lucky guy who got to you first."

"Shut up," she said, swiping her nose with the back of her hand.

He glanced at Phoebe. "Please tell me you have a tissue. She's a mess."

Phoebe stood and ran a hand down her slim figure. "Have you seen this dress? Where exactly would I be hiding a tissue? Don't answer that, she said pointing a finger at him. She turned him around, lifted the back of his jacket, and yanked his shirt out of the waistband of his pants. "Let her use your shirttail."

"Ga-roooss. Stella is *not* using my shirt to blow her nose," he growled, trying to turn back.

She held his waistband in a fist. "She'll just wipe, not blow."

After Stella cleaned her face and nose on his shirttail, she allowed Leo to drag her onto the dance floor. The band was playing a slow tune, and Leo pulled her into his arms. Growing up, he'd been the calm in their hormonal storm of a house. He still oozed calm. She buried her face against his chest, not caring if her mascara blotched his shirt. A small price he'd have to pay for making her dance. The song switched to a fast two-step, but Leo continued to rock her slowly as if the tune hadn't changed. Why couldn't she have fallen for a man like sweet, extremely handsome, constantly irritating Leo instead of cheating, lying Jerry?

When she first met Jerry, he came on strong, but in a sweet way. He called for a date the very next day, and she couldn't wait to see him again.

Leo turned her slowly, and she spotted Rowdy near the stairs to the deck. Some blonde was chatting him up. He glanced around, caught her eye, and winked. An unexpected tingle ran up her spine. Rowdy belonged in the days of pirates, plundering villages and kidnapping maidens in the dead of night. All he needed was an eye patch, a sword, and a ship. She could picture him in his knee boots, a white shirt opened to his nav—

"You okay now?" Leo looked down at her when the second song ended.

"I was okay before."

"Riiight. That's why I'm wearing snot on my shirttail and black streaks on my chest."

"You're the one who insisted on a dance."

"At least your head doesn't look like it's going to explode from your shoulders for a lunar landing."

Lunar talk made her glance around for Rowdy, but he was gone. She patted Leo's cheek. "You are such a treasure."

He led her off the floor. "Taking care of you is cramping my style, so I'm going to hand you off to the next lonely schmuck. You'll flash your beguiling smile and make his night."

"First of all, you're *not* taking care of me. Second," she looked him up and down, "you have no style."

Her little angel fanned her face with a hand. *That is a complete lie.*

Yep. Leo looks as heart-stopping in jeans and a tee as he does in a suit and tie.

"I'm going to pick up one of the lovely single ladies here tonight. That's all the style I need." Leo laughed. "One of these days, you're going to roll your eyes and they're going to get stuck."

She jabbed him in the ribs.

"Rowdy, you look lonely. How about taking this—"

Stella held a finger in front of Leo's face. "Think very carefully before you utter your next words."

Leo gave her a brotherly hug and headed straight for a brunette in a red dress.

Stella glanced at Rowdy. "Don't worry. I can entertain myself."

Rowdy, who was suddenly standing very near, minus the blonde, turned her by the shoulders. "Let's take a quick turn around the dance floor. Then we can head over for some of the cake JT and Carolyn just cut. Maybe a piece will sweeten your mood."

"My mood is fine," she grumbled.

"Yep. I can tell you're as happy as E. coli on room-temperature chicken." Rowdy laughed. "And your eye-rolling does nothing to thwart me, Stella Adams."

Stella snorted, grateful she hadn't just sipped a drink or she'd have to wipe her nose again. "Did you just say thwart?"

"Yep, I did. And I used it in the right context, too."

Stella genuinely smiled for the first time since JT and Carolyn said "I do." Rowdy had always been able to make her laugh. She looked him up and down as she had Leo. "You clean up nice for a hippie."

He frowned. "Just because I have long hair doesn't make me a hippie."

Nope, her little angel fanned her face again. *He's definitely a pirate.*

"No, I guess it doesn't."

He twirled her into his arms, and she rested her cheek on his chest. He was tall, and she was middling, but somehow they fit together nicely. He was also a good dancer, which surprised her. Another plus, he smelled clean, woodsy, with a tiny hint of lavender.

"Why have you always worn your hair long?"

"When I was a kid I didn't like the way Glen the barber spit through his teeth."

She glanced up and laughed. "Oh, my gosh, he does do that."

"Yeah, try sitting in a chair in front of him while he's cutting your hair and spitting. No, thanks. I'll wear my hair long."

"Misty would cut your hair."

"I didn't like Misty well enough until very recently."

"She's your sister-in-law, so you have to like her now."

"Luckily she's growing on me."

The song ended and she stepped back. "Thanks for the dance, but I think I'll skip the cake."

He took her elbow. "What's a wedding without cake?"

"Five hundred calories less than a wedding with cake."

"It's good luck to eat a piece of cake at a wedding."

She narrowed her eyes. "You just made that up."

Rowdy crossed his heart with an index finger. "A sliver isn't going to be five hundred calories. And who doesn't want good luck?"

A piece of good luck was exactly what she needed. She held up her finger. "Just a sliver."

She and Rowdy walked over to where Carolyn and JT were feeding each other slices of the beautiful creation the bride and Patsy Douglas made. Carolyn graduated from culinary school in San Francisco and worked her way up to sous chef in a fancy five-star restaurant. Her specialty, though, was pastries.

Rowdy let go of her arm when someone called his name, and she took the moment to escape back to her dark corner of the yard.

"Hey!" she heard him call. "Where are you going?"

She turned around, but continued to walk backward. "Somewhere quiet."

Rowdy palmed her elbow again and steered her into the dark forest surrounding JT's property. "I'll come with."

"I'd rather you didn't."

"I know a great spot."

"I'm sure you know a lot of great spots in the woods. *My, what big teeth you have, Grandma.*"

He chuckled while he continued to guide her through the trees.

"These aren't exactly hiking shoes I'm wearing."

Suddenly, a path seemed to appear out of nowhere. The crickets were making a comforting racket tonight. An owl hooted overhead. The sound moved over her, triggering goose bumps. Despite what went on in the world, life moved on. Something in that haunting hoot calmed her uneasy spirit. Even though she had told Alice she would be okay, a peace settled deep, assuring her it was true. She would be okay. She tried to spot the owl, but couldn't see its outline against the darkness surrounding them.

Rowdy slid his hand down her arm to grasp her fingers, leading the way another fifty paces before the trees opened up to reveal a small clearing.

"Wow. How did you find this place?" She glanced at him from the corner of her eye. "Or shouldn't I ask?"

"My grandpa used to bring me here. He liked stargazing too." Rowdy pointed to the sky. "They're hard to see tonight because of the moon."

"I like crescents."

"The word crescent is for kids," Rowdy scoffed. "The provocative smile of a woman is a grown-up description."

Stella groaned. "Only you."

"Only me, what?"

"Only you would compare the moon to a woman's smile. It's obviously a fingernail."

"Where is your imagination?"

"Taking a break over the summer."

~

Rowdy didn't know much about love, but he did know a lot about the brokenhearted men and women who came into his bar and grill to self-medicate.

He didn't want to be the rebound guy, but he also didn't want to stand back while another man swooped in and took Stella away from him. He knew enough about Stella to know she never stayed single for long.

He had a self-imposed summer assignment: *Your mission, should you choose to accept it... Secure Stella. If you should be caught or maimed during this mission... This crazy notion will self-*

destruct in ninety days. Good luck with your mission, should you decide to accept it.

Like all Stella's friends, Rowdy had suspected there was something weird about Jerry from the first time they met. He rarely made eye contact and, other than mentioning teaching, he was evasive when questioned about his life. A simple internet search would have revealed marriage records easily enough, yet none of them had taken the initiative.

"You don't have to babysit me, Rowdy. I'm not going to do anything stupid."

With his eyes adjusted to the darkness, he could make out her features pretty clearly. "Not your style."

"What does that mean?"

Her tone had turned defensive, which was good. A feisty disagreement would get her mind off the cheater ex. They'd sparred many times over the years, and she was a worthy opponent. "You're more of a woe-is-me-type person. Kind of like Eeyore with your big, sad eyes."

Stella turned, hands fisted on hips. "What you know about me, Rowdy Garrett, wouldn't fill a shot glass."

Wrong, Stella. I know a whole lot more than you think. You love teaching, but also love working in the flower shop during summer break. You hate your curvy figure, because you're not pencil-thin like half of your friends. Rowdy liked Stella's curves.

You get your hair cut in Harrisville so you won't hurt Misty's feelings by going to one of the other girls in Dahlia's salon. Your eyes flash when you disagree. You enjoy helping others. You wear shorts and dresses with sandals in the summer, jeans with boots in the winter. You choose hot chocolate or tea over coffee and pie over cake.

"I'm *not* a woe-is-me-type person. I haven't tried to get anyone to feel sorry for me, and I don't moan on and on about what Jerry did. If everyone would leave me alone, I'd get over what happened by myself, on my own time."

"Get over what? The guy is cheating on his wife. You *know* what happened. That poor woman is still in the dark. She's the victim. Not you."

Her hurt expression told him he'd gone too far. But the hurt transformed quickly to anger, flashing eyes and all.

"How dare you! You, who have no idea what love even is, are telling me I have nothing to get over after dating a guy for two years." She jammed a finger toward JT's house. "Go back to the reception, find some girl, and break her heart like you always do. Men," she said, her tone brimming with disgust. "If a woman leaves you, you just move on to the next one. Women are different. We can't just turn off our feelings and pretend like the relationship never happened."

He was well aware of the differences between men and women. He'd listened to many melancholy stories. He knew men had a tendency to bounce back faster after a breakup, but not all men were the same.

Rowdy risked life and limb when he stepped closer. "*Jerry* showed up to events one out of about eight times. Now you know the reason was because he had to rush home to his wife and kids. In truth, your relationship was a farce. You can't lose something you never had. He's a waste of time, Stella."

"You don't know anything about women."

He knew one thing. He knew how to kiss a woman until her knees buckled. Before he took the time to think it through, he hauled Stella against him. Too surprised to resist, she let out a little gasp, and he took that moment to lower his mouth to hers.

She tasted of spearmint. He turned his head to deepen the kiss. She didn't resist, so he began a tongue tango, and she met him move for move. The kiss exploded through his brain, igniting every nerve ending in his body. His heart pounded hard enough to punch a hole through his chest.

He'd waited for this moment for so long, and still he'd jumped the gun. Any second she'd come to her senses and shove him away, but until then, she was his. Her arms circled his neck, her fingers diving into his hair and coming to a halt because of his ponytail. He pulled her curvaceous figure closer, cupping the back of her head. Lost in the feeling of her against him, he—

Crack!

Stella catapulted out of his arms at the sound of a twig breaking.

He sucked in a ragged breath. "I might not know everything about women, but I do know how to kiss them," he said, without turning to see who'd interrupted their moment. "Compare that to your cheating boyfriend."

Stella shoved past him to the sound of Beam's chuckle. "Sorry to interrupt."

"You didn't interrupt anything," she snapped breathlessly before scurrying in the direction of the reception.

Rowdy turned to his brother, who stood close enough that his grin, stretching from ear to ear, was visible. Rowdy rubbed a spot on his chest which felt strangely empty as soon as Stella was out of sight. He'd been wanting to kiss her for a long time, but never imagined a simple meeting of lips would be far more potent than anything he'd ever felt before. He inhaled and shoved his hands into his tux pockets. "Don't say anything."

Beam's booming laugh echoed through the night. "Yeah, sure, I'm not going to say anything about you and Stella locking lips."

"It just happened."

"Stella *just happened* to fall into your arms, and you decided kissing her was the smart choice. Do I have that right? Or was it you who did the falling? I sure don't want to get the facts wrong."

"There are no facts. It wasn't planned." Even in the dark, he could see Beam's smirk. Rowdy looked skyward. "I was trying to get her mind off her scumbag boyfriend."

"Yeah? Did your plan work?"

Sure worked for me. He blew out a breath. "How would I know?"

Beam closed the distance between them and wrapped a big hand around the back of Rowdy's neck. "Simple, little brother. Did she kiss you back?"

The thought of her tongue dancing with his flashed through his mind. "Yeah." He glanced at Beam. "She did."

"Friendly peck or full-on kiss?"

"You saw. What do you think?"

"Full-on, with tongues tangling."

"Something like that." Rowdy shuffled his feet, releasing the scent of pine into the air.

"Sophia has decided she doesn't like to sleep in her crib. She's up half the night or in our bed. Misty and I are like walking zombies. I need details."

"You saw all the details you're getting."

Beam clapped him on the shoulder. "You're a very good Samaritan, bro. Way to step up to the plate." He turned on his heel. "Better fix your hair before coming back."

Rowdy watched his older brother saunter back to the reception, still smirking. Of all the people to catch him, Beam was the one who'd give him the most flack.

With a smile, he realized he would do the same, because that's what brothers did.

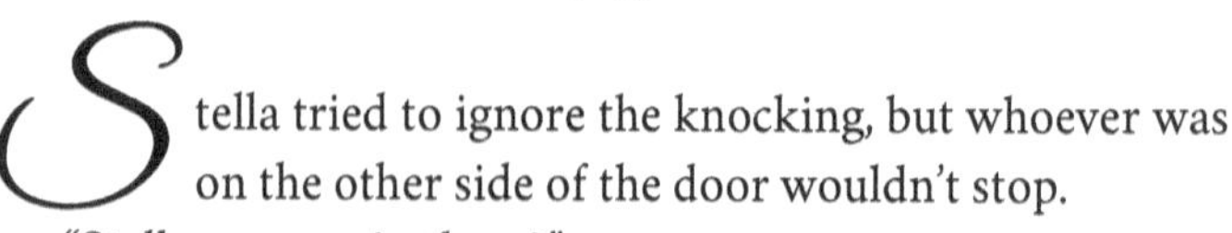

*S*tella tried to ignore the knocking, but whoever was on the other side of the door wouldn't stop.

"Stella, are you in there?"

She stood, unlocked the door, slid back into the tub, and yanked the shower curtain closed. She knew she couldn't stay here forever, but she was determined to stay hidden in JT's upstairs bathroom until Rowdy left.

The door opened and the curtain slid away. "What are you doing in here?"

Stella touched her lips with her fingertips. She'd kissed Rowdy Garrett. Well, he started it, but she hadn't put up much of a fight.

No fight.

Stella closed her eyes. *No fight at all. I acted like I was starving for affection.*

And Beam saw that starvation.

Fudge brownie with frosting on top!

"Stella." Alex tapped her on the top of the head. "Why are you in the bathtub?"

"I'm soaking."

"Kinda hard to soak with clothes on and no water."

Stella slid farther down. "Have you ever tried it? No? Then don't knock it."

"I think what you're doing is called sulking." Alex sat on the edge of the tub.

"Potayto, potahto."

"Why are you letting Jerry do this to you?"

Jerry. She hadn't even been thinking about him, but she sure couldn't tell Rowdy's cousin who *was* on her mind.

So change the subject.

Right. "I'm sick of everyone asking me the same question or telling me the same thing. Do you think I'm feeling horrible on purpose? I'm mad because I didn't see the obvious signs."

Alex opened her mouth, but Stella held up a hand. "And don't start making lame excuses for me. I know them all. *You didn't know. You can't blame yourself.* When in truth I was stupid, and I was blind. All the warning signs were in front of me and I ignored them. I ignored my skeptical friends. I was in love." *Or I thought I was.* "So I overlooked the obvious. How do I get over what I did to Jerry's wife?"

"You didn't knowingly do anything to his wife. He did. Stop being so hard on yourself. If you'd known he was married, you wouldn't have dated him. You know that. I know that. Everyone who knows you knows that. Enough with the self-abuse."

Maybe you are being hard on yourself. Her little companion patted her shoulder.

I can't excuse my blindness, my total self-absorption. If she was truly honest with herself, deep down she'd known something wasn't right, but she never suspected he was married.

And here she was, feeling sorry for herself again, when she should be worrying about Jerry's wife. Just that selfish thought humiliated her to her toes. Rowdy was right. Anna was the true victim of this game Jerry was playing. And their sweet, innocent little children.

No amount of consoling would lighten her heavy load of guilt.

You're thinking of yourself again.

Stella gritted her teeth. *Feeling guilty isn't thinking of myself.*

Potayto, potahto.

"Have you talked to him?" Alex asked.

Rowdy popped into her mind, but that wasn't right. She and Alex were talking about Jerry. "No. He keeps calling, but I haven't answered. I think he's worried I'll tell his wife."

"Will you?" both her white-clad shoulder-sitter and Alex asked at the same time.

Stella closed her eyes, wishing she knew the answer. "I don't know."

Alex knelt on the floor and wrapped her arms around Stella's shoulders. "You've got to stop beating yourself up over this. Len's a master manipulator. He tricked you. This is on him, not you."

Stella shrugged Alex's arms away. "His name is Jerry Winters. He's been married for eight years. He and his wife have three children. Benjamin is seven, Michael is five, and Zoe is two. Yes, I finally did an internet search," she said, keeping her eyes averted, her voice choking on a sob. "His wife has a Facebook page with pictures of her family on outings, at the beach, playing at the park, her sons splashing in a pool, her family celebrating birthdays, carving pump-kins, posing in front of a Christmas tree. A recent picture was taken of her and Jerry celebrating their wedding anniversary."

She looked at Alex. "If we hadn't walked into that restau-rant, he'd be here with me tonight instead of at home with his family."

"I know," Alex said, her voice oozing sympathy. "I'm sorry."

Stella laid her head on the back of the tub and squeezed her eyes shut. "Me too."

CHAPTER 8

Stella sat through the hour-long church service the next morning wondering why she even bothered to come. She stared at the preacher as he droned on and on.

"Forgiveness is not forgetting. Forgiveness is not reconciliation or condoning or dismissing. Forgiveness is not easy. Blah, blah, blah…" Stella wanted to scream.

It's not good to hang on to anger.

One sermon a day is all I can take. She wiggled her shoulder to unseat her shiny-haloed irritant. *Go away.*

She was careful to keep her eyes forward. Rowdy always sat with his parents, across the aisle, two rows behind her family's usual spot. She didn't want to get into a glaring-smirking match with him.

When she closed her eyes, memories of the kiss they shared seared the back of her lids. Heat rose over her cheeks, and she blinked her eyes open in case someone—*Rowdy*—was watching. To add to her embarrassment, Beam, who married one of the biggest blabbermouths in town, found them while they were lip-locked and breathing like they'd just run an uphill footrace.

Beam probably told Misty before they left the wedding. She would undoubtedly confront Stella after church.

Instead of Jerry popping into her head first thing this morning, Stella woke up thinking of Rowdy and the slow, deep—so deep she felt it in her toes—kiss. Not only had she let him kiss her, but she'd kissed him back—which she'd never admit aloud. To anyone. Ever. Insanity was the only answer she could come up with. Discovering Jerry's secret had driven her over the edge, because she'd completely lost her mind last night.

Her thoughts bounced back to their knee-trembling, earth-shattering moment. Just thinking about that kiss made her short of breath. Rowdy told her to compare his kiss to her cheating boyfriend's and she had. Rowdy's won hands down.

Double fudge brownie!

Her angel rubbed her tummy. *Yum...warmed with a side of vanilla ice cream.*

After the service, while everyone met in the fellowship hall to visit over coffee and donuts, Stella walked outside. She and Phoebe were expected at their parents' house for Sunday dinner, but Phoebe was on duty today, and dinner was hours away.

We could just reflect on the kiss...

Let's not!

She turned when a throat cleared behind her. Preacher Brenner stood ten feet away, hands folded in front of him. Any other day, he was Josh Brenner, Eden Falls resident, fisherman, and lover of pastries. On Sundays, he stood at the pulpit and suggested she might be psychologically and physically damaged by her refusal to forgive.

Her angel sat at attention and adjusted her wings. *Be nice.*

"Hi, Stella. I just.... I want to say I'm sorry about what happened with Len."

"Jerry." Josh met her ex-boyfriend on a couple of occasions when they were out and about and happened to run into him, but never at church functions. Jerry refused to go to anything church-related.

Now we know why.

Josh bowed his head with a nod. "Jerry."

"Obviously you heard."

"Yes." His smile was serene, his brown eyes kind. "Rita Reynolds."

Of course, Rita—first only to Misty—would happily spread the word. The small, birdlike lady, who worked at the post office, ate gossip for breakfast and spit it back out before lunch.

"I would have heard anyway." He took a couple of steps closer. "Small town."

They followed the flight of a bee as it buzzed around their heads. She swatted, sending it on its way. "Nice sermon."

His wide-eyed look of surprise was entertaining. "You were listening?"

"Sure. You talked about how we're commanded to forgive. Holding onto bitterness only hurts us. We should let our grudges against those who've wronged us go. We shouldn't be so easily offended." She rubbed a spot between her brows that started to throb. "Write it for me?"

"No. It was written before I heard about Jerry." His closed-lipped smile appeared. "Inspiration, maybe?"

"Yeah, well, Jerry did a little more than offend me."

Josh nodded again, not quite meeting her gaze. "What he did was very wrong."

She snorted. "You think?"

Over Josh's left Shoulder, she saw Rowdy and his parents come out of the church. He glanced her way, his smirk in place, just as she'd predicted.

She hoped he took her narrow-eyed, stay-away-from-me glare seriously.

That grin is a big nope.

Don't need any help from you right now.

Preacher Brenner rocked back on his heels. "So, Stella, would you like to come to my office and talk?"

"No, I don't want to talk, and I'm not even close to forgiving. Jerry can rot in— Well, you know where he can rot."

"Maybe with time…"

"With time he'll rot? I sure hope it takes a nice long time. Years, in fact. I hope pieces of him started flaking away and falling off one at a time."

Josh tried to look stern, but he couldn't quite pull it off. "I meant, maybe with time, you'll feel like talking."

She knew what he meant. Stella's traitorous gaze strayed to the parking lot to watch Rowdy climb behind the wheel of his truck. "Doubtful, but if the thought makes you feel better, go for it."

Josh glanced toward the parking lot when Rowdy shut his truck door.

"Do you think I should tell his wife?"

"That's a tough question." Josh rubbed the back of his neck. "One I don't have an answer for."

Frustration bubbled through her. "I know it's a tough question. That's why I asked you. I need to know what to do."

Josh toed a weed growing out of a crack in the sidewalk. "You don't tell her, and she lives with her children in ignorance. You do tell her, and you possibly break up a family." He looked up to meet her gaze. "Do you think there's only one answer to that question?"

"No. You just suggested the only two options I can think of—which I already knew. That's why I asked you." She glanced at her shoulder, hoping for guidance from her pesky little friend, who was inconveniently quiet.

"I think the answer is something only you can decide. I know that doesn't help much." He took another step closer, looking into her eyes. "What does your gut tell you to do?"

Stella looked up into the flawless azure sky. Not a cloud in sight. Today was the perfect summer day. Not too hot, a soft breeze ruffling the leaves overhead. "That I should tell her."

"And what does your heart tell you?"

Stella tried to swallow around the sudden lump in her throat. "If I tell her, I'll hurt her even worse than Jerry hurt me. I have two years invested. She has at least eight. I have a broken heart. She'll have a broken world which includes three children, a home, and the façade Jerry has built."

He pressed his lips together, his kind eyes not offering her any answers.

She crossed her arms. "You haven't been much help."

"Have I made things worse?"

She thought a moment, then shook her head. Not sure why, but she did feel better for having talked to him. "I'm sure you can't answer this question either, but how do I get past the guilt of being 'the other woman'?" she asked, making quotation marks with her fingers

"Service. There's nothing better for the soul than helping others."

"What kind of service?"

"Look around and you will find numerous ways to help. Babysit for a friend. Volunteer at the shelter or the Senior Center."

"For how long?"

"You're back to another question only you can answer."

"Have you ever been in love, Josh?"

His smile turned sad. "Yes, I have."

"What happened?"

"She decided she couldn't be the wife of a preacher."

"I'm sorry." And she meant it. Being a preacher had to be very lonely at times.

The doors of the church opened again, and Josh thumbed over his shoulder. "I need to get back."

She nodded. She didn't want to talk and yet they had.

"Take care of yourself, Stella. Remember I'm here if you need to talk to someone." He took a couple of steps back. "I might not have all the answers, but I have experienced a broken heart. And I'm a great listener."

Stella watched Josh approach his congregation as they began to emerge from the friendship hall. She didn't think service would eliminate her overwhelming shame, but maybe helping others would lighten the load a bit.

When Stella got back to her apartment, she loaded the dishwasher, wiped the kitchen counters, swept the floor, vacuumed and dusted the living room, straightened the bathroom, but ran out of steam by the time she reached her messy bedroom.

Standing in the doorway, she sighed at the chaos. Phoebe organized the other rooms, so she had a starting point. Here, she didn't know where to begin. Maybe she should start by weeding out the closet or cleaning out her drawers, although either task seemed daunting. Maybe she could start with a simple task like making the bed. That alone would shock Phoebe.

Saved by the ringing of her cell phone, she pulled it out of her back pocket. A selfie of her and Jillian lit the screen. "Hey, Jillie."

"Where are you?"

"Robbing a bank. How much do you need?"

"It's Sunday. Banks are closed."

"Oh. Right. So I'm..." She snorted. "I got nothin'."

"Very unlike you to run out of material so quickly," Jillian said with a laugh. "Are you having dinner with your parents tonight?"

Stella had to move several things on her nightstand to see the clock. "I'm headed there in about thirty minutes."

"Want to go to a movie afterwards?"

"Let me check my spinster calendar. Nope, not delivering doilies to the senior center until next week."

"You are not a spinster."

Stella dropped to the bed. *Close.*

Being the last single of the group doesn't make you a spinster.

What do you know? Stella wiggled her shoulder. *You're not even real.* "Is your fiancé working today?"

"No. I just thought we could do something."

"You don't have to entertain me, Jillian." Before discovering Jerry's secret, she wouldn't have thought twice about Jillian's invitation. Now she considered it a pity call.

"I can tell by your silence that you're overthinking this, Stella. We haven't done anything together in a few weeks. I didn't call because Brandt is working. I called because we're friends. We haven't been to a movie in a long time. If you're free, let's meet in front of the cinema at seven-thirty. We can drool over Tom Hardy together."

Stella laughed. Jillian drooling over anyone but her hot fireman fiancé was ridiculous. Brandt Smith was a modern-day Hercules. "Okay. A little after-dinner drooling sounds like a great plan. I'll see you at seven-thirty."

Now was that so hard?

Stella glared at her haloed buddy. *You're not invited.*

~

*S*ophia squealed when Rowdy walked through the door of East Winds. She and Beam were waiting for him in a booth by the window.

"Hey, Cricket." He leaned down and kissed the top of the one-year-old's head, the only place that wasn't a gooey mess. "You know the cracker goes in your mouth, right darlin'?"

She grinned and blew a raspberry. Bits of soggy cracker spattered the table in front of her high chair.

"Sometimes I wonder how much food actually makes it to her stomach," Beam said.

"You can tell by the pudgy cheeks and plump thighs that something is getting to the right places." Rowdy slid onto the bench opposite his brother. "Where's Misty tonight?"

"Dahlia called a mandatory meeting at the salon."

Rowdy had warmed up to Misty after years of bare toleration. He'd been stunned when Beam asked her to marry him, convinced his brother had lost his ever-loving mind. Yet he tamed her wild, mean-girl ways. An explanation of the gentle giant and the wicked witch's relationship could go either way, but their marriage seemed to work. Misty smoothed Beam's rough edges and he calmed the black-clouded storm that was Misty. Much to Rowdy's surprise, despite a rocky start, Misty turned out to be a doting wife and a loving mother to his adorable, blue-eyed niece who'd wrapped her little palm around Rowdy's heart and made him want to settle down and have one of his own.

The concept stunned him. He'd never considered himself father material until little Sophia entered his world. He'd never held, bathed, burped, or diapered a baby, but after a year with Sophia, those things came naturally.

Rowdy accepted the wet wipe Beam held out and wiped cracker goo off his jeans after his niece blew another raspberry. "Who taught you that disgusting trick, baby girl?"

Beam set another cracker in front of Sophia. "It's a kid thing."

Rowdy dipped the corner of his napkin in his water glass

and dabbed at Sophia's mouth. "How's the hardware and lumberyard business?"

"Busy. Better than I ever expected. Since we advertised the grand opening beyond the boundaries of Eden Falls, we're getting business from all over the area. There's so much new construction we can barely keep up with the demand." He pulled another wet wipe out of the handy diaper bag and attempted to clean Sophia's hands. "I have to admit, I wasn't sure we'd recover after the fire. People got used to driving to Harrisville for their hardware and lumber needs."

"Harrisville is only fifteen minutes away, but when you only need a few nails, the distance seems to grow. How is working with the father-in-law?"

"You know Mason. He's so easygoing he agrees with every change I suggest."

Sophia reached out and Rowdy handed her a spoon. She stuck it on her mouth, pulled a pouty face, and dropped it over the edge of the high chair tray.

"That's her new trick. Throwing everything that isn't edible on the floor."

Rowdy leaned close to the raven-haired baby. "I don't blame you a bit."

The waitress arrived, placed a plastic placemat in front of Sophia, and dumped a small bowl of noodles down before the placemat joined the spoon on the floor. "That should keep her occupied."

Sophia took enough time to blow a raspberry before she stuffed a noodle in her mouth.

The waitress scooped the spoon off the floor and dropped it in one apron pocket while tugging an order pad from another. "What can I get you tonight?"

"I'll have the shrimp and garlic sauce with wonton soup." Rowdy handed over his menu.

"Good choice," she said with a pretty smile. She glanced at Beam.

"I'll take the Dragon and Phoenix."

"Spicy?"

"Yes, and egg drop soup. Can I get a side of mixed vegetables for the munchkin?"

"Sure. Anything for the munchkin." She smiled at Rowdy before turning from the table.

Beam laughed as soon as she was out of earshot. "Looks like Stella has some competition."

Stella doesn't have any competition. Rowdy shook his head.

"Speaking of competition," Beam said as Mac and Noelle Johnson approached their table. "You two are supporting the competition by eating here."

"The café is closed on Sundays, and we're celebrating."

Noelle ran a hand over Sophia's flyaway black hair. "Hi, sweet girl. Is your dinner yummy?"

"You're celebrating without Beck?" Rowdy asked, referring to Mac's ten-year-old son.

"He's at Grandma and Grandpa's house for the evening." Mac wrapped his arm around his wife's waist and patted her flat belly. "Ask what we're celebrating."

Noelle smiled. "Mac."

Rowdy knew immediately, but could tell by his brother's expression that Beam didn't have a clue. Still, he left the news for them to tell. "What are you celebrating?" he asked.

Mac couldn't contain the grin that spread from ear to ear. "We're having one of those," he said pointing at Sophia.

"Why?" wide-eyed Beam asked at the same time Rowdy stood. He hugged Noelle and shook Mac's hand. "Congratulations. And excuse my uncouth brother. He and Misty aren't getting much sleep these days."

"He's right. We're not. Sorry," Beam said, standing to

congratulate the couple. "What I meant to say was that's great news."

"Is Beck excited to be a big brother?" Rowdy asked.

"Shhh," Noelle whispered, index finger at her lips. "Beck doesn't know yet. Besides the in-laws, you're the first to hear."

"We won't say a word," Beam said.

"Rance and Lily must be excited to have another grandchild." Rowdy could imagine Mac and Noelle's excitement when they discovered their news. They married quickly last fall when Mac's first wife tried to get full custody of the son Mac raised alone. This baby would be Mac and Noelle's first together.

After the couple exited the restaurant carrying a bag of takeout, he and Beam discussed a company looking to develop a tract of land on the other side of the river.

Beam scrubbed a hand over his jaw. "Not sure how I feel about a golf course so close to Eden Falls."

"It sure would boost the economy."

"Maybe."

Rowdy glanced out the window just as Stella strolled past. She hadn't been far from his thoughts...like white noise, there but not. The scent of her hair as they danced, the sweetness of her kiss, the feel of her body pressed close to his. He would have missed church if the alarm hadn't jolted him out of an arousing dream of Stella. He'd been so busy staring at the back of her head during the sermon he couldn't remember a thing Josh said from the pulpit.

"Speaking of Stella." Beam laughed. "You just rolled your eyes like she does."

"I didn't roll my eyes, and we weren't talking about Stella."

Beam pointed at him, laughing harder. "You just rolled them again."

Rowdy held up his left hand to hide the right while making a gesture Sophia shouldn't see.

"You realize Sophia has no idea what that means."

"And she won't be learning from me."

Beam nodded toward the window. "Stella's headed for the cinema. You could meet her for some more lip-locking."

"She's already meeting someone," Rowdy said when Stella joined Jillian in front of the box office.

The waitress set their plates in front of them and leaned so she could see out the window. "Who are we looking at?"

"Woman watching," Beam said at the same time Rowdy said, "No one."

"I'll assume the short *girl* since the tall one was in yesterday with her fiancé." She straightened, hands on her hips and looked at Rowdy. "Isn't she the one who threw up on you a few days ago?"

"You haven't met the town's Good Samaritan?" Beam asked, waving a hand toward Rowdy.

"No, but I'd like to." She held out her hand. "Hi. I'm Juliette."

Rowdy was tempted to kick his brother under the table. Instead he shook the waitress's hand. "Rowdy."

"It's very nice to meet you, Rowdy. I've been in your place several times. You're always so busy, I haven't had the chance to introduce myself."

"Are you new in town, Juliette?" Beam asked.

"I live in Harrisville."

Rowdy nodded and picked up his chopsticks. As a bartender, he could make small talk with the best of them and Juliette was pretty, but his heart was committed elsewhere. He glanced out the window just as Stella and Jillian went inside the theatre.

The waitress waited a beat, then flashed a tight smile. "Okay, well, enjoy your dinner."

"Looks like you've survived your dry spell," Beam said after Juliette walked away. "Between Stella and Jul— If you're going to throw food at me, throw the shrimp."

"If you don't shut your trap, I'll throw the bowl of rice." Rowdy lifted his niece out of the high chair, sat her in his lap, and handed her a carrot to gnaw on. "Your daddy's an idiot, Cricket. If he keeps it up, he's going to get himself into trouble with Uncle Rowdy."

"You don't scare me, little brother. Don't give her that." He grabbed for the sucker Rowdy pulled from his T-shirt pocket. "Misty will kill me."

"Should have thought of that before you opened your big mouth." He unwrapped the sucker and handed it to Sophia. "Who's your favorite uncle, baby girl?"

She flashed four-toothed grin.

"That's right, Uncle Rowdy."

CHAPTER 9

Stella let herself in through the back door of Pretty Posies, still smiling over the comedy she saw with Jillian last night. Her talk with Preacher Brenner had helped too. Even though he didn't tell her what to do or even give her much direction other than to serve others, she felt better.

The question of whether or not to talk to Jerry's wife still troubled her. One part of her said, "Not my problem." But another part despised the idea that Jerry would get away with what he was doing unless she said something. She rarely struggled with indecision, but the results of her choice would impact other people's lives, which included innocent children.

She'd taken Preacher Brenner's suggestion of service to heart. Before coming to Pretty Posies, she stopped at the senior center and signed up to serve lunch on Tuesdays. She also volunteered to help at Eden Falls Shelter on Thursday. She doubted helping others would be enough to alleviate her guilt, but service might take her mind off herself and direct her focus toward others for a while.

Grabbing an apron from a hook by the door, she slipped

it over her head and tied the strings around her waist. She heard voices in the front of the shop and assumed Tatum was helping customers. Alex not only owned the flower shop, but she was mayor of Eden Falls. She usually spent Monday mornings performing mayoral duties in her town hall office, but always left a list of things Stella could work on.

She began washing the eight vases Alex left out. A familiar chuckle from the front of the shop made her breath catch. Her heart thumped hard several times. A giggle followed, like fingernails down a chalkboard.

Abruptly, her temper flared to life.

Two nights ago, Rowdy kissed her silly under the stars amid the scent of evergreens and summer. Everything about that kiss had burned a memory so deep, she actually dreamed about him. Now, he was in the flower shop flirting with gorgeous Goth girl Tatum Ellis like their kiss never happened.

What is it with bad-boy attraction?

I am not attracted to Rowdy. Sure, he's good-looking and has the self-assurance I love in a man. And he is a good kisser—

Good? Her pest fell off her shoulder laughing.

Stella conceded. *Okay, phenomenal.*

And you do enjoy a good kiss.

Right. But Rowdy's love 'em and leave 'em attitude made her eyelids twitch. She stuck her head around the corner, and sure enough, both he and Tatum were leaning on the counter with their heads together like two lovebirds.

How did a guy kiss a girl the way he kissed her, then turn around and flirt with another girl as if it never happened? Not that she and Rowdy were a thing, but still….

She didn't think her snort was loud enough to hear, but Rowdy looked up. He straightened and flashed his wickedly handsome grin. Other girls probably fell to their knees when he smiled like that, but it did nothing for her. Well…maybe a little something deep down in the pit of her stomach. And lower.

Her white-clad friend shook a fist in the air. *Only because we're vulnerable right now, bud.*

"Hey, Stella."

Tatum turned. "Oh, hi. I didn't hear you come in. Alex just called. She finished early at town hall, so she's stopping at Noelle's Café for sandwiches. She said if you don't want turkey to call her."

"Turkey's fine." Stella ducked back into the workroom. She tried to shut out Rowdy's chuckle and Tatum's giggle while she finished washing and drying the vases. What did she care who Rowdy flirted with? His reputation for being a ladies' man was well known around town. He'd certainly never been with a woman long enough to fall in love with her.

A thought stopped her. Other than trying to pick up bridesmaids at weddings, she couldn't remember ever seeing Rowdy out on an actual date. Ever. Word around town was he dated out-of-town girls. That way, when he broke their hearts, he wouldn't have to make small talk when he ran into them at One Scoop or Two.

Still, she was livid that he'd kissed her like it was their last day on earth two nights earlier and was flirting like it never happened today.

What does it matter?

It doesn't.

Seems like it does.

Go away.

She pulled buckets of roses out of the cooler and started plucking off the damaged outer petals. The blooms were a beautiful yellow with orange edges. When the centerpieces were finished, they would grace the tables at a fund-raising event in Harrisville.

She heard the bell over the front door jingle and more voices drifted into the workroom. Normally she'd check to see if Tatum needed help, but she wasn't going anywhere near Rowdy. She heard the squeak of tennis shoes on the concrete floors a moment before she felt a finger run along the back of her neck where her hair was pulled up into a ponytail. Goose bumps popped up along her flesh, probably making her look like a plucked chicken.

She spun around and glared into Rowdy's mossy green eyes. "What are you doing?"

"Tatum is helping customers, so I thought I'd come see you."

Yeah, one girl is busy so let's go flirt with another.

Right on, sister. Her shoulder sitter punched a fist in the air.

Stella turned back to the table so she wouldn't look at his tempting mouth. "I'm up to my elbows in rose petals, so go away."

His cologne's different today. Grapefruity.

Mmm...grapefruit. Her conscience took an exaggerated breath.

Stella rolled her eyes.

Rowdy pulled a stool close and sat so she was positioned between his knees. "I thought I might get in on this lunch thing if Alex is bringing sandwiches."

Oooh, your stomach is doing funny things again.

"It's the past-expiration-date yogurt I had this morning."

"What is?" Rowdy asked with raised brows.

Did I say that out loud?

Stella flicked her laughing annoyance off her shoulder. "Look, if you're going to stay you have to stop talking. I work better when it's quiet."

Rowdy laughed.

She narrowed her eyes. "What?"

"You work in a room full of second graders from September to May. When is your life quiet?"

"Here. During summer break, I look forward to peace and quiet." She flapped a hand at him. "Go back out front and flirt with Tatum so I can get some work done before Alex gets here."

He flaunted his absurdly white teeth with a grin. "Are you jealous?"

She snorted.

That's attractive.

I don't care. Rowdy's heard me snort before.

Still, she should work on a more feminine laugh. Alex had a musical laugh, and Carolyn's was so sweet. Maybe she could giggle like Tatum. Rowdy seemed to like that.

She didn't like where her thoughts were taking her. Why did she care what kind of laugh Rowdy liked? "Jealous of what? You flirting with Tatum two days after kissing me doesn't affect me at all."

His smile grew as he turned her chin with an index finger. "You *are* jealous."

This time she snorted on purpose. "Don't be ridiculous."

His hand settled on the small of her back, which felt way nicer than it should. "How about we compromise, darlin'? I'll leave if you admit you're jealous."

"In your dreams."

He waggled his eyebrows. "Now that you mention dreams...."

She held up a hand, her own dream popping into her mind. "Let's not go there."

The hand at her waist pulled her a step closer. "Ahh, you're jealous because you're dreaming about me. Tell me everything."

"Oh ouch, your ego just bumped its big head on the ceiling. I never said I dreamed about you."

"But you did, didn't you?" he said inching her close enough to stick his nose against her neck. "You smell good, citrusy." He breathed her in. "Like oranges with a hint of lavender."

There's a match made in heaven. Oranges and grapefruit.

Shut up. Stella demanded. Not that her irritant ever listened. She glanced down at the rose she'd stripped of petals.

He grazed her jawbone with his lips, his warm breath snaking over her skin. "You can kiss me again. Any time."

Geez, she'd even tilted her head to give him better access to her neck. She tossed the rose stem in the trash and picked up another. "I didn't kiss you." To her horror, the words came out raspy.

"Really?" he murmured against her skin. "Because that's definitely the way I remember it. A romantic wedding and me in a tux, I can understand why you'd be tempted to express your feelings—"

"I was not tempted." However, she was tempted to step away now, but he was tucking her hair behind her ear to give him better access to her neck, his finger triggering more goose bumps.

"Don't get me wrong about that kiss," he continued as if she hadn't tried to interrupt his babble. "Let me just say, I'd be happy to offer the use of my lips any time you need help getting over your sad."

She narrowed her eyes, trying to look as menacing as possible. "I promise I'll never need the use of your lips—"

"When were you two kissing?"

Stella whirled toward the back door, and there stood Alex. Her cheeks blazed with sudden heat. "We weren't. I mean we did, but it wasn't…" She glanced at Rowdy for help. He grinned. She turned back to Alex. "It was a complete accident, like contracting chickenpox or the bubonic plague."

Rowdy frowned. "You comparing our kiss to a plague?"

"If the shoe fits."

That's harsh.

I don't need any help from you right now.

"When were you guys kissing?" Alex repeated, not at all fazed by Stella's reference to an epic illness.

"It wasn't like that." Stella rolled her hand and her eyes at the same time. "It was more like, oops, I tripped, and Rowdy was in the way, and our lips bumped together."

Alex set a box from Noelle's Café on the worktable, an eyebrow raised. Her glance bounced from Stella to Rowdy. "Oops your lips bumped together?"

Rowdy seemed to be enjoying Stella's stumbling explanation as much as Alex. This was his fault in the first place. If he hadn't brought up the subject of their kiss, Alex wouldn't be questioning her now. "It wasn't"—she rolled her hand again—"romantic or anything. It was more like…" She glared at Rowdy. "…going to the dentist."

Rowdy wrapped an arm around her waist and pulled her closer still. "The truth is, Stella dragged me into the dark at JT and Carolyn's wedding reception." He had the audacity to put his hand over her mouth when she started to disagree. "Under the light of the moon, she kissed me like she was starving for a real man's kiss. It was spontaneous, and very romantic, and would have led to other unmentionable things if Beam hadn't interrupted us."

Stella shoved his hand away. "I'm not starving for *any* man's kiss."

"You're pretty cute when you're mad."

Her head about shot off from her shoulders. She glanced at Alex. "Okay, I'll give him the romantic, because we were in the moonlight," she said, more breathless than she liked. "But we were nowhere close to unmentionable-ing." She turned to

Rowdy. "And I did not drag you into the dark. You dragged me. I wanted to be left alone."

"Don't get so worked up, darlin'. You're getting all breathless and flushed." Rowdy stood and took her face in his hands. "My flirting with Tatum doesn't mean anything."

"You arrogant, pompous…. How dare you come in here and…."

He stopped her tantrum with a quick, completely knee-quaking kiss. When he pulled back his wink was so slight, she almost missed it. His thumb, the one Alex couldn't see, ran back and forth along her jawline, sending delicious tingles down her neck. "I better not stay for lunch, cuz. When Stella gets worked up like this, she can't keep her hands off me."

Stunned into silence, Stella couldn't manage to do anything but gape. Not only had Beam caught them kissing, Rowdy had just kissed her in front of Alex. He left by the back door with a wave.

"You and Rowdy were kissing at JT and Carolyn's reception? Was this before or after I found you in the bathtub?"

Stella sank onto Rowdy's stool without meeting her friend's eyes. "After. And he kissed me once," she said, holding up and index finger.

"Uh, he just kissed you."

"Okay, twice." She glared at Alex. "Since when are you so literal?"

Her honest little pain in the neck patted her shoulder. *Might as well admit the whole truth.*

"And I kissed him back." She shook her head. "Not this time. Just the first time."

"You know what this means?"

Stella swiped a hand through the air. "Nothing. It means absolutely nothing."

"Wrong. It means I was right."

"Right about what?"

Alex leaned forward conspiratorially. "Rowdy has been crushing on you since you started dating Jerry."

The laugh that burst out came from deep in her belly. "Oh my gosh, did he tell you that?"

Alex shrugged a shoulder. "He didn't actually say the words, but I've caught him staring at you many times."

"He's just goofing around, trying to get my mind off Jerry. He probably knew you were watching."

Alex smiled.

"Stop. You're creeping me out. Even if he was serious—*which he's not*—he would be the last man on earth I'd be attracted to."

"What's wrong with Rowdy?"

Of course Alex would defend her cousin. "Come on, Alex, you know Rowdy has never been serious about a woman in his life. He's probably never had a relationship that lasted longer than a weekend."

"True." Alex unloaded the sandwiches. "But there's always a first."

"Well, that first isn't with me. He kissed me like…" Unexpectedly, the memory of their seconds-long kiss took her breath away. She shook her head. "I don't know, but I do know two days later he's out front flirting with Tatum."

"You're blushing and getting all breathless."

Stella felt her cheeks heat. "I'm not—okay, I am blushing, but I'm not breathless. I'm irritated." She jabbed a finger at Alex. "There's a difference."

Alex pointed at the table. "How many roses have you denuded?"

Stella looked down at the second naked stem she held. She swiped the petals into the trash with the side of her hand.

"He's telling the truth about Tatum. They've been flirting

since the day I hired her. Something would have happened by now if either of them was truly interested."

"It doesn't matter. Rowdy can flirt with Tatum all he wants." Stella leaned over and picked up a wrapped sandwich. Turkey was written on the wrapper. "Mine?"

Alex nodded.

"I'm not interested in another heartbreaker. Besides he is so *not* my type."

"Not your type?" Alex asked sarcastically.

"I know. After Jerry, maybe I don't know what my type is, but I do know it isn't Rowdy." She rested both elbows on the table, her head in her hands. "I'm tired of dating, Alex. I want to find *the one* and settle down. Look at me. I'm the old maid of our group. The last woman standing."

Alex moved around the table and rubbed her back. "Most of the time being the last woman standing is a good thing."

"Not if you're single and standing alone. I want babies before I'm forty."

Alex laughed. "You're not even thirty yet, Stella."

"I'm close." Stella unwrapped her sandwich. "Speaking of babies—and yes, I'm changing the subject because I'm done talking about Rowdy—how are you feeling?"

"Good." Automatically, Alex cupped her nonexistent belly. "Still having occasional morning sickness. Right now, I'm starving. In an hour, I'll be ready to throw up. Hey, I just heard Noelle is pregnant."

"That's just the news my old ovaries need to hear."

"Would you stop? You're not old and neither are your ovaries." Alex leaned through the door that led to her shop. "Tatum, lunch is here."

Stella rubbed her own stomach, where she imagined her ovaries were shriveling into raisins. "Hear that? You still have a few years left in you. Hang in there."

~

*W*hile his mind lingered on Stella's neck, Rowdy spent the first hour at work in his office going over applications and setting up interviews for Friday morning. He'd fired his busboy two nights ago for smoking funny cigarettes before his shift.

He always scheduled interviews early. If a kid wanted a job badly enough, he'd get here on time or he wouldn't be hired. Luckily, it was only the second week of summer vacation and plenty of kids were looking for jobs.

With that task completed, he dug into a plate of the chicken enchiladas Juan was serving for the special tonight. He was halfway through when his tiny cousin marched in. After the kiss in Pretty Posies, he'd expected her to show up sooner or later.

"What brings you in, Low-Rider?"

She cocked a hip and folded her arms. "I think you know."

He set his plate aside and linked his fingers behind his head. "Since you're all puffed up, trying to act taller than you are, why don't you tell me?"

"You can't play with Stella's emotions right now, Rowdy. She just experienced a shocking breakup."

He waited, because he could see she had more to say.

"I'm serious. She's vulnerable right now." She leaned forward, palms on his desk. "You can't mess with her."

He continued to wait.

"Stella is different. She'd not like one of your many... hookups, for lack of a better word. She'd not a hookup kind of girl."

Irritation rushed through him, yet he had no one to blame but himself. He hadn't done anything to change people's minds about the reputation he created in high school. One broken heart—his own—a few years ago had opened his eyes to the way he'd been abusing emotions and relationships. "What do you know about my *many hookups?*"

Alex straightened, looking surprised by his question. "I know you bounce around from woman to woman, never being serious enough to make a commitment."

"How do you know that?" Rowdy dropped his feet to the floor and leaned forward, crossing his arms on the desk.

"Everyone in town knows your track record. It's not like you've kept your *rowdy ways* a secret."

"Yet *I've* never told anyone about all these women I've dated."

Rowdy could almost see the wheels in his cousin's mind spinning.

"You mean…" She narrowed her eyes. "No. You can't be telling me we've been assuming all this time."

He sat silent, allowing Alex to draw her own conclusions.

She held out her hands, palms up. "Say something."

"You're the one who encouraged me to ask Stella out."

"Yes, but I didn't encourage you to go from zero to one hundred in one night."

"It was a kiss, Alex. One kiss."

"Hey, Rowdy. Can you sign for this delivery?"

"Sure, Kyle." He stood and walked around his desk. "Gotta go, cuz."

"We're not done here, Rowdy."

"Oh, but we are." He dropped a kiss on the top of her head. "You should take a plate of Juan's chicken enchiladas home for dinner. They're amazing."

～

Stella walked home from Pretty Posies with the early evening sun on her back. They finished all the centerpieces today, so Alex didn't need her tomorrow. Serving lunch at the Senior Center would only occupy about two hours of her time, and then she'd have the rest of the day to….

What? Finish cleaning? Phoebe had been thrilled with the little bit she'd accomplished on Sunday. She hadn't started her bedroom though. That would take her all day. If only she had some idea where to start.

The closet.

Yep. Tomorrow she'd follow through for Phoebe. A tidy apartment and a clean bedroom would make her sister's day. Phoebe had been there to help her through this heartbreak, so the least she could do was clean up.

On a whim, she turned down Jillian's street, thinking she could stop by for a chat, maybe talk her friend into joining her for dinner. As she approached Jillian's basement apartment, she noticed Brandt's truck parked out front. Nope. If she knocked, Jillian would invite her in, but she didn't want to interrupt the two lovebirds. Jillian and Brandt were new enough a couple that there would be lots of kissing and touching, and she'd be the spare tire.

She turned the other way and headed for home, but stopped in front of Mike Stettler's apartment. His car was parked out front, so he was probably home. Time to apologize for the way she'd treated him at Rowdy's a few nights earlier. She swallowed any remnants of pride she had left and knocked on his door. No answer.

The sound of running footsteps turned her toward the street. Mike jogged toward her. When he looked up, he came to a stop and removed an ear bud.

"Hi, Stella," he said from a safe distance.

"Hey, Mike."

"How are you?"

"Medium…rare."

He smiled at her lame joke and motioned toward the door of his apartment. "Do you want to come in?"

"No." She waved a hand, hating that their usual easy banter had turned awkward because of her dumb decision to drink herself into oblivion.

"Kyle said you came by looking for me."

"I did. I want to apologize for the other night. I don't remember much, but I'm pretty sure I yelled a little. Or a lot. I'm sorry."

"I accept your apology."

"You do?"

He smiled. "I came to Eden Falls to escape Boston after my fiancée left me for my best friend."

So, the rumors were true. "Wow."

"Yeah, wow." He tugged the other ear bud free. "I know what it's like to hurt."

"Your best friend?"

"Ex-best friend."

"Sorry."

He shrugged. "It's okay. I'm okay. If I'd married her, I wouldn't have come to visit Noelle. I wouldn't have fallen in love with Eden Falls. I wouldn't have my dream job with the forest service. Things happen for a reason. Maybe what happened to you will change your life in an unexpectedly great way."

Doubtful. "Thanks, Mike. Next time I come into Rowdy's I won't order anything, but I'll leave a giant tip."

"Not necessary. Let's forget the whole thing."

Sadly, she couldn't remember what she was supposed to forget. She waved goodbye and headed for home, feeling a thousand pounds lighter. Alex's comments pressed in on her, but she laughed them away. The notion that Rowdy was interested in her was ludicrous. Rowdy was interested in

Rowdy. He was a player, and got away with it because he was handsome and charming.

Like Jerry had been in the beginning.

That thought turned her stomach sour. How many women had men like Jerry and Rowdy hurt without a thought? What was Jerry's long-term plan? Did he just love 'em and leave 'em like Rowdy? Did he make promises he never kept? He never made her any promises. He alluded, but never voiced anything permanent aloud.

What a dope I am.

She had no one to blame for her stupidity but herself. And Jerry. He needed to accept responsibility for what he'd done.

CHAPTER 10

Stella climbed out of her car in the parking lot of the Eden Falls' Shelter and ran to help Jillian's mom, Amy who was unloading boxes from a Saunders' Orchards pickup truck. Amy and her husband owned a successful orchard just outside of town and donated boxes and boxes of fruit every year. Blossoms in the spring, fruit during the summer, and all the colorful leaves in the fall. Jillian hadn't enjoyed all the chores that came with her family's business, but running through the orchard and eating fruit right off the trees were still favorite memories for Stella. She used to help Jillian man the fruit stand on the main road that ran past the orchard. Lots of cute boys stopped by on their way to lake for a day of summer fun. She'd spent a lot of hours flirting at that stand.

Amy dropped a box by the back door and greeted Stella with open arms. On top of operating a fruit business, Jillian's mom supervised at the shelter, scheduling meals and volunteers for those in need. By the warmth of the hug, Stella suspected Amy knew about cheating Jerry. Maybe she should be upset she was being talked about behind her back, but the comfort of Amy's arms felt too good. She didn't tell Stella "everything will be okay" or "he's not worth your tears." She just held on tight.

After hugs and lugging boxes into the kitchen, Amy put Stella to work peeling the biggest pile of potatoes she'd ever seen. The kitchen was a hive of activity, everyone scurrying about with a purpose. Just like Tuesday at the senior center, Stella felt guilty about taking so long to volunteer. She'd enjoyed chatting with the men and women she served at the senior center, and she especially enjoyed the time she spent with Mrs. Bingham, who owned the most beautiful rose garden in town. She taught a weekly gardening class at the senior center, and her roses were the highlight of the annual garden tour each summer. Carolyn's family used to live next door to Mrs. Bingham. Whenever Stella visited her friend, the elderly lady always sent her home with a single rose or a whole bouquet from her garden.

Before she left the senior center, Mrs. Bingham asked if Stella could stop by her house the next Tuesday to help move a few furniture pieces around. Stella liked the feeling of being needed by someone, even if it was only to move furniture.

The back door of the shelter opened and Rowdy walked in carrying a box of green beans. His look of surprise when he spotted her was comical.

"Hey."

He'd caught her off guard twice in less than a week. Now she'd returned the favor. "Hi yourself."

He set the box on the counter. "You helping out today?"

"Smart deduction. You're wasting your private investigative talents behind the bar."

Amy buzzed into the kitchen. "Oh Rowdy, I'm glad you're here. Can you help Rance with the tables? I forgot the floors were cleaned last night."

"Sure."

Amy showed Stella how to put the peeled and washed potatoes into a slicer. Then she grabbed bags of grated cheese and two jugs of milk out of a large refrigerator. "When you get all those potatoes sliced, layer them in these greased pans with the onions Rowdy sliced earlier."

Stella was surprised Rowdy was so at home here. He didn't seem the volunteering type.

She felt a sense of satisfaction and maybe a little too much pride as she worked along with a handful of other volunteers. She wasn't much of a cook, but Amy walked her through the steps of making au gratin potatoes.

"I know you help Alex during the summer, but we could sure use you on Thursdays if you're free," Amy said.

"If Alex doesn't need me, I can come in until school starts."

Rowdy walked into the kitchen and lifted the heavy pans of potatoes and cheese into the oven without any direction from Amy, which piqued Stella's curiosity. She was snapping the ends off green beams when he joined her.

"Do you volunteer here often?"

He picked up a handful of green beans. "Every Thursday."

She turned toward him. "Why only Thursdays?"

"That's the only day the Eden Falls' Shelter serves lunch. Every town in the area takes one day a week. Harrisville is Monday, Glenwood serves on Tuesday—"

"How do the homeless get here?"

"Bus."

She stared at him while he continued to snap beans. "When did you start volunteering?"

He shrugged. "A couple of years ago."

"But…"

"But what?"

"I just…"

"I know I'm extremely good-looking, but you've got to stop staring or we'll never get these beans finished."

"Extremely good-looking is pushing it." Stella picked up a handful of beans. "I'll give you cute in a…baby hippo kind of way."

He looked down at his T-shirted chest. "A baby hippo?"

With muscles.

Not now. Stella shook her head. "I never took you for a volunteer kind of guy."

"What kind of a guy do you take me for?" He reached around her for a metal colander, his tall body brushing against hers—intentionally—when he did.

A silly tingle rippled through her. "That kind. A player. A guy who leaves a trail of broken hearts because you can't or won't commit to a relationship."

Rowdy took a step back. A line appeared between his brows. His mossy green eyes narrowed. "That's what you think of me? That I go around having affairs and breaking hearts like your ex-boyfriend?"

It was her turn to take a step back. She glanced around to see if anyone was listening. The other volunteers were too busy to be paying any attention. She looked back at Rowdy, who scrutinized her for a long, uncomfortable moment, then dumped the beans they'd snapped into the colander. The silence between them hung as thick as fog while kitchen sounds clanged and clanked around them.

Rowdy turned back to work.

After a good washing, the beans went into a pot, and Amy swept Stella away to cut pies so they would be easy to serve when the time came. Stella sliced cherry, apple, peach, and blueberry pies, and put each serving on a plate before adding a dollop of whipped cream. She loaded the plates onto trays and the trays onto carts, which she pushed into the walk-in cooler. The work kept her from thinking about Jerry. Instead, she was haunted by Rowdy's expression.

You hurt him.

Rowdy is unhurtable.

Unhurtable is not a word. And no one is unhurtable.

Rowdy's reputation is legendary around Eden Falls. She wiggled her shoulder to unseat her little friend. *Haven't you heard the saying, the truth hurts?*

Maybe the legend is wrong.

Rowdy worked at the sink, washing pots and pans, wiping down the kitchen counters, moving around the kitchen like this place was a second home. Proof that what he said about volunteering was true.

At noon, Amy led Stella out front, where she dished up servings of meatloaf for an hour. She lost track of Rowdy during cleanup. When she finished wiping down the last table and walked out into the bright sunshiny day, his truck was gone.

~

*E*ntering Pretty Posies always conjured bittersweet memories for Rowdy. When his Grandma Garrett owned the shop, he'd stop by after school to help her move the armoires she used as display cases or unload a fresh delivery of flowers. He and JT would clean out the walk-in cooler, or he and Beam would help decorate the shop for the holidays by hanging garlands and lights higher than his tiny-as-Alex grandma could reach. She always had homemade cookies tucked away for her grandkids who visited often.

Alex hadn't changed the interior much since she inherited the shop. That alone kept their grandmother alive in his heart. He could still picture her, watering can in hand, making her way around to the many potted plants.

Alex was also a supporter of local artists, and always displayed and sold their goods. As mayor, wife, and mother, life kept his cousin busy. Yet she'd found a comfortable balance between running a town, a business, and a home. She was behind the counter helping a customer when he entered. He waved, and she shot him an unfriendly glance. She was probably still peeved because he dismissed her from his office Monday afternoon.

He was looking over a collection of metal artwork when she appeared next to him.

"Are you here to order flowers for someone special?"

"Have you ever known me to order flowers for anyone besides my mom?"

She shrugged. "There's always a first."

"I just finished up at the shelter and thought I'd stop by."

"Unusual. I could count on one hand the number of times you've stopped by since Grandma Garrett passed." Her smile broke out. "But this is your second trip in this week."

He picked up a metal fish and turned it over, searching for the artist's name. "I was here to order flowers for my mom's birthday."

"Yet you didn't, or I would have known."

"You were busy that day."

She pointed out the signature on the back of a fin. "I'm never too busy for birthday flowers, except your mom's birthday isn't until next month."

"I was going to order early so I wouldn't forget."

"You know I would have reminded you."

Searching for an exit from their back and forth conversation, he said, "I didn't know Maude was into metal art."

"She took a class at the community college. Pretty good, huh?"

"Yeah." The thought of spunky, red-headed Maude holding a welding torch scared him a little. He set the fish next to a purple orchid. His grandmother had taught Alex the Victorian language of flowers, and people said she used it in most of her floral arrangements. "What do orchids mean?"

"Beauty. Refinement. In ancient Greece, orchids represented virility. Victorians collected them as a sign of luxury."

Rowdy had always admired Alex for her longtime friendships and her ability to care for those around her. She'd found out her husband was killed in Iraq the same day she discovered she was pregnant with her first baby. After years of raising her son alone, she'd stumbled across love again and remarried. She and Colton were now expecting a baby. Besides his mom, Alex was probably the strongest, most honest, hardworking woman he knew.

"Does everyone in town think I'm a player? That I go around having meaningless hookups?"

Alex tipped her head. She was more than a foot shorter than him, but she still carried herself with authority. "Didn't we already have this conversation?"

"Yes, but Stella just told me I leave a trail of broken hearts because I can't commit. Is that what people think of me?"

When she didn't answer, he came to his own defense. "I haven't been on a date in two years."

"How would anyone know that? You've never dated anyone from town. We've never seen you with a woman, only heard rumors. What do you expect? People think you're a player because you've led us to believe that's how you roll, Rowdy."

"They're assuming the worst. Anyone who knows me knows I serve on the town council, I volunteer around town, and I run a successful business. Sure, I've broken up with women when things didn't work out, but I haven't left a trail of broken hearts. I've had plenty of women"—*one in particular*—"break up with me, too. It hasn't always been one-sided.

And you know the reason Beam, JT, and I never dated girls from Eden Falls."

"I do. Others don't." Alex took his arm and led him to a stool near the counter. She pulled another close and sat beside him. "Why does what other people think bother you? Or is it just what Stella thinks that has you worked up?"

Truth? Only Stella's thoughts bothered him. He didn't care what the rest of the town thought. He never had.

Maybe that was part of his problem. He and Beam had been a little wild as teens. They'd gotten into their fair share of trouble, but they were both respectable businessmen now, and had been for several years. It wasn't like they were racing through fields on their motorcycles or shooting off illegal fireworks. They'd sowed a few wild oats, but they'd settled down. What happened in the past shouldn't affect how people saw them now. They'd both proven themselves.

"So only Stella's opinion truly matters."

He glanced at Alex. She was wearing an I-knew-it smirk. "Stella's opinion matters."

"Let's clear the air."

"About?"

"You and Stella. I know you've been interested in her for a while." She held up a hand when he opened his mouth. "Don't try to deny it, Rowdy. I've seen the way you look at her. You care. You two have bantered back and forth like a married couple for years."

He gave up the fight. Why argue with the truth? "She compared me to her ex-boyfriend just now."

"Ouch."

"Yeah ouch. How do I change her opinion?"

"Show her you're not Jerry. It may take some time for her to trust after what he did. If you really are interested, ask her out. Take her somewhere people will see you. Prove to her you're willing to put yourself out there for her." She placed a hand on his knee and squeezed. "You might decide after only one date that she's not your type. Wouldn't that be awful after secretly admiring her for two years?"

"Not gonna happen."

"Maybe you just wanted something you knew you couldn't have."

Rowdy shook his head.

Alex's smile was big and bright. "This is serious for you. You're serious."

"Yes," he said without hesitation.

She leaned close. "Wow."

"Wow what?"

Alex wiggled a finger between the two of them. "Is this the first time you've ever talked to someone about a girl."

"Yes." Then he narrowed his eyes, going for gravity. "And I expect this conversation to stay between us."

Alex spit in her hand and held it out. When he lifted a brow, she took his hand in hers and shook. "I've wanted to do that ever since I saw you and JT do it as kids."

He wiped his palm on her jeans. "When we were kids it wasn't gross."

"Is my spit worse than Stella throwing up all over you?"

"No, that was pretty gross."

~

Stella noticed Rowdy's truck parked on the square as she circled around looking for a parking spot, and wondered where he'd gone so quickly after leaving the shelter. She circled the square twice wanting a parking spot as close to Dahlia's salon as she could get. Finally, someone backed out and she zipped in before she changed her mind.

Misty turned from the client in her chair. "You decided to grace us with your presence?"

Stella ignored her and stepped up to the front desk where Dahlia Dallas sat. She smiled. "Hi, Stella."

"Thanks for working me in."

"Not a problem. I had a cancellation so your call was perfect timing."

"Can we start now? Before I chicken out?"

Dahlia stood and moved around the desk. "Come on back."

Stella's knees wobbled as she followed Dahlia to the first chair in the line of four. Dahlia's was the only salon in town, and all chairs were full but hers. Stella had expected the pungent scent of chemicals, but the salon smelled like fresh laundry. Once she was seated, Dahlia turned her toward the mirror and lifted Stella's long hair off her neck. "What do you have in mind?"

Stella had always worn her hair long. With plenty of natural curl, she didn't have to fuss with it much—just wash and go. Jerry had loved her hair, running his fingers through it often. "Something new and completely different."

"What?" Misty asked, instantly next to her chair. "You can't cut your hair."

Dahlia threaded her fingers through the hair at Stella's temples. "You want to go shorter?"

Stella stared at her reflection. "Yes."

"Shoulder length?"

"Stella, you *cannot* cut your hair," Misty insisted.

Dahlia gathered her hair in a way that gave Stella an idea of what a shoulder length cut would look like on her.

"Will shorter hair make me look fatter?"

"You are not fat," Dahlia said at the same time Misty interjected a quick yes.

Dahlia pinned Misty with a glare in the mirror. "Don't you have a client, Misty?"

"Shoulder length," Stella said decisively.

"You don't want me to do anything with the color, do you? Your natural highlights are beautiful."

"No. One huge change at a time." After Dahlia washed her hair, Stella watched with fascination and trepidation as her locks began to fall on the cape snapped around her neck. What-am-I-doing alarm rattled her brave nerves. *Am I cutting my hair to spite my face?*

Relax. Short hair will be so much easier.

Dahlia put a hand on her shoulder. "You okay?"

"I don't know."

"Do you want me to stop?"

"No." She caught sight of Misty texting madly. Who would be the first to find out about her rash decision? Knowing Misty, she was probably sending a group text to the whole town. She'd beat Rita to this piece of news.

A minute later Phoebe stalked into the salon wearing her police uniform. "Where's Stella? What's the emergency?"

Misty pointed. "You have to stop her."

Phoebe glanced from Misty to Stella, back to Misty. "You can't text the station that there's an emergency because you don't agree with a haircut decision."

Misty jammed a hand at Stella. "This is an emergency. Look what Dahlia is doing to Stella's hair."

Dahlia turned, hand on hip. "I take offense to that."

"I ought to arrest you for scaring me, Misty," Phoebe said jangling her handcuffs.

"Relax Misty, short hair will be so much easier," Stella said trying to channel her haloed friend's calm nature as another lock hit the floor.

Phoebe walked over and watched Dahlia chop another lock. "I love it. You look adorable."

Stella studied her sister's expression in the mirror. "Adorable as in 'look at that dog, it's so ugly it's cute,' or adorable as in 'you look years younger, much thinner, and mildly attractive with shorter hair.'"

Everyone in the salon but Misty laughed. "Adorable as in you are going to wow everyone you know. Mom will love it."

Her friend fluttered her wings. *The cut does make your face look thinner.*

Thanks my sweet friend. Stella wondered what Rowdy would think. Didn't most guys like long hair?

You're thinking about Rowdy again.

Just in general.

The angel rolled her eyes. *Whatever.*

$\mathcal{C}$ ars lined Rowdy's long driveway and the road leading up to his house by the time Stella's dad parked for the Father's Day barbecue. Phoebe planned to join them after her shift, but the other three Adams sisters couldn't make the celebration.

Stella was tucked into the back seat like that extra tire. She'd decided to list the benefits of being single last night and came up with four. At Halloween she only needed to carry an extra wheel to have a hilarious costume. If she added one more person, she'd be on a double date. She didn't have to share her food. And best of all, she could consider herself a lagniappe—a small bonus gift given to a customer, like a thirteenth donut with the purchase of a dozen. She was the extra donut. *Yay, me.*

"Leo's already here," her mom said as they climbed out of her dad's car.

Stella's father always stood in as Leo's dad at the annual barbecue. Leo's own father argued that coming would be conforming to society. He insisted the holiday was designed to make greeting card and barbecue grill companies richer and refused to cater to the system.

They walked around a bend in the driveway and Rowdy's house came into view. Stella's mom paused. "Isn't this lovely?"

Stella studied the house, which sat on a hill surrounded by pines. Unlike Leo's commanding log and glass house, Rowdy's was traditional and unpretentious. A simple ranch with a wide front porch framed in river rock. Five asymmetrical peaks added interest to the roofline.

Her mom turned to her. "Have you been here before, Stella? I had no idea Rowdy built such a charming place."

"I told you in the car I've never been here." Stella had to admit the house was charming…and completely out of character for the Rowdy she knew. Or at least the Rowdy she thought she knew. Trees and low-growing shrubs were planted in three berms around the front yard, and the lawn was thick and green.

A sign on the front door invited guests to enter. The interior was just as amazing as the outside. Arched beam ceilings led the eye to a river rock fireplace. Colors of earth and sky lent a cozy feel to the place. On either side of the fireplace, a wall of glass overlooked a backyard full of people.

"Oh, my goodness," Stella's mom said on an outbreath. "This is gorgeous."

"Gorgeous isn't exactly what I was aiming for, but thank you," Rowdy said coming down a hall to their left. Followed by his horse-sized dog, Moose.

Stella's dad reached around her to shake Rowdy's outstretched hand. "Very nice place you have here."

"Happy Father's Day, Neil. Glad you could make the barbecue."

"We haven't missed one of JT's barbecue since he started the tradition," her dad said.

Rowdy took the covered bowl her mom carried, set it aside, and hugged her. "How are you, Beverly?"

"Wonderful. I just can't get over your home. Living here must feel like you're on vacation every day."

Rowdy flashed his devastating grin. "Would you like a tour?"

Her mom smiled. "We'd love one."

Stella waited for a hello or a nod of acknowledgment. Better yet, a *Wow your hair looks great,* but Rowdy didn't even glance at her. Quite a feat, since she was standing between her mom and dad. He didn't offer to take the plate of brownies she carried. Moose, however, was very interested.

"Moose, behave," Rowdy commanded as he led them down the hall.

Two bedrooms in the front of the house had doors that opened to the beautiful porch. Each had a wall of old barn wood, and traditional furniture with a rustic twist. Simple quilts in muted colors adorned the beds. Stella was surprised by the order and tidiness. No wonder he seemed so appalled by her messy room. Everything was so perfect and pristine, so not what she expected from Rowdy. Phoebe would love this place.

Moose stayed right next to her, bumping up against her hip and gazing at her—or was he looking at the plate of brownies?—with hungry brown eyes.

Across the hall, a bathroom fitted with rough stone double sinks had a door that closed on rollers.

"Is that barn wood in the shower?" Stella's dad asked.

"Actually, it's tile."

Stella's mom ran a hand over the surface. "Amazing. I love this."

Stella followed along like a puppy. She assumed Rowdy was angry about her comments on Thursday, but what did he expect, given his lifestyle?

The last room down the hall was the master bedroom. Spacious and beautiful, it opened onto a back patio with the mountain peak standing majestically behind. This room, like the great room, had cathedral ceilings with arched beams. The wall behind the king bed was barn wood. The opposite wall displayed another floor-to-ceiling river rock fireplace.

Stella couldn't help but stare. She'd heard his place was a rustic mountain home, but she'd expected mounted deer heads, antler furniture, and outdated posters of rock bands and barely clad women leaning against muscle cars. This house was magazine-perfect. Another side of Rowdy she didn't know stood up and took a bow.

You misjudged him. Her irritant was busy shining her halo. *Again.*

So he's a neat freak.

He's more than a neat freak. He has excellent taste.

While her parents gushed and cooed, she looked around for evidence of a woman—a picture, a dog-eared romance novel, or a pair of undies peeking from under a pillow. Nothing.

Rowdy opened a sliding glass door that led to the back patio. "Beam has been grilling up a storm. Hope you enjoy the eats. Again, happy Father's Day, Neil." He thumbed over his shoulder. "I'll get the dish you brought, Beverly."

"Your place is spectacular," Stella said after her parents walked outside.

He blocked her exit with a hand across the door. "And unexpected. I can tell by your shocked expression. What exactly did you think you'd find?"

She laughed. "I thought I'd have to shield my mom's eyes while my dad shielded mine when you suggested a tour." Her laugh died away when he didn't smile at her attempt at humor. She cleared her tight throat. "So about Thursday…" She usually said what was on her mind, which sometimes got her into trouble. Seeing Rowdy's hurt expression made her wish she'd kept her thoughts to herself. "I want to apologize for my player remark. I shouldn't have said anything."

"But you believe it to be true."

She pressed her lips together, biting off any comment.

He straightened his shoulders, his face free of any expression. "Can you name one heart I've broken?"

Her laugh sounded more like a croak. "How can I when you date women from other towns?"

"Then how do you know it's true and not a rumor?"

"I guess I don't."

Rowdy raised a brow.

Stella pulled at the neck of her T-shirt. *Is it hot in here? Nope. Just Rowdy's incinerating stare.*

"I said I was sorry."

"But you still believe it's true."

Not sure what she believed anymore, she lifted his hand so she could go outside.

"You have a little Rita Reynolds in you if you spread rumors before confirming their truth."

She stopped. Turned. "You're comparing me to Rita?"

"If the shoe fits." He slid the door shut.

～

*R*owdy was angry and amused at the same time. Angry because Stella assumed, and amused at the look he'd put on her face. Small town gossip frustrated him, but he'd never corrected the rumors, which was now a mistake on his part.

He was also surprised Moose had warmed to Stella so quickly. His dog was usually a little more standoffish at first.

In the kitchen he pulled another container of hamburger patties out of the fridge, the reason he'd come inside in the first place. The Adams' arrival sidetracked him. And Stella. He'd been wanting to show Stella his house for two years. And, yeah, he'd been hoping she'd like it, possibly feel at home. *Probably not filthy enough.*

He looked out the bank of windows framing the back of his house. People were milling around enjoying the sunshine and good company. A volleyball game was in progress in the far corner, croquet was set up on the side yard, and a crowd had gathered to witness a heated battle between his dad and Uncle Denny on the horseshoe court. Aunt Alice and his mom sat in the shade of a pine entertaining his niece.

Stella made her way across the yard to the food tables. She glanced toward the house, then looked away just as quickly. His Rita remark, though funny, wouldn't go down as his finest moment. Instead, he should have said her haircut looked nice, because it did. He liked the way it framed her pretty face and curled around the neck he'd like to nibble.

Alex's son bolted through the door. "Uncle Rowdy, Uncle Beam says where are the hamburgers? Hi, Moose!"

Rowdy ruffled the seven-year-old's head of thick black hair and handed him Beverly's bowl. "Set this on the table by the other salads and tell Uncle Beam I'm on my way. I got waylaid."

A tiny frown line appeared between big brown eyes. "What is waylaid?"

"I had to talk to someone, but I have the hamburgers." He held out the container. "Let's get these to Uncle Beam before he turns into a growly bear."

Charlie laughed. "Mom already calls him *a bear of a man.*" He said the last four words with a growl. Charlie, who was born smiling, brought joyful enthusiasm to any situation. Everything he said ended with an exclamation point.

Outside, Rowdy set the container on a table near the grill.

"About time. You went in for those fifteen minutes ago."

"I was giving a house tour."

Beam smirked. "To Stella? I saw her come out of the bedroom door."

"Her parents were with us. Need any help?" he asked, not in the mood for teasing or sparring with his brother.

"Take this platter of burgers to the food table. Colton said he'd help me here. Go mingle with your guests—but no sneaking off into the woods," Beam shouted, loud enough for everyone in the yard to hear.

Rowdy had a large tent delivered and set up yesterday for shade, and he and Beam hauled tables and chairs borrowed from the church fellowship hall into the yard so his guests would have plenty of places to sit. People milled about or rested in the shade of pine trees around the perimeter of his property. The food tables were weighed down with salads, chips and dips, relish trays, and yummy desserts.

Rowdy did as Beam suggested and mingled with his guests, which wasn't out of his element. He did the same at his bar and grill when he had the time.

He joined the crowd to cheer his uncle to horseshoe victory. Last year at JT's barbecue, he'd let Stella win their game of horseshoes, a mistake he wouldn't make again. She was a terrible loser and an even worse winner.

Through all his wanderings, he kept Stella in his sights. And she kept him at a safe distance.

~

Stella watched Rowdy make the rounds of his backyard, shaking hands, greeting guests, and making everyone feel welcome. Still in awe of his house and the surrounding property, she couldn't quite imagine Rowdy here alone, not after she'd pictured him with so many women for all these years.

How dare he compare her to Rita Reynolds, the biggest gossip in Eden Falls. Sure, she listened to what other people said about Rowdy—and believed it—but she never passed that gossip around. He was free to see whomever he wanted, wherever he wanted. If he kept a harem, that was his business.

He had no right to judge her.

Though you've been judging him for years. Alex said he's been crushing on you since you started dating Jerry.

Ridiculous. He hasn't looked my way since he came outside.

The angel smiled down at Moose. *At least his dog likes you.*

Stella looked at the huge Saint Bernard leaning against her like she was a tree. He'd been following her around since he came outside with Rowdy.

Rowdy scooped little Sophia from her mom's arms. Misty looked grateful for the reprieve.

Stella smiled. *He's good with Sophia and Charlie.*

You could have thought to help Misty.

Now you're *judging?* Stella lifted her shoulder, trying to unseat the tiny messenger of guilt. *You could have planted that thought in my head.*

The angel hung on tight. *I shouldn't have to plant good thoughts. Start thinking them for yourself.*

"You can go away."

"I just got here." A heavy arm landed on her shoulder.

Stella looked up into Leo's ridiculously blue eyes. "I was talking to myself."

"Isn't that a sign of senility?"

"You should know."

Leo lifted her chin with a finger. "You're in a snit today. What has you all riled up?"

Stella ducked out from under his arm. "Nothing."

"I like the short hair. Looks sexy."

"You think so?" Stella fingered her curls. At least one guy

liked her cut. Rowdy hadn't said anything about it. "How's Willy?"

"Settled in like he's always lived at my place."

"He seemed well-behaved. Why didn't you bring him to the barbecue?"

Leo pointed at Moose. "I was afraid Rowdy's dog might eat him for lunch. When's your sister getting here?"

"You talk to her more than I do." Stella reached out to touch a stain on Leo's T-shirt.

Leo swatted her hand away. "I was busy this morning and didn't get a chance to call her."

She snorted. "You couldn't have been busy with a woman or she would have told you to pick a clean T-shirt."

"I was busy visiting my dad on Father's Day and this T-shirt was clean before breakfast." He frowned. "What is up with you?"

Jillian joined them before Stella got a chance to voice her opinion of men in more detail. "Oh my gosh, Stella, your haircut is darling. I wish my hair curled like that."

"She looks like a Shirley Temple doll."

Stella tugged at the ends. "It's not that short or that curly."

"Isn't Rowdy so cute with Sophia?" Jillian said, always quick to defuse a tense situation.

"Adorable."

Jillian frowned. "That didn't sound at all sarcastic."

"Be careful, Jillian," Leo said over his shoulder as he turned away. "Stella's in one of her moods."

"Sorry," Stella said when they were alone. "Rowdy and I had a…disagreement earlier. "He compared me to Rita."

Jillian's mouth formed a perfect O. "Ouch. Fighting words."

"Exactly!" Stella pointed a finger in his direction. He was making faces at Sophia. Her cute giggle floated around the yard. They *were* pretty adorable together.

"Why'd he make that comparison?"

"I called him a player." When Jillian didn't say anything, Stella glanced at her. She could see the doubt playing across her friend's face. "Everyone says so."

"That doesn't make it true." Jillian lifted a shoulder. "Besides, I haven't seen Rowdy out with anyone in a long time so it wouldn't be fair to agree."

"But his reputation—"

"Again, gossip doesn't make it true."

Stella felt a little betrayed and a lot foolish. What Jillian said made sense and concurred with Rowdy's argument, but how did you just stop believing something that was legend? "Did you just get here?"

Jillian nodded. "Yeah. I had to work this morning."

"Where's Brandt?"

"He has to work all day. The fire department doesn't get holidays off."

"Right." Not only was Jillian marrying a fireman, but he was also the only paramedic in town. Poor Brandt was on call even on his days off.

Stella realized she was still watching Rowdy and Sophia. She turned her back. "Have you eaten yet? I'm starving."

She and Jillian filled plates and found a shady spot on the grass to sit. Jillian stretched out her long, toned legs. Stella stifled a sigh. If only she were four inches taller. Jillian's mom had always called their group of friends the stairstep girls. Stella was only second to Alex as the shortest.

Moose stretched out beside her and rested his gigantic head in her lap. Slobber ran down her bare leg. "Eww. Moose, scoot over." Stella swiped at the inside of her thigh with a napkin. "Gross."

Jillian pointed at the dog with a carrot stick. "He sure has attached himself to you."

"Yeah, lucky me." Stella took a bite of a dill pickle spear. "So, how are plans for the engagement party coming?"

"We're keeping things simple. Dad is grilling chicken to go with Mom's pasta salad and homemade rolls." Jillian looked at her from the corner of her eye. "You don't have to come, Stella. I know it isn't the best time for you."

"Of course I'm coming. I love your mom's pasta salad almost as much as I love you."

Jillian picked up another carrot stick. "I just mean…I'll understand if you change your mind about coming."

Stella dredged a chip through the dill dip on her plate. "I appreciate your concern, but I'll be there." She popped the chip in her mouth. "I saw your mom Thursday."

"She said you helped at the shelter." Jillian cut the hamburger she'd wrapped in lettuce in half.

No wonder she's so skinny.

That and she works out all the time. Stella looked down at her own loaded burger, which didn't look so appetizing anymore.

"Yeah. I talked to Preacher Brenner. He suggested service to help relieve my guilt."

"You shouldn't be the one struggling with guilt, Stella."

She popped another chip in her mouth. "Yet I do."

"Well, you shouldn't." Jillian picked up half her hamburger. "I know my mom appreciated your help."

"She kept me busy enough to forget about everything until I got home to two missed calls from *The Jerk*."

"I wish there was something I could do to help."

Ask her opinion.

Good idea. "You could answer a question that's been bugging me. If you were in my shoes, would you tell Jerry's wife?"

"Yes."

Stella was surprised by Jillian's immediate response. "You would?"

Jillian set her plate on the grass and leaned back on her palms. "If I were in her shoes, I'd want to know. Imagine being in the dark about your cheating husband."

"On the other hand, imagine her hurt when she finds out."

"Would you want to know?" Jillian asked. "Or would you rather go on in ignorance?"

"I'd want to know." Stella set her plate aside. Before she could grab it back, Moose had wolfed her burger down. "Oh boy." She glanced at Rowdy. "I sure hope it's okay if you eat human food."

"Rororoo woof."

Rowdy looked toward her with raised brows.

"How would you tell her, Jillian?" she asked turning her attention back to her friend. "Would you find out where she lives and visit in person, or would you try to get her phone number and call?"

Jillian rolled both shoulders forward and wrinkled her forehead. "I'm not sure I could tell her face-to-face. That would be the most awkward conversation ever."

Stella agreed. She couldn't imagine anything but a phone conversation, but how would she tell a woman she didn't know that her husband was cheating? Maybe an anonymous call?

Chicken.

Shut up.

"I hope you're not letting Stella pull you into her gossipy ways, Jillian."

Stella glared up at Rowdy towering over them. "Since you snuck up on us to eavesdrop, you should know we weren't gossiping."

"I love your house, Rowdy," Jillian said, jumping in to calm the brewing storm. "You have a beautiful view."

Rowdy turned toward the mountain behind his house. "Thanks. I was lucky the property was available when I started looking for a building site."

"Well, the inside is as pretty as the outside. Did you have help with the decorating?"

Stella felt as well as noticed his pointed stare. "Yes. One of the many hearts I've broken was an interior designer. She helped me pick colors and some of the furniture."

"The bed?" Stella mumbled loud enough to be heard.

"As a matter of fact, yes. She did help me pick out the bed. Sadly, I broke her heart before we got the chance to try it out."

"One of many."

"Stella," Jillian reprimanded quietly.

"You and Rita should know."

Stella jumped to her feet. "Stop comparing me to Rita."

Rowdy leaned down until they were nose to nose. "Then stop acting like her."

She fought to keep her eyes off his mouth. "Sorry."

"For acting like Rita?"

"No. For calling you a jackass."

A puzzled expression moved over his face. "When?"

"Just now. In my head."

He straightened with a shake of his head. "Can I get you anything, Jillian?"

"No, thank you," she said, her glance bouncing from Rowdy to Stella. "The burger was great."

"You can get me another burger. Your dog just ate mine."

"Come on, Moose." Rowdy patted his thigh, ignoring her request.

Moose rose. *"Rororoo woof."* He nudged Stella, almost toppling her over. Rowdy grabbed her arm before she stumbled and fell. His jaw bulged like he was grinding his teeth before he turned and stalked away.

"Geez, he makes me nuts." Stella plopped down next to Jillian again.

"What's going on between you two?"

Stella rolled her eyes. "He's just so…annoying."

"He sure seemed to annoy you." Jillian pulled her knees up to her chest. "Did I miss something?"

"He kissed me at JT and Carolyn's wedding."

Jillian's eyes widened. "As in a friendly little peck or—"

"Yep, the *or* one. And I kissed him back."

"Wow."

"Yep, it was pretty wow all right."

"Seriously?"

Stella nodded.

"Are you ready for another relationship so soon after Jerry?"

"Ha! I don't have to worry about that. Rowdy doesn't do relationships."

~

*R*owdy stopped next to his brother. "I'll take over."

"I just put on the last patties. Hope everyone has eaten."

Rowdy glanced around. Of course his attention stopped on Stella. She was lying on her back in the grass. She frustrated him like no one else he'd ever met, yet at the same time he wanted to pull her into his arms and kiss her until she forgot all about the idiot she'd been dating. The thought that she might still be pining over Jerry infuriated him.

Beam's laugh irritated him further.

"You have it bad."

He'd had it bad for a long time, made worse since Stella caught her boyfriend with his wife, because nothing but her stubbornness kept them apart now.

"Great party, Rowdy," Colton said as he and Alex joined them. "You're giving JT a run for his money."

"How's the house coming?" Beam asked.

Alex threaded her arm through her husband's. "Slow and steady, which is nice. I'm going to miss my little bungalow."

"We're tripping over each other in that *little bungalow*," Colton said looking down at Alex. "We've needed more space since we got married and now, with a baby on the way…"

"As you can tell, Colton isn't as nostalgic as I am." She patted his arm. "We shared our first kiss in that kitchen."

Colton laughed. "Yeah, right before you threw me out."

"You were an egotistical, city-dwelling pig back then."

"And you were a prim and proper prude."

Rowdy watched the oddest couple he knew banter back and forth. Best-selling author Colton McCreed had flown into town from LA to study small town life for his next slasher murder-mystery. Alex caught his eye, and her son, Charlie snared his heart. Now, they were expecting their first baby around Thanksgiving and building a new house on the other side of the ridge near JT and Leo.

"How's the movie coming along?" Beam asked of Colton's book turned movie.

Colton bent and ruffled Moose's hair. The dog woo-woo-wooed in ecstasy. "The movie and the baby are due out about the same time. The studio wants to do a big premier in LA, but I talked them into having one here."

"Wow," Rowdy said. "Movie stars in Eden Falls."

"Maybe you can find a special lady to take with you," Alex suggested with a wink.

Rowdy rolled his eyes.

Beam pointed at him, his bellowing laugh grabbing the attention of pretty much everyone at the party.

CHAPTER 12

*S*tella entered Pretty Posies Monday morning by the back door. She listened for any sign of Rowdy. Instead she heard Tatum talking wedding bouquets with another female. She glanced into the front of the shop to make sure Tatum didn't need any help before picking up the to-do list Alex left on the worktable.

She'd avoided Rowdy for the rest of the afternoon on Saturday, and found not looking around for him on Sunday extremely difficult. She'd never thought of Rowdy as anything more than Beam's brother, Alex and JT's cousin, Glenda and Dawson's son. He was as much a part of Eden Falls as Patsy's Pastries or The Fly Shop. Jillian's skepticism about jumping into another relationship so soon after Jerry made sense, but there would be no jumping with Rowdy.

So why do you keep thinking about him?

Because I don't want to think about Jerry anymore.

She was so tired of picking through and ruminating about the past two years. Trying to justify her feelings and reactions. Trying to make herself innocent when she felt anything but. Late last night she decided what she had with Jerry couldn't be called a relationship when all her emotions had evolved from lies. She hoped the simple explanation would assuage her guilt, but it didn't work, because for those two years she believed she *was* in a relationship.

Her emotions had shifted from disgust to pure hate. She truly hated Jerry for putting her in a position that caused overwhelming culpability and had her questioning everything she'd done, every decision she'd made. He'd duped her and she'd followed right along like a trusting puppy.

She nearly hit the ceiling when a hand touched her shoulder.

"Oh, sorry hon." Patsy Douglas hugged her from behind. "I didn't mean to scare you."

Hand to heart, Stella glanced down at the two daisies she'd denuded while thinking of Jerry.

"You were so deep in thought you didn't hear me say your name."

"Busy morning." Stella swept the petals into her hand and dumped them into a nearby trashcan. "What can I do for you?"

The proprietor of Patsy's Pastries, who looked near tears, dropped onto a stool. Her teased and sprayed-to-perfection platinum hair was tousled, like she forgot to check the mirror before she left home, which was very unusual for perfectly put-together Patsy.

"I've got a huge problem and thought maybe a second grade teacher could help."

"What happened?"

"Did you hear about Ben Jensen's barn roof caving in this spring from that wet snowstorm we had?"

Stella vaguely remembered hearing the news.

"Most of us business owners kept our parade floats in his barn. They were all damaged." She laughed without humor.

"Damaged is putting it mildly. Except for the trailer, my float is destroyed. Alex let us move everything to the abandoned canning factory at the edge of town, which Mason helped me do today. Two high school girls working for me thought they could come up with an idea for a new float, but I can tell they're in way over their heads. I don't know who else to ask. The fourth of July is only two weeks away, so I don't have time to contact a professional float builder."

Stella had never thought of building floats as a career choice, but hey, why not? Towns all over America held parades. She pulled out her cell phone calendar. "You actually have two and a half weeks until the Fourth."

"This isn't a joking matter. I've had a float in the Fourth of July parade every year since I opened the shop. I can't miss this year. You know crafts. You work with kids. Please tell me you can help. I'm begging."

Stella rubbed a hand over Patsy's back. "I wasn't joking, just the practical part of my brain giving you a few more days." She glanced over Alex's to-do list. "Alex didn't leave me much work today. When I finish here, I'll run over and take a look."

Patsy hugged her tight. "Thank you, thank you, thank you. You have no idea how much this means to me. I can pay you by the hour or—"

"You don't have to pay me, Patsy. Just cover the cost of supplies, which I'll run by you before I buy them."

"Money is no object. Buy anything you need."

After lunch Stella drove to the abandoned canning factory. The number of cars parked out front surprised her. The doors and windows of the factory were open, allowing a cross breeze to cool the interior.

Luckily, the temperatures hadn't reached scorching in

western Washington state yet. Even better, most of the building was shaded from the worst of the sun by towering cottonwood trees, their white fluff floating through the air like snow, drifting into piles against the building.

The interior was a beehive of activity, people hard at work building new or refurbishing old floats. The high school cheerleaders were decorating an old Ford pickup with red, white, and blue bunting. They always rode in the bed and threw candy to eager children. Rowdy sat on top of the cab, securing the school mascot to a post. One of the cheerleaders giggled at something he said.

He grinned down at the teenager wearing cutoffs short enough to be illegal and winked.

"Cradle robber," Stella mumbled.

That's unkind, her little friend whispered.

The guy has no shame.

Says the woman who dated a married man.

Hey! Aren't you supposed to be on my side? Stella swiped her shoulder.

The angel fluttered her wings enough to carry her out of reach.

Leo walked from one end of a flatbed trailer to the other, duct-taping a wire for a sound system. The Tiny Twirlers' instructor was following along, watching him like he was a yummy piece of chocolate cake. A geek all through school, Leo had definitely changed his looks and style. Gone were the black-framed glasses, high-water pants, and Live Long and Prosper T-shirts. He glanced up and yelled, "Stella," *A Streetcar Named Desire*-style.

She waved and moved on to the next float, where Colton was working alongside a few members of the town council to construct a patriotic float with his stepson's help. As a member of the town council, this was where Rowdy should be concentrating his attention.

"Hi Stella!" Charlie exclaimed with huge brown eyes. "Me and Colton are building a float for the parade. Veterans are going to ride on it."

"It looks great. What part are you doing?"

"I'm holding this fringy stuff up and Colton is stapling it on. It's almost long enough that it will touch the road. See the big staples?" He held one out in his small palm. "They go through the wood."

"Wow, those are big. Good job." She glanced at Colton, who was grinning at the adorable kid. "Looks like you have a super good helper."

"Charlie is always a super helper." Colton lifted his chin. "You here to work on a float?"

"I told Patsy I'd look at hers."

"Oh," Colton said with a chuckle. "Good luck."

"Bad?"

"A complete redo."

As she rounded the float 4-H kids were working on, Patsy's cake float came into view.

Oh, boy. Her bright-eyed friend plopped down in a cloud of white. *This is going to be a big job.*

You got that right.

The cake on Patsy's float was completely crushed. Two teenage girls stood on the trailer looking helpless and confused. Patsy paced nearby, wringing her hands. When she spotted Stella, she threw her arms in the air. "Oh, thank heavens you're here."

Stella tugged a piece of the demolished confection off the trailer. "What was the cake made of before?"

"It looks like it was all cardboard," one of the girls said.

"I don't know. Maybe," Patsy added. "The float was built so many years ago, I can't remember. The whole thing is ruined. The girls don't even know where to start."

"If we could get cardboard and rebuild the cake, we could use balloons for frosting," the second girl suggested.

"Cute idea, but balloons lose their air after a few hours or pop." Stella rounded the trailer, again. *A cupcake tower might be cute.*

Her little companion clapped her hands. *Oh, good idea. Thank you.*

"Is there a dumpster we can use?"

"Alex had a large one dropped off." Patsy pointed. "It's on the east side of the building."

"Do you ladies know any strong young men who'd be willing to haul all this out to the dumpster?"

"I'll pay twenty bucks an hour," Patsy chimed in.

"I'll call Aaron," the first girl said with smitten eagerness.

"Great. Once the boys get the flatbed cleaned off, you ladies wash it down with soap and water so we can paint it a pretty pink. We'll let it dry overnight. I'll go shopping for supplies."

"Please tell me you can get this float done in time."

"We can." Stella flashed Patsy what she hoped was a reassuring smile. "Trust me. I teach second graders. You are going to have a fabulous float by the Fourth of July."

After she left the factory, Stella's first stop was a fabric store in Harrisville. She bought all the tulle they had in a variety of pastels and three bolts of pink and white gingham. Next, she visited a big box store and cleared the shelves of their largest round laundry baskets. A craft store provided the poster paper she needed. She'd score the paper, fold it accordion style, and secure it to the laundry baskets. Her last stop was Eden Falls Hardware and Lumber.

Beam Garrett was behind the front counter when she entered. "Hey, Stella. What brings you in today?"

"Me."

She jumped at the nearness of Rowdy's voice. "You pop up more often than a Whack-a-Mole."

"Funny, I was thinking the same thing about you."

"Last time I saw you, you were flirting with a cheerleader young enough to be your daughter."

"Jealous again? You have no reason to be, darlin'." He hooked an arm around her neck and looked at his brother. "Stella's been following me around town ever since that kiss at JT and Carolyn's wedding."

Her groan was audible enough that Beam laughed. "Why would you want anything to do with this long-haired lowlife?"

"*I don't.*"

Although what Rowdy said was true. Not that she was following him around town, but on average she ran into Rowdy once a week, maybe twice at the most. Now it seemed like she saw him at least once a day, and sometimes more.

Rowdy and Beam's smirks were mirror images of each other, like their mossy green eyes, narrow noses, and height. The resemblance ended there. Beam was broad as a bear, with muscles bulging under his T-shirt. Rowdy, while still muscular, was more slender in build.

He smells nice.

You always think that.

Well, he does.

Stella had to agree with her little friend. He did smell extremely nice. *I'm as bad as that lovesick cheerleader.* She shrugged out from under the weight of Rowdy's arm. "Point me in the direction of chicken wire."

"Chicken wire? You live in an apartment," Rowdy said.

"Come with me." Beam rounded the counter. "Keep an eye on the register for me, bro."

Beam led her to the back of the store, which had just

reopened after burning to the ground a year earlier. Poor JT still hadn't caught the arsonist responsible.

"How much do you need?" He picked up a roll from a bin. "This is a hundred and fifty feet."

Stella looked at the sign over the rolls. Twenty bucks would be well within Patsy's unlimited budget. She bent an exposed end, which was easy enough to do with just her fingers. "I'll take it and some wire cutters."

"Mind if I ask what you're doing with it?"

"I'm making cupcakes."

Beam's wide-eyed expression sent Stella's little friend tumbling off her shoulder in a fit of laughter.

"Cupcakes?"

"Look for Patsy's float on the Fourth of July. I also need two to three gallons of pink paint, brushes, trays and rollers."

～

*R*owdy watched Stella climb into her car at the curb. When he turned back, his brother grinned like a court jester. "I never thought I'd live to see the day when a woman caught you."

"No one's caught me."

Beam threw back his head and laughed. "You should see your face. You're a goner."

Rowdy's punch to his brother's chest was lightning fast. Beam might outweigh him by sixty pounds, but he'd never be as fast as Rowdy.

"The truth hurts." Beam rubbed the muscle over his heart. "I remember the day I realized I was in love with Misty."

"You mean the day you lost your mind?"

Beam moved behind the counter. "One and the same. I took my bike out for a long ride to try to clear my head and came back more in love than when I left."

"I didn't say I was in love."

"You don't have to. It's written all over your face." Beam pointed to the door. "Go take the bike out and see what you come back with."

Rowdy already knew what he'd come back with. He'd been crazy about Stella for a long time now. A bike ride wouldn't change that. He'd decided this huge, expanded feeling in his chest was love, and he sure wasn't going to ask his brother to verify if love felt too big to contain.

He walked out into the bright sunshine, waved to two men washing a fire engine in front of the station across the street, then climbed into his truck and headed back to the canning factory. Halfway there, he made a U-turn back to the hardware store for the wire he forgot because Stella had interrupted all rational thought. Beam, still behind the register, held up the wire while getting in another roaring laugh.

The factory, which had been vacant since he was a teenager, was bustling with activity. People were either building or refurbishing a slew of bulky kid-pleasers. As soon as he walked in, he searched for Stella. She and Patsy Douglas were watching two teenage boys pull yards of damaged cardboard off the trailer. Apparently Patsy's rain- and snow-damaged float was the reason for Stella's chicken wire. He stopped next to Patsy and hung an arm around her shoulders. She, her pastry shop, and her float were Eden Falls' icons.

She snaked her arm around his waist. "Hello handsome."

"Hey yourself. Time for a little repair work?"

Patsy shook her head. "Total overhaul is more like it."

"You *are* following me," he said when Stella glanced his way.

She rolled her eyes. "I was here first."

Patsy raised perfectly arched eyebrows, sudden interest

buzzing in the look she sent Stella and then him. "Hmm, do I detect a little interest zinging—?"

"There is no zinging, Patsy," Stella interrupted, holding up a hand.

Patsy flashed her fuchsia smile at him. "What about you, handsome? You finally ready to settle down and give your mama another grandbaby?"

"Settling down would cramp my style, Patsy. Just ask Stella." He thumbed over his shoulder. "I gotta finish up the high school truck."

"He's leaving out that he has to trifle with a young girl's heart."

He took Stella's chin between his index finger and thumb. "Jealousy puts a line between your eyebrows, darlin'."

She jerked away from his touch and he laughed.

Patsy's eyebrows rose even higher.

"Let me know if you need any help, Patsy."

"She doesn't," Stella shot back.

Rowdy finished wiring the high school mascot to the top of the old truck. On his way out, he found the owner of The Fly Shop staring at his fish float, hands on hips.

"Hey, Rance. Congrats on the new grandbaby in the works."

"Thanks, Rowdy." Rance ran a hand over his bald dome, a grin on his face. "That sure is something, huh?"

"Sure is. Mac and Noelle were beaming when I saw them the other night." He nodded at the fish float. "What's going on?"

"My fish has flopped."

"What's wrong with it?"

"The engine won't start, and without the VW, the fish is out of the parade."

Rowdy knelt to see how the fish was attached. "Can we attach the trout to something else?"

"That rainbow has been attached to that VW since time began. It ain't goin' nowhere."

Rowdy couldn't remember a parade that didn't include Rance's fish snaking along the route. Time was too tight to build another. "Did you call Nate Klein?"

"Yep. He ordered the part he needs, but it's being shipped from who knows where and won't arrive until the end of next week. Too late for the parade."

"Hey, Rowdy."

Rance's son, wearing his police uniform, joined them. "Hey, Mac. Just getting off duty?"

"No, I've got the night shift. Any idea how we can repair this fish in time for the parade?"

"If Nate can't get the car running before the Fourth, why not push the whole thing onto a trailer?"

"I suggested that. Dad doesn't like the idea," Mac said.

"Pulling the VW around on a trailer won't be the same as driving her through town."

"No, but at least your fish will be in the parade advertising The Fly Shop, Dad."

Rance ruffled a hand around his fringe of white hair. "I guess I don't have much choice." He looked at the fish-covered car in an I've-lost-a-longtime-friend way. "I knew ol' Jezzie wouldn't hold out forever."

"Jezzie?"

Rance flashed a grin at Rowdy. "Short for Jezebel. Me and Lily had some fun times in that back seat before we attached the fish."

"TMI, Dad," Mac groaned.

Rowdy glanced through the open window of the Volkswagen. "How did you both squeeze in back there?"

Rance ran a hand over his belly. "That was back in my fit days. Boy, we'd—"

"Enough." Mac held up a hand. "I don't need more than

the mental picture I already have of my dad having his way with my sweet mother in the back seat of a VW."

Rowdy laughed at Mac's pained look and the light in Rance's eye. "Nate will get Jezzie up and running by the Christmas parade."

~

Stella put her hands on the small of her back and bent backwards, stretching her tight muscles. Straightening, she rolled her neck and shoulders, then leaned forward until she touched her toes. She'd been attaching domed chicken wire to laundry baskets for three hours. Dark had fallen, and the warehouse, almost empty of people, had grown quiet.

She glanced over her work. *Enough for tonight.* She had wired the bones for four huge cupcakes. When finished, instead of one large cake, the float would hold tiered layers of cupcakes. Hopefully, Patsy would be okay with the design change. Tomorrow, Patsy's two teenage employees would slap a new coat of pink paint on the trailer. The next day, they would attach the gingham bunting she'd coaxed Alex's mom into sewing for the drop between trailer and ground. She just had to figure out how to make the tiers and where to place the pastry shop banners Patsy ordered.

The next step was to call in reinforcements.

While she waited for her dad to answer his cell phone, she wandered outside and breathed in the sweet summer air. If Alex was here, she'd be able to identify the something wonderful blooming nearby.

Jerry flitted through her mind. She couldn't even think of him as Len anymore, and Jerry was a stranger to her. Their time together had been a complete farce.

"Hey, number four daughter."

Hearing her dad's voice sent a shot of warmth through her. "Hi, Daddy."

"How are you, cupcake?"

She smiled at the endearment. Very fitting for her project. Her dad called all five of his daughters by a sweet nickname. She'd always been cupcake, Phoebe went by cotton candy, Isadora was sweet roll, Georgiana, candied apple, and Adelaide, aka Oops, was sugar plum.

"Better," she said, pleasantly surprised by her answer. She'd only thought of Jerry twice today, which was less than yesterday, and much less than the day before. And none of those times had she felt the sting of tears.

Her angel nodded with a smile. *Progress.*

Yay, me.

"I'm glad to hear that. You seemed distant yesterday at dinner."

"Temporary setback. I'm good."

"Is Alex keeping you busy with summer weddings?"

"Alex *and* Patsy, which brings me to the reason for my call. Do you have plans after work tomorrow?"

"I was going to mow the lawn, but that can be put off for another day. What do you need?"

She heard his eagerness. She loved that about her parents. Nothing was more important than spending time with loved ones. "Can you meet me at the old canning factory? Patsy thought my second-grade teaching skills included building parade floats. I have an idea how to replace her dilapidated cake but need help with the support."

"Ah, I heard about Ben's barn collapse. Was Patsy's float damaged?"

"Destroyed."

"What time do you want me?"

She looked up into the night sky, thought of Rowdy, and

looked away. "I should be finished at the flower shop by five. Can you meet me then?"

"I'll see you tomorrow, cupcake."

"Bye, Daddy. And thank you."

"Does a girl every get too old to call her father daddy?"

Somehow, she'd sensed Rowdy was nearby, so she wasn't startled by his voice. "Not at my house."

"Rororoo woof."

"The stars are really showing off tonight."

When she turned, she could barely make out Rowdy's outline leaning against a brick retaining wall about twenty feet away. "I think we've had this conversation before. If memory serves, it didn't end well."

Rowdy pushed off the wall with the heel of his boot. "I disagree, but that's me."

She had to disagree too, but she'd never say it out loud. In quiet moments, she was still comparing his kiss to Jerry's, who had taken the joy out of kissing for her. Why had it taken two years for her to realize that? She should have picked up on little annoyances sooner. Instead she'd settled. Accepted—even appreciated—the little Jerry had offered.

Stella held out her hand and Moose trotted over. She ruffled his fur. "When did you get here, Moose?"

Rowdy was beside her now. "He wanted to go for a ride and we ended up here."

Moose nudged her, nearly knocking her down with his weight. Rowdy reached out and steadied her.

"Next month the Milky Way will be very visible."

Stella looked up. "I'm not sure I've ever seen the Milky Way."

She could tell he was smiling by the flash of white teeth. "Sure you have. You probably just didn't know what you were looking at." He pointed skyward. "Can you find the Little Dipper?"

Moose bumped her leg, and she dropped a hand to his huge head as she looked up. The Big Dipper was easy to spot, but she had no idea where to look for the Little Dipper. "No."

Hands on her shoulders, he backed her against him and pointed. "Just northeast of the Big Dipper's bowl is the Little Dipper."

She snorted. "Knowing that doesn't make it easier to find."

"This time I'll help, Miss Impatient." He fingered her hair. "By the way, I like your haircut."

Her tiny companion did a victory dance as a silly thrill shimmied through Stella.

"Thank you."

"I noticed Saturday. I should have told you then."

She glanced over her shoulder at him. "Instead you were all mean and grouchy."

"I'd describe my mood differently, but we're all entitled to our opinions." He turned her head back to the stars.

Not because she was determined to find the blasted constellation, but because she liked Rowdy's nearness and his voice so close to her ear, she stood still. He was close enough that she could feel the sparkling silver energy flowing between them. The *zinging*, as Patsy called it, was very real. She wondered if he could feel it too.

"Dubhe is the top outside star of the Big Dipper's bowl. It's known as a pointer star, and points to Polaris."

"Got it."

"The star directly under Dubhe, forming the bottom edge of the bowl, is Merak, also a pointer star."

"Got it."

"Draw an imaginary line connecting those two stars, then extend the line to a point that is about five times longer than the distance between Merak and Dubhe. At the end of that imaginary line is Polaris."

"The North Star."

"The second-grade teacher in you is shining through."

Moose bumped her again. She teetered, almost losing her balance, but Rowdy steadied her with an arm around her waist.

"Behave, Moose," Rowdy said in a soft but firm voice.

Moose whined and lay down, resting his head on her foot.

"Rowdy, I see it."

"Good. Polaris is the first and brightest star in the Little Dipper, and the outermost star of the handle. Now look for Pherkad and Kochab."

"Wait, I haven't seen the Little Dipper yet."

His chuckle rumbled from his chest, which was nestled all nice and warm against her back. "Pherkad and Kochab are the two stars that make up the front edge of the Little Dipper's bowl, and the only two that are pretty easy to see with the naked eye. Pherkad is the top corner, and Kochab forms the bottom corner."

"How do you know all this?" She started to turn, but he stopped her by cupping her face in a heated palm.

"Keep looking. Don't lose the Small Dipper."

"I haven't seen it yet."

"Patience. You've probably seen it a thousand times and just don't realize. Have you found the top and bottom corners yet?"

Stella leaned slightly forward. She was having a hard time concentrating with Rowdy so close. The warm air, his masculine scent, and a sky full of stars were all creating a heart-pounding, light-headed effect. An effect she liked. A lot.

"Stella?"

She gasped. "I see them."

"Those two stars are called the guardians of the pole

because they march around Polaris. Now connect the dots. Once you've spotted the three brightest stars of the Little Dipper, you can gradually find the other four stars to complete the picture."

"This is a waste of—" She stopped as the Little Dipper came into view as plain as day. "I see it," she said on a whisper of breath.

"Good girl." His other arm circled her waist and he squeezed lightly.

"I do. I see it!" She leaned into him, her arms resting on his, their fingers intertwining. "I can't believe how clear it is. I'm afraid to look away for fear I'll never find it again."

"You'll find it now you know what to look for."

"Thank you."

"Is that all I get, a measly thank-you?"

She turned until she faced him, their bodies pressed together. "What do you want?"

He turned his head and tapped his cheek.

She stood on tiptoe to give him a peck. At the last second he turned his head and their lips connected. She didn't move away as her breath quickened. Instead, she allowed him to gather her even closer, let him deepen the kiss. She relaxed and let herself enjoy the moment. Her heart thumped a steady beat as her blood moved as slow as honey through her veins. An unusual weakness shook her upper thighs and invaded her belly, which seemed to float upward, making her breathless.

The kiss grew more demanding, and then ebbed into sweet sensations of fulfillment. Rowdy was talented at creating a sense of belonging, of inducing a need that overwhelmed common sense.

He broke the kiss and dropped his forehead to hers, an unexpectedly intimate gesture. He lifted a tendril of her hair to his nose. "You smell of summer and oranges."

She didn't trust her voice to come out as smoothly as his, so she remained silent.

He tucked the tendril behind her ear and exhaled a ragged breath, something she hadn't expected. His fingers trailed from her ear to her jaw. The sheer pleasure of his touch sent lovely tingles up her spine.

As her breath leveled, a morsel of responsibility returned. She stepped away from his hold. "We can't do this," came out raspier than she planned.

"Sure we can. We're all grown up and can do whatever we like. No one is going to send us to the principal's office for kissing in the dark."

"You're reckless."

"How am I reckless, sweet Stella? You've known me your whole life. I am who I am."

She didn't know who he was anymore. Either he was changing or her opinion of him was. She'd started to think of him in ways she never had before. They'd bantered together for years, but that was being altered slowly into… She wasn't sure what, but her shifting feelings were scaring her for some reason she couldn't explain. "I have to go."

He reached out and took her fingers. "No, you don't."

"I don't, but I'm going to anyway." She tugged from his grasp and almost ran to her car. When she pulled onto the road, she glanced in the rearview mirror. Rowdy stood exactly where she'd left him, Moose leaning against his leg.

CHAPTER 13

Rowdy breathed in the fresh mountain air. The surrounding forest came alive with early dawn sounds as the mists started to dissipate. He was a morning person by nature, but his business didn't allow him the luxury of enjoying it very often. The nearby river splashed over rocks while birds competed to be heard from the branches overhead. Tangy scents of pine and rich soil wafted along on the breeze.

Colton's Range Rover pulled into the trailhead parking lot, and he and JT climbed out. He met them here on the trail a couple of times a week when his schedule permitted. They didn't exchange more than a few words while they stretched their muscles.

"Any more on our arsonists?" Colton asked after they started jogging on the groomed trail.

"They were in town yesterday." JT flipped his baseball cap backwards. "That tall kid brings his little gang and parades around just to push my buttons. The little one with the orange hair taunts the shop owners, pretending to stick things in his pockets."

"He's probably pretending with one hand while actually shoplifting with the other," Colton replied.

JT shook his head. "If that's true, no one has caught him in the act."

Two years earlier the lumberyard caught fire and soon spread to the hardware store. Neither survived. The fire was ruled arson, but no one was caught. The next summer, the largest pine in the square—always decorated as Eden Falls' Christmas tree—also burned to the ground. Though evidence linking the Goth group of kids from Harrisville was found, JT couldn't prove they set the fire. Two more fires were set, but both were extinguished before much damage occurred. The group was very good at covering their tracks.

"I hear you're helping Rance with his float," JT said.

"Not really. The old VW won't start, and Nate can't get the part he needs in time. Rance found a buddy with a flatbed trailer. We'll load the car up tonight. He'll have to pull the fish through town this year."

"Bet Rance isn't happy," Colton said. "He loves that VW as much as he loves to fish."

Rowdy pictured the old man's disappointed expression. "Without the part, there's nothing Nate can do. At least the fish will be in the parade."

They finished their eight-mile run in companionable silence, then met at Noelle's Café for a quick breakfast. Afterwards, Rowdy headed to Mrs. Bingham's house before going home to shower. The men in his and JT's family took turns mowing the widow's lawn each week. Today was his turn.

∾

*S*tella stopped at Mrs. Bingham's as she'd promised at the senior luncheon. The sweet lady sat on the porch, a pot of tea on the table next to her, reading their little local paper that was delivered once a week. On the front page was a picture of Rowdy kneeling with Charlie's little league baseball team, his smile as big as Charlie's. The article stated the importance of sponsoring local sports teams.

One more surprising fact about Rowdy.

Stella stared at the picture. *Yep, his surprises are sprouting as fast as weeds.*

While Mrs. Bingham complimented her haircut and poured her a cup of tea, Stella read over the article. Seemed Rowdy supported several teams around the area.

"Isn't that a handsome picture of Rowdy?"

"Um-humm." He had a nice smile when he thought to use it rather than his typical smirk.

"That boy should find a nice girl and settle down."

Stella folded the paper and set Rowdy facedown on the table. "Patsy said almost the same thing yesterday. Problem is, Rowdy isn't a settling down kind of guy. He told Patsy it would cramp his style."

Mrs. Bingham's musical laugh made Stella smile. "He's such a big talker. When he finally falls for a girl, he's going to fall hard. The big talkers always do."

"Was Mr. Bingham a big talker?"

"Oh my, yes," Mrs. Bingham replied with wide eyes. "He liked to throw out his chest and proclaim that he'd never get married. I knew he was interested in me the second our eyes met, but he fought the attraction harder than two dogs going after the same bone."

"How'd you finally convince him?"

"I baked him a pie." Mrs. Bingham's smile twinkled of mischief. "He asked me to marry him the next day."

The romantic story warmed Stella's bruised heart, reinforcing her belief that love could have a forever-after ending. "Did you say yes right away or make him work for it?"

"We were married two weeks later."

Stella's parents' story was similar. They married quickly and were still happily married after thirty-five years. "Was Mr. Bingham romantic?"

Mrs. Bingham's expression grew serene. "He could be very romantic at times."

Their conversation turned her thoughts to Rowdy. Alex's comment played through her mind again. She pushed the words aside. Even if Rowdy did like her, it wouldn't last. He was out to have fun and then move on. That she kept thinking about him made her antsy. Thoughts of their last kiss made her even antsier. She was up half the night thinking about his lips against hers. Now, she was tired and grouchy and wanted caffeine, which she wasn't getting with the decaffeinated tea Mrs. Bingham served.

"Did you hear me, hon?"

Stella shook herself from her stupor. "I'm sorry?"

Mrs. Bingham pointed at the street as a truck—Rowdy's truck—stopped at the curb. "I said it's going to get noisy in a minute. Rowdy is here to mow my lawn."

Wow! It's eerie how often he appears.

Like an annoying fly that just won't go away.

Rowdy unloaded a lawnmower from the back of his truck. He glanced toward the porch and waved, then did a double-take when he spotted Stella, his green eyes so intense the air was squeezed from her lungs.

Mrs. Bingham's glance bounced from Rowdy to her. "Maybe you're wrong about Rowdy. He just might be the settling down kind."

"No. He just likes to torment me. He aims for an argument or a blush."

Mrs. Bingham patted her thigh. "You don't seem the blushing type."

"I'm not. He usually goes for the argument with me."

Once they finished their cup of tea, they went inside, where Stella helped move several light pieces of furniture. Then Mrs. Bingham walked her through the different rose gardens in her yard. Stella was very aware of Rowdy going back and forth just beyond peripheral vision. *Whack-a-mole.*

Roses from pale yellow to deep gold or bright orange lined her driveway. On the side of the house the colors ranged from blush to burgundy and every shade of pink and red in between. Stella was amazed by all the different varieties. Mrs. Bingham talked about their general care, fertilizers, and watering. She was in her element, and Stella was intrigued enough to listen.

"How much time do you spend out here each day?"

"As much as I can. I love the outdoors."

"Why only roses?"

Mrs. Bingham's smile was slow, a dreamy look in her eye. "Mr. Bingham gave me a rose bush as a wedding gift. I made him plant it before I would leave on our honeymoon." She crooked her finger and Stella followed her to the backyard. At the corner of the patio, Mrs. Bingham pointed.

"That's the bush?" The blooms were deep, velvety red against leaves of dark green.

Mrs. Bingham nodded. "It blooms just in time for our anniversary every year."

Stella was so touched her throat tightened. To have that kind of love and devotion was unimaginable. Though it shouldn't be. She loved the idea of forever with someone. Someone who would know everything about you, from your favorite food to your shoe size. Every intimate detail. And you would know them just as well.

Jerry had been the "here's your cup of coffee" kind of

guy, but never remembered to add the cream she loved so much. Another small detail, important to a relationship, which she conveniently overlooked because she was in love.

Thought she was in love….

She was so confused at this point. How could she be in love with someone who didn't exist? Let alone someone who knew nothing about her likes and dislikes.

"I heard what happened to you, and I'm so sorry you were hurt," Mrs. Bingham said, as if reading her mind.

Stella glanced around Mrs. Bingham's beautiful backyard. Roses grew in flowerbeds everywhere, vivid colors blooming in heights short and tall. Miniatures to bushes to small rose trees. Climbing roses clinging to an arbor, and wild roses spilling over the back fence. From white to orange to variegated. An explosion of colors. "I was stupid."

"We're all a little stupid when we're in love." Mrs. Bingham took Stella's hands in her own gnarled ones. "Life is funny. Sometimes we have to take a wrong turn to find the right path."

Mrs. Bingham tugged a pair of scissors out of her apron pocket and clipped a red rose from the bush her husband gave her. Holding the bloom under her nose, she smiled sweetly, sadly, her brown eyes moist. She held the rose out for Stella. "Love will find you when you least expect it, Stella. A sweeter, truer love than you've ever imagined possible. I know it's hard to believe right now, but one day you will be so grateful things happened the way they did."

Too many people had repeated that same sentiment to her. As much as she wanted to believe it her pride and dignity were too wounded to embrace the notion.

Rowdy came around the corner to the backyard sans shirt. Stella's breath caught as she watched the muscles in his arms and along his back bulge and flex as he turned the mower in their direction. He glanced up and winked. Her cheeks heated.

"Oh, my," Mrs. Bingham muttered.

Sucking air into oxygen-deprived lungs, she turned back to Mrs. Bingham, who grinned like a kid with a cupcake. Stella felt her cheeks burn brighter.

"Since you're not a blusher, you must be getting a sunburn. Your cheeks are very red."

"Thanks for the tour of your garden, but I have to go."

"Will you be serving lunch at the senior center again today?"

"No. Alex needs me at Pretty Posies. I'll talk to you again soon." She rounded the house in the opposite direction from Rowdy as Mrs. Bingham called out, "Thank you for your help, Stella."

~

*R*owdy went around Mrs. Bingham's yard with a weed eater, cleaning up the edges before he joined her for a glass of iced tea and a cinnamon roll he didn't really want, but ate so he wouldn't hurt her feelings. He usually finished her yard with a leaf blower to get rid of the grass clippings, but she'd pulled out a broom, which she did when she wanted to chat.

The shade of her covered patio felt good after working in the intense sun, though he'd hoped Stella would still be here for the requisite visit after mowing.

"I love the rain," Mrs. Bingham said.

Rowdy glanced at the mountain peaks where dark clouds were building. "We sure could use it."

"Yes, though we had a beautiful spring. The temperatures were perfect." She studied him for a long moment. "She had to go."

"Who?"

Mrs. Bingham's laugh filled the air. "You know exactly who I'm talking about, young man. Don't play dumb with me. I saw the way you kept looking at Stella."

"And on that note," Rowdy stood. "I've got to go."

Mrs. Bingham pushed to her feet. Moving fast for an old girl, she blocked his path. "Just so you know, she was watching you too, but you'd better act quickly if you're interested. Stella is a beautiful girl."

I'm not the one holding things up.

"Oh, and Rowdy?" She put a hand on his arm. "If you do catch her, don't you dare hurt her or you'll answer to me."

~

By the time Stella arrived at the abandoned factory, a light rain was falling. Her dad was already there when she arrived, surveying all the different floats.

"Hey, cupcake. How come Alex doesn't have a float in the parade?"

"I don't know." Stella kissed his five o'clock shadow, which reminded her of Rowdy. "I guess because she owns the only flower shop in town, she doesn't need to advertise."

He pointed at Rance's fish. Rowdy, Mac, and Beam were pushing the VW up a trailer ramp.

I can't get away from this guy.

Her silly little friend fanned her face. *Look at those muscles.*

I saw them plenty today. Stella tugged on her dad's arm, but he resisted.

"Rance owns the only fishing shop in town and he advertises."

"Next time you see Alex, you can ask her."

"What happened to Rance's trout?"

"The engine won't start." She tugged on her father's arm again.

"That fish has been a part of the parade for as long as Rance has owned The Fly Shop."

Stella didn't get the big deal. The fish would still be in the parade, whether it was driven or towed. She supposed the fuss involved tradition. "Nate is a genius with engines. He'll have the car running by the Christmas parade."

Her dad shook his head as Stella towed him across the floor. "The parade won't be the same without it."

"I'm pretty sure we'll all survive." She stopped next to the pastry float. Patsy's high school helpers had painted the flatbed a shiny coat of pink, which looked great. "I need some engineering advice. Making a bunch of cupcakes stacked on tiers will be easier than trying to construct a whole cake, but you know I'm not any good at construction. Is there any way you could build some platforms for me? The cupcakes won't be heavy. They're just laundry baskets with chicken wire tops, so the platforms don't have to be very sturdy, but they also can't topple over if the driver suddenly hits the brakes."

"I think I can handle some platforms." Her dad walked around the trailer. "How many do you need?"

"I was thinking three." She held up one of her laundry baskets. "The top one would need to hold six of these. The next tier will hold eight, and the bottom will hold thirteen. I'll paint them pink to match the bed of the trailer."

"Platforms shouldn't be too hard to construct."

"Does that mean you'll do it?" When he nodded, she hugged him tight. "Thank you, Daddy. You're the best."

"It'll be fun working on a project involving cupcakes with my cupcake." He circled the trailer again. "How much time do we have?"

"The parade is in two weeks."

"I'd be happy to help," Rowdy said from right behind her.

Stella jumped and put a hand to her heart. "Would you quit popping up out of nowhere?"

"I didn't pop up out of nowhere. You were staring at me a couple of minutes ago."

"I was *not* staring."

Rowdy chuckled. "You rolling your eyes won't change the fact that I caught you watching me twice today."

"Why were you watching Rowdy?"

Stella waved her dad's question away. He was a sweetheart who didn't understand females, even though he'd had a houseful. "Don't you have a bar to run?"

"Actually, I'd appreciate the help," her dad said at the same time. He wrapped his arm around her neck. "I don't have the summer off like a certain school teacher I know."

She smiled at her dad, glared at Rowdy, and decided to wire a few more cupcakes while they discussed platform details. They laughed several times, and her dad patted Rowdy's shoulder more than once. Her poor dad was probably thrilled to have a little male companionship, even if only for a week.

She lost track of time as she wired laundry baskets. A planner, she wanted the float completed with time to spare in case they ran into problems. And she wanted her debut float to be as perfect as possible.

Patsy rushed in, raindrops spotting her My Husband's Sexiness is Distracting T-shirt, which made Stella laugh. Mason Douglas had been an awkward, almost stodgy man before he married Patsy. She had definitely put a kick in his step and a smile on his face.

"Please, please, please tell me you have a plan, Stella."

"Relax. I have a plan"—she indicated her dad and Rowdy —"and some help. Your float will be ready before the Fourth of July."

"Stella's as good as her word," her dad said. "She always has been."

"I don't doubt her. It's just a big job."

"You and the girls getting the trailer painted today is a huge help."

"All the credit goes to my darling husband. He sanded and painted all morning."

"Tell Mason thank you."

Patsy winked. "Oh, I'll be sure to thank him my own way."

Rowdy joined them, tucking his cell in his jeans pocket. "I just got off the phone with Beam. They have almost everything we'll need at the lumberyard, and he'll order what he doesn't have. Everything should be in by Thursday."

Patsy looped one arm around Stella's dad's waist and the other around Rowdy's. "Thank you both for helping. Stella's talented, but this job is overwhelming."

Her dad patted Patsy's shoulder. "Your float is as much a part of the Fourth of July parade as Rance's fish. We'll get it fixed."

Patsy sighed with relief. "Now that Stella has a plan and reliable help, I believe rebuilding this float is going to be great fun."

Rowdy winked down at Stella.

Stella rolled her eyes.

Yippee. Her little friend cheered.

～

On Friday Stella rushed through the door of Rowdy's Bar and Grill for an impromptu girls' night out. She hated to be late, but she'd lost track of time while wiring laundry baskets. Before she glanced around for her friends, she looked for Rowdy, which wasn't good. Him taking precedence in her thoughts had to stop.

When Alex called to say they were welcoming Carolyn back from her honeymoon, Stella suggested they meet somewhere else for a change. Alex vetoed her proposal, arguing that they'd been celebrating girls' night at Rowdy's forever. Stella suspected Alex just wanted to push her and Rowdy together as often as possible.

He'd been at the factory every day before going to work at the bar and grill, either helping her dad with the cupcake platforms or busy with someone else's float. He annoyed, she glared, he laughed, she snarked, he grinned, and she fought hard not to smile back, because that was what she and Rowdy did. It was who they were with each other. One day, he was leaving as she was coming. As they passed without exchanging their usual banter, she experienced a severe twinge of disappointment that she didn't dare analyze.

Inside the bar and grill, country music competed with the noise of the crowd. Both tourists and locals filled the place to maximum capacity. All five of her friends were already here, including Misty, which was a rarity. She was always the late one, thinking her time was so much more important than theirs.

Rowdy stood at their table.

Of course it couldn't be Mike or Rachel or any number of employees helping her friends. Nope, has to be Rowdy.

She reached the table just as he settled a huge platter of loaded nachos in the middle. Stella slid into the only chair left, determined not to make eye contact with him even though she felt him staring.

"Hey. Sorry I'm late. I was—" She waved a hand. "Doesn't matter." She reached for a loaded chip. *Welcome to my hips.*

"Ohmygosh! You cut your hair," Carolyn exclaimed. "It looks darling."

Stella tugged on the ends. Because she was on her honeymoon, Carolyn missed her debut at the barbecue. "Thank you."

"Dahlia did a good job," Misty admitted grudgingly. "I was convinced you were making a huge mistake."

"Hence the emergency call to Phoebe," Stella mumbled around a mouth full of food. Passing by a mirror, she still did a double take when she glimpsed her short hair. She met Rowdy's gaze. "I needed a change."

He said he likes it.

I didn't do it for him. I did it for me and that's all that matters. I'm through doing things to please a guy.

"That was an interesting little eye exchange you two just shared," Misty said, studying her, then Rowdy. "Is there something you want to tell us?"

Stella deliberately looked at Rowdy and batted her eyelashes. "Yes, we're getting married next weekend. Hope you all can make it."

"What?"

"Joke, Carolyn." Stella rolled her eyes.

"What can I get you to drink?" Rowdy asked, standing way too close.

Breathe.

I am breathing.

Her little white-clad friend patted her shoulder. *Yes, but it's coming in short little wisps.*

Stella sucked air into her lungs. Everyone at the table was staring at her. "I'll take a Diet Coke with a lime twist. So. What did I miss?" she asked a little too enthusiastically.

"Carolyn was about to tell us *everything* she and JT did on their honeymoon." Misty moved a finger between her and Rowdy's retreating back. "But whatever is going on between you two might be more interesting."

"Nothing's going on. Carolyn, tell us everything."

Carolyn, the blusher of their group, turned crimson. "Not everything."

While Carolyn described the places she and JT visited, Stella glanced around the table at all her married and engaged friends.

Fudge brownie with chocolate sauce.

She reached for another loaded nacho, this time with extra cheese dripping off. She had two donuts for dinner last night, and this morning Phoebe's talking scale had literally groaned under her weight.

"Let's get a talking scale," Phoebe had said when they moved in together. "It'll be so much fun."

Stella was ready to throw the moaning machine out the window.

In the middle of Carolyn's description of paddleboarding on a beautiful lagoon, a waitress delivered a tray of drinks. Stella took a sip of hers and winced. Coke with cherry. She tried to catch the waitress, who'd already moved on to another table.

"Hold that thought. I got the wrong drink." She pushed back from the table.

Rowdy was behind the bar, not looking in her direction. Mike was working the other end, so Stella headed for him. "Hey, Stella," he said cautiously.

"Don't worry. I'm alcohol-free." She held out her glass. "I ordered a Diet Coke with lime and got a cherry Coke."

"Sorry about that." He took the glass from her. "I'll get it changed out."

Turning her back to the bar, she glanced around. Rowdy had turned this vacant building into the busiest place in town. He'd foregone chrome and glass for wood that lent coziness to the bar and grill. The prerequisite behind-the-bar mirror made the space look double its size. Best of all, Rowdy's wasn't a relationship landmark, one of those places where memories of time spent with Jerry overshadowed fun. She was glad she'd never brought him here and at the same time wondered why she hadn't.

At least half the faces crowded around the bar were familiar. The rest were out-of-towners enjoying a night in Eden Falls.

"Heard you got the wrong drink, Stella."

She turned to Rowdy with an eye roll. "I can see how you'd get Diet Coke with lime mixed up with cherry Coke. They sound so much alike."

He held out a glass with a grin. "Here I thought you were coming to ask when you could kiss me again."

"You're not that lucky." She sipped her drink and wrinkled her nose. "Lemon. I asked for lime."

"You weren't supposed to sip your drink until you got to the table, then you'd have to come back again."

"Why?"

"So I can look into your pretty green eyes." Rowdy leaned as close as the bar would allow. "About that marriage proposal…."

"Oh, right. Sorry to spring that on you. Are you free next weekend?" She laughed.

He didn't. "I can be."

His gaze was so powerful, her skin sparked in reaction. "Can you imagine yourself married, Rowdy?"

"Yes."

Someone next to her vacated a stool, and she fought the urge to slide aboard so she could stay close to him. "You can actually see yourself with *just one woman* for the rest of your life?"

"Yes."

She studied his mossy colored eyes, blade nose, jawline with a scruff of whiskers, and….

I think sensuous lips are the words you're looking for.

Yes. All the Garrett men were so darn handsome, but Rowdy….

Heart stopping.

Stella took a deep breath and rolled her eyes as dramatically as possible. "Well, good luck finding a woman to put up with your clean freak expectations."

Finally a smirk.

Whew. Her angel swiped a hand across her forehead. *That was getting intense.*

He reached out and threaded a strand of her hair between his fingers. "I really do like your haircut."

Stella's heart fluttered at his sincerity. "I'm surprised. Most guys *love* long hair."

His smile fell away. "You mean your cheating ex-boyfriend guy?" He straightened. "Don't lump us all together, Stella. I'm not him."

Stella studied his eyes for a long moment. Dead serious. She felt her cheeks heat and turned toward her table.

"What about your lime?"

"Lemon is great. I love lemon," she said over her shoulder in her haste to escape.

~

*R*owdy watched the dark-haired firecracker all the way to her table. He liked the haircut, her sharp words, her cute figure—everything about her. He loved to make her blush, which was hard to do. And he loved to see her eyes flicker from indecision to flame.

"Staring at a table full of women. Who's caught your eye?"

Rowdy turned his attention to the platinum blonde leaning against the bar. "Eeny, meeny, miny, moe." Patsy flashed a grin at him before glancing at the table of women. "We'll skip Alex since she's your cousin, and Misty since she's married to your brother. We better slide past Carolyn—her new husband carries a weapon. JT would not be happy if you were dreaming about his new wife. Jolie and Jillian are out too—those engagement rings and wedding bands can be such a nuisance." She slid onto a barstool. "Catch a *Stella* by the toe. I detected a little something between you two the other night. Smart choice. Stella is feisty enough to hold her own against you."

"You detected wrong, Patsy."

"Silly boy, I just saw the way you were looking at her." Patsy lifted an arched brow. "I love her new haircut. So fresh and flirty, don't you think?"

Yes I do. He suspected she'd cut another piece of Jerry out of her life by chopping off her hair. Based on her remark, the SOB must have preferred it long.

Patsy turned back to him. "Stella's a beauty no matter what."

Rowdy tapped his fingertips on the bar. "You want your usual?"

"Yes please, and a second for Mason. He'll be here soon." She fluffed her hair. "Stella got her heart broken pretty bad. You don't want to be her rebound guy."

Rowdy decided to level with the pastry shop owner, who'd been married four times before finally tying the knot with Misty's dad. She'd been floating around town on cloud nine ever since. So had Mason for that matter. "How long does one have to wait to not be the rebound guy?"

She rested her elbows on the bar. "I guess it depends on the circumstances. Stella dated Len—"

"Jerry."

"Right," Patsy said, pointing a bright pink fingernail at him. "Anyway, they dated for two years, so I'm guessing she was pretty serious."

Rowdy slapped two napkins on the bar in front of Patsy.

"She was. He wasn't. Don't you think deep down that Stella knew?"

"Denial is powerful."

"Got any advice?"

Patsy clicked her nails on the bar while looking somewhere above his head. "Do something fresh. Surprise her a little. Be a friend."

"She has friends."

"She has girlfriends. She has to learn to trust the opposite sex all over again. Be her friend first."

He planted his palms on the bar and locked his elbows. "What do you mean fresh?"

"Something the old boyfriend didn't do with her. You still have your Harley?"

"You know I do."

"There you go. Take her for a ride. Get her out into nature. Let her enjoy the wind in her hair. And your company." She covered his hands with hers. "Give her a reason to smile again, Rowdy."

He could do that. "Is our talk going to be all over town by tomorrow?"

Patsy mimed locking her lips and throwing the key over her shoulder.

"I can do fresh." He glanced Stella's way and caught her watching him. He winked.

CHAPTER 14

Stella finished applying her makeup and then studied her reflection, Rowdy front and center in her thoughts. She knew he'd be at Brandt and Jillian's engagement party, thus the primping in front of the mirror, which was so ridiculous. Rowdy had seen her a million times. No amount of extra eye shadow or lycra would make her look different or....

Or what?

I don't know. Rowdy has always been there, a part of Eden Falls, a part of me. He's... Rowdy. Reliable, teasing, fun-loving, long-haired Rowdy.

Except now, after Alex said he was interested and the two kisses they'd shared, she was thinking of him differently. And way too often.

A knock on her door interrupted her thoughts. Everyone who might show up at her door would already be at the party. Another knock—a little harder. Stella grabbed her sandals and ran down the hall. She was already late, so she'd have to get rid of this solicitor fast.

When she opened the door, her heart stopped. Anna

Winters stood in front of her, purse held to her chest like a protective shield.

Oh, no. Oh no, oh no.

Stella glanced beyond her, but Jerry's wife was alone.

Anna offered a weak smile that wobbled around the edges. "I can tell by your reaction that you remember who I am. Your worried expression tells me even more."

Stella opened her mouth, but nothing came out.

Anna nodded toward the apartment with a wince. "Can I come in?"

What could she do but open the door wider? "Yes. Of course."

Anna stepped inside and glanced around, her attention settling on Stella. She gestured toward the sofa. "Did Jerry come here often?"

Stella face flushed so hot it physically hurt. "Uh...."

"I know." Though Anna lowered her purse from her chest, she still clung to it like a lifeline. "About you and Jerry. You don't have to cover for him. Are you still seeing each other?" Her rushed sentences melded together as one.

"No." Stella shook her head for added emphasis. "We aren't." She motioned to the sofa. "Would you like to sit down?"

"Not really, but I will. My knees are shaking."

Anna started to sit on the sofa but, after a look of distaste, she opted for an adjacent chair. Stella assumed she was imagining her husband there with Stella.

Wise choice.

I don't need any help from you right now. Stella dropped into a chair opposite Anna. "Mine are a little shaky too."

Anna set her purse on the coffee table and folded trembling hands in her lap. "When did it end?"

"The night I saw your family at dinner in Seattle." She

kept eye contact, willing Anna to believe her. "I didn't know he was married."

Anna looked down at her clenched hands.

"Can I get you a glass of water?" Stella asked as she stood. She needed a moment, some space, a defibrillator.

"Yes please. That would be nice." Anna's smile, while tight, was a little more stable this time. "Thank you."

Out of sight of Anna, Stella sucked in a shuddering breath. What could she say to the woman besides apologizing profusely, which seemed so insufficient given the circumstances?

She glanced at the clock on the stove. Even before she opened the door she was late for the party, but she couldn't exactly rush this conversation along.

She filled a glass with ice and water carried it back to the living room. She set a coaster close to Anna, handed her the glass, and sat on the edge of her chair, prepared for the worst. Jerry's wife didn't look like the type who'd resort to fists, but one could never be sure.

Anna took a sip of water and set the glass down. "I came because…" She closed her eyes and swallowed. "I don't know why I came. Curiosity, I guess." Her tear-filled eyes opened, and Stella's heart broke. She jumped from her chair and came back with a box of tissues.

"Thank you." Anna blotted her eyes. "Can I ask a few questions?"

Even as dread filled her, Stella nodded. How could she not answer every question Anna threw at her?

"I know your name is Stella and that you teach. Have you always lived in Eden Falls?"

Not the question she'd expected. "Yes."

"Did he come to Eden Falls often?"

"No."

"Once a week? Twice a week?"

"Maybe once every two weeks. He broke a lot of dates. Probably for family obligations, though I didn't know that at the time."

"Do you have a summer job?"

Another unexpected question. "I help a friend who owns the local flower shop."

"Jerry does some bookkeeping over the summer."

Stella knew that, but didn't respond.

"Have you ever been married?"

"No."

Anna picked up her glass, but set it back in place without drinking. "You called Jerry by another name that night in Seattle."

"He told me his name was Len."

"Len. I wonder where that came from?" Anna said, talking more to herself than to Stella. "He told you he was single?"

Stella started to nod, but stopped. "Actually, no. It never occurred to me to ask. I just assumed he was single when he asked me out." Stella couldn't believe how naive she'd been. "I should have asked. He wasn't wearing a ring."

Anna sat quietly, which somehow made Stella feel worse. If that was possible.

"I wouldn't have gone out with him if I'd known he was married."

Anna lifted a shoulder in a half shrug. "Jerry can be very persuasive."

Stella leaned forward. "I'm telling you, persuasive or not, I would *never* have gone out with him if I'd known."

Anna studied her for a long, agonizing moment, then dropped her chin. "I believe you. I'm sorry he hurt you."

Her comment stunned Stella. Jerry's wife was apologizing to her for something her husband did. "I'm the one who's sorry. I feel so awful. Have felt so awful since that night. I wish there was something I could do to turn back time and fix this."

"I haven't told him I know. Maybe I'll do that tonight. Or tomorrow. I'm not sure what will happen when I do. I think I'll tell him to leave." Anna laced her fingers together and glanced around. Again, she seemed to be talking more to herself. She looked at Stella expectantly. "Do you think there are others?"

The thought had never occurred to her, but now…her guess would be yes, though she'd never say that to Anna.

Anna must have read her mind. "Yes. Most likely there were—*are*—others."

Jerry had finally stopped calling incessantly. He'd probably moved on to his next conquest, which made her heart hurt for Anna.

"How insensitive of me to barge in when you look so pretty." Anna stood, clutching her purse as a shield again. "Do you have a date?"

Stella glanced down at her dress. "No. An engagement party for friends."

"You must have a lot of friends. When we met in Seattle, you were at a bridal shower."

"Just dinner after our dress fitting for a friend's wedding."

"Jerry has made it hard for me to have friends. If I make plans with someone, he somehow interrupts. Did he do that to you?"

Stella had put off friends several times to make room for Jerry, but she would never have let him come between them.

Her non-answer seemed to be enough for Anna. She nodded. "That's a pretty dress."

"Thank you."

Anna walked to the door, but turned before going outside. "I truly am sorry Jerry hurt you. I could see it in your eyes that night. The pain."

"I'm sorry I hurt *you*. I've had a hard time living with what I've done to you and your family. I couldn't decide if I should find you and tell you the truth or hope you'd never find out. I hope you'll forgive me."

"There's nothing to forgive. We're both Jerry's victims." Anna offered a little smile. "Take care of yourself, Stella. I hope you find happiness."

Stella sat in her quiet apartment long after Anna left, the kitchen clock reminding her how late she was with every echoing tick. Anna's words tumbled through her head as she replayed their conversation. *I hope you find happiness.*

Jerry hadn't brought her any happiness. The two years they dated had been one disappointment after another. Time and time again she'd been hurt by him.

What is wrong with me that I was okay with that treatment? Why did I continue to put up with him and his excuses?

Just talking to Anna had helped relieve some of the guilt. How many times had she unknowingly taken Jerry away from his family? How many of his children's events had he missed because of her?

You handled that well. Her friend hugged her neck. *Time to let this go.*

Much easier said than done.

*J*illian's parents' backyard was breathtakingly beautiful. Several rows of trees in the surrounding apple orchard were draped with hundreds of twinkling white lights. Beautiful bouquets, which she helped Alex put together, sat in the center of tables covered with white cloths whose edges rippled in the breeze. A band was already playing on the large patio that extended from the house.

Stella grew up running barefoot through Saunders'

Orchards, climbing trees to get to the fruit, swimming in the pond at the edge of their property. Memories of lazy summer days flooded her. She and her friends would lie under the tree branches watching the clouds float by as they discussed fingernail polish, girlhood crushes, and first kisses. They talked about careers and how many babies they would have. They shared their hopes and dreams for the future under the apple trees. How many of those hopes and dreams had come to fruition? How many had fizzled?

One afternoon long ago, she and her friends had sealed their secret plans and dreams in a metal box Jillian's dad found in the barn. They buried their little time capsule under an apple tree laden with fruit. Did any of them remember which tree roots sheltered their secrets? Maybe Jillian would know. Would their girlhood aspirations ever be found?

She searched for Rowdy while trying not to look obvious. Instead she spotted Jillian and Brandt with their arms around each other. He, a fireman and paramedic, her, a physical therapist and personal trainer, both so physically fit, they matched perfectly.

Stella moved through the crowd toward the couple. Her heart pinched uncomfortably as a painful awareness moved through her. She'd been so positive that she loved Jerry while they were together. Jillian radiated a happiness that Stella had to fake many times to convince her friends everything was fine between her and Jerry. She was positive Jerry had never gazed at her the way Brandt was looking at Jillian.

Jerry had needed her in the same way her students did. His ego needed to be stroked. He thrived on reassurance, and she'd showered him in positive reinforcement just like she would a second-grader who needed an encouraging word. *You're handsome. You're talented. You're fun to be around.*

He'd never reciprocated any of those sentiments. He'd

taken and taken and taken, depleting her energy, but he'd never given back. Amazing how she'd overlooked all that.

When she reached Jillian, she pulled her into a tight hug. "Congratulations, my beautiful friend. I'm so happy for you."

"Thank you for coming to share this with us, Stella. I know—"

Stella held up a hand to stop Jillian. "There's no place I'd rather be."

"Thanks for coming, Stella," Brandt said.

She returned his hug. "Thanks for making my friend so happy."

Brandt smiled at his fiancée. "Your friend makes me happy."

"Icky, ick, ick," Misty said from behind Stella. "You guys are as nauseatingly sweet as Colton and Alex."

Beam bent Misty over his arm. "I'll take some of that ick. We have a few hours without a baby girl crying out for attention."

Misty narrowed her eyes. "Later, honey," she said seductively.

Stella breathed out a sigh. *Yep. Surrounded again by lovey-dovey crap.*

Her annoying nuisance patted her cheek. *Be nice.*

Jillian leaned close to Stella. "Go get something to eat. My mom has been cooking for days."

Stella glanced toward the food tables, more than ready to escape the love besieging her from all sides. "Good idea."

She made a small plate and wandered around the crowd, waving and talking to acquaintances as she went.

Still no sign of Rowdy.

Maybe he had to work.

The night was warm, with just enough breeze to set the twinkling lights swaying. Beautiful. Magical. Enchanting. All words that described the setting perfectly. Everything was so simple, yet so wonderfully elegant.

Once she reached the edge of the party, she threw her paper plate in the trash and let her feet carry her deeper into the orchard with only the stars and a partial moon to light the path.

She thought about her own dreams. Her desire to be a teacher was buried in that time capsule. In fourth grade, she had the best teacher ever. Mrs. Hemming had set the bar for her. She instilled the love of reading with books like *Where the Red Fern Grows* and *Charlotte's Web*, which she read after lunch recess when her students were sated and sleepy. She made learning fun, allowed creativity in her classroom, and showed her students she cared. Teaching was more than a job to her. Stella had grown up aspiring to be the same kind of teacher.

Stella took a deep breath of sweet night air. Jillian and Brandt chose a wonderful night to celebrate outside.

And thanks to Anna's visit, she felt lighter than she had in three weeks. The relief edged under her sadness, giving her a spark of hope. The decision of whether to tell Jerry's wife had been lifted off her shoulders by an unexpected visit. Still, she hurt for the woman she barely knew.

A giddy feeling swept over her when she heard approaching footsteps. A moment later, a male arm wrapped around her neck and pulled her against a lean body. But it was the wrong arm and the wrong body.

"Why are you out here all alone?"

Her little ray of hope diminished her need to utter a snarky response. She smiled at Leo. "It's such a beautiful night, I couldn't help myself."

The moon cast an eerie, unreal glow over the orchard, and she half expected to see fairies flitting through the air, or orchard gnomes darting from tree to tree.

"The night is pretty spectacular," Leo said. "Like Brandt commanded it for Jillian."

Leo has a romantic streak.

She glanced at him. "Why don't you have a nice brother?"

He chuckled. The familiar sound surrounded her comfortably. "My parents could barely handle one kid. Can you imagine them with two?"

His parents were so far out in left field, Leo had pretty much raised himself. She grabbed the wrist of the arm around her neck. "Despite what everyone else says, you're pretty amazing, Leo."

"Don't let that get around or my reputation will be ruined."

"Oh, I wouldn't dream of telling anyone."

"Want a piece of cake?"

"My hips don't need any cake, but thanks." She ducked under his arm. "You don't have to babysit me tonight. Go eat cake."

He stuffed both hands in his front pockets. "You're okay?"

"I am," she said, truly meaning the words for the first time since seeing Jerry with his family. "I'm good." She shooed him with a hand. "Go. Eat cake. Have a piece for me."

After he walked off, she moved a little deeper into the trees. The smell of grass and bark and earth were strong and soothing. Music from the party floated around her, soft and sensuous.

You're going to be okay, her little angel whispered, or she just sensed the voice. Either way, she believed the declaration was true.

A second set of footsteps approached on the soft grass.

Her little friend rubbed her stomach. *A piece of cake does sound good.*

Stella smiled. "Did you bring cake, Leo?"

"I'm not Leo, and I don't have any cake."

Stella put a hand over the sudden thudding of her heart. Rowdy's voice was becoming as familiar as Leo's. "No cake, no kisses."

"You're assuming I came out here for a kiss."

She turned to him. "Why did you come out here?"

"The view, of course."

Does he mean the sky?

Stella's heart thudded a little harder. *He's not looking at the sky.*

Funny that it took a kiss for her to notice Rowdy as more than just…Rowdy. She now saw him in such a different light.

Moonlight. Her angel sighed.

She'd always thought of him as fun, even if he was shallow and self-serving, but he kept proving her wrong. What she had learned recently was the complete opposite. He donated food and volunteered at the shelter, he mowed lawns for widows, supported sports teams, and helped repair parade floats. And he liked gazing at the night sky. Instead of being shallow, he was a man of many caring, community-centered layers.

He took her hand and tugged her into his arms. She did nothing to stop him.

"You could just ask if you want to dance," Rowdy said softly.

"I didn't—I don't."

"You're swaying to the music."

She laughed. "I didn't realize…"

He started swaying along with her under the light of the moon and stars. "Are you too embarrassed to ask because of your attraction to me?"

She pushed against his chest in an unconvincing attempt to step away. "You are so arrogant."

"Your skin glows under the moonlight."

When she looked up, she expected his usual smirk.

Instead she encountered a dead serious expression. "False flattery will get you nowhere." *Or everywhere.*

"I'm not into false flattery. I give a compliment when I see one to be given. You look beautiful in moonlight, but then you look beautiful in sunlight too."

Stella's heart bumped erratically as reality tried to wiggle out from under the romantic static. "Jerry said those kinds of words to me. Pretty words that I believed."

Rowdy's hold loosened. "I've already told you, I'm not Jerry. I don't look like him or talk like him, so don't compare us, Stella."

"You're right. You're not Jerry." But how did she know he wasn't just toying with her as Jerry had? "I'm sorry."

On the other hand, two could play the kind of games Rowdy played. He was good-looking and entertaining. If he wasn't looking for love, just someone to spend the summer with, why not? Leave emotions at the door and enjoy some fun. If their hearts weren't involved in the equation, no one got hurt.

"Apology accepted."

Take the lead.

She stood on tiptoe and kissed his neck, then the corner of his mouth. The surprise on his face made her bold move worth it. She kissed the other corner of his mouth, and his arms tightened, pulling her against his hard body. He lowered his mouth to hers, his kiss like a flame igniting her from head to toe.

Her little companion fell off her shoulder in a dead faint.

~

*R*owdy wasn't sure what had changed with Stella, but suddenly she was the aggressor. Arms around his neck, fingers in his hair, she pulled his head down and kissed him with abandon. Their connection was beyond anything he'd ever experienced before. Like lightning flashing through the sky right before striking something tangible.

He gathered her closer, reveling in how they fit together so nicely. She took the lead, and he was right behind her, move for move.

She tilted her head and his mouth found the hollow behind her ear. The intoxicating scent of her perfume made him dizzy. He'd never allowed himself such unrestricted freedom with his emotions. He was always careful to hold back just enough of himself to avoid getting lost in the passion, but Stella was different. He'd waited for her for a long time.

She finally pushed him back a step and inhaled a shaky breath. "That was fun, but we should get back to the party."

"We could, or we could stay here and have even more fun."

"People will miss us."

She was right. He didn't want Leo—or worse, Beam—stumbling upon them again.

"I'll go back first." She ran a finger long her bottom lip, then pointed to him. "I messed up your hair."

Rowdy pulled the leather strap free and finger-combed his hair. "Why can't we go back together?"

"People will talk. Rita Reynolds is here."

"So? Let them talk."

"Rowdy, I'm already the talk of the town. I don't need everyone thinking I'm in the orchard with another guy so soon after dating a married man."

He didn't see the point of waiting to make their interest in each other known, but he wasn't going to argue with her tonight. He wound the leather strap back in place while watching her smooth a hand down her dress. "You might want to check your face for lipstick. I was wearing some when I came out here."

Rowdy ran the back of his hand over his mouth, not bothered by the thought of lipstick on his face either. Before he could say so, she disappeared among the trees.

He emerged from the orchard a few minutes later, immediately looking for her. She was on the dance floor with his bartender, Mike. They laughed together, and an unsettling and very unfamiliar shot of jealousy streaked through him.

Beam appeared at his elbow, his big brother's smirk in place. "You have lipstick on your Adam's apple, and Stella is just short enough to have left it there."

Rowdy wasn't in the mood for Beam's joking, but again, that's what brothers did. He rubbed his neck.

"Kissing you one minute and dancing with another guy the next. You sure you aren't going to get your heart broken over this one?"

Rowdy hadn't suffered a broken heart since college, when Alison Stark dumped him for a guy with money. He'd vowed then, he'd make something of the inheritance his grandparents left him.

Misty took her husband's arm. "Let's dance." She leaned toward Rowdy with narrowed eyes. "You have lipstick on your neck."

"That's already been established, dear wife. And you're right. We're at a party and have one more hour before we have to go home and pay the babysitter. Let's dance."

"Wait," she argued as Beam towed her away. "Who's been kissing Rowdy?"

"Yeah, who's been kissing Rowdy?" Alex asked, eyeing his neck.

He rubbed at the spot where Stella had kissed him, if only to get everyone to shut up. "Hey, Low-Rider. The flowers look nice."

"You're trying to change the subject." She got up on tiptoe and touched his neck. "Stella's lip print is still there."

"Honestly, I don't care."

Alex glanced toward the dance floor. "Does Stella?"

The idea that Stella didn't want to be seen with him made him mad. They would either be a couple and be seen around town together, or they wouldn't be a couple at all. He wouldn't sneak around like Misty and Beam had done. People would know Stella was his.

Rowdy glanced down at the tiny cousin who was so good at making her presence known. "She's a big girl, Alex."

"I'm as worried about you getting hurt as her."

"And I'm a big boy. You don't have to worry about either of us."

The music ended. "Gotta go, cuz." He stepped onto the deck and took Stella's hand before Mike had the chance to ask for another dance. When the opening chords of the next song rang out, he enveloped her in his arms. As they moved around the dance floor, Rita Reynolds gawked behind her coke-bottle glass lenses. Stella's mom and dad stole a few glances their way.

Misty didn't try to hide her curiosity. As soon as the music stopped, she was next to them, staring at Stella's mouth.

"Who've you been kissing, Stella?"

"Unlike you, I don't kiss and tell."

Misty pointed at Rowdy's neck. "No, but your lipstick does."

Rowdy looped a protective arm around Stella's shoulders. "She can't help herself. Every time she gets near me, she goes a little crazy."

"You're moving from a cheating boyfriend to a guy who's never had a serious relationship in his life?

Stella rolled her eyes. "Relax, Misty. I'm not moving on to

anyone. Rowdy and I bumped into each other and my lips hit his neck."

"You seriously think I believe that?" Misty scoffed.

"I seriously don't care what you believe."

While Misty and Stella debated back and forth, Rowdy staggered from Stella's "I'm not moving on to anyone" comment.

Beam lifted you-need-to-be-careful eyebrows at him.

CHAPTER 15

Stella shut the door of her apartment and kicked off her sandals. She peeled out of her skirt on the way down the hall, dropping it on the floor of her room. Her blouse soon joined the growing pile.

Her haloed friend shook her head. *Sorry, Phoebe.*

I'll clean tomorrow.

You work for Alex tomorrow.

Afterwards. I'll come home and clean.

You have a float to finish.

I'll clean. One day. Soon.

The weather had turned hot, so Stella chose a pair of knee-length shorts from her drawer and a T-shirt from a hanger in the closet. Falling back onto the cool sheets of her unmade bed, her mind whirled to Rowdy. Dancing under the stars, kissing with only the moon watching.

What was she doing getting involved with a guy who made her feel like she was the only girl in his life when really she was just one of a dozen? Last night she'd told herself it would be exciting and harmless, even amusing. But dawn's light drenched her with a cold bucket of reality.

Normal people didn't escape a toxic relationship one week and fall for another guy the next. Normal. After dating Jerry, she wasn't sure what normal was anymore. First, Rowdy could choose anyone. That he was zeroing in on her didn't make sense. Second, Rowdy was reckless and free. He would never be interested in a long-term relationship, let alone playing for keeps.

Maybe letting her guard down for a summer of lusty fun wasn't a smart idea.

Maybe he wants more.

Stella rolled her eyes. *This is Rowdy. He'd never want more.*

What are you going to do?

She shoved the question aside. Today was too beautiful to worry about Rowdy and his motives. She was meeting Alex, Colton, and Charlie for a picnic at the waterfall that shared its name with the town. She could entertain Charlie in the pond at the foot of the falls while Alex and Colton snuggled under a pine tree.

A knock sounded on her door. She bounced off the bed and gave a cursory look around her messy room. *One of these days, Phoebe...*

Who are you kidding?

Stella brushed at her shoulder. *I don't need any grief from Miss Goody Two-shoes today.*

She opened the door just as Jerry raised his fist to knock again. She waited for a heartbeat, then two. Nothing. She felt nothing. No feelings of love or loss or even guilt. Anna's chat eased that debilitating sensation. "What do you want?"

His face screwed in distaste. "What did you do to your hair?"

What did I see in this guy? "Why. Are. You. Here?" she demanded through gritted teeth.

"You told my wife about us after you said you wouldn't. She left me."

"I didn't tell your wife." Stella tried to slam the door, but Jerry's foot over the threshold was faster.

You really need to work on your reflexes.

You really need to go away.

"If you didn't tell her, who did Stella? You're the only one—"

"I have no idea, *Len*. Maybe your lies finally caught up with you. Deal with them yourself and get your foot out of my door."

He gave the door a hard shove, throwing her off-balance. She released her hold and he stepped inside. "She said she talked to you."

Stella heard an engine and wished it was Colton and Alex pulling up to the curb. Or Leo. He pestered her constantly when she wanted to be alone, but when she needed him, he was nowhere to be seen. But no, this was a motorcycle.

Stella drilled a finger into Jerry's chest. "She did, but she already knew about you when she came. Now get out of my house."

"Not until you tell me what you said."

"Hey, darlin'."

Rowdy.

Stella's heart fluttered when she looked past Jerry and saw him coming up the walk, motorcycle helmet under his arm.

Her angel fluttered her wings. *Knight in shining armor.*

On a motorcycle instead of a white steed.

Jerry glanced over his shoulder, but Rowdy ignored him as he stepped inside, pulled Stella against him, and kissed her like they'd shared hundreds of kisses rather than just a few.

His arm around her was firm and possessive, yet his kiss was gentle. As he explored her mouth with his tongue, she almost giggled with the pleasure of knowing Jerry was probably gaping like a beached fish.

When Rowdy lifted his head, his black pupils were dilated, stealing room from his mossy irises. She sucked in a shaky breath. Everything missing with Jerry was right here in Rowdy's eyes. A burning chemistry she'd never felt with anyone before.

Does he feel the connection?

Intense green eyes, tight jaw…

Yes.

"You sure moved on quickly."

She glanced Jerry's way. Next to Rowdy, he appeared weak and silly. *Your poor family.* The weight of Rowdy's arm around her lent a sense of security. "Go home, Jerry. Try to make things right with your wife. Be a dad to your children."

"Were you seeing him while we were dating?"

Rowdy stepped forward, backing Jerry over the threshold. "Don't come around again, Jerry. Your stint in Eden Falls is over."

Jerry puffed out his chest. "Are you threatening me?"

"Nope. Making a promise." Rowdy pushed the door shut in Jerry's face.

"Your timing is impeccable," Stella said with a smile. She'd remember the look on Jerry's face for a long while.

Rowdy pointed to his cheek. Stella suspected he'd turn his head at the last second and their lips would meet. Stark disappointment unsettled her when he didn't.

"Change into jeans and grab a jacket. Let's take a ride."

"You're kinda bossy," Stella complained, but ran off to do as he said. The idea of racing over the streets on the back of a bad-boy bike excited her. She skidded to a stop halfway to her room as another wave of disappointment scuttled through her. She plodded back into the living room. "I can't go. Alex, Colton, and Charlie are on their way over to pick me up for a picnic."

"Go change. I'll call Alex."

When she nearly skipped back into the living room, jacket in hand, Rowdy was shoving his cell phone into the front pocket of his jeans. "Alex conveniently invited me to join you for the picnic. I told her I'd pick you up."

One of her high school boyfriends owned a motorcycle, but she hadn't been on the back of a bike since then. Excitement shimmied through her. Rowdy handed her the helmet strapped on the back.

How many women have worn that thing?

"How many women have worn this thing?"

Rowdy raised a brow. "Are you sure you want to know?"

She hesitated about five seconds before she pulled the helmet over her head.

Rowdy tugged her close, fastened the strap under her chin, and took that moment to satisfy her desire for a kiss. Long, slow, and just what she'd been hoping for. Her skin heated as sparkling, effervescent desire surged through her. When he drew back, she pulled him in for one more quick kiss, then met him smirk for smirk. He threw a leg over the bike and patted the seat behind him.

She leaned close. "Wait."

He held up a hand. "Stella, you don't have to yell."

"Oh! You can hear me okay?"

He chuckled. "Loud and clear, darlin'. Just talk normal."

"Okay."

He waited a beat, then rolled his hand. "Wait what?"

"Oh right!" She laughed when he looked skyward and shook his head. "I mean, oh, right," she said in a lower voice as she settled on the seat behind him. "No crazy tricks. I don't want to throw up on you again."

"I don't want you to throw up on me again either. Did you have blueberry pancakes for breakfast?"

"Not today."

He turned a knob, flipped a switch, and pressed a button.

When the engine rumbled to life, the thrill of excitement sizzled like drops of water on a hot skillet.

"Time to hold on."

She responded by wrapping her arms around his waist. He revved the engine and they were off. He drove through town, around the square and she didn't care who saw them. She even waved to Rita Reynolds, who craned her neck around so quickly she dumped the top scoop of her triple-decker ice cream cone on the sidewalk. Stella laughed. When was the last time she'd enjoyed a genuine, deep-in-her-gut laugh? It felt so wonderful she laughed again.

They headed up the mountain, past the turnoff for his house. The trees grew thicker and taller, and she marveled at the beauty of nature. Her mom and dad had taught their girls to appreciate the world around them, but Stella seldom took the time to really look. Today she would. She threw her cares to the wind, and tilted her face to the sun.

Their ride came to an end too soon when Rowdy turned into the parking lot for Eden Falls. He parked next to Colton's SUV, and held her hand as she swung her leg over the seat, her thighs still vibrating from the powerful engine.

Charlie charged toward them, waving madly. "What took you so long to get here? I've been waiting and waiting. Come and see the giant caterpillar I just found."

"Okay!"

Rowdy turned her by the shoulders, unclipped her helmet, and lifted it from her head. "Still don't have to yell."

"Right." She took Charlie's hand. "Show me this giant caterpillar."

~

owdy lifted his own helmet off and stored both on his bike while watching Charlie drag Stella along the path leading to the waterfall. He could still feel her arms around his middle and decided they'd have to go for motorcycle rides at least once a week, if not more often.

He made his way through the trees and spotted Colton and Alex spreading out blankets in the shade of a pine. Stella and Charlie were bent over a large boulder studying Charlie's discovery.

People crowded the grassy area at the foot of the falls. The spray of the water cascading from above glimmered in the sunshine like a bucket of rainbow glitter thrown in the air.

Alex waved him over.

"Hey, Colton." He plopped down on the blanket next to Alex. "Thanks for letting me tag along, Low-Rider."

She handed him a clump of red grapes. "You're always welcome as long as—"

"Alex," Colton said in a warning tone.

Alex frowned at her husband. "Stella has been my friend forever. I don't want to see her hurt again."

Rowdy popped a grape in his mouth. "We've been over this, Alex. I'm serious about Stella."

He could see by her expression that his cousin didn't fully believe him. Sure, he'd been around the block, so her concern was valid. He didn't have any way to convince her otherwise. In time, everyone would know how he felt about Stella.

Lunch was ham and cheese sandwiches, chips, and home-made cookies for dessert. Charlie kept them entertained with stories of baseball, bugs, and birthday plans. He'd be eight in a couple of weeks.

The day Charlie was born, he emerged with a head full of long, flyaway black hair and a smile instead of a scream. He'd been smiling ever since. Rowdy hoped he'd keep his positive outlook throughout life.

After lunch Charlie pulled his parents away for a little hike and Rowdy lay back with his hands behind his head. Stella stretched out on her stomach, propped up on her elbows. He could tell she wanted to say something, so he waited, imagining she wanted to discuss her ex-boyfriend's visit. He was pretty sure Jerry wouldn't be bothering Stella anymore after today. He only wished getting the idiot out of her mind was as easy as warning him to stay out of town.

"Thanks for saving me today."

Time to lay things on the line. "I wanted to spend time with you, so my coming when I did was more self-serving than gallant."

"Why?"

He could feel her eyes on him, so he turned to look at her. "Why what?"

"Why did you want to spend time with me?"

"I thought you'd be familiar with how the boy-girl thing works by now. Boy likes girl, boy goes after girl, girl falls madly in love with boy, and they live happily ever after."

"Didn't you forget a step?"

"Like…?"

She rolled her hand. "Like isn't the boy supposed to fall madly in love with the girl too?"

"That step already happened."

She sat up, a frown drawing her cute little brows together.

"Your mouth is hanging open."

She closed it.

"I never thought anyone could render *you* speechless."

And just like that, she looked like she might cry. He reached over and took her hand. "What?"

"Don't mess with me, Rowdy. I've always liked you. I like

competing and arguing with you and giving you as much guff as you give me, but I don't think I can handle this kind of joke. At least not after what happened with Jerry."

"I'm not messing with you, Stella. I'm here. Right in front of you." He watched several emotions move across her face.

"But…why are you interested in me all of a sudden?"

"There is nothing sudden about it, Stella. I've been interested for a long time."

She rubbed her forehead. "Why didn't you tell me?"

"You were dating someone else."

"But you could have said—"

"You weren't ready to hear or accept what I had to say. I know you have to get over Jerry. I'm in no rush. I've been waiting for two years, and I don't mind waiting a little longer."

More emotions played across her features before her narrow-eyed, stubborn expression appeared. "How do you know I'm interested?"

He reached for her arm and tugged her until she lay across his chest. Her special Stella scent filled him with heady contentment. "You wouldn't kiss me the way you've been kissing me if you weren't interested."

"How do you know I'm not *toying* with you?" she asked, fluttering her eyelashes.

"You're not the toying type."

She looked at his lips, and he smiled. "Go ahead. Alex and Colton are over by the waterfall. No one will see."

Leaning closer, she touched her lips to his. He relaxed and let her take the lead again. She tasted and teased until he opened his mouth. Then they were tilting heads and tangling tongues until someone snickered. Stella jerked back, and Rowdy frowned up at Charlie. "Nice timing, buddy."

"I catch my mom and Colton kissing all the time."

Stella jumped up and grabbed Charlie's hand. "Come on. Let's go look for more giant caterpillars."

~

*A*n hour later Stella was clinging to Rowdy's waist as his bike carried them higher up the mountain. The things Rowdy said earlier were rattling around in her mind like marbles in a metal bucket. As the motorcycle tipped when they rounded a curve, all the marbles rolled to one side of her brain, not causing any damage, but loud enough to wake her dead emotions.

Jerry was bleak tans and browns against Rowdy's vivid blues and greens. Jerry looked at the negative side of everything, while Rowdy turned bad into good. She could picture them long-term, something she'd tried to do with Jerry but never could quite accomplish. In her imaginings, there'd been no white picket fence, no parting in the morning with a kiss, or sharing kitchen duties after a romantic dinner at home. Somehow, with Rowdy those things were easy to see.

Aren't you getting a little ahead of yourself?

When I said the boy was supposed to fall madly in love with the girl, he said that step had already happened.

Still...the breakup with Jerry was three weeks ago.

Between the motorcycle's roaring engine and the silky wind rushing past, there was too much noise to talk, so she just held on and took in the scenery. After Rowdy's hair tickled her nose several times, she stuffed his ponytail down his T-shirt with one hand.

She'd only been this high within the confines of a car. Everything was so green and beautiful. Small pockets of wildflowers lined the road here and there, and once in a while there was a break in the trees and she could see their town below.

She loved Eden Falls, the whole area where she lived. With a business and a beautiful home, Rowdy was here to stay. As crazy as his declaration was, and much to her surprise, she believed him.

She wasn't sure how much time passed before Rowdy pulled off the road. Peering over his shoulder, she realized he was stopping at a scenic overlook. He killed the engine and heeled the kickstand down. She held onto his shoulders to climb off.

"Careful," Rowdy warned, grabbing her arm when she stumbled on wobbly legs, then chuckled when she rubbed her butt.

After a frustrating couple of attempts to release the chin-strap, Rowdy pulled her close and unclipped the helmet.

"Does this dizzy feeling go away?"

"Yes." He lifted the helmet off her head.

Stella put a hand to her mouth and stood in awe of the valley before her. She turned back to Rowdy, who still strad-dled the motorcycle holding his helmet. "How did you ever find this place?"

"Beam and I rode all over these mountains as soon as we got motorcycles. Our parents decided we were safer up here than in town where we kept getting speeding tickets." He climbed off the cycle and tugged his ponytail out from under his T-shirt. "Did my hair bother you?"

She rolled her eyes. "Would I have stuffed it down your shirt if it didn't?" She started for a nearby granite outcrop. "My dad always warned us to never date a guy with hair longer than ours."

"Guess I'll have to cut my hair."

"Don't you dare. You wouldn't be Rowdy without a ponytail."

He followed her, and they sat side by side looking over the vista. Other than an occasional bird calling or chipmunk chattering happily in the surrounding forest, their world was quiet. Peaceful. Stella's agitated mind settled on Anna. Jerry said she'd left him, but she suspected Anna would stay close so the children could see their father. What a sad situation for all of them.

"Jerry's wife came to see me yesterday before the engagement party. Her name is Anna."

Rowdy turned to look at her. "I'll bet that was awkward."

"A little. At least at first." She picked up a pinecone. The top half was missing. She should have brought a bag to collect some for her second-graders. They could make turkeys for Thanksgiving with real feathers for the tails and acorns glued on for heads.

She broke a pinecone scale off. "She left him. That's why Jerry was at my apartment today."

Rowdy rested a reassuring arm behind her, barely touching her back. There, but not.

"Jerry thought she left him, because I told her about us."

"Did you?"

Stella shook her head. "She already suspected. She came last night to confirm. She believes I'm not the only one."

"I can just about guarantee you aren't the only one."

Rowdy's comment did nothing to assuage her ego or soften the blow. No getting around the fact that she'd been a dunce.

She threw the pinecone, watched it drop over the edge of the rocks where they sat.

"Do you feel better after talking to her?"

"Yes." She believed that Anna knew she would never have dated Jerry if she'd known he was married, which eased some of her angst. Love was hard enough without adding all the elements Jerry had heaped on her.

There I go again, thinking only of myself and my hurt rather than considering Anna's unhappiness. Stella had never thought of herself as a selfish person until Jerry came along.

"Stella?" Rowdy prompted, moving a lock of her hair behind her ear. His touch was gentle, soothing.

She glanced at him. He'd put on reflective sunglasses, and all she could see was her own distorted image. Which was exactly how she'd been feeling for a long time now. Twisted. Hollow in some bizarre way that was unrecognizable. She'd allowed Jerry to alter everything about her, from the things she believed to the length of her hair. She ran fingers through her short, windblown curls. "I feel pardoned but not absolved. Does that make sense?

"It does."

She leaned back against Rowdy's sturdy shoulder. "I've tried to put myself in Anna's shoes. I nailed the coffin shut. I destroyed her confidence in her husband, the one man she should be able to trust more than anyone else in the world."

"No, Stella. Jerry did that." He took her hand in his. "The situation would be different if you'd known he was married, but you didn't. What he did is cowardly."

Stella looked out over the surrounding mountains and the green valley below. "Thanks for bringing me here. I needed this."

"You're welcome."

"Am I keeping you from something today?"

"Nope." Rowdy twisted his watch. "Mike is working this afternoon, so I don't have to be at the bar and grill until seven."

Stella tugged out her cell phone. "I usually go to my parents' house for dinner on Sundays. I should call them so they don't worry."

"You're not going to get any reception up here." He took the phone from her hand and touched the camera icon. "Smile," he said, holding it at arms length.

She smiled and so did he. Their face, his slightly behind hers, frozen in time.

"You look happy,"

Staring at the photo, she decided he was right. She did look happy.

Rowdy stood and held out his hand.

She wasn't ready to leave. This place soothed her soul and calmed her mind. She reluctantly placed her palm in his. "Are we going home?"

"I have one more place I want to show you." He handed her jacket over. "You might need this."

Rowdy put on his own jacket, his ponytail tucked inside—which she thought was so sweet—and started the bike. She settled behind him, deciding she could get used to lazy Sunday drives on the back of a Harley. After about twenty minutes, he turned off on a dirt road barely wide enough for a car.

When they passed under a canopy of trees, she felt a visceral connection with the forest. The shadows and the rumble of the engine made her sleepy, so she rested her cheek against his back, closed her eyes, and enjoyed the closeness of Rowdy. He was solid and dependable enough that she could excuse his teasing ways.

She liked spending time with him. He'd taught her how to dive rather than belly-flop when she was seven, and showed her and Alex how to shoot a gun when they were thirteen. She learned to drive a stick-shift at sixteen with Rowdy by her side. He had been a big part of so many things she'd done. Things she'd always remember.

They suddenly broke through the trees and Stella was wowed again by the view.

Rowdy pulled off the road into a small meadow, and Stella was off the bike in a heartbeat. Spinning in a circle, she could see for miles and miles in every direction. "We're on top of the world."

He flashed a smile and she smiled back.

"This is amazing, Rowdy."

He tapped his lips.

She narrowed her eyes. "I'm on to you."

"Don't you think I deserve a reward?"

She leaned forward and planted a kiss on his cheek.

"I think you can do better than that," he scoffed.

Yes, she could. She cupped his cheeks with her hands. "Did you mean what you said earlier?"

"Every word."

She lifted his sunglasses so she could see his eyes. "Would you be willing to wait so I can catch up?"

"For as long as it takes."

She brought his mouth down to hers and kissed him with enough passion to let him know how much his vow meant to her.

CHAPTER 16

Stella groaned when a hand grabbed her leg and jiggled her awake. She twisted under the covers and pulled a pillow over her head. "Go away, Phoebe."

"Not happening until you spill the beans about you and Rowdy."

"No beans to spill," she mumbled, tugging her leg out of Phoebe's grasp.

"Lots of people saw you on the back of his motorcycle yesterday. Rita is telling everyone who walks into Noelle' Café this morning. She said Rowdy owes her an ice cream cone for revving his bike next to her."

"Only one scoop, and he didn't rev his bike. She was gawking."

"Stella…"

"We met Alex and Colton for a picnic at the waterfall."

Phoebe shook her other leg. "Charlie is backing Rita's story with a little ditty of his own. He told Noelle he caught you and Rowdy kissing."

Stella pressed her lips together, the memory burning

bright, just as Phoebe yanked the covers down. She gasped and pointed at Stella's face. "You did kiss him!"

Stella struggled against a smile and lost. "There might have been some kissing involved."

"Have you lost your mind? You just got out of the worst relationship in the history of relationships and the first guy you go out with is Rowdy?"

"I'm pretty sure my relationship with Jerry wasn't the worst in history," Stella grumbled.

Close.

Don't you start.

"And we didn't go out. He just gave me a ride up—"

"A ride that involved kissing. That's a date, Stella. You know Rowdy has never been serious about a girl in his life."

Stella sat up. "Do you know that for a fact, or are you just listening to rumors like everyone else? Just because we've never seen Rowdy around town with a woman doesn't mean he hasn't had serious relationships."

Phoebe laughed without humor. "Oh, I've seen him with plenty of women many times, sometimes multiple women in one night. Don't forget I went to school with Rowdy. If you think Rowdy is serious, you're setting yourself up for more heartache."

Stella felt a little—actually, a lot—crushed by her sister's harsh comments. "He says he's been waiting for two years to date me."

"Awfully convenient that you didn't find out until you were alone and vulnerable." Phoebe stood, shaking her head. "You can *not* be stupid enough to fall for another two-timing Lothario."

"Who's Lothario?"

"Look him up." She glanced around at the mess on the floor. "And clean your room."

Phoebe crossed the hall to her own bedroom and slammed the door shut with a bang.

"Yes, Mom." Falling back on her pillows, the same niggle of doubt worked its way under her skin. She pictured Rowdy's face, his eyes when she'd removed his sunglasses yesterday. Either he was telling the truth or he was a very convincing liar.

Just like Jerry.

Stella plugged her ears. *He's not like Jerry.*

Are you sure?

What happened to sunshiny attitudes?

Phoebe has a point.

Yeah? Well...

"Hey Phoebe, when was the last time *you* had a serious relationship with a guy? Huh. Maybe you shouldn't be so judgmental," she hollered before jumping up and slamming her own bedroom door.

~

Rowdy printed out the schedule he'd been working on and closed his laptop just as Phoebe swung into his office. By her expression, he guessed she wasn't here for a friendly chat. Nope, she was in big-sister-looking-out-for-little-sister mode.

He leaned back in his chair and lifted his heels to his desk. "Hi, Phoebs. What brings you here?"

She tossed her blond braid over her shoulder and stuck out her chin in an attempt to look threatening. He'd gone from kindergarten through twelfth grade with Phoebe. He knew she hated lima beans, got her first bra on her eleventh birthday, and learned to kiss by practicing on Mac Johnson. She was about as scary as a hummingbird batting its wings in anger.

She narrowed her eyes for emphasis. "You know exactly why I'm here, Rowdy. Don't play dumb with me."

He blew out a breath. "How about you just say what you're here to say so I don't have to play a guessing game."

"You need to stay away from Stella."

He deliberately looked at her hip. "You're not wearing your gun, are you?"

"I can get it quick enough."

He lowered his feet and sat forward. "Want to have a seat?"

"I don't plan to be here that long. Just do as I ask. Stella is fragile right now. She doesn't need you messing with her emotions."

He stood up and moved around his desk. "Sit down for a minute, Phoebe."

Indecision moved across her face as she glanced from him to the sofa. He took her arm and pulled her down next to him. "This is going to be hard for you to hear, but I'm not messing with Stella's emotions. I'm in love with your sister and have been for a while."

A tiny line appeared between Phoebe's brows, then she snorted as only an Adams sister could. Another glance at him, and she doubled over in laughter. He crossed an ankle over his knee and waited for her to realize he wasn't joking, even handing her a tissue to wipe her tearing eyes as she snorted twice more.

"Oh, that's a good one. For a split second you had me there." She crossed her arms over her middle as she continued cackling.

He rested an arm behind her on the sofa and waited, not the least bit insulted because she found the idea of him in a long-term, committed relationship ridiculous. Phoebe had been around for most of his highs and lows, not to mention the in-betweens.

She finally leaned back against his arm, still wiping her eyes. "You're a hoot."

"I'm serious."

She glanced his way, and he watched the humor leak from her face. "No, you're not, Rowdy. You are not going to decide to be serious with my little sister. You go find someone else to play house with and get this"—she circled a finger in front of his face—"whatever this is, out of your system. She just got out of a crazy situation, and she doesn't need you screwing her up even more."

"I'm serious about Stella, Phoebe. I love her, and I plan to see her unless she tells me otherwise."

Phoebe jumped off the sofa. "You listen to me, Rowdy Garrett. I do have a gun and I will use it if you don't stay away from my sister."

"Go get it. I'll wait right here."

"I'm serious."

"As I've told you twice, so am I. I plan on seeing Stella unless *she* tells me no. Your best course of action is to try to talk some sense into her. My mind is made up and has been for a long time."

"No, Rowdy." She stamped her foot like a child. "You can't do this to her. You've never been in love in your life. How do you even know what it feels like?"

He just gazed at her, the best way he could think of to let Phoebe know just how determined he was.

She dropped next to him on the sofa and he wrapped his arm around her neck. "I won't hurt her, Phoebe."

She looked at him, her concerned expression so much like Stella's. "Tell me the last time you were in a serious relationship."

He lifted a shoulder. "Never, but I can tell you I'm serious about Stella. I know she's been through a lot recently and may need some time to recoup. I'm fine with that. She can take all the time she needs. I'll wait."

She pushed to her feet and held out her hand to help him up. As soon as he stood, she punched him in the stomach, fast and hard.

He doubled over, gasping for air.

"That's a fraction of what I've got. You hurt her, and you'll wish I'd used a gun."

He dropped back onto the sofa, eyes tearing too much to watch her stalk out of his office.

~

*S*tella reached the warehouse just after five. Her dad and Mason were hard at work on the platforms, and she had too much to do to be disappointed Rowdy wasn't there. They hadn't talked since yesterday, and her self-doubt reared its ugly head, but she stomped it flat. She would not obsess. Rowdy said he wanted this to work and she *would* believe him.

"You've taken a weight off Patsy's shoulders, Stella. Thank you for agreeing to rebuild this float," Mason said.

"I hope she'll still feel that way when it's finished. I've never built a float before."

"Your dad explained your idea, and I think Patsy will be thrilled with the end result."

Since the bare bones of her cupcakes were finished, she started cutting the tulle into large squares and stuffing tufts into the openings of the chicken wire. All around her, people were busy working on floats. Maybe the roof of the barn collapsing was the best thing for the weathered and time-worn parade favorites.

"Hey."

Stella looked up at Phoebe in surprise. "Hey, yourself."

"I thought you could use some help."

She glanced at her dad and Mason, who were back at work. "You're not still mad?"

"I was never mad, just…" Phoebe lifted a shoulder. "Just concerned."

"Don't be, and I would love some help. Thank you."

Stella couldn't remember the last time she and her sister had worked side by side on anything. She loved that Phoebe had stopped by. She told Stella about a couple who'd fallen asleep buck naked by the river. A Cub Scout troop discovered them before the leaders caught up and could shield young eyes. She also told her about a girl who hauled off and smacked her boyfriend for looking at another girl coming out of The Roasted Bean.

"Knocked him out cold." Phoebe pointed to her face. "Put a big old lump on his forehead."

"What'd she hit him with?"

"Her purse."

Stella laughed. "What's she carrying around, rocks?"

"She'd just bought a couple of hardback books from Pages Bookstore and stuck them in her bag."

Even though they lived together, she and Phoebe spent very little time with each other, which made her even happier that Phoebe had stopped by to help. "Where's Leo tonight?"

"On a date with a girl who laughs like a seal. Scares the daylights out of me every time she's near."

"Kind of like Rita?"

Phoebe jabbed an index finger at Stella. "Exactly like Rita, only younger and much taller. This woman is as tall as Leo."

"Wow." Leo was about six-two, about eye-to-eye with Rowdy. Stella laid a two-by-four-by-eight her dad had cut for her on a piece of the poster board she bought. She scored it with a pencil she'd stuck in her purse, then folded the scores back and forth accordion style. Once she finished the folds, she circled it around the laundry basket to look like a paper cupcake holder. "What do you think?"

"I think you're a genius."

Stella stepped back and studied the cupcake from a distance, pretty pleased with her efforts. She'd drilled four holes in the bottom of each basket and threaded wire through so they could be anchored to the platforms, ensuring no toppling cupcakes.

"How's Willy?"

"Leo loves that mutt, and the mutt loves him. He follows Leo everywhere."

"Aww, you've been replaced as Leo's best friend by a four-legged, one-eyed mongrel."

"I know. I'm kinda hurt. About this morning…" she added without a pause.

Stella shrugged. "Don't worry about it. I know you're just being a protective big sister."

"So you're not mad that I went to see Rowdy?"

Stella's thoughts screeched to a halt. She'd always thought of Phoebe as perfect. She was beautiful and smart and tough. Stella had idolized her older sister her whole life. At this moment, though, that adoration flew out the window on wings of how-dare-you-get-involved. "You went to see Rowdy?"

"He didn't tell you?"

She didn't want to admit to her sister that Rowdy hadn't called. Was Phoebe's visit the reason? "No. Why did you go?" Stella held up a hand. "Never mind. I know the answer."

"Remember the protective big sister—"

Stella stood over Phoebe, hands on hips. "You had no right to interfere. What did you say to him?"

"You girls okay?" their dad asked from the other side of the trailer.

"Fine, Dad," Phoebe answered her eyes on Stella.

"Tell me what you said," Stella demanded, lowering her voice.

"The same things I said to you."

"And what did he say?"

Before Phoebe could answer, her gaze moved past Stella. A sudden bump nearly knocked her flat.

"Moose, sit." A hand grabbed her around the waist to keep her upright. "Hey, darlin'. How's your day going?"

When Rowdy pulled her against him and kissed her temple—in front of Phoebe—Stella's heart did a crazy dance that included a couple of backflips as her little angel pumped a fist in the air.

Phoebe's glance bounced from Rowdy to Stella, her disgust visible. She stood up from the makeshift bucket she'd been using as a stool and walked around the trailer. "I've gotta go, Dad. See you Sunday for dinner."

"I'll walk you out."

After Phoebe and her dad left the building, Rowdy turned to her. "Something I said?"

"Depends. What did you say when she came to see you this morning?"

"Nothing but nice things." Rowdy nodded a hello at Mason. "I even told her I'd wait in my office while she got her gun."

"I can't believe she's being so stubborn."

Rowdy nipped her bottom lip between his index finger and thumb. "You look pretty cute when you pout."

"I'm not pouting. I just think"—she looked away from him—"maybe she could be happy for me. For us. I mean if you're serious."

He blew out a breath. "She filled your head with doubt, didn't she? I'll tell you again, Stella. I'm serious, but not in a hurry. I've been waiting a long time, and I can wait some more."

Stella was angry that Phoebe had, indeed, planted a little doubt. After two years of questioning and doubting, she was tired of uncertainty. She wanted to be sure. She wanted to feel comfortable and in some kind of control instead of waiting on a guy.

"Give her time." Rowdy's rare smile touched her heart. "Me being serious is new territory for all of us. In fact, if you want to help me change people's attitudes, agree to go out with me this Thursday night."

Stella opened her mouth and then closed it as tears burned her eyes.

Rowdy leaned close and whispered near her ear. "No crying, darlin'. Just a simple yes will do."

She swallowed and took a deep, deep breath. "Yes."

~

Rowdy didn't have to be at the bar and grill until late on Tuesday, so he loaded Moose into his truck and drove to Riverside Park to get a little exercise. He'd rescued the Saint Bernard as a pup three years earlier. He was in Seattle visiting Beam, who lived there while flying tourists around on sightseeing expeditions. He'd taken a walk and passed a kid who was selling six puppies on the sidewalk. Not that he was interested, but he stopped to take a look—who couldn't resist a puppy? The smallest one caught his eye. The ball of fur squirmed and squiggled and licked his chin when he lifted it to take a closer look.

"He likes you."

Rowdy laughed. "I bet he likes anyone who pays him attention. These puppies don't look old enough to be away from their mama."

The boy looked down sheepishly. "Come on, mister. My dad won't let me keep them. I have to sell them all today."

"Sorry, kid. I don't have time for a dog," he said, putting the puppy back in the box.

Two hours later when he passed again, the smallest puppy was the only one left. The sign on the box that read twenty dollars earlier, now said Free and the boy was gone. Rowdy squatted down and picked up the whining puppy. The brown and white bundle of fur tried to gnaw on the tip of Rowdy's finger. He knew right then, busy or not, he was a dog owner.

Moose barreled out of the truck when they reached the park while Rowdy grabbed a tennis ball and lobbed it to the far side of the green. Moose took off as fast as his legs and girth would carry him. Rowdy found a bench in the shade. Soon Moose was back, slobbering all over his jeans. "Get back, Moose." He grabbed the ball at his feet and lobbed it out again.

"Hey, Rowdy. Mind if I join you?"

He glanced over his shoulder, then scooted on the bench to make room for Noelle. "Not at all."

She sat next to him. "Your monster dog won't eat mine, will he?"

Rowdy looked at the dog at the end of the leash in Noelle's hand. "Moose might cover him in slobber, but he won't eat him or her."

"Him," Noelle said.

Moose galloped over like a small pony, and Noelle's dog hopped onto the bench and cowered against her. They laughed.

"What's his name?"

"Quincy. He's about nine months old. I've never seen him act skittish, but he's also never been around a dog quite as intimidating as yours."

"Intimidating but very friendly."

Moose dropped his ball and laid his head on Rowdy's knee. Slobber ran down both sides of his leg.

"Yuck," Noelle said on a laugh, her brown eyes shining.

Rowdy ruffled the fur behind his dog's ears. "You get used to it."

Noelle shook her head. "*You* might get used to it, but I wouldn't. Is he an indoor dog?"

"He's restricted to certain parts of the house."

Moose looked up at Noelle, and she petted his huge head. "Keep your slobber over there, fella."

"How are you feeling?" Rowdy asked, throwing Moose's ball again.

"Good. Pretty good… Horrible morning sickness. I've had to cut out most of my early shifts at the café. Had to hire some help for Gertie."

"Despite her age, Gertie could probably run the café twenty-four-seven."

Noelle flashed her pretty smile. "You're right, she could, and would if Albert let her."

"I've been hungry for Albert's meatloaf. Juan is a great cook, but no one makes meatloaf like Albert." He held up a hand. "Don't tell my mom I said that."

Noelle crossed her heart with an index finger. "I won't."

"Is Mac working?"

"No. He and Beck took a little camping trip. They needed a little father-son time, but haven't been able to get away because of Beck's baseball schedule."

Mac Johnson and Noelle had married last fall, and she became a doting stepmother to ten-year-old Beck. Mac didn't know he was a father until Beck's mom dropped the six-month-old baby on his doorstep and didn't contact him again until she showed up last fall wanting Beck back. Noelle had worked behind the scenes, and now Beck's mom visited her son in Eden Falls every few months. Everyone was happy.

"You don't camp?"

"I'll go once my stomach settles down a bit. Though I'm a little nervous. I've never been camping before."

"Really?"

She tapped fingertips to her chest. "City girl."

Moose was back with his ball. Noelle's dog leaned forward, sniffed, then jumped to the ground, but stayed next to Noelle's leg. Moose got close, and Quincy whimpered, which caused Moose to howl.

Noelle laughed. "I have never heard such a pitiful sound in my life."

"He likes attention, and uses every available tactic."

"He's kind of endearing, isn't he?"

"Has been since he was six weeks old." Rowdy lobbed the tennis ball toward the river.

"So, I heard a rumor you and Stella are dating."

Rowdy shook his head. "Not a rumor."

"I'm surprised, but very happy for you."

"I think you're the first to say that." Rowdy chuckled.

"Why?"

"Not a lot of people know, but the ones who do have been pretty negative, though I'm not surprised. I haven't exactly been a showcase for romance."

"Well, I think it's the best news I've heard since Brandt and Jillian's engagement. I hope things work out for you two. After what happened to Stella, she deserves some happiness."

Rowdy felt a little lift in his spirits, which had sunk pretty low after his talk with Phoebe yesterday. He hoped he could change even more opinions when he and Stella showed up on their first official date.

owdy helped Mason and Neil attached the last tier of Stella's platform. The three of them stood back to evaluate the placement.

"Looks good to me," Mason said.

Neil nodded in satisfaction. "Better than I expected."

Rowdy had to admit. Stella's plan was coming together better than he'd expected too. He shouldn't have doubted a teacher coming up with creative ideas. He'd caught sight of one of her cupcakes last night and could imagine how the finished float would look.

"I ran out of paint on the trailer," Mason said. "I'll pick some up in the morning and finish the platforms tomorrow. That will give the paint time to dry before we attach the laundry baskets this weekend."

JT, in police chief uniform, stopped next to Rowdy and ruffled Moose's fur. "Hey. Heard you were making cupcakes."

"Stella's making cupcakes," Neil said. "We're making the cupcake stand."

"Patsy was going on and on about this float at the pastry shop this morning, so I decided to have a look for myself."

Mason pointed at a finished cupcake nearby then waved a hand at the trailer. "Imagine lots of those stacked on this."

JT nodded. "I can see that."

"Okay," Mason said. "I've got to get to the hardware store so Beam can take a lunch break."

"And I have to get to work. I have a couple of houses to show this afternoon," Neil said.

"Got a minute?"

Rowdy turned to JT. "Sure. What's up?"

"I was going to ask you the same thing about you and Stella."

Hands on hips, Rowdy dropped his head back. "Not you, too?"

"Phoebe came to my office and wanted me to talk to you."

"So, talk. Fair warning though, nothing you say will make a difference."

JT leaned against the trailer and Moose followed hoping for more loving attention. "When did this happen? Stella just broke up with her boyfriend."

"She caught him cheating four weeks ago."

"Don't you think that's a bit fast to be moving on already? Aren't you worried she's just using you to mend her broken heart? I'm as concerned about you as I am her?"

"You don't have to be concerned about her or me. I won't change my mind." He shrugged as he moved around the trailer to retrieve his water bottle. "If she decides this isn't right for her, I'll live." It had taken some time, but he'd survived his last broken heart.

"I just hope you're not making a mistake."

Rowdy hadn't been so sure of anything since he purchased the property for his bar and grill. "I'm not."

~

S tella put a hand to her nervous stomach.

She'd seen Rowdy almost every night while he, Mason, and her dad worked on the platforms. He'd been at the shelter helping her serve lunch earlier today, and he stopped by Pretty Posies twice during the week while she was working.

Still, tonight would be their first official, public date. He made it clear several times that he wanted to take her to dinner and a movie *in Eden Falls*, where people they knew would see them together. He wanted to prove to Phoebe, and to her, that he was serious. She hated to admit it, but she did need proof.

Phoebe walked into the apartment while unbuckling her utility belt. She looked Stella up and down. "You look nice."

"I have a date."

Phoebe went into the kitchen and filled a glass with water, then leaned against the doorjamb between living room and kitchen. "With Rowdy?"

Stella nodded.

"On a Thursday?"

"He owns a bar and grill, Phoebe. It's kind of hard for him to get away on busy weekends."

"Where's he taking you?"

"East Winds and then a movie."

She expected a sarcastic or reproving remark, but Phoebe simply took a sip of water. Stella jumped at the knock on the door. After a long moment, one corner of Phoebe's mouth turned up. "You going to answer that, or do you want me to?"

Stella stumbled on the way to the door and swung it open to an unsmiling Rowdy. His intense green eyes moved over her, taking in her breezy summer dress and sandals, making her tingle all over.

"You look pretty."

Jerry hadn't given compliments. "Thank you. You look nice too."

He looked past her. "Hey, Phoebs. Just getting off work?"

Still leaning against the wall, water glass in hand, she nodded.

"Don't wait up. We'll be late." Rowdy put one hand on Stella's waist and pulled the door shut with the other.

On the way to East Winds, which was only a few blocks, Rowdy asked her a few questions, things that didn't matter when they were just friends. Their conversation was stilted at first, but became more comfortable as they ate dinner. Stella loved Chinese, so she enjoyed every bite. She got a kick out of the number of times people did a double-take when they noticed Rowdy was with her. Word spread quickly, and soon East Winds was packed with people stopping by their table of picking up takeout.

She had a hard time paying attention to the action-adventure at Eden Falls Cinema, never more aware of another person in her life. The way Rowdy smelled, the in and out of his breath, the way he looked at her, all small things that were making a huge impact on her own rapid breathing. He linked their fingers, their hands fitting together perfectly. He kissed her temple tenderly, touched her waist or the small of her back often. He made her feel special and safe with just a smile and a wink.

She didn't want to get her hopes up, allowing herself to only imagine a summer romance. Once September hit, she'd be back in school, surrounded by her kids. They'd keep her mind busy so her heart could heal when Rowdy moved on.

After the movie, she expected him to drive her home. Instead, he headed out of town, turning on the road leading to his house. Her stomach jumped anxiously. Even though it was almost ten o'clock, the sky was still light enough that she could see him. "Where are we going?"

"I want to spend more time with you. Neither of us has to be up early."

She half turned in her seat. "I…"

Rowdy steered to the side of the road, shifted into park, and rested his wrist over the steering wheel. "Would you rather I take you home?"

Stella's heartbeat kicked up a notch.

Just say it, her little friend insisted. *Get how you feel out in the open.*

But what if…

It doesn't matter.

Right. "I'm not sleeping with you, Rowdy."

He stared at her for a very long, extremely uncomfortable

minute, then he looked down and shook his head. "If you think so little of me, why did you agree to go out?"

"I don't—"

"Yes. You do, Stella."

She swallowed while trying to gather her thoughts. "I don't think little of you. I've just heard the rumors, lots of rumors"—*years of rumors*—"about you and all the women you've dated. If you were me, what would you think?"

The intensity of his stare hurt her heart, but she'd survive. After what happened with Jerry, Rowdy dumping her on the side of the road would be easy to handle.

He blew out a breath. "I hope I'd give you the benefit of the doubt, but…I probably wouldn't."

"You'd assume?"

"I might… Yes, I would assume." He shifted into drive and turned the truck around. "I'll take you home."

Even though disappointment settled deep in her stomach, she decided going home was for the best. At her door, he tugged her close and kissed her until she was breathless.

"I'm in this for keeps, Stella. I'm putting my heart on the line here by telling you that you're all I think about. Night and day. From the first thing in the morning until I fall asleep, you are on my mind."

His words made her heart pound in ways she'd never experienced, and she wanted to trust him.

Too soon," her little friend whispered.

Under the porch light, his green eyes held hers captive for a long moment, taking her hostage, examining her heart, her soul. In that moment, she saw love.

"Good night, Stella."

He kissed her again, just a gentle brushing of his lips against hers, and then he was gone. She felt a stirring deep in untouched places of her heart. His promises were true. He loved her. Something new and so completely delightful unfurled in her chest. A sob escaped. She'd never cried from too much happiness.

Don't you love when that happens?

She smiled at her little winged friend. *Yes.*

Phoebe and Leo were on the sofa watching a movie, a bowl of popcorn between them, when she entered the apartment.

Phoebe held up her phone. "Eight callers giving me a blow by blow account of your date."

"Only eight?"

Leo laughed. "I told her to turn her phone off, but she loves to live vicariously, since she's going through a dry dating spell herself."

"Phoebe has never had a dry spell in her life. What happened to Maude's insurance guy?"

"Too serious, too fast."

"Enough about Phoebe's love life. I've been wanting to see that movie. How was it?"

She sat next to Leo and reached for a handful of popcorn. If she said great, she'd be lying. She hadn't paid enough attention to the film to have an opinion.

He glanced at her and laughed. "You didn't watch the movie, did you? You and Rowdy sat on the back row and swapped spit like a couple of teenagers."

"No." She shoveled a handful of popcorn in her mouth.

"She's telling the truth or I would have gotten more than eight calls," Phoebe chimed in.

"So?" Leo prompted.

Stella stood, ready to escape. "Save your money. You can see the movie when it comes out on cable."

In her room, she spun around the mess. The clutter in her closet was spilling out onto her floor. Dust covered almost every surface. Her jewelry box was empty, because every-thing she owned was on her dresser or nightstand. Books littered the floor. She paid attention to the details, really looked as if seeing through someone else's eyes. Her room, her space, her life was a complete disaster.

She changed into shorts and a T-shirt, and dropped her dirty clothes in the hamper.

Her little pal jumped up and down clapping her hands. *Good for you.*

Just a baby step, but it's time to clean house.

Hallelujah! Hallelujah!

Stella started wading through her closet, bagging up clothes she hadn't worn in a long time. She pulled down boxes of shoes and boots, tried them all on and gave half away. Belts, scarves, jackets were set aside. When she dropped into bed three hours later, she'd filled two garbage bags with trash and six bags to give away.

CHAPTER 17

Stella met her mom and dad at their usual spot along the parade route, eager to see her hard work in the light of day. It was well after dark when she put the finishing touches on Patsy's float last night. She loved the results. And most important, Patsy was thrilled.

Now, she was anxious to see the crowd's reaction.

JT approached on horseback. This year Charlie sat in front of his uncle waving madly and calling her name. Stella waved back and blew him a handful of kisses.

A couple of clowns with shovels and a rolling waste can followed. She couldn't tell who they were under the makeup, and wondered how they were unlucky enough to get that job. Maybe students working off detention left over from the school year.

The Tiny Twirlers came next. Hair curled to perfection, red, white, and blue tutus bobbing with every step, they marched down the street, twirling batons to a blaring rendition of *Yankee Doodle* from speakers balanced on the hood of a pickup truck.

"I remember standing here watching you," her mom said, clapping for the tots.

"And I try to forget. Baton twirling was not my thing."

Her mom glanced from the corner of her eye. "I hear you've had a couple of dates with Rowdy."

Rowdy had taken her out a couple of times, so Stella wasn't surprised her mom knew. Too many people saw them for her not to know exactly what Stella ordered plus all the other details. What surprised her was that it took her mom so long to say anything.

"What's going on?"

"He asked me out and I said yes."

"Did you have fun?"

"Sure. We've always been easy around each other. At first it was a little weird, because we've been friends for so long. Dating threw us into a different scenario, but we hit our groove and things smoothed out." She turned to her mom. "You know Rowdy. He's laid-back, comfortable, and as unchanging as peas in split pea soup."

Her mom laughed.

Stella glanced around for him, but caught sight of Phoebe instead. She stood across the street in the square. Stella felt pretty sure that, despite the mirrored sunglasses, Phoebe was watching her. After a week, she still hadn't warmed to the idea of Rowdy dating her little sister.

"Phoebe came over last night. She's worried," her mom said.

"I know. She's voiced her opinion." Several times.

"Be patient and try to understand where she's coming from."

"I understand. Two weeks ago, I was teasing Rowdy about his prowling ways."

Teasing?

"Teasing isn't the right word. Actually, I was accusing." She glanced at her mom. "Do you think people can change?"

"Yes."

Her dad wrapped his arm around her mom's neck. "I was a Rowdy before I met your mom."

Stella lifted an eyebrow while fighting a smile. Her dad was the least likely player in the world. He was devoted to her mom.

Her mom's lips pressed together, but a smile still lifted the corners of her mouth.

"What?" Stella glanced from her mom to her dad. "No way."

Her dad kissed her mom's temple, gently—*like Rowdy kisses mine.*

"Yes, way," her mom said. "Look." Her mom pointed at Rance's trout. Rance honked the VW's horn and waved. The part came in Tuesday morning, and Nate worked around the clock to get Rance's car running. The fish made its way around the square. Judging by the pictures snapped by Jace Dickson, Rance's grin would be front and center in this week's Eden Falls Chronicle.

Stella glanced across the square at Phoebe. Someone or something else had caught her attention. Stella followed her line of sight and spotted a pack of Gothic-garbed kids standing near The Fly Shop.

Stella looked back at Phoebe, who'd been joined by Mac Johnson. He crossed the square while Phoebe went at them head on. On the other side of the street, Layne Yancy, another police officer, worked his way through the crowd toward the kids. Once the Goth gang spotted the three cops converging on them, they scattered like bats taking flight.

The float for One Scoop or Two passed, and Stella's thoughts traveled to Jerry. He'd never been able to make it to Eden Falls' Fourth of July celebrations. Now that she knew why, she was glad she didn't have those plaguing memories plodding through her mind.

She hoped Anna was okay, hoped she had family support, friends who would rally around as Stella's did. As much as she hated Jerry at the moment, she hoped, for their children's sake, that he and Anna could work things out. And for Anna's sake. After Alex's husband was killed, Stella knew the struggle her friend went through raising a son alone. She couldn't imagine Anna having to raise two boys and an infant daughter all by herself.

Sadly, Stella didn't believe Jerry would change. He was too comfortable with his cheating ways. The two times he showed up at her door, he'd shown no remorse, no real desire to fix things with his wife.

She shook off her gloomy thoughts. *Enough about Jerry.* He was out of her life, and today was a celebration.

She glanced around for Rowdy again. He'd helped her last night until he had to leave for the bar and grill. His last words were, "I'll see you tomorrow." They were going to Denny and Alice Garrett's annual barbecue together, then they'd watch the fireworks in the square with the whole town surrounding them.

The junior high school band marched past playing a summertime tune. Luckily, they'd improved greatly from last year's parade. This time, she could make out the tune of a popular song.

Happy faces surrounded her, and Stella realized she was one of them. Ever since her motorcycle ride with Rowdy, her whole attitude had changed. Or maybe it was the talk with Anna that had changed everything. It could even be that she'd completely cleaned her room over the last week. Amazing how a dust free environment could lighten your spirits. Phoebe was astounded. So was Rowdy. Stella had to admit, freeing herself from clutter had also freed her from something much deeper. Something…. Divine was the only word she could think of to describe the feeling.

As Patsy's cupcake float approached, Stella couldn't contain her delight when the crowd stood up and cheered.

Her dad gave her a tight hug. "Good job, cupcake."

"Good job to both of you." Her mom clapped. "The float is adorable, Stella."

"Thanks for all your help, Dad."

Someone tugged Stella's arm and she turned to Jillian's smiling face. "Hey, girlfriend. The float is perfect. Great job."

"Thanks. I'm feeling kinda proud at the moment." Stella glanced past her. "What are you doing here without Brandt?"

Jillian pointed to the fire engine coming in their direction. "He's throwing candy," she said just as Brandt showered them with a handful of miniature Tootsie Rolls. Stella's favorite.

"Aww. Look at the love shining from Brandt's eyes."

Jillian blushed. "He is pretty cute."

"You're both darling," Stella said, hugging her friend.

The second time he threw candy, they caught a couple of pieces, but left the majority for the kids scrambling around them. Stella waved to her parents as she and Jillian walked away arm in arm.

"I haven't had a chance to tell you how much I appreciate you coming to our engagement party. I know it probably wasn't easy to be there."

"I wouldn't have missed it for the world," Stella said as they crossed the street in front of the high school cheerleaders, who were throwing more candy from the back of the pickup Rowdy helped decorate. "You two picked a beautiful night, and the setting almost made me break into song. Don't take that the wrong way," she said when Jillian looked like someone had just stolen her teddy bear. "I'm being serious.

Your parents' backyard looked enchanting, and you two truly are the perfect couple. I'm so glad you found each other."

Jillian dropped onto a bench. "I found Brandt way before he found me."

Stella sat beside her. "Maybe earlier wasn't your time." Her own words rang true. Maybe earlier hadn't been her and Rowdy's time either. "Sometimes we don't see what's right in front of our own noses."

"Like you and Rowdy? Yes, I've heard the rumors, though I haven't spotted you two out and about yet."

"Exactly like me and Rowdy, except I'm not sure we're meant to be forever like you and Brandt."

"Pessimism isn't like you. What's up?"

Before she had a chance to explain that she was afraid this Rowdy thing was only a summer stint, Rowdy appeared as if conjured.

"Hey, Rowdy," Jillian said.

He set something on Stella's head, which slid off and landed at their feet when she doubled over laughing at his headband, which sported blue stars attached to slinky wires that bobbed up and down with his every move.

"It's not that funny." He handed Jillian a red, white, and blue plastic tiara with long streamers in the same colors curling down the back.

"Thank you."

"I thought you ladies deserved a crown for the Fourth of July, but I think I've changed my mind about Stella."

Jillian picked the other tiara off the grass and perched it on top of Stella's head. "She loves hers too."

Stella nodded, wiping away tears. This laughing thing was something she'd have to get used to again. Especially with Rowdy. He'd always been good at making her laugh.

Rowdy sat beside her and settled an arm around her neck.

"What are you ladies discussing before I so hilariously interrupted?"

Jillian's glance bounced from Rowdy to her. "I was going to tell Stella about Brandt's cute single friend, but it looks like the rumor you two are dating is true."

"That's really sweet of you, Jillian, but Stella's already involved with someone."

Jillian pressed her lips together to suppress a smile and glanced at Stella. "Are you?"

Rowdy lifted her chin with an index finger and kissed her right there on the square for everyone to see. "Are you?"

Stella kept thinking she'd get used to his kisses and her body would stop its jumpy, somersaulting nonsense. But nope. An electric current zipped through her from head to toe.

Double fudge brownie with chocolate sauce.

When he leaned away, she looked into his beautiful green eyes, then reached over and patted Jillian's hand. "Thanks for thinking of me, though, girlfriend."

"Forget I mentioned it." Jillian waggled a finger from Rowdy to Stella. "So, when did this actually happen?"

"The night of Carolyn and JT's wedding," Stella said at the same time Rowdy said, "Two years ago."

~

Rowdy felt a violent rush of blood every time he kissed Stella.

Her mouth was soft, her lips full, and she always smelled like oranges with faint, slightly spicy lavender undertones. Her kisses erased all common sense, made him think crazy thoughts like marriage and kids and forever.

From where he stood at the grill in his aunt and uncle's backyard, he could watch her play with his dark-haired niece. She blew a raspberry at Sophia, her lips all puckered up and pretty. Sophia giggled and blew a raspberry of her own.

"Would you stop doing that, Stella," Misty commanded, hands on hips. "We're trying to break her of that habit. She spits her food all over me every time she eats."

"Sorry, but introducing bad habits is what aunties do, huh, cutie?" she said, breaking off a bite of cookie and giving it to Sophia. Stella glanced at Misty. "We feed our nieces and nephews too much sugar, teach them bad habits, and then hand them back to their parents."

"But you're not her aunt."

"Down, boy." Beam slapped Rowdy on the back. "You're in public now. Tame your thoughts."

If he wasn't holding a spatula in one hand and a platter in the other, he would punch his brother.

Beam knew it and punched him instead. "You gotta give me this, bro. After all the razzing you gave me about Misty, and here you are, looking like it's your last day of summer vacation."

JT joined them. "I just heard through the Eden Falls grapevine—aka Rita—that you and Stella were seen necking in Town Square earlier. *In broad daylight!*" JT said the last three words, perfectly imitating Rita's scandalized tone.

"Yep, they were. They've been getting cozy all over town. Took her for a ride on his Harley, tangled tongues during a picnic at the waterfall with Alex, Colton, and Charlie. A couple of people have seen them lip-locked. Me included. Isn't that right, bro?"

"I think that's great, except she's pretty vulnerable right now," JT said, concern etching his brow. "Maybe you should slow down a bit."

"She's a big girl, and she knows how I feel."

"And how is that?"

"None of your business, JT."

"Except it is. Stella is like a little sister to me."

"Well, she's not your little sister. Phoebe already punched me after threatening my life, so you can relax. She's on the job," Rowdy said, trying to soothe JT's irritation and his own. "I'm not going to hurt her. I know she's been through a lot. We'll take things as slow as Stella needs to." He knew going in that he couldn't mess this up. Eden Falls' residents would run him out of town if he did anything to hurt their favorite second grade teacher.

JT glanced toward Stella. "You two always have squabbled like a Mr. and Mrs."

Beam rested an elbow on Rowdy's shoulder. "They have. Stella will definitely give little bro here a run for his money. She's small, but feisty."

Stella kissed his niece under the chin like he always did. Sophia squealed in delight.

"Hey, keep your eyes on the grill." Beam grabbed the tongs from Rowdy. "You're burning the burgers."

Rowdy patted his brother on the back. "Then you take over and I'll spend time with Stella."

~

Sitting by a man for the Fourth of July fireworks was like that moment in the middle of a dream when you realize you're stark naked and can't find any cover. People are staring while pretending not to as you search for a fig leaf. She felt completely exposed because everyone—including her parents and Rowdy's—was here. She sensed every eye in Town Square on them.

She'd dated a lot of guys, starting when she was sixteen, but she'd never had a date for Independence Day before. Kind of fun and kind of scary at the same time.

Moose misinterpreted her leaning toward Rowdy to mean she wanted a slobbery kiss, so he obliged. Saliva dripped off her chin.

"Yuck!"

Her white-robed friend toppled off her shoulder in hysterical laughter.

"Moose," Rowdy chided with a chuckle. "Back off."

Moose's tail thumped against her leg. *Woo woo wooo roof.*

Stella wiped her face with a corner of the blanket they sat on.

"Like Moose, I thought I was going to get a kiss."

"I wasn't going to kiss Moose or you. I was going to tell you I'm not sure this is a good idea."

Rowdy glanced around with his smirk. "Why?"

"Everyone is staring." He leaned close enough that her knees tingled. She looked at his mouth. "That's not a good idea either. Your parents are watching."

"Then it's the best idea. They've never seen me kiss a woman before."

That was hard to believe, given all the rumors. "Never?"

He dropped a kiss at the corner of her mouth. "Tonight's a first."

Her winged friend sighed.

Rowdy lifted her chin with an index finger and kissed her full on the mouth. Butterfly wings fluttered in her chest, leaving her a little breathless. As he deepened the kiss, the butterflies moved low in her belly.

Her angel covered her eyes with both hands. *The whole town is seeing this.*

Fudge brownie with chocolate sauce.

"We are no longer a secret," Rowdy whispered before nipping her lower lip.

Topped with a scoop of vanilla ice cream. Stella knew her grin was as goofy as a kid with a bag full of Halloween candy.

Let's add whipped cream and a cherry. Her angel swooned dramatically.

Soon they were surrounded by friends and family stretched out on blankets, kids running in circles with sparklers lighting the night. This was Eden Falls' Fourth of July.

Rowdy's aunt and uncle had a card table set up in their usual spot, sharing fried chicken and apple pie with Rowdy's mom and dad. Jolie was here with Nate and their darling baby. Alex and Colton sat two blankets away, snuggling like newlyweds. Beam was smoothing out a blanket for Misty and Sophia. Jillian waved as she and Brandt made their way through the crowd. Carolyn and JT were enjoying a spot on the other side of Alex and Colton. Charlie grinned as he ran past with a sparkler.

This could be her life forever after if what Rowdy said was true.

After what Jerry did, trust wasn't coming as easily as it once had, but she believed it could…in time.

The night air was warm and alive with laughter and cheers once the fireworks started shooting into the sky. Stella oohed and aahed right along with the crowd when one shattered into a thousand colorful sparks, cascading through the darkness. Another spiraled up and spewed a glittering silver shower overhead before bursting into mini explosions of red, white, and blue.

When Rowdy kissed her goodnight at the door of her apartment, he boosted a wonderful day into gloriously perfect.

CHAPTER 18

Stella spent the next two weeks in the pulse-throbbing excitement of a new relationship while waiting for the other shoe to drop. For the moment when Rowdy would come to her and say, "Okay, this isn't for me after all" or "I thought I'd give it a try, didn't work" or "What was I thinking?"

She felt guilty for expecting the worst, but planning would save her a portion of the heartache when the breakup came. Live in a state of preparedness rather than a fool's paradise was her new motto.

Her friend plopped on her belly, chin in hands. *You are full of clichés today.*

I just don't know what to make of the situation. Instead of breaking up, Rowdy called every day—sometimes twice. He showed up at the flower shop to make out in the back room when no one was around, and even cooked dinner for her. They went for Harley rides and star-gazing outings. Through it all, she made comparisons, last summer to this one, her happiness then compared to now. And wondered again why she'd been so blind to the way Jerry treated her? The comparison between Jerry and Rowdy—well, there was no comparison. She was amazed by the way Rowdy treated her. He was attentive and sweet and a complete surprise every day.

Even if Rowdy did come to his senses, she'd be grateful for this summer. She discovered a lot about herself over the past month. When Rowdy decided it was time to move on, she'd be grateful *he* was her rebound guy. Not only because he was fun and exciting to be around, but because she learned she'd been wrong about him for all these years. He was completely unlike the person she had assumed. She liked knowing he was different. Even if they never dated past September, she was glad he was nothing like Jerry.

She was out front of her apartment when he pulled his truck to a stop at the curb. They were meeting the gang at the river for a tubing party. The back of his pickup was heaped with inflated tire tubes. He jumped out and helped her load a cooler filled with lunch goodies. Then he gave her a sound kiss. "We have to start this adventure out right."

Rowdy opened the door and she climbed into the passenger seat. "We've been on this adventure before. Many times."

He ran around and slid behind the wheel. "But not as a couple. That makes this a brand-new adventure. In fact, I've never been tubing with a date."

"Another first?"

"For me." He took her hand across the console and kissed her fingers.

So many of his small but intimate acts surprised her. Like kissing her fingers or tucking her hair behind her ear or just touching her face.

"I imagine this isn't a first for you."

"No. I went tubing with high school boyfriends."

"Who?" he asked as they pulled away from the curb.

Stella had to think back. Tubing was something she'd been doing since she was a kid, a summer pastime with friends and relatives. Guys were usually involved. She'd been at the river with Leo, JT, Rowdy, even Alex's first husband, Peyton, too many times to count. "I went with Max Klein a couple of times when we dated over a summer."

"I didn't know you dated Max. Does it feel weird running into him around town?"

"No. We parted friends. There was never much of a spark between us. We had fun for three months, then we both moved on."

Rowdy had the windows down. Stella kicked off her sandals and propped her bare feet on the dash, enjoying the ride. They didn't talk much, which was fine with her. With Rowdy, silence was comfortable. For some odd reason, she'd always felt the need to fill the silence with Jerry. She used to rack her brain for something of interest, something to get him talking.

Maybe searching for something in common?

Stella flicked her winged annoyance off her shoulder and laughed aloud when she flew out the window like a bug. *Don't need your input today, sweetie.*

Rowdy reached across the console again to rest a big hand on her knee. She loved his habit of touching. It made her feel wanted and desirable, emotions she rarely felt with Jerry.

Enough. Today is beautiful and Rowdy is beautiful. Have fun.

Right. She glanced from beautiful Rowdy to her tiny pal who'd found her way back into the car—just like a bug. *No more comparisons.*

~

*M*ost of the gang was already at the drop-off point before he and Stella arrived. Rowdy felt conspicuous being here with a date. Like Stella, he'd been here with friends many, many times, but never with a specific girl.

He waited for the teasing that didn't come. Maybe people had seen them around enough to put their fairly new relationship on the back burner. Everyone treated him—or them—as if Stella had just hitched a ride up here with him, which had happened several times before.

Phoebe must have finally accepted him as her sister's boyfriend. She wasn't exactly friendly with him, but she wasn't shooting him the stink eye every time they ran into each other either. She showed up with someone besides Leo.

When Leo pulled into the campground where they always put their tubes in the water, Rowdy recognized the woman with him as soon as she stepped out of his SUV. By the look on her face, she recognized him, too.

With Beam's help, he got the tubes out of the back of his truck. Stella got busy with the rest of the girls, covering picnic tables with plastic tablecloths and setting out all the fixings for lunch. JT already had a charcoal grill started.

Rowdy couldn't quite relax with a previous woman-friend around. Stella already thought the worst of him. He didn't need her questioning his feelings for her, not this early in their relationship. When Leo introduced the woman, Rowdy said they'd already met. Stella looked at him long and hard before going back to her lunch.

Leo laughed. "I should have known I'd eventually ask one of your *previous companions* out."

The woman blushed. "We didn't date that long."

"Rowdy never dates anyone for long," Phoebe mumbled, loud enough for him—and Stella—to hear.

He expected Stella to ask questions once the picnic goodies were packed away and they were floating down the river. Instead, she lay back in her tube and seemed to enjoy the day. He clung to her tube or her ankle to keep her close. She didn't seem to mind his possessive hold. Most of the other couples were doing the same, including Leo and his date.

This impromptu party had been Alex's idea, and all five of her friends, plus others with their partners, were here. He'd never been a part of something like this. When he dated, the woman was never an Eden Falls local. They'd date a few months, then either he would move on when she became too graspy, or she'd call things off when he didn't.

What he had with Stella was different. He wanted this to last, but he didn't want to be so clingy that he drove her away.

He gazed at the blue sky. The slight breeze pushed white cotton-candy clouds eastward. He and Stella rounded a bend, out of sight of the others, but their laughter floated through the air. Charlie and his buddy Tyson were soaking Colton and Beam with water guns.

"What are you thinking about?" Stella asked.

He glanced from the trees above to his gorgeous girl-friend. She'd raised her sunglasses to the top of her head and was looking at him with a pretty smile lighting her face. "You."

She rolled her eyes, a staple for Stella. "Seriously."

"I am being serious. I'm thinking about you. Us. How nice it feels to relax with my girl."

She lowered her glasses and glanced away. "Both of *your* girls."

He pulled her tube around so they were closer and lifted her glasses to see her eyes. "I only have one girl, Stella. Leo's friend and I dated a long time ago. Way before me and you.

Remember, this thing goes both ways. Do you think I can look at Max Klein again without thinking of you two kissing?"

"Max and I only dated for three months."

"And I probably only dated that woman three times. It doesn't matter. What matters is us. Here. Now."

Stella looked away from him again. He suspected she was sizing up Leo's date. "What's on your mind, darlin'? Talk to me."

She bit her lip.

"Stella…"

"Sometimes this"—she fluttered a finger between them—"us…seems surreal. Like I might be dreaming, and I'll wake up soon."

He propped an elbow on his tube, leaned forward, and kissed her. "Then we're both experiencing the same dream, sweetheart. Only it's not a dream. It's as real as this water is cold. Don't overthink the situation. Let's just enjoy what's happening."

"What's your definition of happy?"

He felt a smile. He'd never thought much about happiness. It had always been kind of a girl word to him. He could see people around him who were happy, but he'd never considered himself a happy person. Content, yes. But at this moment, he was happy. Stella made him happy, and he hoped she felt the same way. "This. Us enjoying a summer day together. Knowing I'm going to kiss you before I have to go to work tonight. Knowing that you'll smile when I do. Being in lo—"

A shot of ice water hit the side of his face, and he immediately tried to shield Stella with his body. She jumped, and they both dumped off their tubes into the frigid water. Stella came up sputtering, and he went after Charlie and Tyson, who shrieked in delight.

～

*C*arolyn poked her head in the back door of Pretty Posies. "Hey, girlfriend."

Stella turned from the vases she'd lined up on the worktable. "Hi, Carolyn. I didn't get to talk to you much yesterday. How's married life?"

Carolyn stepped through the door, her smile sweet, serene, so full of joy. "Fabulous. Maybe you should try it."

Stella laughed. "I don't see marriage anywhere in my near future." Which wasn't quite true, because she'd been imagining the possibility for a couple of weeks now. Especially after yesterday. She would give her eyeteeth to know what Rowdy was about to say before Charlie and Tyson pelted them with cold water.

She pictured herself in Rowdy's beautiful house with its spectacular views. Moose loved her, and she loved the slobbery lug right back. Raising a family in that picturesque home would be heavenly. She'd read to their children and help them with homework, Rowdy would teach them how to fish and to appreciate the beauty around them. Even though the fantasy was so incredibly vivid and detailed, she would never voice her thoughts aloud.

"Really?" Carolyn's look of disbelief was pretty vivid too. "You and Rowdy looked pretty close together at the river yesterday."

"Yeah, but...we're just starting out, dating casually." She stopped short of adding *just for the summer*, because maybe...

Carolyn moved around the table, tugged a rose from a bucket of water, and held it to her nose. "Rowdy wasn't looking at you like you're just dating casually."

Stella turned to the sink to hide any hope that might show in her expression, but couldn't stop her question. "How does he look at me?"

Carolyn's mouth was hidden by the rose, but the crinkling at the corners of her eyes gave her smile away. "Like he's in love."

Her little pest nodded vigorously. *He does look at you that way.*

Stella forced a laugh. Sure, he'd said as much at their picnic to the waterfall and seemed about to say it again yesterday, but the thought of Rowdy actually, *truly* being in love with anyone but family was too…

Preposterous?

I was thinking impossible, but both words work. She shook her head. "You know Rowdy isn't the type of guy who falls in love. He's always been wild and free, and has probably dated a million women, so why me? I mean…you saw his old girlfriend yesterday. She was gorgeous and I'm…me. I'm like the ugly duckling next to her."

"Stella," Carolyn reprimanded as she came to stand next to her. "You are just as gorgeous if not more so. Rowdy has known you his whole life. Maybe he picked you because he knows exactly what he's getting and he likes that idea."

Stella rubbed her chest where her own crazy feeling of love had begun to blossom. She was experiencing emotions she'd never felt before. Even for Jerry, who she thought she might one day marry. This was something different, something stronger. More permanent. Something that left her breathless.

She glanced at Carolyn, who was as sweet as the pastries she produced every day for Patsy's bakery, and her eyes filled with unexpected tears. "But forever is a long time and he's not a forever kind of guy, so what am I going to do when summer is over and he moves on?"

Carolyn wrapped her arms around Stella. "Because you're falling in love?"

"I-I think I a-already have."

Carolyn squeezed her tight. "I think you're wrong about Rowdy. I believe he is capable of a very deep, everlasting love. The forever kind. He may be just as surprised by it as the rest of us, but after watching him yesterday, I think he's going to prove all us naysayers wrong."

I hope you're right.

~

*R*owdy sat in his office long after the bar and grill closed. Yesterday's river trip was great. Most days he spent with Stella were great.

He was pretty confident her feelings for him were deepening. She wasn't in love, but hopefully he'd change that with time. Leo showing up with an ex was inconvenient, but bound to happen eventually. And now he knew Stella had dated Max, who else was out there? Inconvenient could happen to both of them.

He pushed away from his desk and walked out into the warm summer night. The crickets were chirping up a storm while the rest of the town lay quiet. He looked up into the night sky. Clouds covered his stars. Around the side of the building, he toed a crack in the asphalt where weeds had sprouted. Next year he'd have to replace the parking lot, but he'd set aside enough money to cover the expense.

A loud clank rang out. Probably a dog dumping over a trash can. Another clank following close behind turned him toward Town Square, just a block away. As he moved down the sidewalk he heard more noise...not loud, but unusual for two-forty-five in the morning. Even a dog wouldn't make that kind of noise.

Low voices made him take a left down the alley that ran behind the businesses on Main. In the dim light he spotted three figures dressed in black. They were struggling to slide a metal garbage bin next to the back wall of The Fly Shop. He couldn't make out whether they were male or female.

Sticking to the shadows, he eased his phone out of his jeans pocket and scrolled to JT's number. At a groggy hello, he whispered, "I have your arsonists behind The Fly Shop." He hung up before JT could respond, hit the camera icon and scrolled to video.

"The old buzzard chained it to the fence," a male voice hissed.

"Don't you have any tools in your car?"

"Yeah, sure, I always carry a bolt cutter around with me."

Even from where he stood, Rowdy could hear the sarcasm dripping from the tallest figure—the vampire-looking Goth kid. Leader of their pack.

"Why don't we go out to that farm we hit last year? That guy had crates everywhere. We can break those apart and use them to get the fire started."

"Let's just use the trash from the ice cream shop. There are a bunch of boxes in their garbage bin."

Rowdy couldn't tell which of the three was speaking, but kept the video rolling as he inched closer. He could see profile outlines but not distinct facial features. *Of all the nights for cloud cover.*

"What are we going to do?" asked a fourth person, a girl by the sound of her voice. She stepped out from behind the dumpster.

The tall figure pointed. "Go get those boxes from the ice cream shop."

The girl and one of the boys walked away as another kid opened Rance's dumpster and started throwing lit matches inside. The glow of orange flared when a box or something caught fire. It wouldn't do much harm, though, since the dumpster stood several feet from the back of the building. *Chaining the dumpster to the fence was smart thinking, Rance.*

Rowdy imagined JT had radioed whoever was on duty by now. They had to be close to The Fly Shop.

The two figures reappeared, each carrying an armload of boxes. "This isn't going to be enough," the girl said, throwing the boxes down by Rance's back door. "We need more."

Rowdy guesstimated his chances of grabbing more than one of the kids were pretty slim. He had all four profiles and voices on video, but would that be enough to nail the little law-breakers?

He heard a car engine and hoped the cavalry had arrived. He stopped the video, shoved the phone in his pocket, and stepped out of the shadows. "I can help." All four figures spun toward him. He thumbed over his shoulder. "I have some crates behind my place. It's just a block away."

He was already running toward them when they scattered. He channeled his high school football days and dove for the one closest to him. The kid went down with an "Ooofff!"

He pinned the kicking, punching teenager's arms behind him. "Hold still, kid. Your fire-lighting days are over."

"Get off me! You don't have anything on us."

"That's where you're wrong. I've got plenty." He held the kid down while the blessed sound of screeching tires cut through the air.

A few minutes later, Mac and Phoebe appeared next to him, hauling two more kids in handcuffs.

"You're a hero," Phoebe said, handing the girl over to Mac so she could handcuff Rowdy's delinquent.

"Far from a hero." Rowdy pulled the thrashing kid to his feet, tightening his hold.

"You're breaking my arm!"

"*You* are breaking your arm. Stop fighting me."

"Please, let us go," the girl pleaded.

"The only place you're going tonight, sweetheart, is jail,"

Phoebe said. "Can you believe that your mighty leader took off in a cowardly cloud of dust?"

Once the kids were locked in a cell, Rowdy recounted what happened and showed the video to Mac and Phoebe before sending it to JT's phone.

Mac stood up from his desk. "This is going to make JT's year."

"I think marrying Carolyn made JT's year. This is just icing on the cake," Phoebe said.

"You're wrong, Phoebe." JT walked into the room with the leader of their little arson gang in handcuffs. "*This guy* is the icing on the cake."

The kid's black eye makeup made his skin look almost transparent, he was so white. Even his lips were black. One arm of his trench coat was ripped off at the seam.

"How'd you catch him?" Rowdy asked.

"I knew I wouldn't get here in time to apprehend, but hoped I could head them off at the pass if they got away. How many of these little arsonists were here tonight?"

"Four. With this one, we got them all." Mac grabbed the kid's arm and pulled him toward the door.

"I want my phone call," the kid growled as Mac hauled him down the hall.

"All in due time, Thorn," JT called.

"Congrats, Rowdy," Phoebe said. She thumbed over her shoulder. "I'm going back out on patrol."

"Thanks, Phoebe," JT said.

Rowdy described what happened again while JT watched the short video.

"The picture is dark, but I think it's clear enough to convict these little criminals. Thanks for thinking of it." JT beckoned Rowdy to his office. "What made you take a walk tonight?"

"I came out of the bar and grill and heard a weird noise."

Rowdy dropped into a chair, his adrenaline rush wearing off. "At first I thought it might be a dog dumping over a trash can, but the sound wasn't quite right."

"Thanks for following your intuition. I just wish the little orange-haired kid had been with them. *Blaze*," he said, using air quotes. "I think he's our real pyromaniac." He shook his head. "You have no idea how bad I've wanted these guys."

Oh, but I do. He'd wanted Stella for as long as these kids had been setting fires in Eden Falls. "Just took a little patience. They were bound to mess up eventually."

"They even admit to setting the fire out at Leo's parents' farm." JT leaned back in his chair and closed his eyes. "I was beginning to think I'd never get these kids. I just have to get them to give up the rest of their gang."

"Well, you can relax. You got 'em...or at least some of them...locked up tight. With their leader in jail, maybe the rest of the gang will disperse." Rowdy pushed up from his chair. "I'm beat. I'll see you tomorrow." He saluted JT on his way out the door.

Stella was in the kitchen when Phoebe came in from her night shift. She stopped in the doorway, arms folded. "You look like you're losing weight."

"I wish."

"I'm serious."

"So am I." Stella turned from the window, a cup of herbal tea in her hands. Not a glutton for punishment, she hadn't weighed herself since the day the scale groaned at her. "You're home kind of late this morning."

Phoebe took the cup of tea from Stella, and sipped. "Thanks for keeping the apartment a little cleaner. I haven't had to follow your usual trail of clothing from front door to bedroom in over a week. And your room," she said with wide eyes. "I never thought it would stay neat after your whirlwind cleaning spree, but it still looks great."

Stella took her teacup back and sat at the table. After the tension between them, Phoebe was offering an olive branch in the way of compliments. She hadn't been trying to lose weight, but if she had dropped a few pounds, she'd take it and celebrate. She *had been* trying to keep her side of the apartment cleaner, though, and appreciated her efforts being noticed. "I'm a long way from perfect."

"We all are."

Phoebe went to the stove and shook the teakettle. Stella heard the water slosh the sides. "It should still be hot if you want a cup."

She listened while her sister went through the steps of making a cup of tea. Phoebe usually came home and went straight to bed after a night shift. Her sticking around meant she had something on her mind.

She finally sat at the table across from Stella. "Your boyfriend was walking the streets at three this morning."

Stella smiled. Phoebe was either accepting that she and Rowdy were dating, or she was mocking. Either way, Stella was in too good a mood to take the bait. "I'm not sure I'd call him my boyfriend."

Phoebe raised eyebrows. "What is he?"

Stella looked into her teacup, careful not to meet her sister's gaze. "We're just dating…casually. If it turns into more, great. If not, I had a wonderful time."

"Huh. Could have fooled me. And everyone else in town."

She glanced up to see if Phoebe was kidding. *Nope.* She wanted to know why her sister felt that way, but she didn't want to make Phoebe suspicious of her feelings for Rowdy. Going for nonchalance, she ran a finger over her teacup's *I Survived Another Day in the Classroom* letters. "Why do you say that?"

"Just seems pretty serious to me. You guys see each other every day."

Stella hoped her snort sounded convincing. She was out to protect her heart. "You know Rowdy isn't the serious type."

"Maybe he is." Phoebe took a sip of her tea. "Anyway, back to your boy—Rowdy walking the streets. He heard a noise behind The Fly Shop. His investigation ended up with us catching four kids trying to set a fire by Rance's backdoor."

"What? You guys finally caught the arsonists? That's great news."

"Yep. JT's pretty happy. When Rowdy saw what was going on, he called JT at home. While he videoed the kids at work with his phone, JT called us. We got three kids at the scene and JT got the fourth on his way out of Eden Falls. Rowdy's the town's hero today."

Stella started to push away from the table, then stopped. If Rowdy was up at three, he'd be sleeping now, but he would be working at the bar and grill tonight. She'd go over right after she finished at Pretty Posies and give him a congratulatory kiss.

Or two.

Stella liked the way her winged friend thought.

~

*R*owdy spent early afternoon mowing his lawn. Alex told him once that she loved to mow lawns. She said mindlessly going back and forth gave her time to rest her thoughts from daily worries and focus on the pleasures of life. Since then he'd looked at mowing in a different light. Except his thoughts were always on Stella.

Moose lay in the shade of a pine, sleeping until Rowdy finished, then he bounded around, ready to play some catch. Rowdy had never been an animal person. Not that he didn't like animals, but he'd never been home enough to take care of a pet. Moose changed all that.

After giving Moose a bath, which was a water-slinging playtime for the dog. Rowdy showered and headed to town. He needed to be at the bar and grill for a meeting before his shift.

Stopping at Pretty Posies would be a waste of time. Stella was helping Alex deliver flowers for an out-of-town wedding, and his cousin said they wouldn't be back until after five. Mike was off, but Rowdy had two other bartenders working, so he planned to take Stella to dinner when she got back. Their time together would be cut even shorter when Stella started back to school. She worked days, he worked nights, a little problem they'd have to navigate around.

Juan offered him a plate of the shrimp tacos on special for the night. There wasn't much Juan made that Rowdy didn't like. He was an amazing cook, and Rowdy was lucky Juan knocked on his door when looking for a job.

For the most part, Rowdy had been lucky with employees. At the moment, he had a full staff that worked well together, which made his job, and life, so much easier. He would hang onto Mike as long as he was willing to give up his weekend nights.

He walked out front and surveyed the bar and grill. At this hour, only a few tables were occupied. The cleaning crew had been in earlier and the place sparkled. He tapped the bar. "Can I get a ginger ale and a JD and Coke, Kyle?"

"Sure thing."

Rowdy took the drinks to a table. His accountant always made his place the last stop of the day and unwound with a drink or two.

~

*A*lex laughed. "You anxious to see someone? You've looked at your watch at least a hundred times today."

Stella let the guard against her heart down enough to smile. "I just want to tell Rowdy congrats on catching the bad guys. I haven't had a chance to see him since last night." Their ride back from Yakima was taking forever. She'd checked Alex's speed as often as she'd looked at her watch. "I bet JT is really glad. The unsolved arsons had to have been a huge distraction for him."

"Yeah, we're lucky Rowdy was wandering the streets in the middle of the night."

That little bit of news still bothered Stella. Why had Rowdy been wandering around at three? Two months earlier, she would have assumed he was making his way back to his truck after hooking up with a woman. Her assumptions had changed over the summer. Still, the news raised questions.

They entered Eden Falls' town limits and her heart bumped against her ribs a little harder.

"Want me to drop you off at Rowdy's?"

"Yes, please."

Alex pulled into the Bar and Grill's parking lot. "Thanks for your help today."

"Anytime."

"You and Rowdy seem to be getting along."

Stella didn't want to discuss Rowdy with his cousin. Not yet. Their relationship was still too new, too uncertain." Simple answer, "Oh, we still have our squabbles."

Alex flashed her sunshiny I-told-you smile. "Making up from a squabble can be fun."

Stella slid out of Alex's delivery van just as a beautiful woman climbed out of a fancy sports car wearing a tight red skirt and jacket. She slipped the jacket off to reveal a silky camisole. Tossing the jacket onto the passenger seat, she shut the door and walked inside.

Pretty lady.

Yep, kind of out of her element here.

Don't be judgmental.

Stella smiled at her haloed friend. *Right. Sorry.*

Once inside, she took a moment to let her eyes adjust to the dim light. Rowdy wasn't behind the bar, but Kyle spotted her and motioned to a booth along the wall. Rowdy sat with his back to the door. She took a step forward, but immediately stopped when the woman in red touched his shoulder. He stood. They embraced, kissed, and Stella's heart dropped to her stomach. She could see Rowdy's profile, the smile on his face.

He moved aside so the woman could slide into the booth, then he scooted in close beside her.

Stella tried to suck in a breath, tried to swallow the pain around the sudden lump in her throat. The room swam in front of her eyes and the white noise from the Seattle restaurant closed in on her. She'd let her guard down, trusted Rowdy with her heart, and he squashed it flat, just as Jerry had.

She glanced toward the bar, her eyes zeroing in on several pitchers of water sitting on the end. Without thinking, she rushed forward and grabbed two. She slid into the booth behind Rowdy and his floozy, and dumped a pitcher on each of their heads.

"What the—!" Rowdy yelled at the same time the woman shrieked.

Stella stormed out of the bar and down the street toward her car, parked behind Pretty Posies. Her vision narrowed to the front of Alex's place as she stalked past the shops that circled around Town Square. A hand on her shoulder jerked her to a stop before she reached the flower store.

"Stella, I said stop. Didn't you hear me calling you?"

She slowly turned to face a soaking wet Rowdy. The woman's red lipstick was still on his face. She jerked out of his grasp.

"What are you doing?"

"Looking at the face of a cheater," she hissed. "You're no better than Jerry."

He laughed, and the red clouding her vision expanded.

"Come with me," he said wrapping his big hand around her upper arm.

The amusement in his voice made her livid. She tried to yank free. "Let go of me."

"I want you to meet my accountant. Natalie has been doing my books since I opened the bar and grill," he said towing her back the way she'd come.

Stella closed her gaping mouth.

"We always meet at my place, in a booth, where everyone can see."

"Your accountant?" she squeaked out.

He towed her inside to the table Kyle was mopping up.

"Sorry," she mumbled as Rowdy directed her to a dry booth.

"Not a problem." She could tell Kyle was trying hard not to laugh. This story would spread around town fast. "Can I get you a drink?"

She shook her head.

"Natalie's in the bathroom drying off," he said to Rowdy. "I gave her the shirt in your office."

"Thanks, Kyle."

He must keep a closet full of those things.

Not now.

The pretty woman came toward them, her once curly brown hair hanging wet and straight. She was taller than Stella, so Rowdy's oxford shirt hit obscenely high on her thigh.

She must carry a boatload of makeup in that gigantic bag.

No kidding. You can't tell I dumped a pitcher of water on her.

The woman stopped next to the table, fist on cocked hip.

Rowdy chuckled. "Natalie, this is *my girlfriend*, Stella. Stella, my *accountant*, Natalie."

"Girlfriend?" The astonishment in the woman's voice was blatant. And annoying. "Wow, Rowdy. I've never known you to have a *girlfriend*. I'm surprised."

Rowdy's eyes narrowed in a slight reprimand. "So is she."

"Well, at least you picked a fighter. She'll be able to keep you in line." Natalie set her bag on the bench on the other side of the booth and glanced at Kyle. "Keep the pitchers of water away from her."

Kyle chuckled until Stella glared at him. "Sure. Want another JD and Coke?"

"No. I'm not staying." She reached into her leather bag, took out a thick folder, and set it in front of Rowdy. "Good thing this was zipped away, or you'd be looking over soggy numbers."

"Thanks, Natalie. Juan has some shrimp tacos tonight."

"I'll take a rain check on dinner." She slung her bag over her shoulder and glanced down at the shirt she wore. "By the way, I'm keeping this as recompense for damages incurred."

Rowdy nodded with a grin. "Not a problem. I'll look these over and get back to you."

"You do that." She nodded toward Stella. "Good luck with her." Her glance bounced from Rowdy to Stella. "And vice versa."

"Sorry," Stella mumbled to the gorgeous woman, then Rowdy after Natalie walked out.

Rowdy slid in next to her, the thigh of his wet jeans soaking through her own pants. "I'm not. Now I know how much you care."

She snorted. "You're reading too much into a simple soaking."

He captured her chin in the palm of his hand, his gaze

boring into hers. "Yeah?" he said, his voice low and sensuous. "Look me in the eye and tell me you don't."

"Of course I care. I mean…we've known each other forever. I don't want you to get involved with the wrong person."

He tipped his head so their gazes connected when she looked away. "You were mad because I was with another woman."

"In your dreams."

"That's the second time you've used that phrase with me, and you were right both times. I think about you when I'm awake. I dream about you when I'm asleep."

She stared into his beautiful, mossy green eyes and knew he was telling the truth. *Why me* ran through her mind for the hundredth time. Rowdy could choose anyone, so why her? Why now? He ran fingers down the side of her face, and his sexy mouth quirked into a genuine smile. "Wow. This is the second time I've rendered you speechless."

"No. Well, maybe I'm just having trouble believing you."

"Why? When have I ever lied to you, darlin'? Name one time."

He never had.

"By the way, that's the second shirt you've cost me."

She lifted her hand, cupped his jaw. His eyes closed at her touch, and she loved that she could do that to him. She finally accepted that she wanted this to work. More than anything she'd ever wanted before.

~

Stella stopped her car outside Rowdy's garage and let herself in his back door. As soon as she entered the kitchen, Moose was *woo woo woofing* in his gentle giant way.

She took him out back for a game of catch. Every time he brought the ball back to her, he almost knocked her over with his huge body. When he was tired of playing, they both plopped down in the shade. He licked his chops, slobber drooling from his jowls, and laid his heavy head on her lap.

Relaxing in the shade with the clouds floating overhead was the perfect way to spend a summer afternoon. Rowdy had a town council meeting, then he was picking her up here for a motorcycle ride and some stargazing.

And kissing.

Yes. Lots of kissing.

She took a deep breath.

But instead of fresh mountain air, she smelled a hint of smoke.

Rowdy didn't have any close neighbors, and it was too hot to be burning a fire. "Get up, Moose."

She walked around the house, the dog close on her heels. From the front yard, she could see black smoke rising over the trees. She pulled her cell phone from her back jeans pocket.

"Nine-one-one. What's your emergency?"

"Hey, Gianna. It's Stella. I'm at Rowdy's house and see black smoke to the west. I can't see if it's a fire or something else."

"Thanks, Stella. I'll call the fire department. Is the smoke close to JT's house?"

Stella stood on tiptoe wishing she could see over the treetops. "I don't think so. I think the smoke is coming from Rowdy's side of the ridge."

"Hold on," Gianna said.

Stella walked to the end of the driveway, but still couldn't see the source of the smoke, which was getting thicker by the minute.

"Hey, Stella, I just alerted the fire department. To be safe, maybe you should come down the mountain."

"I think you're right. See ya, Gianna." Stella turned around quickly, completely forgetting about Moose. He jumped sideways when she fell over him. The huge dog stumbled and landed on her ankle. Stella heard a sickening snap before pain shot up her leg.

"Owww…Moose."

Woo woo woof.

She laid back in the dirt driveway trying to catch her breath, then twisted to the side to throw up from the pain.

Now what?

"You're the guardian angel. Aren't you supposed to do something?" Stella said with a moan.

A guardian angel and a conscience are two very different things.

Well, tell the guardian she's up.

Moose paced anxiously, probably smelling the smoke. He nudged her arm with his nose.

A second grader in another class broke his ankle last year, and she'd about fainted when she saw his foot facing the wrong way. The poor kid did faint. Her ankle was already swelling, but her foot wasn't flopping.

Thank you for small miracles.

You're welcome.

I thought you weren't a guardian angel.

I'm not, but you didn't know that until just now.

Stella pushed to one foot, hopped to the edge of the driveway, and fell on the grass. Her back pocket vibrated. She pulled her phone out. The ringer wasn't working, but Rowdy's number showed up on the shattered screen. She connected the call. "Hello? Hello? Rowdy, if you can hear me, I'm at your house with Moose. I fell. I think I broke my ankle, and there's a fire burning somewhere, but I can't see because of the trees." She looked skyward. The smoke was thicker and closer. Moose whined and nudged her again. She wasn't sure Rowdy could hear her, though his number still lit the screen. *What should I do?*

She shoved the phone in her back pocket and started crawling toward her car.

Stay calm.

I'm trying. "Come on, Moose."

The dog thought Stella was playing a game and started prancing around. He bumped into her, knocking her on her side.

"No, Moose. We don't have time to play. We need to get down the mountain." She'd hurt her left ankle, so she'd probably be able to drive if she could get to her car. The smoke was thicker now. Moose whined again and ran ahead of her.

When she reached the side of the house, she found a short shovel leaning against the garage. Not an ideal crutch, but she could use it to hobble to her car. When she opened the door, Moose hopped into the back seat. Once she was in, he rested his head on her shoulder, slobber dripping down her front. She looped her arm around his neck. "It's going to be okay, buddy. We'll get out of here."

At the foot of the driveway, she turned toward town, but only got around the first bend before flames shot high into the sky right in front of them and black smoke billowed, obliterating the sun. Panic sent her heart into overdrive. *WhatdoIdo?WhatdoIdo?* ran nonstop through her mind. This road ended at Rowdy's house, so going higher was out of the question. And the fire would follow. She glanced around searching for an answer, but nothing came. With a broken ankle, she couldn't outrun the blistering flames.

Don't panic.

Kind of hard not to at this point.

She could barely make out the other side of the small

ridge. Leo and JT's houses would be safe unless the fire jumped.

Stella turned the car around and drove back to Rowdy's. Smoke was thick now, and she could hear the trees down the hill exploding as they caught fire. She climbed out and Moose followed. He leaped to the far end of the yard, away from the fire.

She patted her leg. "No, boy. Come here. We can't go up."

Moose ran back to her, grabbed the tail of her T-shirt, and yanked her toward the trees. She glanced behind her. They had nowhere else to go but up. She hobbled back to the shovel she'd thrown on the lawn when she climbed into the car. Using it as a cane, she followed Moose into the trees.

CHAPTER 20

$\mathcal{R}$owdy raced out of Town Hall, phone still to his ear, and looked at the side of the mountain. Flames rose above the trees, and black smoke billowed high into the sky. "Stella!" he yelled, even though he knew she couldn't hear him.

Her voice was muffled as she talked to Moose. She must have dropped her phone or put it in a pocket. Sirens blared through town as two fire trucks rounded the square. He could see from here that the fire was already out of control, racing up the hill he lived on, and Stella was up there with Moose.

Tires squealed to a stop next to him. "Gianna said Stella is at your house," Phoebe shouted out the window of her patrol car.

He jumped into the front seat. "I have her on the phone. She said she dropped hers and can't hear me."

"Is she okay?"

He held his cell to his ear with one hand and pointed with the other. "She must have put it in her pocket. I can barely hear her, but she's still talking. Go! Let's get up there."

He couldn't tell what Stella was doing by the sounds he heard. Moose was whining in the background. Rowdy wanted to push Phoebe aside and drive himself. She had the siren on and was going over the speed limit, but not fast enough for him. Stella was at his house because of him. He rubbed his chest where his heart squeezed painfully. The fire was going uphill. Stella said her ankle was broken. She had nowhere to go. "Hurry, Phoebe."

Phoebe pulled into the left lane, racing past the fire engines.

He rolled down the window and glanced skyward when a helicopter carrying a bucket passed overhead. "Can you radio them? Tell them where to drop the water or fire retardant or whatever it is they're carrying?"

Phoebe grabbed her cellphone from the dashboard. "No, but I can call the fire chief."

Rowdy half listened to the conversation as she explained Stella was at Rowdy's and the helicopter needed to drop everything it carried on the house. They reached the turn off and Rowdy jumped out of the car as soon as Phoebe stopped at the roadblock. He started running up the hill, but hit the ground hard when someone tackled him from behind. He immediately lashed out, but JT flipped and pinned him.

"Get off!"

"Stop, Rowdy. You can't go up there. It's too dangerous."

"Stella's at my house!"

JT released his hold. "What?"

"Stella's up there. She broke her ankle. I have to go."

"No." JT sat back on his heels. "The fire's jumped the road. There's no way up."

Rowdy covered his face with both hands and released an animalistic sound. JT grabbed his arm and pulled him out of the way as Beam's truck screeched to a stop, kicking up a cloud of dust. Rowdy's brother and dad jumped out as another helicopter buzzed overhead. The fire chief approached from the other direction.

"I told them to hit the house, Rowdy. They radioed back to say it's already on fire."

Rowdy's panic rose to epic levels. "Tell them to hit it anyway. Stella's up there."

Beam turned him by the shoulders. "She's at your house?"

"Yes. We were going to take a ride after the town council meeting. She went up to let Moose out." He glanced at the fire chief. "I have to get up there."

"Stella's resourceful," his dad said. "She'll be okay."

Rowdy jabbed a hand toward the mountain burning before them. "Where's she going to go?"

"Hey, Chief," a fireman called out. "We found a starting point for the fire, and we have a couple of eyewitnesses."

JT spun toward the fireman. "Where?"

Rowdy followed JT around a bend, where a charred gas can lay on its side. Apparently the fire had moved uphill from here.

"We're in luck there's no wind," the fire chief said.

JT pointed at a couple of backpackers. "Are they the witnesses?"

The fireman nodded.

JT jogged down the hill towards them and Rowdy started to pace. He couldn't see his house from here, but he could see the two houses below his were engulfed in flames. The chief said his was burning. He needed to be up there looking for Stella.

He glanced at JT, who'd pulled out a notebook while talking with the couple. He held his hand a little below chest height, and Rowdy knew he was asking them about the orange-haired kid who hadn't been with his fire-starting partners three nights ago.

He didn't want to think a teenager would go this far to avenge his buddies.

His dad approached, put his arm around Rowdy's shoulders. "Phoebe called her parents. They're on their way. They've been trying to call Stella. She's not answering."

Rowdy tugged out his phone and listened. Even Moose wasn't making a sound anymore, but the call was still connected. "When I called, she said she fell and broke her phone. I could hear her, but she couldn't hear me." Rowdy scrubbed his stinging eyes. "When she fell, she said she broke her ankle, so how is she going to get away? I need to get up there."

"As soon as they open the road we'll go, son."

"She's alive." Rowdy rubbed the spot on his chest, right over his heart. Then he glanced up the blackened hillside where a fire crew worked at dousing a blaze. "I know it sounds crazy, but I feel it." He just couldn't imagine how. The two houses he could see from the road were still burning, flames and black smoke billowing high. The helicopter buzzed overhead again. He watched as it dropped its load.

Sick to his stomach, he bent at the waist and rested his hands on his knees. The shadows were growing longer as the sun dipped behind the mountain peaks. It would be dark soon, which would make it even harder for him to find her.

His dad rubbed his back. "Here comes JT. Maybe he has some news."

JT tucked the small notebook in his pocket. "The backpacking couple ID'd Blaze. They saw him lugging the gas can up the road from a small blue Honda and set the fire. They got a license plate number and gave a perfect description."

"Blaze?" Rowdy's dad asked.

"The orange-haired kid who hangs around with the gang of Goths from Harrisville. He wasn't with them the night they tried to set the fire behind The Fly Shop. Makes me wonder if he's on the outs with them."

"Maybe this was his revenge for you picking up his friends," Rowdy's dad suggested.

"Possibly. Or his attempt to get back in good with the group." JT pulled his cell phone out. "I've got to call Harrisville police. See if they can pick this kid up." He touched Rowdy's shoulder. "Then I'll check with the fire chief to see when we can go up the hill."

When JT stepped away, Rowdy looked up at the mountainside. Nothing was holding him here. JT was busy on the phone, and the chief was barking orders into a radio. If he made his way up to his house on foot, he'd be there in twenty minutes, but the ground was still smoldering…

"We'll go as soon as it's safe, son. I know you're anxious."

"Rowdy!"

Stella's dad and mom jogged toward him, Phoebe and Leo close behind. Her dad reached him first. "Have you heard anything?"

"I keep trying to call, but I'm getting a busy signal," her mom said.

Rowdy held up his phone. "She said she'd dropped her phone. I could hear her, but she couldn't hear me." He left out the broken ankle part. No need to scare them further.

He lost track of time as it slipped past at a crawl. Two more fire engines and a truck full of smoke-eaters headed up the hill. He spotted the fire chief's truck and walked toward it. If the keys were inside… They weren't, but the chief's gear sat on the front seat, his boots on the floor. Without thinking, Rowdy opened the door and grabbed the boots. These would get him up the hill.

Rowdy couldn't wait any longer. He slipped his own boots off and jammed his feet into the fire boots, which were a tight fit, but he'd deal. He quickly cut across the mountain toward the burning houses, hoping to reach Joe Eglin's detached shed where the man kept a four-wheeler. If the fire hadn't destroyed it, Rowdy could hotwire the vehicle and get up the hill faster. The ground was still hot and smoldering in places, so he worked his way to a dirt trail that crisscrossed the road in several places. Once he hit the trail, the going was easier.

Any number of people would have noticed his absence by now. He looked down the hill but didn't see anyone following. Luckily there were enough ridges to keep him hidden until he reached the Eglin place.

When he arrived, firefighters were spraying water on the burning house. All that was left of the shed was a pile of ashes, the four-wheeler a wreckage of charred metal. Okay. *Uphill by foot it is.* He started jogging, grateful the smoke was rising and moving westward, away from him.

Around a bend in the road, he caught the first glimpse of his house still burning. His jog turned into a full-out run. Good thing he was a regular exerciser. Racing uphill where the dirt path allowed, he said a silent prayer for Stella and Moose's safety, which didn't seem possible or adequate. He wanted to shout at the top of his lungs. They had to be safe. There was no other alternative. No other outcome was acceptable.

He rounded another bend and lost sight of his house, but saw a fire engine and a small pumper truck. He recognized Brandt Smith with a group of firefighters from around the area. They were putting out hotspots along the road. The poor guy's wedding was days away and he was up here risking his life because of some dumb kid's decision.

"Rowdy? What are you doing here?"

"Stella was at my house when the fire broke out. I have to get up there."

Brandt glanced in the direction of Rowdy's house, then

the small pumper truck that sat nearby. "Get in. Guys, we have a woman in a house up the road."

Rowdy slid into the passenger seat as Brandt turned the engine over. Dirt spewed behind the tires as they spun off. The closer they got, the more Rowdy's stomach twisted into knots. When they rounded the bend closest to his house, he saw the damage. Two supporting outer walls and the rock fireplaces were still standing. Flames licked at what was left.

"Oh, man, Rowdy. Sorry about the house."

"I don't care about the house." He pointed to the left. "Go around back." When he spotted Stella's scorched car, his stomach turned over.

As soon as Brandt came to a stop, he threw Rowdy a pair of gloves and an oxygen mask before he jumped out. Brandt backed the truck to the house and yanked a hose free. The other fire engine arrived and they doused the flames as Brandt and Rowdy worked their way through the house, lifting smoldering beams and searching through the remnants of closets. Anything they could safely move, they did. Nothing.

"Good news," Brandt said.

Rowdy knees quaked with relief as adrenaline leaked into a puddle at his feet. He walked around the house, searching the tree line. The fire had moved up and over the ridge, far above his house. Luckily, the trees on the back side of this peak were sparse, which might give firefighters a chance to get ahead of it.

Where is she? Would she go up the mountain?

"Are you sure Stella was here?" Brandt asked, joining his search of the surrounding area.

"She said she was here with Moose." Rowdy walked around the back of what was left of his home. Dark was descending fast.

If Moose was anywhere near, he'd come when called.

Rowdy put finger and thumb in his mouth and whistled. "Moose!"

He waited for any sound, heard nothing. "Have you got a flashlight?"

Brandt tugged one free of his utility belt. "I've got another in the truck."

Rowdy moved into the charred trees and whistled again. He still felt sure Stella and Moose weren't in the house. He and Brandt had checked it pretty thoroughly. They had to have moved up the mountain, which would make them harder to find.

He touched his heart again. He didn't know how he knew, but they were alive.

He walked farther up the hill along the path he and Moose took so often. Suddenly, he knew where they were. "Brandt, grab some oxygen! Get an ambulance up to my house. They're in a cave. Just follow this path. At the fork take the trail to the left."

He ran as fast as he could to get to the mouth of the cave. "Stella! Moose!"

He heard a whimper. *Please. Please.* Smoke lingered at the cave entrance, but the deeper inside he went, the staler the air became. Luckily, the bat's entrance high above allowed the smoke to filter out. He flashed a beam of light around a corner and spotted Stella on her side. She'd pulled off her T-shirt and tied it around Moose's nose and mouth. The dog's tail flapped from side to side when he spotted Rowdy, but he didn't lift his head from Stella's thigh.

Rowdy knelt next to him and ran his fingers along the dog's legs and body. "Hey, buddy. You okay? Are you hurt?"

Woo, woo woo, came out muffled.

"Good boy." He moved over to Stella. She was unconscious, but breathing. Slow and shallow. He checked her limbs just as he'd checked Moose. She didn't seem to be burned anywhere, although her left ankle was swollen to twice the size it should be. He lifted her and carried her out. Brandt ran toward him carrying a black bag and a canister.

"Is she breathing?"

"Yes. Labored." Rowdy tugged his T-shirt off and covered Stella.

Brandt pulled out an oxygen mask and hooked a plastic tube to the canister. He placed it over Stella's nose and mouth. "Where's your dog?"

"He's still inside the cave."

"I'll watch Stella while you get him. An ambulance is on the way."

Rowdy went back inside and knelt next to his dog. "You are a good boy for taking care of Stella, buddy. Good job for leading her here."

Once he untied Stella's shirt, the dog jumped to his feet.

Rowdy chuckled. "Really? Was the T-shirt muzzle keeping you down?"

Roo woo woof.

"You sound a little gravelly. We'll visit the vet once we know Stella's going to be okay. Come on, boy."

Moose led the way out of the cave. Two EMTs had joined Brandt, and the three of them loaded Stella onto a stretcher. Brandt had started an IV. "We need to get her down."

"Has she opened her eyes?"

"Not yet."

"Is she going to be all right?"

"She's breathing and her vitals are good."

"Stella, can you hear me? Open your eyes, baby."

He held her hand, Moose trailing behind, until they reached the bottom of the hill where his family and Stella's waited. After fluttering around the stretcher, asking questions that couldn't be answered yet, Beverly climbed into the back of the ambulance after Stella was loaded aboard.

He watched it make its way down the hill followed by Neil, Phoebe, and Leo in a car. His family gathered around, consoled him about Stella, who might be seriously injured, and a house that could be rebuilt.

"Dad, can you give me a ride into town to get my truck?" Rowdy asked. "I rode up with Phoebe."

"Of course."

Rowdy turned to his brother. "Beam, would you call Doc Stevens and see if he'll meet you at the clinic?"

"Sure, bro. Want a ride to Harrisville Regional first?"

"No, I can drive." Rowdy led Moose to Beam's truck. "Tell Doc I'll pick Moose up tomorrow."

"I'll take him home with me after the doc checks him over. Sophia loves the hulk."

Rowdy put his forehead to Moose's. "Thank you for helping Stella, boy. I'll come get you in the morning."

Woo woo woof.

Rowdy shut the passenger door. "Thanks, bro."

Beam nodded. "Call us with an update on Stella."

"Will do," Rowdy said holding up a hand.

~

Stella opened her eyes to noise, bright lights, a burning throat, and her mom smoothing her hair off her forehead. She coughed, wincing at the raw pain.

"Neil, she's awake. Honey, how do you feel?"

Her mind was as fuzzy as the dust bunnies had been under her bed. She looked around the room. "W-where am I?" she rasped out.

"Hey, cupcake." Her dad stood on the other side of the bed. "An ambulance brought you to the hospital in Harrisville."

Her stinging eyes and throat brought panicky memories

back. Fleeing uphill with the fire on her heels. Moose leading her to a cave where she thought they'd die. Tying her shirt around the dog's nose and mouth to keep him from breathing the smoke filling the cave.

"We've been so worried. You were at Rowdy's when the fire broke out."

"Where's Moose?"

"Rowdy said the vet is checking him over, but he seems fine," her dad said squeezing her hand.

Her mom hiccupped a sob. "That gigantic dog saved your life. When Rowdy found you, Moose was protecting you. He didn't leave until Rowdy carried you out of the cave."

"Moose knew where to go. When I saw the cave, I thought the smoke would come in and"—her throat closed up, choking her worse than the smoke did—"we'd die from smoke inhalation rather than burning." She rubbed her nose where the oxygen tube tickled. "But most of the smoke rose and disappeared. There must have been another entrance I couldn't see."

"Smart dog." Stella's mom sat on the bed and took her other hand, tears running down her face.

"This fire was set by one of the arsonists JT's been looking for," her dad added.

Stella coughed, then pressed fingertips above her eyebrow where a headache pounded. "I thought he and Rowdy caught them a couple of nights ago."

"The orange-haired kid wasn't with the group that night. A backpacking couple spotted him lighting this one," Phoebe said from a spot by the door. "It's about time you woke up. The waiting room is crowded with visitors asking how you are."

A man in a white coat walked in, giving Phoebe a second glance before stopping next to the bed. "You've had quite an ordeal. I'm Dr. McKay. How does the ankle feel?"

She looked down, surprised to see a cast encasing her foot and ankle. "I forgot I hurt it."

"Closed fracture of the fibula, no surgery necessary. It should heal quickly." The doctor rested a forearm against her bed rail. "I'm more worried about the smoke you inhaled. How does your throat feel?"

"Sore. Swollen."

"Do you have a headache?"

"Yes."

"I'll have the nurse bring you something for that." He glanced at her mom and dad. "I'm going to keep her overnight, make sure her cough doesn't get worse. I'll check on you in the morning," he said to Stella. "I'll send the nurse in with something for your headache. And keep that oxygen cannula in your nose."

"Can she have visitors?"

The doctor and Phoebe stared at each other a moment before he smiled. "Sure. I've heard she has quite a fan club in the waiting room. Just don't let her overdo it."

Phoebe leaned out the door to watch the doctor walk down the hall. Stella imagined the good doctor would have Phoebe's phone number before her stay was over. "I'll let your friends know they can come in."

"What do I look like?" Stella asked, having never been on the receiving end of a hospital visit.

"Pretty as ever." Her dad kissed her cheek. "Your mom washed your face earlier."

Her mom kissed her other cheek. "We'll go get dinner while you visit with friends."

Soon after her parents left, the room was full of friends and good wishers. Everyone but Rowdy.

She visited and answered questions while Leo and Charlie drew elaborate pictures on her cast. All the while, she waited impatiently for Rowdy. In the cave, after some discussion, she and Moose had come to the conclusion she was madly in love with the roguishly handsome Rowdy Garrett.

"I didn't know you were such a creative nuisance, Leo. You'll have to help me decorate my classroom next week."

"I can help, too," Charlie chimed in with his usual enthusiasm.

"I'd love your help Charlie."

Leo shook his head. "My tremendous talent would be lost on your little hoodlums."

"They're not hoodlums," she said with a laugh, which made her cough.

Leo held out a cup of ice water, which felt absolutely wonderful going down her parched throat. She'd had so much to drink in the last hour she felt waterlogged.

Slowly her friends and sister trickled out, leaving her alone. The magnitude of what happened hit her then. She very nearly died today. If Moose hadn't known about the cave or been smart enough to lead her there, she—*they*—wouldn't be alive.

She hoped Moose was okay. As the fire moved closer, she'd done the only thing she could think of to save him from the smoke, which was to tie her shirt around his nose and mouth. Even with the small opening at the top of the cave, the smoke still filtered in, making it difficult to breathe. She'd leaned against Moose and tried to use his fur as a mask. Luckily, they'd been around a corner, which shielded them from the worst of it. Most of the smoke rose before it reached them.

Lucky.

Stella smiled through the tears that wet her cheeks. *You haven't shared your opinion since I woke up. Where have you been?*

Polishing my halo.

Oh, cheeky comeback.

Her friend fluffed her wings. *I have my moments.*

When the door opened, she expected a nurse to poke her head around the curtain. Instead Rowdy walked in and she burst into tears. In seconds, he'd kicked off his boots and was in bed next to her wiping her face with tissues. "Baby, why the tears?"

She couldn't admit she was crying because everyone but her *boyfriend* had visited her as soon as possible, or that she'd fallen madly in love with the man she least expected to ever fall in love with.

"My eyes still burn from the smoke," she sobbed.

"Your raspy throat sounds sexy."

She snorted. Sexy schmexy. She sounded like a croaking frog.

He smiled. Not his usual smirk, but a genuine smile, his beautiful green eyes dancing with amusement.

"What?"

Shaking his head, he ran his fingers through her hair. Even though a nurse said she'd helped Stella's mom wash it, Rowdy's fingers still stirred up lingering smoke.

Her glance skated away from his handsome face. "I'm sorry about your house."

"We can live in Alex's rental until we rebuild." He tucked her hair behind her ear.

His comment caught her off guard and she looked at him. "We aren't living together."

"We will be after we're married." He reached into his hip pocket and pulled out a black velvet box.

A hundred emotions flashed through her, so fast she felt sick to her stomach. Rowdy couldn't be proposing. He wasn't the marrying type, yet he just said—

Open it, open it, open it!

She heard herself swallow loudly as she took the ring-sized box between shaking fingers. "What is this?"

His smirk was back. "What do you think it is?"

"I"—she shook her head, not wanting to make a fool of herself by assuming—"I…uh… Well, it's too small to be a car. Mine met the same fate as your house."

"We'll get you a new one. We can go shopping as soon as you feel up to it."

She twisted to face him. "You sure are throwing around the *we* word a lot."

"Isn't that what we are? The we word?" He glanced from her to the box she held between two fingers like dirty underwear. "Are you going to open that?"

Her heart was beating too fast, making her gaspy breaths even gaspier. They couldn't be a forever couple. He was too clean. She was a mess. Her car had probably burned fast and hot because of all the junk she kept in there. She would never be able to keep up with his standards. She'd always be an overweight disappointment.

Open it, open it, open it!

"How did I get out of the cave?"

"I carried you."

"How's your back?"

His frown smoothed out. "My back is fine, Stella. I've told you before, I love your curves." He bounced his eyebrows up and down.

"They aren't going away, Rowdy." She ran the pad of her thumb over the box, wanting to remember the feel, wanting to remember this moment. "Believe me, I've tried. Neither is my messiness. I've tried to change that too, for Phoebe, but cleanliness is not one of my virtues."

Rowdy blew out a sigh and rested his elbow on her pillow. "I'll clean. You can help me."

"I'm not a great cook either."

He chuckled. "I'll cook."

"What am I supposed to do?"

"Teach school if you want to continue, and have babies."

"Barefoot and pregnant?"

"If you like bare feet, that's fine with me. Personally, I think you have cute toes." He ran a finger down her cheek to her jaw. "I should have known you wouldn't make this easy. You can't just say a simple yes like most women do."

"How would you know what most women do at a moment like this? This is big. I probably still have some soot on my face from the fire. I'm not even wearing makeup. Plus, my hair smells like smoke—"

"You look beautiful."

"—and you haven't actually *asked* the question."

He got up on a hand and searched her face. "You don't have black on your face. You don't need makeup because you're breathtaking without and I love your hair, smoky or not. Rolling your eyes isn't going to change the way I feel, Stella. I love you. You love me—"

She sat up a little straighter. "I never said I loved you," she croaked then doubled over in a coughing fit.

He reached for the cup of water. She sipped until her throat felt some relief. "Couldn't you have waited for a more romantic moment?"

"We can make this a romantic moment. How about you open the box, darlin'?"

Open it, open it, open it.

Stella slowly opened the lid and gasped at the beautiful diamond circled by smaller diamonds. Her eyes filled with tears. "It's like a starburst," she whispered hoarsely. "The bright North Star surrounded by smaller but not less bright stars."

Rowdy rolled to his stomach and, supported by his elbows, took the box from her. He pulled the ring free. "Stella Adams, will you marry me?"

"We haven't dated very long, Rowdy. Our first official date was only a month ago. People will talk."

He laughed and she enjoyed the sound. He was a positive person, but he didn't out-and-out laugh very often. "We've known each other our whole lives, and what do you care if people talk?"

True.

"The ring is beautiful. Did you pick it out by yourself?"

"Yes. See how easy that word is. Yes. Say yes."

"Aren't you supposed to get down on one knee? I mean… I've been waiting for you to break up with me. Instead, you show up with a ring."

An incredibly adorable look of confusion parked itself on his face. "Why are you waiting for me to break up with you?"

"Because you're you. You're Rowdy."

"So, if I get down on one knee you'll think of me differently? Instead of the old Rowdy, I can be the new—in love with Stella—Rowdy?"

"Everyone was here earlier. Everyone but you."

"While I was waiting to be allowed in, I decided tonight was the night. Do you have any idea how hard it is to find the perfect ring at this time of night?" He wiggled the ring between his finger and thumb. "I knew you had plenty of friends to keep you company."

"And then you just show up and pull a ring out of your pocket and expect me to say yes."

Rowdy looked up at the ceiling with a groan. "Stella, will you just say yes so we can move on to the kissing part?"

Time to put on your big girl panties and accept that he's not breaking up.

Stella pointed at the floor.

"If I get down there, are you going to say yes tonight?"

She pointed at the floor.

Rowdy slid down on one knee and held out the ring. "Stella Adams, will you marry me?"

"Oh, my gosh, Rowdy. Couldn't you find a more romantic place to propose than a hospital room?"

"Get. Out. Phoebe."

Stella stifled a laugh behind her hand. Her and Rowdy's romantic moment was supposed to be exactly like this. Him on one knee in a hospital room, her in bed with a broken ankle and smoke in her lungs, and Phoebe and Leo standing in the doorway with gaping mouths. This was their perfect moment. One to share with the grandkids. "Yes."

Rowdy smiled. "Yes?"

"Yes," she said, adding a nod to confirm. "Yes."

Finally! Her little friend jumped up and down, clapping her hands. *Okay, now get to the kissing part.*

~

Two weeks after Jillian and Brandt's wedding, and a week after school started, Stella stepped out of the car followed by all four of her sisters.

They'd spent the past couple of days together picking out dresses and planning a quick reception. Except for Phoebe, each had come from their faraway places. Isadora traveled up from her Northern California home. Georgiana was here from Chicago. And sweet little Oops, or Adelaide as everyone else called her, came from New York. They were so rarely together all at once that Stella suspected her mom and dad were more ecstatic about that than the wedding.

She and Rowdy had chosen the ridge he took her to see on their first motorcycle ride as the setting for their wedding. Only family and very close friends were here, waiting just over the small rise. Her dad met her and kissed her cheek.

"You look…"

"Daddy, don't you dare cry, or you'll make me cry."

"Sorry, cupcake." He wiped the corners of his eyes. "I just love seeing daughter number four so happy."

She took his arm and snuggled into his side. "I love being this happy."

As they crested the rise and started down the incline, she sought out Rowdy. He stood next to Preacher Brenner with the surrounding mountains and valley below as their backdrop.

The fire left a scar on one hillside that would take years to recover, but Rowdy said they would rebuild soon.

Until then she, Rowdy, and Moose would live in town in Alex's cozy little two-bedroom rental where she and her first husband lived until his death. Stella was looking forward to chilly nights—at least the nights Rowdy wasn't at the bar and grill—cuddled in front of the cute fireplace.

For some odd reason, her mind turned to Anna. After a summer of working and service, Stella had let the guilt over dating a married man go. She couldn't change the past and, like everyone told her from the beginning, she hadn't known he was married or she never would have dated him. She felt certain Anna believed her on that point.

The next thing to pop into her mind was her dad's words, *I know it's hard to believe right now, but one day you will be grateful things happened the way they did.* Funny how often her dad was right.

Rowdy stood next to his brother Beam, both wearing a suit and tie. They wanted to go more casual, but her mom and Rowdy's wouldn't allow it. They accepted the venue but were adamant about no jeans and T-shirts.

Stella was glad. She loved the white tea-length dress she and her sisters—well, actually, her sister Isadora—found in a vintage shop in Seattle. Isadora was all about vintage and antiques. Stella wished she knew the history of the dress, but only if there was a happy ending attached.

"Beautiful day for a wedding," her dad whispered close to her ear.

The day was beautiful. Birds were singing in the surrounding trees. Bees buzzed in the wildflowers that clustered around the clearing. The blue sky didn't share any space with clouds today.

She, Rowdy, and Moose were surrounded by family and friends.

When she and her dad reached Rowdy, her dad kissed her cheek and Rowdy took her shaking hands. He squeezed her fingers reassuringly before lifting them to plant a kiss on each knuckle.

So romantic.

She'd never felt like she belonged in this particular spot at this particular time so strongly in her life. She and Rowdy. This was where they were supposed to be.

If only Rowdy had approached her two years— No. She wouldn't have taken him seriously back then. She'd needed to experience heartache and emerge from her little "me" shell first. Serving at the shelter and the senior center had opened her eyes to life outside her box.

Preacher Brenner started talking, and Stella hoped Adelaide was recording as she promised, because all Stella could do was gaze into Rowdy's mossy green eyes, notice the crinkles at the corners when he smiled, and watch the breeze flutter a petal of the rose he wore on his lapel.

Alex had chosen their flowers with great care and insight. Orange roses stood for desire and enthusiasm in the Victorian language of flowers. She'd picked calla lilies for beauty and aster was a symbol of love. She'd tied everything together with sprigs of sedum for bonds of affection. Simple, yet so significant.

Preacher Brenner said her name, and she looked at him. He smiled indulgently and repeated the question to which she was supposed to reply "I do". She glanced at Rowdy. He smirked. How was he not nervous? They were getting married, and he was as calm as if he was standing in the river casting a fly.

Rowdy squeezed her fingers again.

"I do promise everything. Except the obey part."

Her little friend raised a fist high in the air. *Well said, sistah!*

Rowdy lifted a brow. "I kind of like the obey part."

A few chuckles rippled through the group, none of them female.

"Won't happen, bro," Beam said, patting Rowdy on the shoulder to more chuckles. "Concede defeat on that one right now."

Rowdy huffed a resigned breath and glanced at Preacher Brenner. "Okay. Forget the obey part."

Preacher Brenner nodded, a smile twitching at the corners of his mouth. He cleared his throat and directed his question to Rowdy.

Rowdy's gaze softened, he smiled, and Stella's breath caught. "I do."

They exchanged rings and kissed to great applause after Preacher Brenner announced they were now husband and wife.

Stella Garrett. Mrs. Rowdy Garrett. Mr. and Mrs—Eek!

Stella laughed when her little friend took a tumble off her shoulder.

~

*O*f course, he and his new wife couldn't sneak off and begin their honeymoon. No, Alex—ever the planner —along with Stella's sisters, organized a reception at The Dew Drop Inn, with food and flowers, and everyone they knew was invited.

"Sorry, Rowdy, but Eden Falls want to congratulate you and Stella."

"I'll give you an hour and a half."

Alex stuck out her chin. "Three hours. I have a band coming."

He shook his head.

"For your moms," she pleaded.

He rolled his eyes, Stella-style. "Two." She opened her mouth, and he held up his hand to stop her. "Two hours, Alex. Stella and I only have the weekend. She has to be back to school on Monday."

Alex's smile, like a beacon in the dark, signaled that she'd get her way. "I called in a few favors. Stella doesn't have to be back until Wednesday morning."

He exhaled loudly. "Two-and-a-half hours."

At the Inn, he and his bride greeted guests who were lined up out the door. Maude Stapleton looked them over with satisfaction. "It's about time you two got married. You give him a run for his money, Stella."

Rowdy draped an arm around Stella's shoulders. "She already has, Maude, but she lost the race this morning when she said 'I do.'"

Stella elbowed him in the ribs. "Don't worry, Maude. I'll keep him in line."

Maude huffed out a breath. "Good luck with that."

After Maude walked away, he bent and kissed Stella's neck. She smiled up at him, and he ran a finger over her bottom lip. "Mrs. Garrett, while you look very tempting, and

I'd love to get out of here, I promised my cousin we'd stay and dance."

"Then let's dance."

She tugged him toward the dance floor, where they fit together so nicely. He couldn't believe after all this time of watching Stella from afar, she was finally his. He couldn't wait to start their life together. "I love you, Stella."

Stella lifted her head from his chest and circled her arms around his neck. "Good. That means you're doing it right."

He laughed, something he figured he'd be doing a lot of in this life with Stella.

"Take me outside and show me the stars, darling husband."

"Gladly." He took her hand and led her down the deck stairs toward the river. The crickets' constant chatter sounded like rotating sprinkler heads *tsk, tsk, tsking* away. The late summer air was soft with a tinge of chill and Stella's particular scents of orange and lavender, which had surrounded him since the wedding. They reached a bench just off the path, and he sat down and pulled her onto his lap. "You said you've never seen the Milky Way." He pointed up. "Now you can say you saw it on your wedding day."

"Oh, wow," she breathed out as she followed the arching line he made with his finger.

"There are between 200 and 400 billion stars in the Milky Way, and at least 100 billion planets."

"Do you think there's life out there?"

He ran fingers through her soft hair, sending out wafts of orange. "Absolutely."

She turned her head. "As in aliens?"

"As in people just like you and me. The neighboring Andromeda Galaxy contains over a trillion stars. It's only reasonable to assume there's life out there."

"I want you to come and talk to my class about the stars this year, Mr. Garrett."

"I'd be happy to, Mrs. Garrett." He pulled her closer. "But first, let's sneak away and start our honeymoon."

If you enjoyed *Stars Over Eden Falls*, I hope you'll continue reading! The next book in the Eden Falls Series is *Fortunes for Eden*

To keep up to date on new releases join my newsletter at TinaNewcomb.com.

Following is an excerpt from *Fortunes for Eden*.

CHAPTER ONE

Isadora Adams waved goodbye to her youngest sister from her parents' front porch. Her mom and dad would be gone all morning on the five-hour round trip to the Seattle airport.

Back inside, she wandered from room to room of her childhood home, lost in memories. Five girls and a wife under one roof—her poor dad was the most patient man on earth. In the kitchen, Izzy ran a hand over the table, which had stood up under countless meals and late-night study sessions. The whole house echoed of laughter and tears, territorial squabbles, hormones, whispered secrets, and screaming matches.

On a small desk in the corner, she spotted a copy of the *Eden Falls Chronicle*. A picture on the front page showed Stella and her new husband, Rowdy, working side by side on a Fourth of July float. Below the article another picture captured the finished product, three tiers of cupcakes advertising Patsy's Pastries. "You always were the crafty one, Stella," she said to the empty house.

After a quick shower, Izzy grabbed a jacket and headed

out the door for Town Square, which was only a few blocks away. She and her friend Joanna were meeting at The Roasted Bean after Joanna dropped her twin boys at school. Izzy and Joanna, along with Ariel, were so inseparable in high school, Joanna's mom had called them Peanut, Butter, and Jelly.

Ariel's devilishly handsome older brother had attended Stella and Rowdy's wedding reception on Saturday night. As hard as she tried not to look in his direction, her traitorous gaze had different ideas. Every time their eyes met, Gunner Stone glared as he'd done since she was sixteen.

Ever since The Kiss.

She turned onto Main Street, enjoying the morning air and familiar sights. As long as she'd lived in San Francisco, she still considered Eden Falls her home.

Outside The Roasted Bean, police chief JT Garrett pulled to the curb in a shiny patrol car. "Hey, Izzy, I didn't get a chance to talk to you at the wedding reception. How's San Francisco?"

"It's still there. I miss running into Carolyn, though. I ate at her restaurant at least twice a month until she moved back here and you made her a better offer. By the way, congrats on your marriage."

"Thanks. Move back to Eden Falls and you can run into Carolyn all the time."

I'm thinking about it.

JT held up a hand. "I've got to go. Mr. Polanski spotted Sasquatch near his chicken coop again."

Izzy laughed. Mr. Polanski had been chasing Bigfoot for as long as she could remember. She waved back, turned to go inside, and collided with a solid mass. The plastic top on a coffee cup flipped off and scorching liquid sloshed down her blouse and soaked the muscular chest in front of her.

Sucking in a gasp and plucking her shirt away from her

skin, she glanced up, apology on the tip of her tongue and froze. *No!* Her mind screamed. Anyone—*anyone!*—but Gunner Stone.

Based on the you-are-the-bane-of-my-existence look on his face, he felt the same way about this fun little encounter.

"I'm sorry, Gunner." She waved a hand at the road. "I was talking to JT and turned…I should have looked…I just…my attention was on him and…" She covered her mouth as a giggle burst out in one of the most awkward moments of her life—a horrible habit she wished she could break.

He cocked his jaw to one side and narrowed his gaze. She found his one brown eye and one green eye mesmerizing. So much so, she'd looked up the term for it—heterochromia iridis—when she was in middle school. They could appear so stormy one minute, so sad, so burdened the next.

"I really am sorry." Another giggle bubbled up, so she pressed her lips together and bit down while she swiped a hand down his T-shirted chest like she could magically dry him off.

He caught her wrist and an energy—so intense, so tangible she felt it in her toes—crackled between them. His nostrils flared, and the look in his eyes hardened like he'd just locked gazes with Medusa.

Ahh, nice job, brain. If only the Medusa analogy were true. Turned to stone, I wouldn't have to put up with Gunner's loathing anymore.

He lowered her hand but didn't release his hold, his palm hot. Was it just him, or was his skin heated from the coffee he was now wearing? When his gaze dropped to her lips, her stomach dipped like she was on a roller coaster. Something flashed across his face…desire? But that couldn't be right. He hated her. She looked at his lips and fire flashed over her cheeks so suddenly it startled her.

"I really am sorry." She tipped her head toward The Roasted Bean. "Come inside and I'll buy you another cup."

He dropped her wrist and, with a look of complete disgust, tossed his empty cup into a nearby trash can and stalked away.

Oka-a-ay. "Good to see you again, Gunner. Have a nice day. Buh-bye."

Anyone—anyone but Gunner.

"I see you ran into Mr. Hot and Handsome," Joanna said, joining her on the sidewalk.

"Oh, now you show up! You couldn't have arrived five minutes earlier? Or two? Thirty seconds?"

Joanna ruffled her still-wet hair with her fingertips. "Sorry. Cody couldn't decide between his black Batman shirt, his yellow Pokémon shirt, or his green Incredible Hulk shirt."

Izzy hadn't seen Joanna's adorable twin boys—the spitting image of their dad—in a year. "Which one did he choose?"

"The blue Spiderman one."

Izzy laughed. The release soothed the lingering Gunner-encounter tension.

"Clothes are an everyday battle with Cody. Everything is too tight, too loose, too scratchy. Food is Caleb's battle. The kid won't eat anything without a fight. If I fix hot dogs, he wants spaghetti. If I fix spaghetti, he wants tacos." She ran a hand over her pregnant belly. "I'm not sure what Troy and I were thinking when we decided to have another baby."

"You were thinking a little girl would calm the snakes and snails and puppy dog tails of a house full of boys." Izzy hated the longing that tinged her tone. The desire for a baby was so deeply embedded, she'd considered adoption—a decision her parents would frown upon if there wasn't a husband. Not her first choice, but not unheard of. "Is your mom still driving you crazy about a name?"

Joanna groaned. "Driving us crazy is putting it lightly."

"Clearly, you should choose Isadora. What little girl doesn't want to go through life being called Isadorable?" she asked, waving a hand down the front of herself like a game show hostess, which got the laugh she'd hoped for.

She glanced down the street. Gunner's scowl was visible from where they stood as he backed out of a parking spot.

"He doesn't look very happy," Joanna said.

"Isn't that the normal I-hate-everyone expression he always wears?"

Joanna looked from Gunner to her with crinkled brows. "Gunner is really friendly around town. He smiled a lot while he and Dahlia were dating."

Izzy closed her gaping mouth. "Gunner and nice Dahlia Dallas dated?"

"For a few months after his divorce."

If possible, her jaw dropped even farther. "I can't believe someone actually married that cranky crosspatch. Why didn't anyone tell me?"

"Cranky crosspatch?" Joanna said with a laugh. "That sounds like something your mom or a four-year-old girl would say."

Izzy opened the coffee shop door and followed Joanna inside. "I learned from the best. So, what happened to the wife?"

"She left after three—or six—months. Not really sure of the details. They were in the Army together."

"Was she pretty?"

"Halle Berry gorgeous."

"Geez, you move to California for a few years—"

"Thirteen."

"—and everything changes."

Joanna looked over her shoulder. "Did you expect things to stay the same as they were in high school?"

"No." But she wasn't sure how she felt about Gunner having been married. Then again, why did it matter to her? He was free to marry anyone he liked.

Joanna pointed at Izzy. "Could that be the reason Gunner looks so angry?"

Izzy pulled her coffee-covered blouse away from her chest. "Could be a small part of the reason."

"Izzy! Wow, I didn't know you were in town."

The second person she'd rather not run into. Ever. She mustered a smile for her high school sweetheart. "Tim. Hi."

Joanna pointed toward the counter. "I'm going to order."

Izzy didn't want to get into a back-and-forth *"You look great." "So do you." "How've you been?"* conversation with Tim.

They hadn't exactly parted on good terms when she left for college. He wanted to keep up a long-distance relationship, but she wasn't interested. She suspected he was seeing someone else, which he vehemently denied, but not quite convincingly enough. College in a new city had been just what she needed for a fresh start.

The man standing in front of her was as tanned and handsome as the boy had been, his smile just as charming.

"Are you in Eden Falls for a visit?"

"Wedding." She winced inwardly. Stella, probably wanting to avoid awkwardness, hadn't invited Tim.

"Right. I heard Stella and Rowdy got married." He reached out like he might take her hand, but stopped. "How long are you in town for?"

"I leave on Friday."

"Do you still live in San Francisco?"

She nodded.

He'd visited once in her freshman year, making her even more certain their relationship had run its course.

"We should get together while you're here."

"Oh…uh…"

"How about dinner tomorrow at East Winds? You used to love that place."

"Ah…" She couldn't think of an excuse fast enough. "Okay."

"I'll pick you up at—"

"Actually, I'll meet you there." She didn't want him coming to the house, where her mom and dad would see him and start asking questions. "Does seven work for you?"

"Sure. I'll see you tomorrow night at seven. Bye Iz."

She waited until he walked out before sidling up to the counter next to Joanna. "Thanks for abandoning me."

Joanna laughed. "You're a big girl. I figured you could handle Tim yourself."

"Being able to and wanting to handle Tim myself are two different things."

"He didn't bite you, did he?"

Izzy fluttered her eyelashes. "Not since senior year."

"He's single, you're single…"

Izzy held up a hand. "Don't go there."

"Why? Tim is a nice guy."

"That flame was doused before I even left for college. There's no going back."

"Thank you," Joanna said when the barista handed her two mugs. She held out one. "Hope chamomile tea is still a favorite. My treat after your two unpleasant encounters."

"Love it. Thank you. And the unpleasant encounters continue tomorrow night. I told Tim I'd meet him for dinner at East Winds."

Joanna slid into a chair at a vacant table. "Why didn't you say no?"

Izzy pulled out a chair across from her. "I couldn't think of an excuse fast enough."

"Why do you need an excuse? Just say no."

Izzy thought of her San Francisco job and all she did for

Baron Van Buren and the Van Buren Gallery. "I've never been very good at saying no."

"You could have used me."

"Nice to know if I need an excuse in the future." Izzy held the mug to her nose and breathed in the lemony fragrance.

Joanna smiled. "The way you say that makes it sound like there's going to be a future in Eden Falls...I say hopefully."

It would feel good to tell someone the secret she'd been carrying around for over a week. "The gallery had a big event last weekend. I planned every detail myself. When I reminded my boss I wouldn't be attending because of Stella's wedding"—Izzy lowered her voice so word didn't get back to her parents before she had a chance to tell them—"he threatened to fire me, so I quit."

"Izzy!" Joanna sat forward and touched her arm. "I'm sorry. You loved that job."

"A long time ago I did." She'd loved every aspect of her job at first. "But after I accepted the manager's position, things changed. I wanted that promotion more than anything, but Baron expects me to be on call twenty-four seven. A day off is rare." Dating the man had only made things worse. He was a major manipulator. Details Joanna didn't need to know.

"Even after gallery hours?"

"I attend fundraisers and cocktail parties and committee meetings representing the gallery. I meet with new artists and organize events and socials. I even plan weddings held at the gallery."

"People hold wedding in art galleries?"

"All the time."

Joanna settled her mug on her extended belly. "What are you going to do?"

Izzy shrugged because she didn't have an answer. "It's only been a week, so I haven't had time to look for another job."

"Do you think you'll stay in Washington?"

She didn't say that the thought had occurred to her more than once. Her mom and dad had tag-teamed her about coming home, even without knowing the situation. The cost of living would certainly be lower here than in Northern California. There were art galleries in Seattle and the surrounding areas, though nothing like the Van Buren Gallery. She had a sizable savings account, but only because she'd been stashing her money and sharing a rickety old house with four other women.

"They're building a big country club and golf course between here and Harrisville. Maybe you could organize their events. Sounds like you have plenty of experience."

The idea of opening her own event planning business had also occurred to her, but she didn't think Eden Falls was big enough to support such a job.

"You should talk to Alex. She does the flowers for weddings all over the area. I bet she'd know if you could make a living around here," Joanna said, as if reading her mind.

"I guess it wouldn't hurt. I have three more days before I go back to California."

Joanna sipped from her mug, then grimaced. "I miss coffee. Herbal tea isn't strong enough to get me through a day with two boys."

"You are an adorable pregnant lady."

Her friend laughed. "I look like a beached whale."

"That's so cliché. Your husband works in advertising. Have him come up with something more original."

"I'll tell him you said so."

"How is Troy?"

Joanna's expression softened. "He's doing well. Business is good and, despite my complaining, life is good."

"I'm happy for you, my friend. Did you think you'd end

up married to your high school boyfriend with two point five kids thirteen years after graduation?"

Joanna laughed again. "Absolutely not." She nodded toward Izzy. "What about you? Where did you picture yourself by now?"

"I thought I'd be married and have the two point five kids. Instead, my career took over my life." She shook her head trying to clear away the melancholy. "Tell me about the boys."

"You mean the heathens? Caleb clogged the toilet yesterday morning before church, trying to flush his plastic Army guys to China, and Cody decided to melt his crayons in the microwave because he couldn't find the watercolors."

Izzy laughed.

"You laugh now. Just wait."

Izzy didn't want to wait. She was anxious for those clogged-toilet and microwave disasters if it meant she got to kiss a sweet forehead goodnight after tucking him or her into bed.

Joanna set her cup on the table. "I thought you'd stick around for social hour after church yesterday."

"Mom and Dad had to take Georgiana to the airport, so I went home to spend time with Oops. She left this morning."

"I can't believe you still call your little sister Oops," Joanna said with a laugh.

"We say it with love."

Joanna pushed back from the table. "I need a donut. Let's walk across the square to Patsy's Pastries."

Gunner backed into the street and drove around the square, flexing and releasing his hands on the steering wheel. Too little sleep had him on edge. Running into Isadora Adams hadn't helped. She'd kept him awake for the last two nights.

Or at least thoughts of her had.

Ever since seeing her at her sister's wedding reception, she'd been front and center in his mind.

His cell phone rang and he grabbed it from the console of his truck, grateful for the interruption. "This is Gunner."

"Hi, Gunner, it's Karen over at The Dew Drop Inn."

"Hey, Karen."

"A maid discovered a hole in a bathroom wall over the weekend. Do you have any time in the next couple of days to take a look?"

He glanced at the clock on his dashboard. "I have a few minutes right now. Is the room empty?"

"Yes."

"I'm on my way."

"Thanks, Gun."

He disconnected the call and waved to Rance Johnson who'd just stepped out of The Fly Shop and placed a sidewalk sale sign on a table filled with tackle boxes. Second Monday in September. Changing leaves and cooler days were ahead. Shop owners would be clearing out summer merchandise and bringing out the fall and winter stock. Porches would soon be decorated with pumpkins and cornstalks.

Once the cold hit, his outside jobs would dwindle, followed by everyone tightening their belts to save for the holidays. Then he'd have to tighten his own belt until spring.

The cons of owning a handyman business in a small town were worth the freedom of setting his own hours and not answering to anyone but himself. He would never be rich, but he'd come a long way from his white-trash upbringing. People who used to look down on him as a thug when he was a kid now trusted him to repair their roofs or fix the leaky faucets—in their homes. Sometimes when they weren't even there.

More thoughts of Isadora muscled their way forward. She was at the wedding reception alone, wearing an orange dress and no wedding ring. She danced with a couple of local guys and her dad, then made the rounds, saying hello to Eden Falls' residents, careful to stay as far away from him as possible.

At one point she and her four sisters converged on the dance floor and gyrated to the pulsing beat of a crazy country love song. Nothing could have torn his gaze away from her. The eyes of every guy in the place were riveted on the sisters as they swiveled and wiggled and giggled to the tune. That's when he decided it was time to leave.

Isadora. Everyone called her Izzy. He knew she'd be at the wedding reception, knew if he attended he'd see her, knew if he saw her it would take weeks to forget her.

She didn't visit Eden Falls often. He'd only spotted her a handful of times over the years since she left for college, and then only from a distance. A quick glimpse across Town Square, going into one of the shops, picking up takeout from Renaldo's Italian Kitchen or East Winds Chinese, coming out of the movies with a sister or a friend.

Rumor had it she ran some swanky art gallery in California. A job that suited her. He could imagine her in fancy clothes commanding a small army of employees. Though he was six years older than she, he knew from his younger sister that Izzy was a leader. Well liked. Surrounded by friends. Heading committees and getting kids involved in causes was her MO even in high school.

She'd befriended his quiet younger sister, Ariel, during her crucial junior high school years, taken her under wing, turned a trailer kid into a fashionable, popular girl. Izzy was there for Ariel when he enlisted in the Army and left her with their unstable mother, something he had to do and wished he could undo at the same time.

Since the wedding reception was held at The Dew Drop, walking through the door made him think of Izzy again. Being so near her this morning, so close, yet so untouchable… She'd be back in California soon, and he'd try to forget her until the next time he spotted her in town.

Karen scanned his T-shirt when he stopped at the check-in desk. "Looks like you're wearing your coffee."

"Ran into someone."

She nodded toward the kitchen. "Let's get you a fresh cup before we go upstairs."

A few minutes later, he followed Karen to a second-floor room where she pointed out a hole behind the bathroom door.

"A group of fishermen got a little unruly over the weekend."

"It will take a few days for the patch to dry."

"Not a problem. I don't need this room until Friday afternoon. I have a big party coming in."

"I can get to it before then. Do you have matching paint?"

"In a storage room in the basement. If I'm not here, whoever's at the front desk can get it for you."

"I have to get to another job, but I'll swing by later this afternoon and start patching it up."

"Thanks, Gunner. Here, take this." She pressed a key card into his palm. "This will get you in when you need to."

He refilled his coffee and walked around the back of the inn to a path that led to the river. Standing on the bank, he watched the water burbling over rocks. The level was low due to the dry summer, but that would soon change with winter snowfall.

A butterfly floated past and landed on a wildflower close by. He took a step closer, but it lifted into the air and fluttered away. The breeze rustling the leaves on the trees brought the smell of rain.

Today would be long and dirty. The team he'd hired would have to wear masks while clearing the damage left by a wildfire that destroyed several mountain homes last month. He hoped the storm would hold off until tonight. Driving a bulldozer through soot would be messy enough without rain making the ground a gloppy mess.

He squatted down and scooped a handful of water. At one point Izzy left the reception and came down to the river. Her father joined her a few minutes later. Gunner had watched them from the windows above, wondering what it would be like to have a good talk with his dad, who deserted his mom and him when he was four.

Gunner had discovered the man had a new family in a town close by. A wife and kids who depended on him. He'd waited outside his father's house early one morning, right before his high school graduation. When his father backed out of the driveway on his way to work, Gunner followed and intercepted before his dad could go into his Harrisville office.

The man recognized him immediately. Their conversation entailed a brief greeting, with no exchange of hugs or even a handshake, Gunner's mumbled request for help with college, his father's denial of responsibility—because Gunner was eighteen by that time—and an exit. The man never gave his mom a dime to help with expenses after he abandoned them.

So Gunner was on his own. The only way for him to generate a steady, reliable income for himself and his dependent mom and sister was to join the Army. He'd serve his time, then use the GI bill to go to college and at least get some business courses under his belt.

He straightened. Enough with the bad memories. Time to get up the mountain to work.

~

Izzy had planned to go back to her parents' house after she and Joanna parted. Instead she walked through Town Square and down a side street to three Victorian houses lined up like pretty sisters dressed in their Easter Sunday finery. She'd loved these houses since she was a little girl. The gingerbread trim, the attention to detail, the original wavy glass in the windows…their history fascinated her.

The first was painted a lovely blue with navy and white trim. Attorney Owen Danielson had refurbished the house for his offices. He'd made slight changes to the interior, but kept the integrity of the house intact.

When the second Victorian, which sat back on the lot a little, came into view, Izzy plopped down on the curb and stared. The house, once painted a soft yellow, was now a garish green, which, along with the black trim, was flaking off in brittle chunks. The beautiful front garden was over-grown with weeds, the lush lawn brown from neglect. A tree had fallen across the driveway. The only pretty feature left on the property was the maple in the front, its leaves just beginning to turn with the cooling weather.

"It's a crying shame, isn't it?"

Izzy turned to find Lily and Rance Johnson standing behind her on the sidewalk. "What happened?"

"We had a fortune-teller move into town," replied the town librarian.

"After painting the house the color of puke and destroying the yard, Madam Venus, *Goddess of Love*, pulled up stakes," her husband added. "I guess not many people in our small town wanted to know what their futures held."

"She doesn't live here anymore?" The sight of the house made Izzy heartsick.

Rance shook his head. "She moved in and out within a year."

"How long has the house been empty?"

"Gosh, going on two years…right, honey?" Lily asked.

Removing his fishing hat, Rance scratched his bald dome. "At least two years."

Izzy stood and got up on tiptoe to see over the weeds that grew as tall as the fence. Had it really been that long since she'd come to admire the Victorians? Two windows above the porch overhang, which sagged on each end, made the house look like it was frowning. "I don't see a *For Sale* sign in the yard. Is she going to keep it?"

Rance lifted bushy eyebrows. "Your dad should have the answer to that question."

True. If not her dad, at least someone in his real estate office should know what was going on with the dismal Victorian.

"Are you staying in town long, Izzy?" Lily asked.

"I leave Friday. How are you both? We didn't get a chance to visit Saturday night."

"We've got a new grandbaby on the way." Rance took his wife's hand and settled it in the crook of his arm.

"Congratulations. I heard Mac got married."

"We're so lucky Mac found Noelle," Lily said. "She's a wonderful addition to our family, such a sweet stepmother to Beck."

"I haven't met her yet. I'll have to stop by her café for breakfast while I'm in town."

After they walked away, Izzy crossed the street. She wrapped her hands around the ornamental iron fencing that circled the yard. The sun-warmed metal felt oddly comforting. She studied the worn, forlorn house and wondered if the interior was as abused as the exterior.

Unhooking the gate, she picked her way over the tangle

of vines covering the walk. She wasn't sure what drew her forward, but knew she had to take a closer look. The steps needed repair work. Pots with plants that had seen much better days, along with leaves and debris, littered the peeling painted porch. The front door screen hung by only one of three hinges. She tried the knob. Locked up tight. Cupping her hands, she tried to see through the oval window, but film over the inside of the glass blocked her view.

After polishing a tiny spot on one of two front picture windows, she peered inside. Trash littered the floor, which looked to be hardwood. The walls were painted black or navy or brown…she couldn't tell for sure. She also couldn't see beyond the one room which looked huge.

The windows on the side of the house were too high, so she picked her way around to the back. The glass in the door was cracked, but she could see into a mudroom. Again, the floor was littered with rags and leaves and trash. Only a small section of the kitchen was visible. The cupboards were painted flamingo pink with lime green walls. She imagined the house sobbing while the painters applied the shocking colors.

She didn't dare climb the rickety stairs that led to some kind of screened-in sunporch.

Disappointed, she stumbled through the overgrowth and around the downed tree. On the other side of the house, she noticed a bird's nest under the eaves and several wasps disappearing behind a shutter.

Izzy crossed the street and stared at the gloomy Victorian, remembering how the house used to look. With a little tender loving care, she could possibly be restored to her majestic glory.

ACKNOWLEDGMENTS

Writing a book is a lonely endeavor. Hours and hours are spent at a computer, pounding away at the keys, developing characters, and researching facts. I belong to a local chapter of Romance Writers of America—Colorado Romance Writers and look forward to the meetings and workshops to mingle with other writers. I wouldn't have seven published books without these two groups and I wouldn't have met my critique partners, to whom this book is dedicated.

To Faith Freewoman, my amazing editor, who encourages and inspires me to be a better writer.

To Hopey Gardner who took my manuscript at the last minute to make sure every i was dotted and every t was crossed. Any mistakes the reader may find are mine.

To Dar Albert who never ceases to amaze me with her cover designs.

To my beta readers who take time from their busy day to help make my books stronger.

And to my wonderful husband who takes care of all the loose ends while I write.

You all have my sincere gratitude.

Tina

ALSO BY TINA NEWCOMB

The Eden Falls Series

Finding Eden

Beyond Eden

A Taste of Eden

The Angel of Eden Falls

Touches of Eden

Stars Over Eden Falls

Fortunes for Eden

Snow and Mistletoe in Eden Falls

Rumors in Eden Falls

Second Chance Romance Collection

When You Love Someone

Endless Love

Rhythm of Love

Second Chance Romance Collection

ABOUT THE AUTHOR

Tina Newcomb writes clean, contemporary romance. Her heartwarming stories take place in quaint small towns, with quirky townsfolk, and friendships that last a lifetime.

She acquired her love of reading from her librarian mother, who always had a stack of books close at hand, and her father who visited a local bookstore every weekend.

Tina Newcomb lives in colorful Colorado. When not lost in her writing, she can be found in the garden, traveling with her (amateur) chef husband, or spending time with family and friends.

Follow Tina on:

facebook.com/TinaNewcombAuthor

instagram.com/tinanewcombauthor

bookbub.com/authors/tina-newcomb

goodreads.com/tinanewcomb

pinterest.com/tinanewcomb